Spectacular praise for the novels of David Poyer

THE CRISIS

"Outstanding...Poyer, an Annapolis graduate, focuses on how his vividly drawn characters behave amid the shifting alliances, while the action inexorably builds to a conclusion that's both tragic and ironic."

—*Publishers Weekly* (starred)

"Riveting." —*Richmond Times Dispatch*

"Dave Poyer has again captured the essence of modern warfare. Not only is this a gripping war tale, but through its rich characters, offers important insights into the roots of the current global conflict of cultures."

—Major General Andrew B. Davis,
U.S. Marine Corps (Retired),
Former Commander, U.S. Marine Corps Forces
Europe and Africa

"Once again, Dan Lenson is a hero among heroes."

—*The Officer* magazine

"A super thought-provoking thriller that will have readers pondering ethical and logistical questions."

—*Mystery Gazette*

THE WEAPON

"Those who relish naval action won't be able to come up for air until they turn the last page of this nail-biter."

—*Publishers Weekly*

"If you like naval action with detailed schematics, this one's for you." —*The Oklahoman*

MORE...

KOREA STRAIT

"The taut tenth entry in Poyer's series...is rich in the naval detail fans have come to expect...a satisfying, fast-paced narrative...Dan Lenson remains a winningly weary hero."

—*Publishers Weekly*

"Realistic and frightening...well up to Poyer's excellent standards. No bluster, no dazzle, just real naval engagements that we may well see before long."

—*Kirkus Reviews*

"Exciting . . . fans of modern naval warfare will relish the details and sea action, as well as the insights into the Korean situation and the Korean people. Recommended for popular thriller collections."

—*Library Journal*

THE THREAT

"Plenty of action, plot twists....frenetically paced...[an] engaging pot boiler." —*The Virginian-Pilot*

"Poyer remains the most thoughtful of the military-thriller set and a master of authentic detail." —*Kirkus Reviews*

"Poyer's forte is storytelling, and *The Threat* delivers a masterful tale that leaves the reader dazzled."

—Steve Berry, *New York Times* bestselling author of *The Third Secret, The Templar Legacy,* and *The Romanov Prophecy*

"[Fans] of *The West Wing*...and political novels will enjoy the author's revealing portrayal of the backroom goings-on at the White House....Recommended especially for fans of Robert Ludlum's political thrillers (although Poyer is a superior writer)." —*Booklist*

"Terrific suspense...perfect authenticity...powerful storytelling and compelling characters...David Poyer is our finest

military novelist and *The Threat* is simply superb."
—Ralph Peters, author of *New Glory* and *Never Quit the Fight*

"There's plenty of danger and gripping action to satisfy his legion of fans."

—Military.com

THE COMMAND

"[An] explosive climax...the reader takes a well-informed cruise on a U.S. destroyer. Poyer knows the ship intimately. Vivid descriptions cover everything from knee knockers to combat information center, radar to computers, wardroom to enlisted quarters. Battle scenes in particular come alive with authenticity...and all that, and more, is in this latest chapter of Commander Daniel Lenson's contentious career."

—*Proceedings*

"Poyer packs the story with both dense technical info and welcome local color. Unique Aisha merits a spinoff series."

—*Kirkus Reviews*

"Plows fearlessly—though with hair-raising effect on occasion—through today's stormy international and social seas... the salvos of nautical expertise also lend flavor and authenticity...the author provides believable insights into Muslim thinking...Poyer's genius for description impresses on page after page. The vividness of his scene-setting grabs you."

—*Virginian-Pilot*

"Lovers of procedural military fiction wait for David Poyer's next installment of the career of Dan Lenson."

—*Roanoke Times*

BLACK STORM

"No one writes gritty, realistic military fiction better than David Poyer. No one." —Stephen Coonts

"A gripping, gritty novel that reads like the real thing. You're with the Marines every step of the way. Poyer knows his stuff."
—Vince Flynn

"Exceptional...A straight-ahead adventure yarn, a frontal assault on the bestseller lists."
—*Boston Globe*

"A must-read...not since James Jones's *Thin Red Line* have readers experienced the gripping fear of what it's like to fight an enemy at close quarters...Poyer's research is impeccable, his characterization compelling, and the Iraqi Desert Storm scenario all too believable."
—John J. Gobbell, author of *When Duty Whispers Low*

"I've been a David Poyer fan for over a decade, and his storytelling abilities—always first-rate—just got better and better. *Black Storm* is a timely, gripping, compelling yarn told by a master."
—Ralph Peters

"Absolutely riveting. David Poyer has captured the essence of what it is like on long-range patrols. His book is distinguished by quick action and continuing suspense that will keep the reader on edge until the very end."
—Maj. Gen. H. W. Jenkins, United States Marine Corps (Ret.), Commander of the Marine Amphibious Forces in the Gulf War

"One of the strongest books in an outstanding series...the remarkably vivid portraits he draws of the variety of men and women drawn to serve their country merit high praise."
—*Booklist*

"One of the best...action fans will be rewarded."
—*Publishers Weekly*

"Poyer's close attention to military practice and jargon will... suit those looking for accurate detail."
—*Newport News Press*

ST. MARTIN'S PAPERBACKS TITLES BY DAVID POYER

The Weapon

Korea Strait

The Threat

The Command

Black Storm

China Sea

Tomahawk

The Passage

The Circle

The Gulf

The Med

THE CRISIS

DAVID POYER

NOTE: If you purchased this book without a cover you should be aware that this book is stolen property. It was reported as "unsold and destroyed" to the publisher, and neither the author nor the publisher has received any payment for this "stripped book."

This is a work of fiction. All of the characters, organizations, and events portrayed in this novel are either products of the author's imagination or are used fictitiously.

THE CRISIS

Copyright © 2009 by David Poyer.
Excerpt from *Ghosting* copyright © 2010 by David Poyer.

Cover photograph of soldiers © Rubberball/Getty Images
Cover photograph of village © Robert Harding/Getty Images

All rights reserved.

For information address St. Martin's Press, 175 Fifth Avenue, New York, NY 10010.

Library of Congress Catalog Card Number: 2009023455

ISBN: 978-0-312-53248-2

Printed in the United States of America

St. Martin's hardcover edition / November 2009
St. Martin's Paperbacks edition / November 2010

St. Martin's Paperbacks are published by St. Martin's Press, 175 Fifth Avenue, New York, NY 10010.

10 9 8 7 6 5 4 3 2 1

ACKNOWLEDGMENTS

Ex nihilo nihil fit. For this book I owe thanks to Steve Biedermann, Harry Black, Joe H. Chaddic, Thane C. Clare, Kimbrew Clayton, P. J. Cook, Jodie Cornell, Cynthia Diggs, Richard H. Enderly, Dave Faught, Suki Forbes, Adam Goldberger, Brian A. Goulding, Chip Harris, David Herndon, Sarah J. Huggins, Michael C. Jordan, Gus Kaminsky, Joan LaBlanc, Marin Larson, Will Lawrence, David Luckett, Leslie Lykins, Hallie Munford, Paul O'Donnell, Katharine Parsons, Steve Ries, and many others who preferred anonymity. Thanks also to Charle Ricci and Carol Vincent of the Eastern Shore Public Library, unendingly patient with my obscure loan requests; Commander, Naval Surface Forces Atlantic; Office of the Chief of Naval Information; the U.S. Special Operations Command; the Spectre Association; the U.S. Navy Parachute Team; and the Library of Virginia. My most grateful thanks to George Witte, editor of long standing; to Sally Richardson and Matt Shear; and to Lenore Hart, my anchor on lee shores and my guiding star when skies are clear. Special thanks on this book to Naia Poyer for her sage advice too.

The specifics of personalities, locations, and procedures

in various locales, and the units and theaters of operations described, are employed as the settings and materials of *fiction,* not as reportage of historical events. Some details have been altered to protect classified procedures.

As always, all errors and deficiencies are my own.

Of all that is bitter for men, cruelest is this: to know so much and to be able to control nothing.

—Herodotus

Prologue:

THE VILLAGE

A turtle crawled into a hole, it crawled inside of an ostrich's hole."

The little girl hops from puddle to puddle, crooning to herself. A tin bracelet jingles.

Diin god gal, god gorey gal,
Gorey god gal, god diin gal.

Mist drifts from gray clouds above the three children in the yard in front of the hut. That morning they ate sorghum porridge sweetened with chopped dates, and their bellies are comfortable.

The roosters crow first, and the dogs bark. Then a low growl grows.

The trucks that come rumbling along the dirt roads between the fields are the biggest things the children have ever seen. Their steel projections snap branches off the young lemon and papaya trees. Their tires crush down the soft moist dirt. A goat runs into the road, baaing loudly. It halts, staring up, and a truck rolls over it without slowing. The soldiers in the truck beds are in dusty green uniforms. They're singing together, shouting out the words.

The family's hut is of hand-patted mud brick. Back of the wattle barn an old cow's tied to a pole buried in the ground. There's a privy with screens of woven branches. The yard faces a field of mangoes, with corn growing behind them.

Ghedi's atop a ladder, pruning one of the mango trees, when he notices the trucks. He doesn't know how old he is, but it's almost time to have a wife found for him. His arms and legs are like a spider's. He's dark, like his father, face narrow around the mouth, but with a wide brow and thoughtful eyes. He slides down the ladder as the soldiers jump down in front of the one house in the village with a sheet metal roof. The old *balabat* bustles out. He bows, then points at the broken branches.

The little girl croons on, oblivious to what's happening beyond her gate. "A turtle crawled into a hole, it crawled inside of an ostrich's hole."

The soldiers shoot and the *balabat* falls. Ghedi stands rooted, not believing it, though it's happened in other villages, the news passed from mouth to mouth across the land. Other guns pop, distant and trivial across the fields. Engines snort from the other side of the *garad*, from across the canals the ancestors dug when the People first came to this land. Lions are growling all around the horizon, a long rope of lions, drawing tight around the village.

Their mother's scream snaps the children around. "Come in out of the yard. Come inside! This instant!"

His little brother and sister look at Ghedi. He shoulders his pruning hook and shouts, "Come!" The children trail in, eyes wide. Chickens run squawking under their feet. His sister Zeynaab's carrying her doll. His little brother Nabil is naked. He keeps pushing at his runny nose with the back of his wrist. Nabil's cute as a baby goat, but his foot drops when he lifts it so he limps when he walks.

"Huyo, huyo," Nabil whimpers. "Mama, mama."

"Mother, they killed *balabat*. Where's *aabbe*? Where's Father?"

His mother doesn't seem to hear. She's looking toward the fields.

"Where's Father?" Ghedi grips her arm, shakes her.

"Gone. He's gone."

"What? Where'd he go?"

She doesn't answer. Just stands looking across at the soldiers, at something they're dragging into the field.

Ghedi turns the hook in his hands. "Mother, what shall we do?"

"They told us to go," she says to herself. "Give up the land and go. But the council wouldn't listen."

A strange humming comes then, and a moment later the air cracks like a whip but louder. His mother jerks and puts her hands to her face. When she opens them her cheeks are bloody. She looks at her palms, then cups her face again. Part of it's gone. There's blood behind her too, all over the wall of the hut.

"Huyo, huyo," Nabil whimpers, clutching her dress where red spots are falling. They rain on his head too. Ghedi slaps his brother's head till he lets go.

Their mother whirls and runs inside. As she moans in there the children look back at the soldiers. The humming drifts above them like angry bees. "Who's taking their honey?" Zeynaab asks. Ghedi pushes her inside the hut, then his brother.

Inside it's dark. Their mother's stumbling about, pulling objects down from places the children couldn't reach. Something falls and shatters. Fragments spin in the dust. He recognizes them. A white bowl with blue birds and rabbits on it. The children ate from it when they were small, first him, then Zeynaab, then Nabil. It would have been the baby's turn next.

The pieces crunch as their mother steps on them. Her blood patters on the dirt. It makes a red apron down her dress. She wraps *muufo* bread and rice in a cloth and gives it to Zeynaab. She takes off her *xirsi* amulet and knots it around her daughter's wrist. At Ghedi she thrusts a knife and a folded packet of dirty paper. He stares at it, not knowing they had money.

She snatches the baby up from where it lies wrapped by the door. Its hand waves in the air, black where the healer burned it. She thrusts it into Ghedi's arms. "Take care of your brother. Never let them see your sisters. Pray to Allah for those killed that He takes them home to paradise. Those who murder, he will put in baskets and burn alive. Go to your family, they'll always feed you. Go to the *magaada*, the great city, find *Abti* Jama. At the Suuqa Haqaaraba. Now *run.*"

"Where is the city?" says Zeynaab, wiping her eyes. "Mama, are you not coming?"

But she's slumping, holding the table with one hand. Melting, like a candle. "Go with your brother," she whispers. "You children stay together. Always stay together."

"Why are the soldiers here?"

"The soldiers take it now, but you will take it back. This land is ours. Our blood is in its water."

"Mama, come with us."

A screech of metal, so close it sounds as if it's in their yard. Forcing herself up, their mother pushes them out the back. She pushes so roughly Nabil falls. She drags him up and shoves him at Ghedi. Then she sits down, and blood runs down from where her teeth were into the bare ground where the chickens pecked. "Hide in the canal. Bullets will not hit you there. Go to the city. Tell Uncle Jama a man's judged by what he does for his kin. Now go!" she screams, face smaller somehow than they've ever seen it. As if it too is a child's, and she's no older than they.

They look back to see their hut, the *balabat*'s, and all the others on fire. The smoke rises black above hills green and golden with groves of lemons and oranges. A bright small red flame rises and hovers before falling again. Shots snap like cattle whips through the leaves of the orchards.

Ghedi's mouth tastes of dust. He left the pruning hook in the hut. How could he do that? He could kill one of the soldiers. He slaps his brother and pushes him along the ditch when he cries and tries to turn back. "What is it to you? Don't complain. You're not hurt!" he shouts, then lowers his voice as men yell not far away. More bees hum over their heads.

Other figures spill from the corn rows. Adults and children, carrying hoes, bundles, babies. Some tow goats, others sheep. A woman waddles with a chicken tucked under each arm, the fowls regarding the children with emotionless eyes. A one-armed elder pushes a rubber-tired farm cart down the bank into the slowly eddying water. A toothless old woman lies on her back in the mud. As the children pass she smiles, reaches out her hand to Zeynaab. Smoke drifts overhead, a dirty drape between them and the misty sky.

When Nabil looks back, the village is already gone.

Three days later, the children lie sprawled in the shade of an acacia. The sun's bright today, and hot. The road is inches thick with yellow dust and they're covered with it, like yellow children. It smells of dung. They're wrapped in castoff clothing picked up along the road. There's plenty to choose from. Bandits discovered the refugees the day after they began walking. Some they beat, others they killed. A boy not much older than Ghedi they simply took. Sharpened sticks are propped against the tree. At their feet is a shallow hole.

Ghedi sits with eyes open, watching the shimmer of heated air on the sand. He sees camels lurching side to side. When he blinks there are no camels there.

"Give her to me," he says.

Zeynaab hands the wrapped bundle over. Yesterday a man offered to buy Zeynaab from her brothers. He offered food for them all if she'd come with him. The sharpened sticks kept him off. He'd laughed, and asked what they were. Samaale? Bantu? "You look like Bantu," he told them. "Scum of shit, offspring of hyenas. Die on the road, then. You'll never reach the city."

Nabil presses the back of his hand to his parched lips. The people who live along the road won't let the refugees use their wells. Yesterday, after he sharpened their sticks, Ghedi traded the knife for water. The rice and *muufo* bread are gone. Zeynaab chewed some up and tried to feed the baby some but it wouldn't eat. It kept its eyes closed, eyelids jerking as if it was having bad dreams. They tried to give it water but it wouldn't drink. This morning when they woke it was dead.

Ghedi lays the bundle in the hole. Each child sprinkles a handful of dirt. They scoop with their arms until it's covered.

"Find stones to pile on," Ghedi says. "Or the dogs will dig her up. Remember this tree. Remember that hill. When we come back with Uncle we'll find her again. Take her to the village and bury her with Grandma. And with—" But he can't say *Mother.*

Nabil's weeping but without tears, just choked gasps. When he rubs his lips they crack into plates that bleed. He wants his mother. He talks to her in his head as they walk.

Zeynaab feels as if there's an empty room behind her eyes. The man yesterday had stared at her as if she were something to eat. For a moment she'd almost said, Yes, give us food and I'll go with you.

Maybe today she'll have to.

All afternoon the dust rises as the road climbs. Their village wasn't the first, or the last. Thousands of others walk the same road. The land of farms and rivers lies behind them, and there are no more trees. This place grows only rocks and twisted gray cacti. The children trudge along, each in his own hell of thirst and hunger. Their ears ring from the heat. One woman gives Nabil a sip of vinegary water. The others ignore them. They move in clots, with those they know, from their own villages or families. They sit apart when they halt. Those who have food don't share; those who have none don't beg.

At last the procession thickens, slows, wends to a halt. From ahead comes shouting. Ghedi jumps in place, trying to see over the crowd. Finally he tells his brother and sister, "Stay here. Stay right here."

"Don't go, Ghedi," Nabil whimpers.

His brother slaps the back of his head. "Shut up. I'll be right back." He twists off between the grown-ups, lithe body and long bare arms and legs like a snake slithering through a rock pile.

A rumble echoes through the stony hills. The crowd stirs. They pick up bundles, pull children closer.

"Bandits," someone says. "Rebels," mutters someone else.

The pickups gun up the slope. Men hang off, rifles in one hand, the other gripping handholds. The vehicles circle inward, trailing dust. The men on them are lean and hard and keen-faced as bronze arrowheads. Ghedi can't make out what clan they are. There's bad blood and bad memories all through these lands, fought over for so many centuries. So much to account for, to avenge or atone. Struggling toward the front of the crowd, he can remember only parts of it. Only what he's been told is his own history.

The cries come on the wind, on the blowing dust. They're high, exultant, mingled with the grind of tires, the noisy honking of the trucks.

Then the killing begins.

I

THE TRANSFORMATION

1

ARLINGTON, VIRGINIA

The symposium ran all afternoon, with papers like "Expert Maintenance Advisory Systems for Deployable Forces" and "Living with OPA-90 Oil Spill Response Requirements." Outside the summer sun blazed down, but the symposium-goers roved an air-conditioned display area. It was indirectly lit, lofty-ceilinged, and corridored into long aisles; its booths featured near-life-size displays of missile launchers, swimmer delivery vehicles, modular radios that frequency-hopped a thousand channels a second.

Dan Lenson was in short-sleeved khaki, the silver oak leaves of a full commander on his collar. They'd glittered once, but they weren't new now. His sandy hair showed silver. The crow's-feet around his gray eyes were deeper. But he was still lean and still managed to run fifteen miles a week.

He sighed, swirling a plain tonic from the complimentary bar, looking at a mockup of yet another weapons system. He didn't think more weaponry necessarily made the country safer. Not the way money was spent on the Hill, a process he'd seen too close up to have much faith in. But he'd also seen too many of its enemies, at too close a range, to believe no weapons were necessary at all.

Grimacing, he kneaded a neck vertebra reinjured in the Strait of Hormuz. An operation involving a Russian-export rocket torpedo that even now wasn't public knowledge. And for good reason.

"Dan. Dan Lenson, isn't it?"

He turned to find himself face-to-face with a small man in service dress blue. His sleeves gleamed with gold, and behind him, silent but attentive, a lieutenant carried a black computer case.

"Admiral Contardi," Dan said, shaking hands. Vincent Contardi was chief of naval education and training, but word on the street had him a front-runner for vice chief of naval operations, and the four stars that went with being the second highest officer in the Navy. They'd met before, though back then Dan had been so junior—just another fresh face holding a pointer—he doubted the admiral remembered. Their last meeting had been—

"At the vice president's party, wasn't it?" Contardi said. His high-domed forehead gleamed. "You were on the National Security Council staff. Before the . . . contretemps with General Stahl."

Dan choked on his tonic to hear an attempted assassination described as a "contretemps." He coughed into his fist. "Uh . . . yessir. Right."

"You were with Blair Titus. I served with her on a medical compensation panel. Sharp lady. I know you're proud of her." Contardi beckoned past him to someone, but added, as Dan started to turn away, "You and I had a chat that evening, as I recall. I complimented you on the Congressional, then we had a few words about a faster, nimbler military."

"I remember that, sir."

"Our ideas were sketchy then. Fuzzy, versus crisp. But since—you listened to our paper?"

"Yessir, I did." It and the Q and A afterward, billed as the highlight of the symposium, had been filled with geekspeak: revolution in warfare, battlespace awareness, decision-making nodes; the PowerPoint slides had flashed by at bewildering speed. Dan had been intrigued, then baffled, and to judge by the faces of the rest of the audience, he wasn't the only one. "But, uh, I wasn't really—"

"I tried to talk Mac out of those equations, but he said anybody could follow it. Anyway, we've put some theoretical meat on the bones. Have you met Dr. Cormac Fauss?"

Fauss was six inches taller than Dan, a scarecrow in tweed jacket and black slacks and tasseled cordovan loafers, with a spiky mustache that wouldn't have looked out of place on a British colonel. Contardi lifted his glass and drifted away, leaving Dan with his new friend, who he assumed was not a medical doctor, but one of the academics who assisted flag-level officers; mathematicians, physicists, the occasional economist. The British called them "boffins," but the genus didn't really have a name this side of the Atlantic.

"Commander Dan Lenson," Fauss said, measuring him like a tailor. "*Reynolds Ryan.* The Syrian incursion. *Van Zandt.* Desert Storm. USS *Horn.* And I heard something from Jenny Roald about your involvement with the Korean navy. Still at TAG?"

Dan nodded. The Tactical Analysis Group was the Navy's think tank, gaming and testing the three-dimensional tactics the fleet needed to fight at sea. He'd been there for two years, with his commanding officer posting him overseas again each time he returned from an assignment. After what had happened in the East Wing, there were still elements in the command structure that might very well want his hide.

"It's really the wave of the future." Fauss's confiding monotone managed to make everyone within twenty yards turn and look at them. "Transformation rests on three legs. One: networking. The transformational shift from industrial-era command structures to a robust network flow that lets co-protagonists self-synchronize decisions. More like a swarm of bees than a rigid hierarchy of information flow."

"Don't bees have queens?"

"We're talking about command, not insect reproduction."

"Sorry. But TAG doesn't get involved in—"

"It will, Dan. Transformation means changing everything—command and control, comms, intelligence, logistics, acquisition. It'll have a resounding tactical impact, especially on the smaller, faster nodes on the pointy end. The units the admiral calls the 'Bar Brawlers'—that make initial contact with the enemy, and act as targeters."

"Uh, I can see that."

"But entrenched forces will resist." Fauss leaned close to Dan's ear. "The 'We've always done it that way' crowd. Your CO knows what I mean."

His commanding officer was Captain Todd Mullaly, who was around somewhere; they'd driven up from TAG together. Dan looked, but didn't see him.

"And that's where you come in."

"Me, Dr. F?"

"I mean, both TAG and the O-5, O-6 community. You'll be our shock troops. Senior enough to see the need, junior enough not to be calcified. Those who comprehend the world to come, and make it happen, will be the admirals and generals of the future. Those who don't—well, 'It is the business of the future to be dangerous.' Alfred Whitehead."

Dan's grip tightened on the glass. Was this fool threatening him? Sometimes he sensed threat where none existed. A doctor had called it post-traumatic. Maybe so, but it meant he had to keep a close rein. Step back sometimes, and calm himself. "You're talking to the wrong guy, Doctor. Making stars hasn't been on my agenda for quite a while."

"But you have something most three-stars would kill for." Fauss gestured at Dan's ribbon bar. "The Congressional gives you credibility. We'd like you on our side. Help us pry boulders aside, shake some foundations."

"But what exactly are you trying to sell, Doctor? I don't get a clear picture when you start talking. Networking—what exactly do you mean by that? I know what the word means, but—"

"That a whiteboard over there? At that booth?" Fauss pushed his way between strolling senior enlisted. "I'll draw it for you."

The dry-erase marker squeaked. A typical org chart took shape, commander at the top, subordinates beneath. Dan noticed each level below the next increased by seven, the proper number for optimal span of control.

"Industrial——age militaries. Weber's bureaucratic hierarchy. Information flows up, decisions down. The most rational and efficient organization. At least, in the nineteenth century."

"Of course. How else?"

"Of course." Fauss looked around the circle of faces that had gathered, attracted by that subtle ozone. "How else indeed."

The marker squeaked again. This time, instead of a pyramid, a circle. Squiggly lines interlocked in its vacant heart. Threads webbed from one boundary to the other, intersecting at nodes Fauss emphasized with thumping dots of the felt tip.

"The outer ring: in contact with the enemy and the environment. They interact directly, through decision nodes that share and store information. The commander sets goals, rather than directing action."

"Then who gives the orders?"

"Outgrow the concept of 'order' and 'command.' In the Weberian Force, only the commander had information, and it was always partial and faulty—Clausewitz's 'fog of war.' In the Networked Force, technology enables perfect knowledge of own force, enemy, and environment. When the chessboard's clear, and each piece selects its own move, no 'player' is necessary."

"The commander withers away?"

"He takes on a new role: system administrator. He defines broad goals; the 'swarm' self-adjusts to achieve them. This is Admiral Contardi's transformative insight."

Dan rubbed his chin as the engineers and consultants around them waited for him to respond. But the circle looked like a pyramid, only seen from above. The "swarm" idea was interesting, but hardly any armed force operated in a vacuum, with only a blank field, a blank sea, just it and the enemy. Setting heavily armed, autonomous actors loose amid a civilian population sounded like a recipe for My Lai or

Wounded Knee. "Uh, but do you—I mean, the admiral—does he really believe perfect knowledge is possible?"

"Given adequate bandwidth, the fog of war is a relic of the past."

"Sun Tzu?"

Fauss smiled, as if he'd found a worthy opponent. " 'If you know the enemy and know yourself, you need not fear the result of a hundred battles. If you know yourself but not the enemy, for every victory you will suffer a defeat. If you know neither the enemy nor yourself, you will succumb in every battle.' For the first time, modern sensor, data-processing, and communications technology makes it possible to know the entire battlefield."

"That's the revolution," one of the onlookers put in.

"Diastrophic change," Fauss said. "Diastrophic—meaning radical. Based on new technology and a new paradigm."

The computer salesmen smiled. Dan cleared his throat, not eager to interrupt the cheerful tone, like that of a church group unleashed on the dessert table. But unable to let it just go unchallenged. "Sun Tzu. All right. 'All warfare is based on deception. Hence, when able to attack, we must seem unable; when using our forces, we must seem inactive; when we are near, we must convince the enemy we are far away; when far away, we must convince him we are near.' "

Fauss tilted his head. "Meaning what, Commander?"

"Meaning whichever enemy we face next has probably also read Sun Tzu. And won't do us the favor of making all that information we're gathering correct."

"They won't have a choice," a woman in a business suit put in. Her name tag read TRANSCRYPT TECHNOLOGIES. "They can run but they can't hide. Not on the electronic battlefield."

Fauss beamed around, then at Dan. "Maybe that's too simple?"

"Maybe that's too simple."

"What about empowering the operators? Is that too simple? Or has every order you've ever gotten seemed wise to you?"

"To tell the truth, that's what appeals to me about what you're describing," Dan told him.

"I thought it would." The doctor pushed through the crowd, which began to drift apart, still discussing what he'd said. Some held out opened copies of a green-covered book, on which Fauss, hardly looking, dashed off a signature. The title, in bold print, read *The Transformation Paradigm*. He took Dan by the elbow, looking around. Caught the eye of the aide who'd been with Contardi a few moments before.

"The admiral's in the greenroom," he said quietly.

Dan's commanding officer was there too, in one of the upholstered faux-bamboo chairs near the silver trays of cookies and the rumbling coffee urn. Todd Mullaly sipped complimentary beer from a Lockheed mug, leaving foam on his upper lip. Beside him Contardi sat with not a hair out of place, a cup of tea steaming at his elbow. He glanced up from a wafer-thin notebook computer as Dan came in. "Mac fill you in on what we're asking you to do?"

Dan sucked air. Had he missed something? He glanced back, but Fauss had vanished. "Uh, did he—no sir, I don't think he did. Not in so many words."

Contardi placed one hand over the other and rested them on his sternum, the slightly old-maidish attitude he'd assumed on the podium. "Our little revolution, on the Navy's level at least, is three-pronged. First comes networking. Robust C4ISR, lateral information flows among operational units. Every commander since Pharaoh's tried to win by concentrating forces at the point of breakthrough. But if we seamlessly link scattered platforms and sensors, we can concentrate *fire* while maintaining *dispersal*. Dominant battlefield awareness buys disruptive, concurrent operations with small, agile forces."

"Yessir. Got it."

"The second is crew swapping. You've heard of that."

"Keeping ships in theater, and flying crews out in rotation. The way the boomer force rotates Blue and Gold crews."

"Essentially." Contardi scrolled; he was reading something

on the notebook even as he carried on the conversation. "We invest a billion dollars in a state-of-the-art destroyer, but it spends only a quarter of its life deployed. We're still crunching numbers, but what seems to be falling out is a four-three model. Four crews for three ships. We rotate back for maintenance and dry-docking, but keep one hull on station at all times. A one-in-four rotation for the ships, instead of a one in three. Eventually we may get to one in two. And don't forget, these will be much more capable units."

"That's the third prong in the trident," Fauss put in, having returned while the admiral was speaking. "How we spend acquisition funding."

"We don't need to go into that here," Contardi cut him off. He tapped keys as they waited. Then looked up, amber gaze flickering among them. "I want TAG to take a piece of the transformation process. Todd, we need several in-depth studies. One will be an evaluation of the crew-swap concept for a squadron of Tornadoes deploying to the Red Sea to surge our force levels there."

For a moment Dan was confused—the Tornado was a British attack aircraft, and he hadn't heard about any surge in the Red Sea—but then realized Contardi must mean the Cyclone-class patrol ships, one of which was USS *Tornado*. Larger and more heavily armored than a World War II PT boat, but shallower-draft and more maneuverable than frigates.

But Mullaly didn't say anything, just waited for Contardi to go on. After a moment he did. "I know Commander Lenson's work aboard *Horn*. He took a challenging concept, integrating females, and made it work. No ordinary crew could have saved that ship, with the damage you suffered."

"Thank you, Admiral."

"Wish we could have recognized you for it. But word gets around. And I know about your accomplishment with Team Charlie, securing the Shkval-K. You have credibility in the Fleet. Engineering experience. You're the most decorated officer we have. I want you to manage the migration, then sum up your lessons learned in a report we can use to expand the crew-swap concept to the rest of the Fleet."

Mullaly raised his eyebrows, watching the ball pass to Dan. Who bought a few seconds by crossing to the coffee urn. The joe smelled burnt, but he'd had worse, in the shaft alleys and chief's messes and engine rooms of a score of ships, here and there across and beneath the watery face of the planet.

"To be honest, Admiral—"

"I want you to be."

"—I'm not entirely certain crew swap's a great idea. What we might get is a fleet that's smaller but costs more. I get that the forward units spend more time on station. But fewer ships and crews at home *reduces* the surge capacity for a major contingency."

"Don't start with a closed mind, Dan," Mullaly put in. "Dr. Fauss asked for the best I had. This issue's right in TAG's strike zone."

"My mind's not closed, sir. I'm just not certain I'd come back with the positive evaluation the admiral might expect."

Contardi's lips thinned. Not exactly a smile, but it might not have been intended as one. "There'll be no command influence on your conclusions. Tell me what's wrong, what needs to be fixed if it's to work on a larger scale. Report directly to me. Your recommendations will be acted on."

Dan looked again at Mullaly, who had laced his fingers over his stomach. Benign but poker-faced.

Contardi pushed a button, snapped the notebook closed. He handed it to the aide, who'd come in so noiselessly Dan hadn't noticed him, and stood. Mullaly rose too. Contardi turned the handle of the teacup in a quarter circle. Then patted Dan's arm, stepping in close. Dan smelled aftershave and fresh cotton and a disconcerting whiff of sweat.

"I want you with me on this, Lenson," he murmured. "There are those who are with me, and those who are against. The same way, they tell me, it is with you. More may depend on it than we know."

Dan had a sinking feeling. He wasn't sure he believed in what this man and his staffers and consultants were selling. Sometimes it sounded like snake oil. At other times, like

Billy Mitchell or Heinz Guderian: other military geniuses who'd had to battle naysayers to change the world. But certainly the way to test it was with a squadron of small boys, before the whole Fleet got reformed willy-nilly from above. Every time that happened, it shot retention and combat effectiveness to hell.

Mullaly was frowning, and Dan remembered: his was not to reason why. He was no longer in awe of admirals. The gloss of unreasoning obedience inculcated at Annapolis had long ago worn off. But he was still in the Navy. Until he wasn't, if a three-star wanted him to stress-test a new organizational concept, his duty was perfectly clear.

"Yes sir," he told Contardi. "If those are my orders, I'll do my best."

GHEDI

The pickups career across the desert, throwing up a dusty smoke that smells of death and terror. It catches in Ghedi's teeth, scratches under his eyelids. He coughs and coughs as he and two other boys slide on the sand that coats the jolting bed. A brown she-goat with a red ribbon plaited around her throat pants at their feet, blood pumping from a slit that looks like another ribbon. Her frantic eyes search theirs. The oldest boy swings himself out of the gate. He hits the sand running, but another truck swerves instantly to smash him down.

Rocks fly out of wheel wells, dust boils, shots crack in the adobe murk. The men shout and gesture to one another as they drive. They're stringy, dark, with white cloths wrapping skulls shaped like ax heads and burning black eyes that turn now and again to look back at their captives like the hungry eyes of locusts.

The goat kicks, the blood pumps. Then it slackens. The animal relaxes. Her gaze goes polishless and fixed, filming with the dust that throngs the dry wind.

Ghedi screams without words, looking back into the boil that writhes and tumbles in their wake, blotting out everything behind them. The road, the clotted multitudes of refugees. Who'd scattered, screaming, clutching their pitiful belongings, their children, their feeble elders, as the trucks first circled, then, seeing no one armed, screeched around to plow into the crowd.

Right into where he'd left his brother and sister. "Let me go," he'd screamed, struggling with the man who'd hauled him up by one arm kicking and struggling into the bed of the truck, like a fish suddenly jerked into a fine thin element where breath itself could not be had.

Now that man smiles, showing yellow fangs like a hyena's. His fingers dig in like the cold claws of a rooster. He leans till his lips brush the boy's ear. His breath smells rank, meaty, like old blood.

"You do not jump off, like that fool. You look like a wise, brave boy. Yes? We will see how clever you are. And how brave."

They ride locked gaze to gaze, Ghedi looking back into those eyes as if reading that which is written and must come to pass. His gaze slides down long bare forearms, scarred and puckered with old burns, to dusty, mahogany-toned hands.

To the weapon they grip, its blued steel worn to silver. The stock scarred where something very hard and moving very fast tore through the fibers of heavy-grained wood. The doubled jut of the barrel. The black curve of the magazine.

The man pulls a fold of fabric up over the lower part of his face, and shoves Ghedi down into the rusty bed.

The camp's a rock-walled ravine only partially sheltered from the rising wind. Heat radiates from it as from a burnt-over field. As the trucks halt beneath an overhang the bandits leap out, carrying the weapons they've picked up from the floorboards. Some pull drab tarps from behind the seats. Others cradle rifles as the boys climb slowly down. They huddle coated with dust like tan flour, sticklike arms and legs quivering, hugging themselves as they wait for what comes next. Ghedi glances at the sun, figuring the direction back to his brother and sister. But surrounded, boxed by steep stone, he doesn't dare make a break.

The fighters' voices are loud. Their dialect's different from that of his village, but he understands them. They pour water into radiators from goatskin bags, pry rocks out of knobby-treaded tires with knives, refuel from battered orange metal cans stacked in the shade. The odor of gasoline tinctures the wind.

Presently, when the trucks are cared for and covered, the tarps pulled tight and then carefully disarranged so no straight lines are left, their attention turns past the captives, to where woodsmoke blows from, and merry voices and music.

And presently, the scent of roasting meat.

The boys wipe their lips with their hands, leaving smudges across their faces. They stand where the smoke blows. They've stood so long their legs shake, their heads spin with thirst and hunger and fear. Two younger fighters, one in a white robe like the drivers, the other in ball cap and T-shirt with interlocking colored rings on the breast, sit with terrible motionlessness against the ravine wall, weapons across their knees. Their jaws contract endlessly, chewing the wads of leaves called qat.

The other rebels are feasting. They toss bones over their shoulders, but none of the boys dares move. The fires crackle. Gradually the sky turns a darker blue. Shadows submerge the ravine.

A boy begs timidly for water. The young guards beat him with rifle butts until his head breaks like a clay bowl. He lies shuddering, eyes rolled up to blank whites, bare feet kicking as if he's running. A darkness grows under him. He jerks, then goes still.

That was hours ago. Since then not one boy's moved from where he was told to stand, not one has spoken.

Ghedi waits with them. His mind is reflectionless as the surface of the canal on a day without wind. He breathes in smoke and the smells of meat and smoke that come now and again like memories half remembered.

The dark comes, and stars sprawl above the firelight as light bleeds from the world. One burns brighter than the rest above the ravine walls. He fixes his gaze on it and listens to hyenas bark far off, the sound carrying across the desert for miles.

At last the man who pulled him off his feet hours before hoists himself from his crouch before the fire like a bundle of sticks wrapped in white cloth reassembling itself. He stretches, looking about, pushing dates into his mouth, sucking the sweetness from each finger. At the sky. The top of the ravine.

At last, as if remembering, he saunters toward the boys. Five are still erect, one lying in the sand, head shattered. The dark puddle has already vanished in the terrible dryness, sucked into the dust that looks white in the firelight, the light of the stars.

"You." Seizing a small bandy-legged lad by the neck, he walks him to the fire, then past it, around a blind curve in the rocks and out of sight.

Ghedi has a sudden sharp memory. A lamb he'd grown to love, that he'd thought had been given to him. Then his father put the knife in his hand, and told him: this was Eid-ul-Zuha, and all belonged to God; and in His name the lamb was to die. He'd cried and begged. But at last, after it was explained, he understood.

God did not need the lamb. God had made all lambs, all human beings too. Ibrahim had been called by God to sacrifice his only son, Ismail. Ibrahim had shown his willingness, and God had not required that death. Now he, Ghedi, was called to do the same. What he loved most was the most acceptable sacrifice.

He remembered his father's hand on the knife with his own. The feel as the blade punctured skin. The bleat, the twisting muzzle, quickly clamped shut by his father's work-scarred hands. The smell of hot blood. The way the beast had looked up, trusting him.

He remembers the she-goat, in the bed of the truck.

And his own mother's eyes.

A staccato of gunfire. The men at the fire glance that way but do not move from their relaxed crouches, their stone perches.

The tall one strides back alone. The folds of his *maahwees* whirl behind him. He swings one of the ugly rifles in one hand, muzzle down.

"Follow me. You boys! This way."

Ghedi's legs pop as he takes his first step in hours. He sways and almost goes down. Another boy catches his hand. They squeeze each other's grip tight and stumble along together. The two guards fall in behind the little group. Curious gazes trail them as they pass the fire. A woman in the long colorful dress of the nomad crouches picking scraps and bones out of the dirt and placing them in a red plastic bowl. Only her eyes show beneath her shawl, and she does not look up as they pass.

"You're nothing," the tall man says conversationally. "You have no land, no clan, no weapons. You've pissed your pants. What sort of men are you? Are you men at all?"

None of the boys answers, and maybe he doesn't expect them to. The smoke eddies around them, hanging in the ravine, drawing stinging tears.

When they turn the corner he lifts the rifle and they shuffle to a stop. Ghedi feels the hand gripping his tighten.

The boys stand shoulder to shoulder, barely breathing. Covered with the dust, they might be terra-cotta statues in the dark. Save for their wondering eyes. Then the guards shove them from behind, rifles out stiff-armed. They swim through the gathering shadows, through the last of the firesmoke.

Gradually he makes out what fills the depression ahead. The mass of blackness seems to crawl, a living blanket.

It's a crowd of women and children, squatting in what little light falls from the stars, from the single burning planet that hangs directly above.

"Yes, look on them. These are your enemy," the tall man says. He doesn't even sound angry. Only tired. "The enemy of all Ashaari and of your country. The government took it in their name. The government, that steals what is ours in the name of fairness. Does this seem right to you? Does this seem just?"

These people don't look as if they took anyone's land. The boys peep at them from the corners of their eyes. The women rock, black-draped, bare heels flashing, holding their children close. One wails, beginning a general outcry. The high thin sounds mount to where the moon rises close and pale.

"The time for blood-compensation is past. When an injury is done to our clan, do we not have blood? Or are we its sons?

"I want all those of noble clan to my right. All those who are *sab*, to my left."

The *sab* are those who are not of the pure clans, the proud tall nomads who come out of the *geelhers*, the camel camps, the high desert.

The boys edge apart. The hand gripping his loosens, then slides free in a whisper of dry skin. There's no possibility of pretense. Each boy holds in his brain the chain of genealogy that defines his clan. More intimate than his bowels, as impossible to disown, this cannot be denied or lied about.

But his people have not been nomads for many generations. He's proud of his line, but what will this man judge, when he asks its name? Time narrows down, narrows down, to a spider-thread glistening in starlight.

He stands where he is. The tall man asks his clan family, and when he says it, nods slightly. "Yes," he says. "You are welcome with us."

"I am proud to stand with you," Ghedi says, the words from which old tale of camel raids and flashing swords he can't recall.

The tall man blinks. "Remember when you were small, and your father and uncles showed you how to give honor to God."

The weapon feels heavy, awkward, for a moment. Then it

seems it's lived within his skinny arms forever. Its weight makes something move inside his chest. Something that lifts, under his heart.

He's pointing it when a short bandit in a dirty Western-style shirt suddenly slaps him on the ear. He staggers, head ringing. The man grabs the weapon back, shows him how the brassy shining rounds lock into the magazine, the magazine locks into the gun, the bolt snaps forward and the lever on the side goes up and down. "Now it's ready to kill," he snarls. "Are you?"

The smoke eddies in his eyes. The whimpers come louder. He aims the rifle again.

Then lowers it. "I have no quarrel with these," he mutters. "Soldiers in trucks drove us from our land. Not these."

The men smile grimly. "Then don't kill those," the short one says. He looks past him, at the boys who stand to the left. The one whose hand he was holding stretches out his arms. Their gazes lock.

"Were you not taught that he who does not strike back when he is offended against is unworthy of the name of Ashaari?"

He remembers his father's face. Wonders why he wasn't there when the soldiers came. If he had been, would they still own their land?

The tall man slaps his face. "Well? Speak up!"

Ghedi's voice sounds muffled in his own ears. "He did so teach me."

"Then show us what he taught."

Before the tall man's finished speaking the gun's jerking in his hands, deafening, like holding thunder itself. Its flashes show him the eyes of those he kills.

2

FENTENI, ASHAARA

Around the compound of trailers and storage sheds the desert stretched shimmering. Despite the knock of a generator and the whine of an air conditioner inside the central lab-and-office prefab, sweat trickled down the ribs of the freckle-armed woman in jeans and short-sleeved bush shirt. The blistering African sun soaked into the polished aluminum roof like rain into a dry dune.

Dr. Gráinne O'Shea noted this only remotely. She was focused three hundred kilometers to the north, sixty meters below the desert surface. She frowned at the monitor, sucking a mint and pushing back a strand of wet auburn hair as the assistant the government had insisted she employ moaned-sang to himself, plotting dots across a graph.

O'Shea had spent all her professional life since graduate school in East Africa. First in the Ogaden, then Ashaara for the International Hydrological Programme, with funding from the UN Commission on Sustainable Development. She was married, but hadn't seen her husband in years. He was in palaeographical assessment at the University College of Cork. She'd had his picture above her computer, but when it had fallen off the wall as the adhesive cooked out of the tape, she'd left it behind the desk. It was too much trouble to move the maps and printouts that stacked and slanted around the narrow space where she wedged her body, her elbows, and her keyboard.

"Crap," she muttered. The screen had stayed blank for five full minutes. Ashaaran Internet service, never better than inchworm-slow, had grown even more sluggish in the last few weeks. Sometimes she didn't get answers to her e-mails for days. Often they vanished, damned to cyberhell.

She leaned back, massaging her lower sacrum. "Abdiwali. Find any fuel?"

"They let me have five liters. But the price, I could not get it for—"

"That's all right. Water?"

"The jerrican's half full. Where are you going? Al-Musa again?"

A knock shivered the flimsy metal door. She waited for Abdiwali to get it. When he didn't she sighed and stood.

A tall dark man she didn't recognize, in the green of the Ashaaran military. A Russian jeep idled, a driver puttering across the hood with a cloth, soldiers sitting in back.

"Vous etes madame le professeur? J' m'appelle Chef de Bataillon Assad."

She shifted to French, the colonial language of northern Ashaara and the one most locals tried first when speaking to whites. *"Bonjour, Chef. Pourrais-je vous aider?"*

Assad looked around the trailer. He wore an automatic in a brown leather holster. "I've come from the capital to see how your work's progressing."

"Excellent. Will you come in? I can heat chai. Or would you prefer Nescafé?"

Assad said neither, but he'd take water. She poured a cup from the container Abdiwali's family kept filled for two euros a week, and invited the major to sit. But he ignored the folding chair and strolled the length of the trailer, turning sideways to skirt boxes of records and sampling equipment, sipping as his gaze roved. Gráinne tried not to frown.

For the first year in-country she'd worked with a Dr. Isdheeb, with the oddly named Ministry of Interior Resources. But Isdheeb had vanished suddenly—"poofed" as one of her UN contacts put it—and she'd been passed from desk to desk until the last time she'd reported to the dusty brickpile that smelled like it was still 1880 no one had been willing to speak with her. They'd watched her stride down the corridors with averted eyes, and most of the desks had been empty. Which was strange for Ashaara, with its top-heavy bureaucracy that was a maddening hybridization of the European love of forms with the African habit of personalizing interactions.

She turned, and caught sight of Abdiwali. He was shaking, backed between two UN-issue filing cabinets, eyes fixed on the officer as if on a lion that had suddenly entered the trailer. Gráinne had encountered a lion once, in the western mountains. The tawny animal had watched her with sleepy eyes for what felt like a century before padding away, back into the broken terrain as if created from it and now dissolved again.

"Who is this man?" Assad asked her, lip curled as if he sniffed a foul odor. "This . . . *southerner*."

"Mr. Abdiwali's my assistant and interpreter." She made her voice firm. "He's been a great help. I hope it will be possible for him to continue working with me."

Assad shrugged. He kept looking at the computer. "He can wait outside. Who does this equipment belong to? The vehicles?"

Gráinne nodded, and her assistant ducked outside, bending his knees as he passed their visitor. A blast of heat entered as he opened the door, then cut off as it slammed, vibrating the walls. The air conditioner whined harder. "Those are the property of the International Hydrological Programme."

"American?"

"Actually Russian funded, mostly. And UN recognized."

"You are a scientist?"

Was he from the ministry? Actually, he'd never said he was. But then, who *was* he? "Uh, correct. I've published in arsenic geochemistry and geochemical modeling at the field scale, and reactive transport modeling of groundwater and surface water. But most of my experience has been in arid-region hydrogeology. And you, Major? Where did you study?"

"Tell me, what is 'hydrogeology'?"

She fought to keep a straight face. "Studying the occurrence, distribution, and effects of subsurface water."

"I'm told you have explosives here."

Was that what this was about? They were afraid their bloody "rebels" might seize it? "We once did, Major. That is, Dr. Kyriazis did." She explained the equipment in the second trailer: the twenty-four-channel digital instantaneous floating point seismographs, the geophones, and the seismic source, a Bison hydraulically accelerated weight system towed behind her Land Rover. "So you see, we haven't needed explosives for years now. Few geologists do."

"What happened to those you had?"

She told him that whatever Kyriazis had brought had been either expended or taken home with him; she had no explosives and for that matter no arms. That was what had confined her to the compound for the last weeks: unrest in the hinterland, lack of security and field support from the ministry. Could he supply escorts and assistance? Fuel? Bond paper, which she was almost out of? (She didn't mention the toilet paper situation, knowing how Ashaarans reacted to any hint of female uncleanness.) The president had assured her the ministry would support her efforts to clarify the country's water resources, especially in the teeth of drought and famine.

Assad listened expressionlessly. He moved to a piece of graph paper taped to the wall. It was frail and darkened, as if held over a fire. A series of broken lines, crossed by a diagonal rising from left to right. "What does this convey?"

"Demographic water scarcity versus a technical use-to-availability ratio."

"These lines have the names of countries."

"Yes, that's correct."

"Why is Ashaara at the bottom?"

She said wearily, "That chart's fifteen years old, Major. From Dr. Kyriazis's report. Do you remember him? Ever heard his name before?"

"Foreigners come and go in Ashaara."

"He was here for twenty years. The horizontal lines denote water supply needed to support a population, including household use, industrial uses, and agricultural production. Yes, Ashaara's at the bottom. He predicted what was coming. Massive drought, drop in groundwater levels, then famine. He laid out how you had to change the way you farmed and how you used water, and advised the president to seek aid to do that.

"Instead, the U.S. and the Russians fed in more weapons, playing you off against the Eritreans. You built a useless concrete industry. Now drought's hit again, and you don't know what to do, any of you. What *will* you do? Do you have any idea?"

But the major's eyes were riveted where her bush shirt gaped, fixed on the claddagh her husband had given her, long ago. "A strange symbol. Is it Christian?"

She told him about the Galwayman captured by pirates and sold to an Arab goldsmith, and how when he had been released he'd set up his shop in the oldest fishing village in Ireland. Knowing all the while Assad must have something else in mind. Abdiwali had brought stories from the marketplace about growing clan friction. The president had to go. That was perfectly clear, even if no one said so in her presence, and she knew enough never to comment on how badly he'd indebted and looted this nation.

Assad nodded, looking around again. "What exactly are you doing in our country, Dr. O'Shea?"

"Do I need to repeat everything I've just told you? I investigate groundwater resources."

"What do you do with these resources?"

"Primarily just now we map them."

"Why do you map them?"

She found this line of questioning both tedious and disturbing. Assad seemed to be probing for some deeper motivation. As if he suspected she was hiding some . . . secret. A drop of sweat rolled down her back.

Could he know?

Impossible. Not even at the ministry had she dropped the slightest hint. She held his eyes until they slid aside. He was sweating too.

Someone fired a shot outside. A flat bark that ebbed away over the desert. "Abdiwali," she muttered. Bolting to the trailer door, shouldering Assad aside, she threw it open.

To a blaze of light and heat like the flare of a welding machine. The major's guards stood a few yards off, aiming at stones piled one atop another. Another shot snapped out. It went wide by five feet, and the men laughed, the shooter too. She squinted around. Her assistant was far off down the road, headed toward the village.

"Why do you map them?" Assad repeated, behind her. She smelled musky sweat and dust and a distinctive scent. Qat, though he wasn't chewing it at the moment.

She lost patience. Would she ever understand this country? "I *map* them because that's my *job.* What's yours, Major? Why are you here bothering me? You know I can pick up my cell and call the president's office, don't you?"

"Oh, you can call. Maybe you can call the president himself, yes? But will anyone answer?"

"What do you mean? 'Will anyone answer'—"

Assad pushed by before she'd assimilated his sentence. "I apologize for 'bothering' you. Perhaps the next time we meet I will convince you of my importance." He stalked toward his vehicle, shouting at the men, who abandoned their game and ambled to join him.

When he was gone she drank down a cup of water, then another. The plastic gave it a musty taste. She stabbed at the air conditioner, but it was already at max. "Feck," she muttered. She threw the cup across the trailer, then grabbed her bush hat and stomped out.

Behind the trailer, at the edge of the gorge. Below her vultures pushed and cawed and fought; something dead must lie down there in the brush. More circled above the compound, cocking an eye her way each time they banked past.

She stood at the edge of an immense emptiness. Miles stretched from the tips of her black Blunnies to where the Western Mountains rose purple and lavender, and beyond them the frost-capped heads of the far Mahawayo. She came here when the stupidity and arrogance became too outrageous. She had no patience. Her mother had told her this when she was small. She saw no signs she'd ever changed.

The gorge was dry, with eroding layers of buff and ruddy sedimentary rock, volcanic ash, and central basin dioctahedral clays. She'd always expected it to yield the bones of tiny protohumans, primordial hairy East African leprechauns, half simian, half hominid. Like Olduvai. Two years ago a small team had come in from Stony Brook, not well funded, and she'd tried to persuade Tim White and Berhane Asfaw to come after that, but they'd refused, said there were no indications. She squinted at the crumbling soil for anything that might be ancient bone. It was supposed to turn almost black, stained with minerals. She was a hydrogeologist, but she'd always wondered about hominids. If you knew where there was water once, wouldn't that have been where the buggers gathered?

This desert reassured her it didn't matter, what human beings did now. What folly and crime. How many millions died, of fever, disease, starvation, war. They'd lived in East Africa for four and a half million years. And they'd still be here long after she was gone.

When she went back in an icon pulsed on the screen. She was back online, and she had a message. In a mailbox she didn't share with Abdiwali, that no one in Ashaara or even at the UN had access to.

She hesitated, hand on the mouse. Got up, checked that the trailer door was locked, and sat again. "Face the music, O'Shea," she whispered. Typed in the password, double-clicked, and sucked a breath as the message opened.

It was from Sweden.

> Ratios of dissolved salts in the four samples submitted were compared. All samples contained a low but consistent content CaSO4 and MgSO4. Ratio of dissolved salts and percentage of sulfate content support the hypothesis of common source.

Isotope analysis: Deuterium excess from the four samples:

Sample A - 21.41
Sample B - 21.38
Sample C - 21.41
Sample D - 21.62

All samples fall near the Levant meteoric line confirming original pluvial derivation from within the Mediterranean basin. Conformity of sample confirms sulfate analysis, again supporting the hypothesis of a common source paleowater deposit dating to 30K BCE. However data on supply and recharge rates are not adequate to speculate on size of common recoverable aquifer as proposed in the letter accompanying samples.

To clarify this further data collection is suggested at the following locations and depths . . .

She exhaled, letting tension ooze out of her fingertips, evaporate out of her wet scalp. Stress she'd carried for months. She felt weak, then immensely strong.

It was there.

But with the same thought came the knowledge: it was superlatively dangerous.

She moved to print out the e-mail, then lifted her fingers from the keys. Instead she closed that window and brought up another file.

A jagged, waist-pinched Ashaara stretched three hundred miles inland from the Red Sea, sticking its elbow deep into Sudan. Just under five hundred miles north to south, it looked like an outline of a human knee, the port of Ashaara City perched at the kneecap. Two river systems bisected it, streaming, at least in good times, toward the Red Sea from the Western Mountains. The red lines of the road network were disappointingly sparse, though not as disappointing as in reality, since whole sections had degenerated into sloughs of mud, dust, or loose stones. The south had been the most fertile region, orchards and farms during Italian times. It had produced agricultural surpluses until collectivization, when the brief but brutal rule of the aptly named Morgue had broken the Bantu and Ashaari farmers.

But she wasn't looking there, but north, to what was perhaps the most striking feature of the whole country.

Haunt of djinns and nomads, repository of myth and legend, the Empty Quarter meant nightmare and death for outsiders. Endless desert, dunes, salt flats; only a few nomad encampments mapped by the British during the Second World War dotted its forty-thousand-square-mile expanse. It was into the dreaded Quartier Vide that the Austrian archaeologist Karl Von Zirkel had disappeared in 1894, seeking a lost city mentioned by the early Coptic Fathers. It was from the Quartier Vide that the infamous Sheikh Dahir had harried the French in the twenties, until their planes wiped out his tribesmen with mustard gas. To this day small bands of *indigènes* roamed its wastes, nomading from seepage to seepage, or hand-dug oasis wells fed by shallow groundwater tables under the dunes.

Tabbing back and forth from her e-mail to the map, she etched numbers beside symbols. Gradually they formed a vast dotted-line oval that stretched to the Western Mountains, nearly to the Red Sea, and across the Sudanese border. The eastern one was marked A. The western, C. The northern, B. The southern, a few miles north of where this trailer sat, was marked D.

The numbers matched the sample names of the results from Sweden.

She saved this in a hidden folder, one invisible to a casual user. Then erased the e-mail from her in-queue. She sat back, blotting her cheeks with a tissue from a dried-out container of wet wipes.

It was real.

What Costa Kyriazis had intuited, and died wondering about. What she'd suspected, inspecting photos taken from space, but never been able to prove.

What had been found before in Libya, in the Sinai, in other regions considered arid and uninhabitable for all recorded history.

The samples she'd sent to Scandinavia had come from wells or artesian seeps at widely separated locations. Yet chemically and isotopically, they were the same.

Which meant they came from the same source, and the same era—an epoch thirty thousand years in the past.

Hundreds of meters beneath the Empty Quarter, in the porous Nubian sandstone that stretched from the Mediterranean deep into Africa, lay a reservoir of "fossil" water. An underground aquifer, a primeval lake. She'd proved it existed, but not how large it was. Perhaps enough to irrigate all Ashaara for decades. Maybe centuries, if the watery lens was thick enough. But only drilling would answer that question.

A more fabulous hoard than any legend of genies and gold. An unexpected, long-sequestered treasure. A secret that, once revealed, could lead to a secure and fertile future for an entire region prone to chronic drought and famine—or to war, mass murder, and genocide.

A secret far more powerful than any explosive, Major, she thought.

One she'd have to keep locked within her brain till she could consider how best to reveal it, and to whom.

Pursing her lips, she took a last long look. Then shut down the computer, and sat in the whirring heat, alone.

ZEYNAAB

When the trucks leave she searches for her brothers through the litter of the crying and the wounded, those hit by bullets maybe not even aimed at them. A sick jerky feeling seeps into her stomach. She wants to claw her family back to her out of the milling dust. She thinks she hears them shouting, and she screams. But how small her voice is, how thin amid the crying and shouting all around. She stumbles. Rocks cut her feet. The dust's too thick to make out the road. She glimpses a shadow with a gun. She turns and rushes away, until her sight reels and the air torches her lungs.

Hours later she wanders an apocalyptic land. The wind's kicked up hot as flames. Not a blade of grass is left on the stony ground. She moans, hands hiding her face. Should she go back to the village? But then she'll never see Ghedi or Nabil again. Her little brother's so small. She saved the last piece of corn bread for him.

When she comes across the road again she sinks into the dust. People trudge by. They look dazed. Before they were all walking in one direction. Now they wander, women without *hijab*, men without shirts, calling in cracked voices to those who've vanished. A blind man totters past, groping the air, scabbed eyes lifted as if he can see. She sits. A man speaks to her. He compliments her eyes, her small feet. She doesn't answer or look up, and at last he goes on.

Toward evening she wakes from wherever she was. She eats the last crust. Her teeth hurt. The stars are coming out. One is so bright, like a candle in the sky. Maybe that's where Paradise is.

She decides to go back to the village. She's afraid to go toward the city now. Even if Uncle's there. She has a confused notion they're still there, she'll push the gate open and there'll be her mother feeding the chickens, the baby on her hip, her brothers wrestling in the shade. This is some evil dream, sent by the Devil.

An old Bantu offers her a ride on his donkey. She's afraid but his kind face makes her trust him. He asks where she's going, and she says the name of her village. His face changes. "That was a sanctuary for the rebels," he says.

We weren't rebels, she wants to say, but doesn't. Still, the old man lets her ride nearly all night before he lifts her down.

For the next two days she walks. She holds out a hand to passing people. Someone throws something from a passing truck. She almost ignores it, then realizes it's a half-eaten banana. She wolfs it down, then staggers off the road, sick to her stomach.

* * *

She's walking along a road that seems to be high above all the lands around it. Then she's not there, that's all, it's as if she's fallen asleep.

When she wakes she's still walking, but now she's with a group of women. They're trudging through a village. All its doors are closed. Not even a cock crows as they plod through. It's so much like a dream she can't believe she's awake. Dust bakes in the noon sun. Something sparkles and she bends. Cartridge casings lie scattered like chickens' corn along the street. There are stains in the dust too. But no people.

The well's capped with a wooden lid. When the refugees drag it off a black cloud rises, buzzing like a rainstorm. So many flies the light fades like a rain cloud's passing.

She can't see what's down there, only the shocked faces of the women around it. She clings to one and says she's thirsty, why aren't they drawing water. The woman pushes her away. She says, "There are too many bodies."

As the days pass she feels less hungry but more ill. Her legs ache as if someone's twisting knotted ropes under her skin. Every few minutes she has to move off the road and squat and lift her skirt. Filth covers the ground. Dirtiness drizzles out of her and she feels dizzy. She feels feverish, then chilled, as if ice encases her even in the sun. She's had fevers before. But at home there was a bed to lie in, and her mother would bring goat's milk and treats. She lies on the ground and moans for her mother, her family, for the smell of the mangoes.

Eventually she realizes this isn't the way to the village. Mountains rise on the horizon, peaks she's never seen before. She trades the *xirsi* amulet to drink from a well guarded by men who murmur that the refugees are unclean, they can't be trusted, they work for the government. She wants to say this isn't true. The government burned our village. But she dares not. The well's surrounded by feces and sick people lying on the ground. Farther away is a pile of things covered with black rags she's afraid to look at.

She no longer knows where she's going. But still she trudges on, singing about the turtle and the ostrich. She wraps her bleeding feet with cloths she finds along the road. She sings all the songs she knows, until her lips bleed. She stares back at two girls who push a cart with bicycle tires.

Her bowels clench in familiar pain and she has to leave the road again.

She's trudging on numb feet when a truck snorts along the road. The refugees part without looking up. The trucks won't stop. Even if they did, bad things happen with the soldiers, with the truckers.

A very strange-looking person leans out of the cab. Her face is white as the clouds. Her eyes are blue as the birds on a bowl Zeynaab used to eat from. Her hair's like the silk of the maize. Zeynaab stops dead, staring. She's never seen a human being like this before. If it *is* a human being.

To multiply her astonishment, the woman speaks words she understands. "Little girl, where's your mother?"

"She's dead."

"Your father?"

"I don't know."

"Have you no family?"

She doesn't cry, only stares.

The woman doesn't need to invite her into the truck. She just holds out something in a bright wrapper.

There are three other children in the back, all boys. For a moment her heart leaps; but none is Nabil or Ghedi. The mountains go in and out of sight, then grow ahead as the truck twists and turns upward. One mountain stays. She tugs on the woman's arm when she needs to go into the brush. When the woman realizes she's sick she gives her a bottle of strange drink. It's salty but sugary too. Zeynaab drinks it all and when she's done the woman gives her another from a box on the floorboards. Then she unwraps the filthy rags from Zeynaab's feet and throws them out the window.

The truck climbs, and the cab, where she rides with the woman and the driver, smells bad. When it overtakes refugees the woman tells the driver to slow. She leans forward, searching as they press through the throngs. Now and then she tells the driver to stop. When Zeynaab realizes what she's doing a chill shakes her.

She's looking for children who are alone. Like the witches in the stories her aunties told her. Is she in a story now? Where are they going? She tries to muster courage to ask, but can't. The truck lurches as it climbs. Enormous rocks loom over the laboring vehicle, throwing cool shadows. Birds she's never seen before dart past. She needs to stop again, but puts it off so long it's almost too late. The woman smells sweet. It comes to Zeynaab that she herself is the source of the bad smell.

At last the truck heaves to a stop, panting like a tired elephant. She's never seen an elephant, only a picture in a book Auntie showed her. Her auntie went to school, when there were schools, in the Italian times. The driver lets down the gate in the back. He calls the boys to come down. He gives each of them a bottle of water. He shows them how to twist the caps off and they drink, eyes searching the sky as they tilt the bottles up.

The woman takes a pair of shoes from a box. They're red as the guava flowers after the rains come. They're plastic, and they *sparkle*. They're so beautiful she can't take her eyes off them as the woman bends and slips them over her torn, nailless, blackened toes. Then comes around to the side and, before she's quite ready, holds up her arms for Zeynaab to jump down.

Her attention's still on the wonderful shoes, so she doesn't notice, at first. The woman tugs at her hand, and she turns. And gasps.

The mountain rears above them, a cliff that goes up to where the sun lives. It's half in shadow, and rocks and stones jut from it. Only after walking for some time, new shoes slippery on the sun-heated scree, does she make out the path.

They climb for hours, until her thighs ache and her head

spins again. The boys trail after them, chattering at first, then silent. The woman halts to rest, but not often enough. They sweat out the water and there's no more. Birds soar, balancing on the wind.

High above and far away, a thread dangles from heaven. It flutters and sways, like spider silk in the wind. Only as they approach does she gradually make out a resting place at the top of the trail, at the foot of a cliff that flies up and up so far she can't tip her head back enough to see the top. When they reach it, wheezing, dizzy, there's an ancient pavement set with bits of colored stone, a picture of a man in a brown robe with a circle around his head, holding up two fingers.

In the center, where the colors are worn, sits a large woven basket. The woman urges her toward it. Zeynaab resists, weeping in terror. The woman tries to persuade her, but all she hears are broken words, like jagged shards of pottery that gouge at her ears.

The woman puts her hands on her. Her voice grows soft. Is this the voice of a witch? Is this the voice of a mother? She struggles, begging the driver to help her. He turns away, his profile hawklike. She shudders, the world spins, the mountain's about to fall on her.

When she comes to again she's curled in the basket. When she peers up, loose strips of blue cloth interlace above her. A rope curves upward until it vanishes. The basket revolves, creaking and swaying in a way that grips her heart.

She knows where she is now: in the bowl with the birds and bunnies on it she used to eat from when she was small. There are the birds, down below her. They're free, released from the hard forever of porcelain.

She stares at the cliff passing a few arm's-lengths away. Strange plants with gray spines grow on it, clinging in the crevices, and around them bright butterflies weave like the colored yarn on a carpet loom.

Then the basket revolves, and she sees only bright blue of empty sky, and below it, so far away she can hardly imagine it, stretch so very many miles of foothill and desert over which they must have driven in the truck. She shivers in the witch's basket gazing out at the whole world, so wide and small now she can't see her village, can't see the road, can't see her old life, which, she finally understands, whatever happens now, is forever gone.

3

ESKAN VILLAGE, SAUDI ARABIA

The air force captain had stopped fighting the night before, after Teddy fucked her for a couple of hours. Zoned out, like they did when you got them quieted down. Turning over when he told her to, doing what she had to, but without a word. When the alarm sounded he lay with an arm over his eyes, listening to the unquiet peep. Then rolled over.

She shifted under his weight, half acquiescent, until she came awake. Then she fought again, trying to kick, scratch, but too late.

When he pulled out, feeling supernaturally alive, the world was still dark outside the curtains of the room in the gated village the Saudis kept the Americans confined to except when they were actually under orders. He shaved and brushed his teeth with quick strokes, then dropped to the slick tile and did one hundred slow push-ups and a hundred sit-ups.

When he went back in, sucking deep breaths, she was sitting up, holding the sheet to her chest and lighting a PX Salem with shaking fingers. Her dark hair was snarled, mascara streaked, face swollen. She was Air Force, some logistics type who got things in and out through Saudi customs. He'd gone down to the pool, swam a few laps, then got out and walked the perimeter, picking the best body out of the baking flesh on display. The Look, a caramel latte at the PX Starbucks, and back to his room.

"Don't smoke here," he told her.

"Fuck you."

"Again?"

"That wasn't fun, you asshole. People don't do things like that to each other where I come from. And why do you keep it so hot in here?"

"Air-conditioning weakens you. And you'd be surprised what people do to each other." He stepped into fresh skivvies, pulled a set of BDUs out of the closet, and laced his boots sitting beside her. She smoked angrily, scattering ash over the sheets. He stuffed the funky shorts and T-shirt from last night into his duffel. Then slid the nightstand drawer open, shoved the retention-clipped Beretta into his belt, and pulled his blouse over it. It was fairly safe here for Americans, but staying alive anywhere in the Mideast meant never going off Condition Yellow. He tried to remember her name, but not very hard. "Gotta go, babe."

Her eyes were wide. The pistol, probably. "Wait a minute. What was your name again? You said you were a consultant. You're enlisted?"

He kept his left side turned away so she couldn't see his name tape, even though she'd picked up on his rating insignia. "Like I told you. Mickey Dooley."

"You used another name last night. What the hell are you, anyway?"

He did a quick scan of the room—the rest of his team gear was still out at the op site, but it never hurt to check, make sure he left nothing with his name on it—and winked. "Know something? When you're sore? Ice works."

"You bastard."

He made sure the lock clicked on his way out.

Theodore Harlett Oberg was six foot even and not as heavily muscled as one might expect, but he could run twenty miles on any given day, swim five miles in the open ocean, bench his weight fifteen times, and do twenty-five pull-ups carrying a weapon and basic load. He wore his dirty blond hair in a ponytail but, unlike some of the guys on the team, shaved whenever the mission permitted. His eyes were light blue and never seemed to blink, but the first thing most people noticed about him were the scars radiating out from his nose. They'd said they could fix the scars, at least make them less noticeable, but he'd told them not to bother.

He was driving the white Caravan the platoon had rented on the OPTAR card in Kuwait, for when they wanted to go places without looking military. The sun wasn't up yet, but the base was bustling. People got up early here and worked until the temperatures hit 110. The air was already blow dryer hot, and he was sweating. He stopped to pick up his guys, a big Hawaiian named Jeff Kaulukukui, and a shorter man, Mickey "Trunk Skunk" Dooley.

The Humvees were warming up when they arrived, desert-tan slantbacks with external water and fuel cans. The lead one was a gun truck with a .50 up for the roof gunner. An older man in three-color BDUs and a boonie hat tilted to shade his eyes was loading long gray equipment cases into the second vehicle. When Oberg came up he turned. Their hands locked and strained against each other.

"Obie, how you? Get to Perry this year?"

"Not this year. How you doing, Master Chief?"

Master Chief "Doctor Dick" Skilley had been Oberg's senior instructor at the nine-week SEAL sniper school at Camp Atterbury, Indiana, two years before. Skilley had barely survived the train-wreck SEAL insertion in Grenada and done countersniper work in Desert Storm and Bosnia. He'd become a legend after taking out fifteen snipers in Mogadishu with the bolt-action M24. He ran an on-the-road countersniper postgraduate course these days, hopscotching around to do refreshers. So when the platoon had gotten assigned to Centcom, headquartered in Qatar but most of the time either on float in the Gulf or back in the desert taking their turn in the barrel, Teddy had put in for him to come out and do some on-the-spot training.

At the moment the Det was gearing up to relieve the Special Forces in Operation Maple Gold, a barrier operation to keep the unrest in southwestern Iraq from spilling over into Saudi Arabia. There was a listening post out there too no one talked about, but Teddy figured it had something to do with ballistic missile detection and reading Syrian radars.

All of which explained what SEALs were doing three hundred miles from the nearest salt water. He released Skilley's arm and introduced Dooley and Kaulukukui. Skilley shook their hands too, but not as competitively.

"What've you been doing, Doc?"

"Pickup team to Afghanistan. Showing the spooks which end the bullet comes out of. You?"

"Got a new Samurai. Did some of that mud bogging, rock crawling, up in Silver Lake."

Kaulukukui was hauling ammo boxes out of the van and handing them into the lead Humvee. "He's got no idea what you're talking about, dude."

"Silver Lake, Utah. Four-wheel drive. Cross country, fun shit, you'd like it."

A driver leaned out to shout over the diesel clatter. "Turn off your cell phones, beepers, any radios." He sounded ticked off at having to truck Navy types around a desert the Army had already pissed on all four corners of. Teddy checked his cell.

The master chief said, "That's right, you were a motorhead, not just a pussy hound. That all you do, chase poon and race them mud cars?"

"Me and Sumo here saw a little action. Chasing that rocket torpedo."

"Catch any?"

"Tell you sometime, buy me enough beer."

"How much is enough?"

"In Saudi? I'm a cheap fucking date, Mas' Chief."

Black smoke shot out the Humvees' stacks. Oberg, Skilley, and Kaulukukui rolled into the lead vehicle and slammed the doors, which had been hastily armored with bolted-on quarter-inch steel. Dooley parked the van in the long-term area, locked it, and jogged toward the second vehicle. Seconds later, the vast rectangles of the base, the glitter of windshields in the rising sun, the flat wavering tarmac of the airstrip, were gone in a cloud of rolling dust.

* * *

Once they left the ring road behind, there was nothing but desert from road to horizon. Tan bedrock covered with sand fine as talcum, and here and there in pleats of the land visible only because the sun was still low, sparse huddles of shriveled brush. Oberg sat with boots on the dashboard, glove wrapped around a handgrip, watching morning wake northern Saudi. Over the curved horizon black smoke rose from Iraq. He liked the dry air, the brilliant sky that was almost blue today, for a change. He'd grown up in the desert, or next to it: in LA, running up in the canyons to get away from the assholes his mother was always bringing home.

The driver said grudgingly there was lemonade in the container in the back, and red licorice, Chex Mix, Slim Jims, and dry-roasted peanuts in the box on the floor. A handheld GPS was cooking on the dashboard but Obie didn't say anything. It wasn't his vehicle, and he had his own GPS.

"Gonna tell me about this torpedo?" Skilley asked. Obie nodded at the driver, and the chief squinted and changed the subject, to a new digital marksmanship training system they were installing at Atterbury.

"Digital? Meaning what? You shoot electrons?"

"Pretty much. Lie on this rubber mat that criticizes your hold. Shoot a toy gun at a screen. Cost five million bucks, I heard."

"Buy a lot of live rounds for five million bucks."

"Tell me about it. But they're talking lead contamination, the air handlers got to be rebuilt on the indoor range, it's gotta be filtered—it's a fucking nightmare. Who let the EPA on base?"

Two hours later the Humvees turned off the highway and began climbing into the hills. Not mountains, but steep enough to make the automatic transmissions take a strain. Goatherds in black cloaks faced away as they passed. The Saudis didn't like Americans in what they called Holy Country. The only locals Teddy had seen since he got here were their Saudi Guard liaison officer for Maple Gold and these distant, aloof goatherds, glimpsed as he sped along the long, line-straight, empty roads.

By ten o'clock it was 115 degrees and heat shimmered up off the baking rocks and ledges. The drivers stayed with the Humvees, the music from their CD players following the SEALs as they climbed. Oberg, Kaulukukui, and Dooley carried Camelback water bladders and sidearms. Skilley carried a black rifle from one of his cases.

Oberg considered it as they climbed, since he was directly behind the master chief. The heavy barrel was longer than the standard twenty inches and ended in the black tube of a sound suppressor. The skeleton stock was covered with foam plastic. The top of the receiver was flat with a backup rear sight that folded down and a scope that wasn't any night vision sight he was familiar with. From time to time Skilley would bend and squint through it up toward the hilltop. A spray can hissed as he colored a six-inch spot of fluorescent orange onto a large rock.

At last, at the top of a rise, Skilley stopped and looked back down the valley. He unslung the rifle and took a knee. He was panting, flushed, and Teddy held out the tube to his water. The older man sucked at it, nodded, and handed it back.

"We use snipers to destroy enemy morale. Nothing saps your motivation faster than seeing your lieutenant's head blow apart, then your sergeant's. We deployed them in two-man teams, shooter and observer, back when we were shooting bolt-action thirties and then when we went to the M14. Problem with the M24 and M14?"

"Range," Kaulukukui said, hunkered on his heels in a way Oberg couldn't believe was as comfortable as the big Hawaiian made it look.

"Well, half right. Problem's really not range, it's dispersion. That 173-grain boattail will only reach out six, maybe eight hundred yards till the cone of fire widens so much you can't count on connecting with a trunk shot. Just not good enough these days, when you're working from a hide in the open, or trying to overwatch an urban area ten blocks in every direction. And more of your high-value targets are wearing some kind of personal armor." Skilley dusted his hands and adjusted the weapon on his lap. "Obie, remember what we did to fix that?"

"Went to the fifty cal."

"That pushed us out to a thousand meters or better. But then we had to go to three-man teams, to carry that son of a bitching rifle and all the fucking gear. And forget trying to conceal it in a hide site."

"So what's this?" Teddy pointed to the black weapon. "A sixteen with some kind of superheavy barrel? What makes this so shit hot, Dick?"

Skilley explained that indeed it looked like an M16. The SR-25 was its big brother. The barrel was a twenty-four-inch stainless steel Obermeyer, cut-rifled and floated to isolate it from sling tension. The trigger was a Geissele match model, and the scope had been improved with larger objectives, higher magnification, and a new stabilization system that reduced tremor and heartbeat. It also had a laser rangefinder built in.

"Caliber?" Dooley asked.

"Still seven-six-two. Standard thirty caliber."

"That the wind pushes around like a piece of dandelion fluff."

"That's been the problem," Skilley agreed. "Plus, velocity dropped so much at long ranges you had to place the shot in the head, the heart, or the spinal column to turn the lights out. So we had to get in to seven, eight hundred meters."

"But this is still a thutty-cal."

"Oh, only technically." Skilley shifted on the rock and pulled a blue plastic box from his trousers. Opened, it showed the tips of twenty cartridges, like filed, blackened teeth. He slapped one into Oberg's glove. "Over three thousand feet per second. Don't try these in your regular chambers. You'll blow pieces of your face all over the landscape."

It was much heavier than even the long-range sniper rounds Teddy was used to. A shiny black, queerly elongated bullet with a dull green plastic tip. He turned it over and inspected the base. "Why's it so heavy?"

"Depleted uranium, with a tungsten core for penetration. Both heavier than lead. So we get a three-hundred-grain bullet, and a ballistic coefficient off the charts."

Kaulukukui whistled. "Who thought of this?"

"Like a lot of the new stuff, it came out of long-range competition. The Army Marksmanship Unit was up against the stops with the Sierras they were shooting. Somebody says, why not go to a denser metal, see what happens. Course, they can't shoot these at Perry. Be over a hundred dollars a round. Plus, anything with the word 'uranium' in it sets the nut fringe off. Next thing, they'd be calling them atomic bullets and yammering to ban 'em." Skilley turned one of the cartridges before his eyes as if admiring some rare ruby.

Teddy looked at Kaulukukui. "So this gives you less wind drift."

"Less drift, a spin of one in five, and image stabilization on the scope. Bottom line: a quarter MOA. A steady hand, you can hold a head shot at a thousand meters."

The Hawaiian whistled again. Skilley stood. He handed the rifle to Oberg. "I run my mouth enough. It takes forty-two muscles to frown, seventeen to smile—"

"But only three for proper trigger control," Teddy finished.

"Hooyah. Shoot the fucker."

He accepted it gingerly. With the long, thick barrel, the suppressor, and the heavy sight, it had to weigh at least twenty pounds. He twisted the sling outward and got his left arm through it and snugged tight under the handguard. He stretched out on the ground and hitched a leg up. As he set the buttstock into his shoulder Skilley reached in to turn a dial on the scope. "Got to load one round at a time. That cartridge won't fit in the magazine. But you can carry another mag full of regular rounds, to slap in if they rush you."

The bolt snapped closed, and his thumb rotated the safety to FIRE.

When he put the scope to his eye the sight picture was the standard reticle. A grid at the top, so you could estimate range by the arc an erect male figure subtended. Below that were aiming dots for various distances. On the right was something new: the laser range finder. He moved back for eye relief, and steadied the sight on the distant orange fleck Skilley had painted. The spot quivered with the involuntary tremor of his muscles, and of the heat waves cooking off the desert floor.

That was the mirage. A subtle shimmer that took training for the eye to read. He focused back and forth, reading that trembling of the atmosphere halfway between him and the target, then a quarter, then three-quarters. Each time he focused, the mirage rolled like surf in a different direction at a different rate, or simply boiled in place, a milling scramble of heated gas.

No bullet ever went where you pointed it. Gravity, spin, the wind, the very rotation of the earth pulled it off track. Some of those you could allow for. Some you could guesstimate, if you fired enough thousands of rounds. But in that boil of the mirage, no one could be absolutely certain where a projectile would go.

"About a three-minute wind? Right to left?"

"Crank it on. Estimate your range," Skilley breathed.

The range finder would be more exact, but Teddy didn't like to put out a laser beam. Protective details were starting to carry laser detectors. He calibrated the top and bottom of the rock against the upper grid, then doubled it, since it wasn't six feet high. The mirage hesitated, then began to roll left to right. Sweating, he adjusted his windage, hoping he wasn't overcorrecting.

"Eight hundred fifty meters."

"Check again. When you have time, use it."

He breathed out, took his eye away, put it back to the eyepiece. "Eight fifty."

"With the laser?"

"Fuck the laser. That's a solid range."

"All right. Check your windage again. The wind never stops changing."

He bit back a retort and checked again. Right to left again, and the nearly invisible moiré pattern eddied more swiftly now. He blinked sweat away and corrected. Kaulukukui and

Dooley squatted, hands dangling. "You guys look like baboons," he said.

"You look like a baboon's prick."

"You suck baboons' pricks."

"Yeah, but not on Sunday."

"Shut up. Watch this," the master chief said.

He reached in past Obie's shoulder to flick a toggle on the scope. It emitted a faint whine powering up.

Teddy blinked. Like magic, the tremor had disappeared. The only motion now was that of the boiling air escalatoring smoothly and silently across the field of view. He checked left, then right, to make sure none of the goatherds were wandering around downrange. Just blank rock, sand, the shrunken shadows of near-noon. He took up the slack in the trigger. Found the second stage. Centered the sights above the eight dot and below the nine. Breathed out and applied pressure, ready to stop if the scope wavered.

But it was rock solid, and the recoil slammed his shoulder like no M16 ever had. The suppressor damped the report, but no way it could silence metal ripping air at three thousand feet a second. The supersonic crack tolled back from rocks and hillsides. He'd stopped blinking when he fired years ago, so he could track the wavering comet of the bullet's trace all the way.

It struck in the bottom half of the fluorescent spot and the rock split apart, exploding into flying fragments and an ocher cloud that hung suspended for a moment, as if contemplating being released from the matrix in which it had spent the last million years. Then uncurled like a blossoming bud and drifted off downwind.

He rolled away from the rifle. The other SEALs looked impressed. "DRT," Dooley murmured. Dead right there.

"If they run, they'll just die tired," Kaulukukui said.

"A little farther than you figured," Skilley pronounced. "But better under than over, if you're going for a head shot."

"I could do some work with this," Teddy said. "This one mine?"

"On the way. Two, maybe three weeks. With a national

stock number, hard case, sling, and butt and handguard weight set."

"And this hot shit ammo?" said the Hawaiian.

"That's different." Skilley laid the plastic case beside Oberg. "So far, the only agency approved to use this has three initials. You won't find it in the supply system. You'd have to depend on what you . . . found lying around."

The case disappeared into Teddy's cargo pocket as he stood. They looked around again, at the blazing sun overhead, the still-climbing column of black smoke far away. Then turned, and began the trek downhill to the waiting convoy.

NABIL

The little boy turns but his sister's not there. Her hand was in his a second ago. Now the air's filled with the black shapes of women but they're not her. Motors snarl from all around. He coughs, digging dust out of his eyes.

"Zeynaab. Zeynaab!"

But nobody answers; in all the screaming he can't even hear himself. A truck roars past so close the hot wind nearly knocks him down. Stones from the tires sting his cheek. Then shots snap. Somebody's shooting! He knows now to fall to the ground, like the people around him. He covers his head and squinches his eyes shut, like on cool nights when he pulls the blanket over his head.

The wind's rising. It scoops dust out of the wheel ruts and blows it along the ground. Dust covers the sky and rasps his squinted eyes. "Zeynaab!" he cries into the ground. "Ghedi!"

When the shooting stops and the motors go away his dread's so deep he can barely jump up. He runs in clumsy circles, so as not to get too far from where he saw them last. He slams into an overturned cart, the wind rotating one wheel with a plaintive squeaking. An old man lies beside it. He's cradling a child, looking away from Nabil. There's a full skin lying next to him. It must have tumbled out of the cart when it went over.

Nabil stops. He blinks away dust, eyeing the skin.

A moment later he's running, wrenching at the cork. The water runs down his face as much as down his throat, but he gulps and gulps. He moans as he drinks. Behind him a faint cry rises, lost in the wind.

All that day he walks in circles. The wind blows, then dies, blows and then dies. Something's burning, an oily stink that reminds him of when he threw a rubber toy into the fire. Now and then refugees trek past. He climbs a hill to look for his sister and brother. The sun burns down. But he sees nothing but a far-off glint in the sky. *Airplane*, his brother told him once. He doesn't know what that is.

Late that afternoon he climbs another hill. This time he sees his sister, far away, headed away from him. A child-sized figure in black. He runs after her, all the way down the hill and then up and then down again. It's a long way, and he's staggering through flashes of light when he reaches her. But when she turns it's not her, it's someone else. She draws a small knife and slashes the air. "Go away!"

"Where's your family?"

"I don't have one! Where's yours?"

He crouches, afraid to say the words. Finally he whispers, so no one but the girl will hear. "They shot my *huyo*. My father, I don't know. My sister and brother, they were here yesterday."

"What's wrong with your foot?" she says suspiciously, keeping the knife out between them and twisting it as if she's boring into something. The blazing sun grinds sparks off it like a wheel when the village toolman sharpens an ax. Nabil stares at it. He wants a knife.

"What?"

"What's wrong with your foot? How old are you? What's your name?"

He tells her he has the limp-foot disease and doesn't know how old he is. "My sister's lost. She and Ghedi got lost when the trucks came."

"Trucks? What trucks?"

"You didn't see the trucks? They came, somebody was shooting—"

"I heard shooting. But it was from over the hill. What village are you from?"

He tells her, but she's never heard of it. She looks hard at him, then tucks the knife away. "Got any food?"

"No. Do you?"

"Bread. You can have a little."

They sit in the shade of a dune and gnaw at the hunk. It's old and hard but Nabil doesn't care. He wishes he'd saved some of the water in the skin.

The shadows lengthen. The searing breeze dies as the desert cool deepens. The sky turns rosy, then hazy brown streaked with golden flames. The two children find a rock that overhangs a scooped-out hollow of dirt. They examine it for scorpions or snakes, then crawl in. Nabil hesitates, then huddles close to the girl, smelling her smells, feeling her warmth. She twitches, and the blade scrapes as it emerges from wherever she sheathes it. But it doesn't prick. Instead she lies still.

Slowly, his arms creep around her.

And he sleeps.

The next day they set out along a high trail. It winds through huge rocks and goes up and down so steeply sometimes they have to scramble on hands and knees. The girl says it's a goat path, but it leads to the sea, where someone said there's food. Nabil doesn't feel good about leaving where he lost his sister and brother, but there's no food and no water and this girl's the only person around who seems to know what she's doing. Only a few other refugees walk the high path. They speak differently than the children are used to, but enough are willing to share water that they can keep going, although hunger gnaws at his belly like an animal.

But the rocks concentrate the sun and there's no wind among them at all. He moves most of the time not knowing what he's doing, and falls often. His knees and hands are covered with scabs that bleed when the next fall tears them off again.

At last they come out onto a plain. So many other refugees are milling around he can't believe it. They cover it like ants, some going in the same direction as he and the girl, others headed crosswise in long lines, and when they meet there's shouting and sometimes fighting with machetes and even guns. He plods after her, thumb in his mouth, stumbling over rocks and dragging his weak foot in the sand.

The air vibrates. Black snakes writhe along the horizon. The girl yanks at his arm. We have to go faster, she says. We shouldn't be out here. She carries the knife all the time now, in a fist so she can stab with it. She's like a black tarantula, Nabil thinks. He dogs her like a shadow of her black dress, panting. He asks where there's water. Up ahead, she snaps. You better hurry up so there's some left when we get there.

There's a pulsing beat in the air, as if the hills are fluttering on a clothesline. As if the whole earth's fluttering in the air.

What's that? he says.

An air-thing. Run.

Are we going to the city?

Just shut up and run, she says. You'd be dead right now if it wasn't for me. Stop crying, you little Bantu worm.

This is so true, except he's not a Bantu, he shuts up and tries to run a few paces, but falls down. He starts to cry, then stops himself. Ghedi wouldn't cry.

He's getting up when the noise comes in the air. The girl whirls, looking into the sun. He sees her from the back, standing in front of him, arms out, head lifted. The sun all around her, so all he can see is shape and light.

All around them the people scream.

When the loud noises stop and the sand and rocks stop flying and the smoke blows away he sits up and looks down at himself. His head's ringing, his whole body's shaking. As he looks down the shaking grows.

From head to toe he's covered in blood and meaty pieces like crushed tomatoes. Whatever struck the girl turned her into this paste that covers him and the ground around him. There's just a crater where she stood, and one shoe.

He cries for a while, but the sobs ebb. Crying doesn't help. Nothing changes when he cries. When he walks, though, things change. Anyway, he doesn't want to be here anymore. The ridge is too skyey. What if the air-thing comes back? He sobs again and tries to brush the meat off with his hands. The blood's sticky. He's so hungry. He sees the knife a few paces away. It's lying on the sand. A small dirty hand's still holding it. Still holding it tight.

He's so hungry. He puts his thumb in his mouth. Then he's licking his hands, before he even knows he's doing it.

Then very slowly everything goes liquid, swirling, like hot bubbling sorghum porridge in a pot, swirling round and round.

Then he's inside something blue, a weird blue with letters on it. Letters, but different from the ones in Auntie's book. The blue moves in waves. He's intensely hot. He's lying on something soft.

Then he's not lying, but sitting with a group of other boys. He puts a hand to his head. Something used to be there that isn't anymore.

Someone speaks in a language he doesn't understand. A black man with a shiny can in his hand. He turns Nabil's head back and forth, looking into his eyes. He says something that sounds like a question. Nabil can't answer. There's nothing in his head to answer with.

The man dips a brush into the can. With one quick motion he paints something sticky on Nabil's head. His hands rise, but the man slaps them down. He says something angry. Then reaches behind him, and shoves a plastic bowl into his hands.

Nabil sits up. He sniffs the yellow mush. The man says things fast, as if he's got to do this over and over. Nabil tastes it. Then he eats it.

He's in a tent. The blue billowing above him is plastic, so thin the sun shines right through it. Boys fill the length of the tent. They lie with spindly legs and arms and knobby elbows and knees. Their eyes are gigantic. On their skulls are painted large Os in pink paint. It looks funny to Nabil, but for some reason he can't remember, he can't seem to laugh.

The man smiles. He leans so close Nabil smells his breath. His fingers move over his legs, then touch him where they shouldn't. Nabil doesn't move. At last the man grunts and leaves.

After a while he tries to get up. His legs don't work, though, and he falls down again. The other boys stare at him unblinking. They don't look like his people.

Where are we? he asks, but they don't move or answer. Flies buzz through the tent. They crawl on one of the boys who doesn't move or brush them away. After a time Nabil realizes that boy's dead.

He rolls over and starts crawling toward the light at the end of the tent. He pushes feet aside. He smells shit and a sweet smell. Some boys kick at him. Others lie shuddering, eyes rolled up in their heads.

He pushes the flap aside and looks out.

The blue tents stretch as far as he can see. A gaunt woman crouches before a fire. An old man staggers under a tin water can. A naked child runs from one tent to another.

Beyond the farthest tent are fine thin somehow spiky threads that lead across the ground. He squinches his eyes to see better in the glare. Far away someone's singing. Someone else is weeping. Something goes *put, put, put,* like the water pumps in their village. He suddenly remembers all the things that weren't in his head a moment ago. They feel jagged, and he wishes they weren't there. His head felt better empty.

He sees what the threads are now, and feels something cold fall down inside his throat, bouncing from side to side as it goes down, like a rock tossed into a well.

The thin black spiky threads, running left and right as far as he can see, are wire.

4

DORALEH, DJIBOUTI

The sun was like the drying lights in a body shop, so bright Dan's lips were burning. His eyeballs felt like bearings being annealed with a torch. The scorching air smelled like the inside of an old toaster. Fat black flies kept landing on his face, no matter how often he brushed them off. Sweat kept running down his neck, and the fine gritty powder so familiar from his previous time in the Mideast rubbed like steel wool against his skin, slacks, his very teeth, as the taxi's wheels jolted over potholes. Dust that smelled like dried vomit rose from the seat and carpet and blew out the window, replaced with no-sweeter-smelling dust from outside.

The Mideast Shuttle flew every other Tuesday. They'd been lucky to get the last seats. After which it had been twenty-six straight hours either fidgeting aboard the 767 or eating plastic-packaged buns and drinking reconstituted coffee from vending machines during layovers in the rubber-matted boxes of passenger lounges. Norfolk to Lajes, the Azores; Sigonella, Sicily; Suda Bay, Crete; Bahrain; and at last and finally, Djibouti International. He'd brought along the read-ins, studies, and position papers Dr. Fauss had sent to TAG, and he and Henrickson and Lieutenant Commander Kimberley McCall had translated them into something resembling a transformation plan for the squadron that would serve as a concept test bed. They'd landed and caught this taxi into town. Their driver had said not one word, just chewed something endlessly, his red-rimmed, spacey eyes hanging in the rearview mirror like a shot from a horror movie.

The pier area, at last, the upperworks of ships ahead. They pitched forward in a painful screech of steel on bare steel. The driver turned slowly. They stared into *Night of the*

Living Dead eyes, and he spoke. "Now you give five tousand Djibouti franc."

Twice what they'd agreed on. Dan handed him the original amount in the damp worn bills he'd changed at the airport, added a generous tip, and got out, ignoring the outraged shouts as McCall and Henrickson bailed too. He hoisted his AWOL and the black nylon sling of his notebook computer, torn between wishing he'd brought more and not wanting to carry what he had.

As soon as he stepped away from the taxi the beggars were on them. One scooted after them along the ground, wooden clogs rattling on his hands. His legs ended at the knees. Another hobbled upright, but with milky vacant eyes and ankles like willow sticks. "Sir. Sir," they muttered, plucking at their clothing. "God *damn*," Henrickson muttered. Dan fumbled in his pockets, handing out dollar bills he'd reserved for tips and baksheesh, one bill to each supplicating palm.

"Five tousand," shouted the driver behind them. "Five tousand! *Ooji, adoon!*"

Dan guessed those were not complimentary adjectives. The halt and the lame desisted only at the head of the pier, where a guard with a slung rifle shouted them away. He led his little party past USS *Mount Whitney*, a gray steel cliffside whose sponsons overhung the pier, whose antennas cast gnomon shadows. He'd report aboard, checking in with the task force commander; but not just yet.

McCall's heels clicked down the asphalted pier as a gaily painted fishing dhow nodded its way out to sea. The glare reflected off the water so brightly Dan had to squint to see her swaying hips, straight back, slender neck. She'd caused him more than a few worries aboard *Horn*, where she'd been the combat systems officer. She was good, but he couldn't always detach her professional performance from the fact that she was a knockout. Tall, professional, smart women were his weakness. McCall wasn't any more attractive than his wife, but she was *here*.

Ten thousand miles away from Blair, he promised himself sex would not rear its ugly head.

Henrickson shambled behind, bent under cases, computers, binders, and what little personal gear he carried. Dan had been amused on previous trips to discover that the little analyst washed his underwear and socks in the sink, dried them on shower bars, and in general, lived like a persnickety stoic. His personal comfort came a distant second to the data.

"That's her, I guess," McCall said as they rounded a shed. Dan pried his gaze off the tight fabric as it stretched and relaxed over her rump, and lifted his eyes to snapping flags.

USS *Shamal*, PC-13, was moored across from several tin-roofed open-sided sheds. A containership with a bright green hull, flying the Saudi flag, was tied up on the far side. Speedboats and fishing craft motored in and out of the inner port through a half-mile-wide entrance. More dhows and smaller patrol craft lay across the inlet, in a basin from which sailboat masts jutted, though he couldn't see their hulls.

The shed was covered with graffiti and colorful hand-painted signs advertising jitney buses and local restaurants. At least fifty locals, all male, sat or stood pierside. Lanky dark men in thin, worn-out short-sleeve button-up shirts, cut-off slacks, some sandaled, others with bony bare feet. They leaned against pilings or walls. A few smoked, but most were doggedly chewing sticks of something green. Part-time cargo wallopers and line handlers, Dan guessed, waiting for the next opportunity to turn a dollar, franc, euro, or riyal.

Shamal was smaller than he'd expected. Only her bridge and mast even showed above the pier. Granted, nothing displacing a whisker over three hundred tons was likely to be huge, but even to his eye—accustomed to frigates and destroyers—she seemed barely larger than a toy. But when he stepped to the edge he got a different impression.

Bow on, she seemed to be straining at her lines, a haze gray pit bull eager to fasten her jaws into something. Her superstructure looked as if someone had planed off all the right angles and painted them sky blue, a pattern that looked garish pierside, but that would break up her silhouette at dusk or daybreak. Her upthrust bow had the heavy-weather flare he'd appreciated ever since a winter cruise into the Arctic Sea. A subdued 13 was painted on it in darker gray. An automatic gun was aligned in the "ready air" position on her foredeck. Aft of that a boxlike hump angled up to an enclosed bridge structure, with a windshielded cockpit above.

Dan noted .50-cal mounts on the wings, sheathed in gray covers, and the glint of cartridge belts. A swept-back mast supported levels of radars and sensors, two of which revolved steadily, flashing in the sun. As they paced nearer, deckhouses came into view aft, with a raised catwalk that ought to be useful getting around in heavy weather, more antennas—one of the electronic intelligence packages, Bobcat or Privateer—and another gun. She had no stack, but when he peered down he caught mascara smeared back from waterline exhausts. She'd spent a lot of time under way at near idle. You didn't get black soot like that when engines were running all out.

A bo's'n's pipe, a flurry of uniforms as the welcoming party formed up on the quarterdeck. Henrickson and McCall fell back. Dan set down his gear at the brow. Catching a photographer atop the bridge, he straightened his cap and pressed his ribbons into his chest with his palm. The pipe went low, high, low, high, and held. When it cut off the 1MC announced, "Commander, United States Navy, arriving."

Dan stepped off the tinny-sounding brow, saluted the national ensign that dangled limply aft, pivoted, faced a chief in khaki. "Permission to come aboard?"

"Permission granted, sir." The chief's salute could have opened cans.

Dan turned to a squat, desert-booted, BDU-trou- and tan-skivvy-shirt-clad black man with a wrestler's neck and a peanut-shaped head whose shaven scalp glistened even under a boonie hat. "Lieutenant Geller?"

"Yessir, Connor Geller. Welcome aboard, Commander." The skipper's grip was hard and his palm wet. So was Dan's, making for a squishy, gritty handshake.

Dan waved his people forward. "Dr. Monty Henrickson, Lieutenant Commander McCall."

Geller shook hands with both, pointedly not looking at McCall's chest. "Welcome to Africa, welcome aboard *Shamal*, welcome to the patrol coastal navy. Want to see where we're bunking you? Or do the tour first? Petty Officer Dugan'll get your gear."

"We could all use showers," Dan said. "Then let's meet someplace cool and get our heads together."

"Excuse me, Cap'n," a radioman said. "Complan for the transit."

Geller scribbled a signature. "Works for me. Except for the part about cool. Dugie, put the commander's bags in my cabin, okay?—Got a shower there, care to use it before you change?"

"Works for me," Dan said.

Geller's stateroom was no larger than those aboard a submarine, porthole-less, and extremely hot despite two bulkhead fans shuddering at max rpm. Dan saw why T-shirts were the uniform of choice. "Not much AC aboard these things," Geller said. "Up forward, where the electronics live, that's about all. Shower help?"

Dan tousled his head with the towel, feeling first gratefully cool, as the moisture on his skin evaporated, then stifling again. "Much."

"Sweet or unsweet?"

"Sorry?"

"Tea. Sweetened or not?"

He said unsweetened. Sucking half the icy glass down at once helped. He sat back and plucked his skivvy shirt off his chest.

"So, understand you're gonna be riding us on patrol. First time you've been aboard one of these?" Geller asked.

"First time. I mean, I've seen them going in and out, but as I said, never been aboard."

"They designed these to deploy special forces teams in

near-shore operations. But the spec ops guys didn't like 'em as much as they thought they would. We draw nine feet; that puts our operational envelope too far offshore. So then the Navy said, who wants these? And started getting rid of 'em."

"Like what happened to the hydrofoils."

"Yeah, and the PTs before that. Some went to the Coast Guard. The Philippines took one. Then we started getting serious about the Gulf."

"They're smaller than I thought," Dan said.

"Yeah, your blue-water Navy isn't impressed. We don't carry the big gun, the sonar, can't land a helo. So what good are we? Well, we've operated off Bahrain, guarding oil terminals. Did antidrug ops in the Caribbean. Did a forward deploy to the Gulf, five PCs and six Coast Guard WPBs. And that worked." Geller nodded toward the porthole, out which the upperworks on the far side of the basin were visible. "And we're training the locals."

Dan pulled khakis out of the hanging bag. "That's them? Across the basin?"

"Well, they aren't seaworthy enough to trust out of the harbor. But we're working on it. The MST's got an engineman warrant over there. Maintenance support team. You'll hear more about 'em on the Mountain."

Dan groped before he realized Geller meant *Mount Whitney*. "What's the outback like? Have you been incountry?"

"Flew over it, sir. It's grim. Sand and scorpions. The Afars and the Issas with their goats and their guns, fucking the goats and shooting the guns, and you really don't want to get in between them. Oh, and there's the refugee camps, full of poor bastards nobody wants. It's like, on the eighth day God said, Crap, I forgot . . . and he made East Africa. I know I shouldn't say this, but whoever got my ancestors out of here, God bless 'em." Geller checked his watch. "Seen the commodore yet?"

"Thought I'd wait till it got cooler. After dark?"

"It's pretty much set on broil all the time. Hit a hundred and forty in the engine room last week. And we're sked to get under way at eighteen hundred. So you better go pretty soon. I'll walk you over. He wanted to see you as soon as you got here."

Dan wasn't looking forward to meeting the squadron commander. All too often, the Visiting Expert was nothing more than a PITA. But you couldn't ride one of his ships without shaking the guy's hand. The Navy didn't pay calls as formally as in 1900, with white gloves and engraved cards, but they were still a reality. "Anybody else I need to punch in with? Base commander? This isn't a U.S. base, is it?"

"Oh, hell no. If anything, it's French. They've got their own flag now, but it's still almost a colony. There's a huge Foreign Legion camp. Usually a frigate or a sweeper at that pier over there. But we have an arrangement."

"I notice you're at Condition Yellow. Live ammo, armed pier sentries."

"There's a civil war going on. Low level, mainly out in the hinterland, but it's there. The whole Horn's boiling. Somalia's been in the toilet for a long time. Looks to me like Ashaara's going the same way. We had an amphibious ready group here for two months. *Inchon*, *Trenton*, *Portland*, *Spartanburg County*. All prepped to run up and evacuate Ashaara City. But things cooled off and they went back to Bahrain."

"Port looks busy."

"Oh yeah. They closed Eritrea to Ethiopian trade. With the drought, that means all the aid shipments for Ethiopia have to come through here. We may have to vacate this pier space. I can anchor out if I have to. Might even enhance security."

"It'll cut down on liberty."

"The guys get as much liberty as they can stand here the first night." Geller grinned. "Okay, pull your shirt on and grab your pisscutter."

The command ship loomed over the quay like a star cruiser. Dan had been aboard *Mount Whitney* before. He was used to its spacious spotless passageways, the icy air-conditioning, the quick, pleasant young crew. It was always a marvel to him, eighteen thousand tons of ship armed with nothing more lethal than a twenty-millimeter self-defense system. Her main battery was her forest of antennas. Her brain was the command quarters, where he sat now, doughnuts and coffee on the leather-covered table, with Geller and Commodore Carlos Goya. *Shamal*'s CO had sweated through his uniform blouse just in the couple hundred yards down the pier.

Goya looked more German than Hispanic, with gangly arms he didn't seem to be able to find a comfortable place for and a small black mustache. Which right now he was plucking at, frowning. He and Dan had gotten past whom they both knew and where they'd both served.

"What I don't understand is why Vince Contardi's interested in the patrol coastal community. I'd think this'd be about the least transformation-izational, if that's a word, community around. Given our lack of advanced sensors and computers."

"Well, yes and no, Commodore." Dan had thought this over in light of Contardi's speeches and papers, most of which he suspected Fauss had ghostwritten. "As best I can tell, you could test-bed two aspects of transformation. The first is the idea we can use, uh, 'sensor nodes,' to target ordnance from larger units via something like a cooperative engagement capability. Those could be small, lightly manned surface craft, operating in littoral environments—like what you do. Eventually some nodes could be robotic, autonomous small craft and subs and UAVs. The second aspect would be crew swapping. Instead of rotating the ship back to home port every deployment, you leave the hull in place and change the crews out."

Goya's quirk of the lips might have been skepticism. If so, it was quickly masked. "I've read a couple of pieces in *Proceedings* and *Surface Warfare*. Sounds like upsides and downsides. But you're here. Tell me what you need."

Dan thought about confessing his own doubts, but undercutting his orders wouldn't be a good way to kick off his stay. He front and centered his notebook. "First, I guess, is the command structure."

"Right now I'm CTG 156.4. Report to COMNAVCENT in Bahrain."

"You have three PCs out of Djibouti?"

"Only temporarily. We had a larger squadron with some amphibs when it seemed like we might have to implement Hasty Exit—that was a NEO from Ashaara City."

NEO was navalese for noncombatant evacuation operation, what the Navy and Marine Corps executed when a country went to shit and the State Department people, residents, and dependents had to be whisked out before being used for target practice. As Dan nodded Goya went on, "I'm running four hulls out of here on the maritime security mission, with an MST of twenty-two guys living in tents north of town. EMs, ETs, electricians, a welder, and a crusty old chief warrant named Wronowicz."

"Fuel? Food?"

"We refuel from *Whitney* and get food through the Foreign Legion out at Camp Limonier. We're actually growing a working relationship with the small navies around the area. The platform's not as threatening as it is when we come in with a Burke-class. It's working peer to peer rather than gawping up at this huge thing you can't even grasp what weapons systems it *has*, much less operate it. We work with them on interdiction ops, antipirate missions, maritime security." Goya cocked his head. "Understand you've had experience along those lines."

"Now and then. Like most surface line officers," Dan said, disguising the particular in the general. "So the infrastructure, if we were to maintain ships on station two, three years at a time—rotating crews—it's adequate?"

"Not for long-term maintenance. Especially how fast bottom fouling builds up here, biofouling in the intercoolers, et cetera. We'd need either a permanent base, which we aren't going to get in this region, or what we used to have in Bahrain—an LPD or an LSD as a mother ship, machine shop, someplace the guys can hang out where there's room to move around. You'll see how true this is"—the commodore checked the bulkhead clock—"once you've operated aboard them, which I guess you'll be doing for the next week. We need to pull the guys off once in a while and let them breathe. Of course"—Goya touched his mustache again—"if we were rotating them every three or four months, they'd be happier with the living arrangements."

Dan went over some other issues, knowing McCall was doing the same thing in greater depth with the chief staff officer, and Henrickson would be huddled with the N-4, going over parts requirements and how the supply system would have to be jimmied to keep a ship on station for three or four years at a time. Finally he turned off his notebook. "Commodore, thanks for your hospitality. We'll have more questions once we get back from our underway, but this should get us started."

For the first time Goya looked ill at ease. "Well, you're all welcome. But there's a little hitch."

"What's that, sir? I thought we had advance clearances, visit approval—"

"Right, but thing is, these PCs are real tight berthing wise."

"We're used to stowing our gear pretty much anyplace—"

"It's McCall." Goya grinned unhappily. "There's no separate berthing on PCs for females. Unless they're CO—he, I mean she, gets a separate stateroom. Everybody else is in bunkrooms."

Geller said, "She can have my stateroom, Commodore. I generally nap in my bridge chair under way. SEAL berthing, if I have to hot-bunk it, no problem."

"We can't take your cabin," Dan told him. "I didn't realize space was that tight. Nice of you to offer, but I'm going to make a command decision and leave Commander McCall here to drill down into the logistics and maintenance, okay? You can bunk her aboard the uh, the Mountain, right, Commodore?"

"Certainly, if you're sure."

Dan nodded, knowing McCall wasn't going to be happy,

but she wasn't being paid to be happy, only to do what she was told. As he'd heard himself more than once since signing on the dotted line those many years before.

"Stand by to test engines," Geller called into the pilothouse, mopping his bare glistening scalp with his bare glistening arm. Not the slightest hint of wind. Heat like Dan had never known broiled off galvanized iron roofs, the mirrorlike glaze of the basin. Behind them the ten-by-ten pilothouse was cheek by jowl with crew. There were no phone talkers looking stoned as they listened to headphones, dragging wires around for everyone to trip on. Instead every crewman carried a black Motorola portable. It looked insecure, but Geller said their range was so short it wasn't an issue. Besides, anything classified still went by naval message over the big white dome of the Inmarsat antenna.

Dan was looking back at several men doing push-ups on the afterdeck, near a rigid-hull inflatable cupped in a well, when a startlingly loud ba-ROOM came from aft. A terrific burst of white-yellow smoke rose between *Shamal* and the pier, mushrooming till it blotted out the sun. Dan blinked as it expanded, shrouding them in a sulfurous murk.

One of Geller's junior officers had the conn, with the CO hovering. Sweating, the jaygee advanced control levers on the bridge wing console. "Ahead thirty on number one . . . back thirty on number four. Cast off the spring." They could control the engines from out here, but oddly enough there was no remote rudder control, so they still had to bawl helm orders in through the door. The sound of a gigantic cat barfing a hairball aft must be the clutch going in.

"Four screws, total fourteen thousand shaft horsepower," Geller yelled. "You can torsion your way in to a pier if you have to. One and two to starboard, three and four to port, and the inner two turn clockwise, so you can actually back down in a straight line."

Dan nodded as the smoke became so dense Geller faded to a yellowish ghost. He sneezed, wondering if something was on fire. But apparently this was normal; no one remarked on it.

"Cast off number one. Then back down and twist out. You don't need your rudder yet," Geller told the conning officer.

Dungareed line handlers from *Whitney* cast off lines that the deck parties hauled in hand over hand. A horn that sounded like it had been salvaged from a Trailways bus went BLAAT. BLAT-BLAT-BLAT. The pier started to move ahead. Geller ducked behind the 01 level superstructure to the far side. Dan followed, keeping tabs. Geller was the skipper, but as the senior officer aboard, if they ran into anything his butt would be on the line too.

The inlet was clear, though, only one speedboat two hundred yards off. The starboard gunner had the big .50 level on its pintle mount, brass belted into the loading tray. His binoculars were aimed at the speedboat.

Geller caught his glance. "Booty's a friendly port, but since that dhow attack in Bahrain we've put more effort into force protection."

Dan nodded and faced aft, sneezing again. *Shamal* was backing slowly, but still lay swathed in a thick bank of her own smoke. The bearing taker was talking into his Motorola, but Dan couldn't see what he was using for marks.

They emerged from the cloud bank, smoke still billowing up, but lighter now, shading to reddish brown, and Dan lifted his head, looking out past only two channel markers, to open water.

The Red Sea. He'd sailed it before, but still felt awestruck at its sere, remote beauty. The Gulf must have been like this before oil and the demands of commerce. But this shallow wide sea was still nearly untouched. Today the sky was all but dustless, so bright it hurt. The sea was a polished golden bronze shading to an opulent green, disturbed only a little, where the sun winked off it, as the waves of *Shamal*'s advent eddied outward. The pintles creaked as the gunner swung to track the speedboat. The engines hairballed again, and Geller murmured to the conning officer, who shouted, "Come right, one five five." The drowsy singsong of the helmsman echoed the order.

"Hold on," the CO said. "You're gonna love this."

A bellow like a dozen diesel tractor-trailers revving to full power came from aft, followed by billows of smoke that made the dose they'd sucked at the pier seem like a gentle mist. The ship accelerated out of it, though Dan, leaning to look over the wing coaming, saw more streaming out of the waterline exhausts. "That'll cut off in a second," Geller shouted over the roar. "They vent underwater once we get past eight knots."

Despite the noise the acceleration was smooth. He felt its tug, though warning him to hold on was overkill. "So, what comms do you have?" he asked Geller.

The CO went down the list: UHF line of sight, HF, UHF satellite communications uplink. "No data link or combat systems. Anything important comes in CUDIXS or on the red phone, HF covered. No Link 11 or 14. No WINSALTS or anything like that."

The wind of their passage was hot and blustery, with swirling effects from the corners of the superstructure. The latched-open wing door vibrated in squeaks and chirps like Morse code. "From stop to flank ahead in under three minutes," Geller yelled. "Full ahead to fifteen knots astern in sixty seconds. In high-speed, hard-over turns, we barely heel. Fin stabilizers. Course, they're CASREP'd right now."

Dan grimaced at the mention of fin stabilizers. He'd been in a typhoon aboard a South Korean frigate when they'd failed, with catastrophic results. "What're we making now? About thirty?"

"Good eye, thirty-three over ground. We can pick up a few more in what they call sprint mode, but it's like every hour is four hours' engine wear."

The sea was flying by, its speed accentuated by how low they were to the water. Only about twenty feet up, as opposed to forty or fifty on the destroyers he was used to. "What kind of range?"

"At thirty-three knots I can run for nine hundred miles. Most economic transit is around fifteen. Generally try to refuel every couple days on patrol. They had us doing oil platform duty in the NAG. We'd rotate out of KNB every couple of weeks. Refueling from *Trenton*."

He was interrupted by a call on the bitch box from the chief engineer, who said the carbon was burned out, they could drop speed now. "Drop to ten, and come to your course for Point Alfa," Geller told the officer of the deck. The ship surged, coming down off plane. This time Dan grabbed for a handhold; the deceleration was more abrupt. "This time out we'll mainly be holding station. That's why I wanted the chief to clean everything out with a high-speed run. That, and impress you. Were you impressed?"

"Sure. What's the patrol plan?"

Geller laid it out above the chart taped to the nav table. The mission was to show the flag and interdict any arms shipments bound for Ashaara. They'd proceed north to the patrol area, then maintain presence on a line covering 120 miles north to south, 20 to 30 miles offshore. There'd be comm drills, and a fast attack craft/fast inshore attack craft drill. He didn't expect much out of the ordinary, but Dan could get familiar with their capabilities.

Just being under way felt good. Who was he kidding—it felt *great*. He climbed another level to the flying bridge and stood leaning on the splinter shield watching the mountains shrink behind them. He looked aft, past the call-sign flags snapping on the mast, down to the catwalk. Two of the BDU-clad figures he'd glimpsed at calisthenics were walking toward the bridge.

Dan frowned. Did he know them?

He believed he did.

5

ASHAARA CITY

From the predeployment briefing, Aisha had expected the airport to be run-down. But she hadn't expected it to be surrounded by tanks.

Well, not tanks exactly, but high-wheeled armored cars with machine guns jutting as men in yellow-green berets lounged in their shade. Armed troops occupied the terminal building, too. The only civilians stood in a double line, heads bowed as they shuffled forward, laden even more heavily with luggage than she was. They didn't look as if they were going on vacation.

The little man was perspiring so heavily his pink shirt was soaked front and back. The terminal was hotter than the Harlem summer, a closed-in, waxy, intimate torridity like a closed-up greenhouse. His knees shook as he bowed, eyes flicking to her, then away. "Welcome, welcome . . . Agent Erculiano, Agent . . . Ar-Rahim?"

"That's correct."

"You are—you are with the Americans?"

"I *am* an American."

"Oh . . . my mistake . . . come this way . . . very glad . . . a car waiting."

Special Agent Aisha Ar-Rahim was used to people mistaking her nationality. Most Americans overseas wore an instantly recognizable uniform of khaki pants and polo shirts. Sometimes the khakis had cargo pockets, or the shirts were button-down, but they were always short-sleeved and wrinkle-free, and their wearers stood clear of the locals as if they carried flesh-eating bacteria. But she swished along in a voluminous cerise silk abaya, clogs, and a lavender pashmina she'd tied in a soul-singer headwrap as soon as she left Washington. In her purse was a cell phone, a gold-toned badge with the seal of the Naval Criminal Investigative Service, and handcuffs. Along with a little prayer rug she'd bought on hajj and a digital Canon.

The little man scurried ahead. Erculiano said again, "I can carry that for you."

Paul Erculiano, of the open-necked shirts worn with Italian slacks, was the assistant agent in charge—her subordinate—but they'd never worked together before. It was the third time he'd offered, and she wasn't sure whether it was politeness, being patronizing, or simple brownnosing. "I can handle it," she snapped, though her suitcase *was* heavy. The computer was in it and her Koran, and she always brought crime-scene gear overseas: a six-ounce spray can of ninhydrin, latex gloves, evidence tape, bags, and a dozen evidence-collection documents.

Down in the bottom, inside a folded Marine Corps duffel bag from the Camp Henderson Exchange, was her body armor and a nine-millimeter SIG Sauer P228 and four magazines of Cor-Bon +P+ hollow points. The pistol was her issue weapon, but the bag had been the suggestion of one of the older agents in the Washington office. "Take along a spare duffel," he'd said. "I always do, on assignments. You never know when you're gonna find something worth bringing back."

The Naval Criminal Investigative Service was the Navy Department's civilian detective force. Most agents focused on traditional criminal investigations, a big problem for a department as huge as Defense, but they also worked counternarcotics, counterintelligence, counterterrorism, and naval security, both aboard ship and wherever sailors or marines were stationed ashore. Aisha was a federal law enforcement officer, like an FBI or DEA agent. Her chain of command went not through the military, but up the civilian side to the secretary of the navy. Whom she happened to know, having been given the Navy Superior Civilian Service Award by him two years before for her work at the Middle East Field Office, breaking a case involving stolen explosives, forged base IDs, and a terrorist attack on a U.S. ship.

In the car the little man sat in back with them, though the

front passenger seat was unoccupied. He kept wiping his forehead, taking deep breaths, and sighing. He said his name was Bahdoon. "First or last?" Erculiano asked, leaning forward so Aisha could see his chest hair. His beard had grown out during the flight, and he reeked of lime aftershave.

Bahdoon explained most Ashaarans didn't have last names, not as Westerners used them. "We have the name we are given. Then our father's name. I am Bahdoon, my father was Abukar, I am Bahdoon Abukar. Then my grandfather, so that is three names."

"Don't you get confused?"

"We have our ways of identifying those we can trust," he said. Before she could ask he added, "Women use their father's names too. They do not change them when they are married."

She blinked out the window, shielding her eyes against the glare. The city—a town really—looked nearly empty. Then, as they passed side streets, furiously active. Here and there a balcony or stuccoed wall reminded her of Italy, but shabbier. The dilapidated, crumbling buildings were one- or two-story, painted either white or bright green or blue. Here and there one had collapsed on itself. A woman in a sarilike robe, colorful as a tankful of cichlids, stared from the shade of a ragged awning. Hundreds of flimsy plastic bags slowly tumbled in the wind, past lean men standing by wooden booths, jiggling something in their pockets. One stepped into the street and spat where they'd just passed.

"What are they selling?" Erculiano said, peering past her. "I don't see anything for sale."

She twisted, trying to see, but caught only dark visages glowering after them. Her face was black too, but there was no acknowledgment of that in those eyes. Her gaze caught on a line of children sitting against a wall. Their thin legs cocked up in sharp angles. She looked after them for a long time, until they were out of sight.

"Is there famine in the city, Bahdoon?"

"No famine. Plenty of rice and bread. The president feeds us all. Unless of course they are a rebel."

A few blocks on what looked very much like a mob pushed and shoved in front of a row of shops. "Is there unrest in the city?" she asked. "I saw something going on down that street we just passed. Were those looters?"

"No, no unrest. That is the Indian Quarter. If there is crime, that is for the police to deal with. I'm sure they are on their way. Only a few more minutes to headquarters." He jerked his neck as if something were biting him between the shoulder blades, and looked away, to the other side of the speeding, lurching car.

Aisha followed his gaze and saw two men beating up a third, who sagged, staring past his assailants as if he weren't participating. All three were in colorful shirts and ragged pants. The victim's gaze followed their car but his expression didn't change as his eyes seemed to meet hers. Probably, given the tinted windows, he hadn't seen her at all.

The mansarded redbrick palace with corner towers was encircled by not just a tall iron fence but a moat. Once it must have been decorative. Now it was a dried-up ring of cracked mud and puddles of scum. The roofs shone the pale green of old copper. More of the troops who'd guarded the airport stood at the gate. A red-and-white crossing barrier from a World War II movie swung up as a guard leaned on the lever arm.

"The Service of Interior Documentation," Bahdoon explained. "You will meet our minister, Monsieur Mukhtar Samatar. He is eager to give you every assistance in your mission."

Samatar however wasn't in, and from the looks of the offices, she wondered if he'd ever return. Despite being ringed by troops, the Palais de Sécurité felt abandoned. Bureaucrats in sweated-through pants and dress shirts sat tensely at desks, blinking, smoking one cigarette after another.

Bahdoon finally found a major who agreed to sit down with them, in a dingy cubby in a subbasement. Apparently a cell block, though now there didn't seem to be anyone in the holding area, which was dark. But the little Ashaaran didn't accompany them, vanishing between the main floor and the basement.

A lower-level policeman who spoke English sat in to translate. An aged, bent, very black clerk or transcriptionist crooned to herself near the door as she bent over an old ledger spidery with ink, which was literally—Aisha looked twice—chained to her desk. A ceiling fan that looked as if it had hung for a century without dusting rocked with a protesting squeal as it rotated at the speed of a clock's minute hand. The major, in starched fatigues, a brown-leather-holstered Makarov automatic at his hip, listened to her without expression. "Here are our passports, visa, and documents," she said, squaring them on the green paper desk protector. "And the letter from your minister expressing his hope we can work together. Perhaps our first step should be to link up with the local police for a background briefing."

The translator spoke around a cud of what Aisha assumed was qat. He had a red-eyed stare, as if looking at someone behind her at whom he was very angry. The major, whose name was Assad, said through him, "Unfortunate, Minister Samatar has left the city. Like big assistant. I am senior officer left in charge."

"I see. Do you know when he'll be back?"

"That major can't talk you. Political situation is . . . *orooyo* at moment."

She had no idea what *orooyo* meant. Fluid? "Well . . . I'd like to begin by discussing the security situation, and how we can help." She hesitated. "*Tatakullum arabi, Ra'id*? Do you speak Arabic?"

"*Shwei*. Not much. *Parlez-vous français*?"

She said she did not. Erculiano said nothing, though she glanced at him, so they continued as they were. Assad spoke, leaning on the desk, and the translator spat, "Major say outsiders, foreigners, they give Ashaara too much help. No. Not little help. When to say when."

"Perhaps I didn't understand that properly. Please ask the major if that is an official comment? For the record?"

Assad shrugged. He said something the translator didn't

bother with. Then added, "Any rate, Major will do what I can. Are Americans considering come?"

"I don't know. I doubt it. Background, that's what I'm principally here for."

"Background . . . background," the translator mumbled. Assad scowled at him.

"Information. Knowledge about Ashaara."

"Intelli-jenz," the man tried. *"Espion?"*

"Not exactly. Uh, can the major tell me what are his principal concerns? As an officer of the Ashaaran national police force?"

"He wants to know what yours. What your concerns."

"Well . . . safety and security of the airport, and the area close to the embassy."

"*Tous les deux sont parfaitement secure*," Assad said in what she guessed was exquisite French. The translator said, "Oather okay."

Oather? "Um, second are what might become personnel safety issues, such as drugs."

"He say, you interest in drugs? What kind?"

She looked at the bulge in the translator's jaw. "What is this gentleman chewing?"

The man grinned, showing her a grassy mass in his teeth. "This qat. Is no big deal. Is like coffee."

"Harder drugs, then. Whatever you find most threatening." She paused, then chanced it. "Monsieur Bahdoon mentioned rebels on the ride from the airport. I knew there was unrest, due to the famine. Food riots? But what is this about a rebellion?"

"Parlero Italiano?" said Erculiano.

Assad looked blank, but the aged transcriptionist, or whatever she was, turned immediately in her backless chair. *"Sì, parliamo Italiano. Che cosa gradite sapere?"*

"*La città è nel corso della divisione.* The city is in the process of being divided," Assad said through her, then via Erculiano to Aisha as he studied her face. "The president has always governed without distinction of clans. All are equal. As are all religions: Christians, Muslims, even the animists of the Western Mountains, all are equal before the state and the law. The rebels reject this. They fight for loot and power, and for their savage interpretation of the words of the Prophet, peace be upon him."

"Peace be upon him," Aisha repeated, earning glances from all three Ashaarans.

Assad cleared his throat. His gaze tracked the creaking fan. "*I ribelli . . . alcuni di loro ora sono attivi nella parte del sud della città.* Some of the rebels are active in the south of the city. Our troops are moving to address the unrest. Meanwhile, normal police activities continue. Would you find it helpful to accompany us on one of our activities? That would give you better background than sitting through a briefing."

She said warmly they'd look forward to doing so. Assad rose and bowed, not extending his hand. He spoke for the first time in English, the sentence obviously prepared before he spoke it.

"Monsieur Bahdoon is . . . unavailable. My driver will take you to your embassy."

Their "office" was a Conex box. The interior was lined with steel shelving, the shelving with canned water, medical and rescue supplies, blankets, and batteries. All too obviously, it had been a storage unit the day before they arrived.

The embassy lay a quarter mile from the sea, which was just visible between spreading acacias the color of dried parsley and sag-roofed tourist cabins or beachfront cottages. Its walls were brick, no doubt the local product, a soft pale rose, darker inside, where it was chipped. It looked like the campus of a moderately prosperous junior college. The grounds were a half mile across, ringed with a security road just inside the wall, though she hadn't seen everything yet, just driven in and taken a quick meeting with the ambassador's staff assistant and the military attaché, a Lieutenant Colonel Jolene Ridbout, U.S. Army.

Sitting in a tilting metal chair with a broken caster, Aisha contemplated a career that had brought her to this.

It had started in Georgia, sixteen weeks at the Special Federal Agent course: crime scenes, firearms proficiency, hand-to-hand, arrest procedures. She'd finished third, then blown the criminal law final. But the service had wanted her all the same. Female African-American agents? She wouldn't be the first, but they were still thin on the ground. *Muslim* agents? The director had offered a deal she couldn't refuse.

Her first assignment had been the San Diego Field Office, and the usual new-agent case load: burglary, larceny of more than fifteen hundred dollars, suicide. Having grown up as sheltered as the Muslim community had kept her, it had been sobering. Her first overseas assignment had been Bahrain. There she'd worked for one of the oldest agents still carrying a shield, a legend in the service: the man who'd fingered Jay Harper, the spy, years before.

Since then she'd served on a protective service detail, providing security for visiting dignitaries, secretary of defense–level officials; then done the obligatory tour of independent duty afloat: in her case, the USS *George Washington* battle group, responsible for not just the carrier, but the whole strike force, destroyers, frigates, auxiliaries. She remembered Commander Candy, and sighed. His smooth mocha skin, in the darkness of his stateroom . . . the only time she'd slipped so far. Then, the Defense Language Institute in Monterey, to improve what was already fairly good Arabic.

She wasn't as naive now. Nor as slim, unfortunately. But she was a GS-13. The next step up could make her a SAC at one of the field offices.

Yet she was no closer than ever to what she really wanted. A family, a child . . . She wiped sweat off her face and tried to concentrate.

She and Erculiano were the lead members of an advance party. The Navy often requested NCIS support in countries where contingency action might occur. Not that it always happened. It usually didn't. But when a landing or humanitarian-assistance mission became necessary, personal relationships with the host government were key to avoiding publics relations disasters, or worse, security problems that could endanger either own forces or the mission.

Of course none of this had been spelled out to their hosts. Her overt orders were to benchmark the host country police on investigational efficiency, respect for human rights, corruption, and technical accomplishment. Then submit a report on what assistance from Justice and DoD might improve their effectiveness in protecting public order and American interests. A carrot that usually prompted cooperation. No one had told her what the advance party was here to prepare for. She suspected another agency time waster, with her report filed for reference. But someone had to do those as well as the big investigations. That was how you got the big ones, after all. By taking on the shit details, and executing them flawlessly.

"Gotta grab a shower," Erculiano told her. "Feel like there's scum all over the inside of my undershirt."

This was so unappetizing an image she squeezed her eyes closed. "You go ahead. I'll wait."

They'd had dinner at the embassy dining hall, sloppy joes and french fries, and were back in the Conex writing up their reports for the day when the phone birred. They looked at each other. He picked up.

"Out front at the gate," he said, hanging up. "Assad. With our weapons."

"Our *weapons*?"

"What he said. You wanted to operate with them? Sounds like he's ready to roll."

She cocked her head, wondering whether the letter of agreement would cover that, then dismissed it: Assad was apparently the ranking security officer in the capital. She bent to her suitcase and found the soft heavy pad of her body armor. Then, the hard heavy outline of the SIG.

"Vests?"

"Absolutely. Whenever we're off-compound," she told him. "At least until we get a reading on what these rebels are up to." He made a face, but pulled his out of its plastic sheath and squirted it with lilac-smelling baby powder.

She turned her back and flipped a fresh blue silk abaya over her head. Once she wouldn't have done that in front of a man. Even wearing pants and a blouse under it. But she wasn't the little Muslim girl who'd grown up sheltered in Harlem anymore. She wiggled her fingers behind her. "Borrow some of that powder?"

She dusted the vest and pulled it on, buckled the side fasteners, pulled the folds of light cloth back down. She chambered a round, decocked and tucked the pistol into the shoulder holster she could get to without anyone on the outside of the voluminous swathe of cloth noticing a thing. She could even shoot through it, though she'd risk setting the fabric on fire.

Rolling through the night took her back to Bahrain, the breakneck dash through the streets to keep USS *Horn* from being attacked. Only this time they were in open pickups, not the unmarked, closed vans the Bahrainis favored.

Night in Ashaara City was even less reassuring than day. The pavements degenerated as they left the vicinity of the embassy into potholes and ledges the wheels dropped from with jarring shocks. In the beds behind them rode sloppily uniformed troops carrying heavy German rifles and old-style French helmets slung over their arms while their shaven skulls gleamed in the occasional streetlight. From time to time shots echoed in the crumbling blocks of low buildings. She and Erculiano rode together, with a grizzled, half-Arab-looking sergeant who'd spoken only in grunts and not once looked her in the eyes.

"You sure this is smart?" Erculiano muttered.

"It's an honor, Paul. To be invited. I'm surprised they're letting us, this soon."

"We're not supposed to operate with them. Only liase."

"The best way to liase is to operate." He wasn't really objecting; he was protesting for form's sake. He looked as excited as she felt.

There wasn't nearly enough excitement in most NCIS work. Most of what she did inside the Beltway was sit in meetings, discuss budgets, suffer through the latest leadership fad, and plot against other agencies. She'd made her bones in the Mideast, though, and cemented the commitment with the Arabic specialization. She'd spend the rest of her career here, and in counterterror watch groups in Washington and Norfolk. To end, probably not as the director—she couldn't see a Muslim in that seat, ever—but maybe as a regional director, or heading up the counterterror bureau.

Though that might be impossible too. There'd always be those who suspected any Muslim had to be a terrorist, deep in her heart.

The headlights bored through darkness. Buildings still rose to either side, but no streetlights lit the increasingly uneven road, which seemed, from the sound of the tires, to have turned to gravel. Behind them the soldiers were singing, a haunting hymn to which they hammered rifle butts into metal. She wondered what the words meant. Her roots were here, but this was the first time she'd actually come face-to-face with real Africans on their home turf. Something shifted in her belly. The boots and butts slammed down, over and over, in a booming roar that must have carried out over the silent houses for many blocks. It felt like fear, but she wasn't sure that was all it was.

The sergeant growled what must have been a command to stop singing. The trucks pulled into a cleared space. Shattered bricks ground under the wheels. She caught whiffs of lime and urine. The troops swung down with only a little murmuring and clanking. She turned her head to catch Assad peering in the truck window, and started.

"Come," he murmured. "You see."

They picked their way down a dirt-floored alley behind a trio of soldiers. She felt inside the abaya and quietly withdrew the SIG. Got a second magazine ready, but kept the safety on and her finger off the trigger. The night was full of smells, faint crepitations, the calls of some sort of insect, up under the eaves of the houses. The hum of a generator a couple of houses away.

Their arrival hadn't gone unnoticed. A woman called from a second-story window, and one soldier, squat, with a scraggly mustache, answered, telling her, Aisha guessed, to butt out. Instead the woman screamed what sounded like curses down at them before she was grabbed from behind and dragged back from the window.

Suddenly shouts burst out ahead, and a bellow she recognized as the sergeant's. She hugged the wall, keeping as much cover as she could between the noise and her body. The surface was crumbly, soft, and she realized what she'd taken for concrete was painted mud. Its peculiar stench, ammoniacal and biting, added to the strangeness of the foreign night.

Assad's voice, carrying in command. Words came drifting back through the chain of police. Then the grizzled trooper was guiding her forward, holding her elbow between finger and thumb as if she were made of spun sugar.

Hand-carried lanterns threw beams around the interior of a corrugated-metal garage. An ancient truck squatted on blocks, hubs dangling, like an old cow with broken legs. A chain hoist swayed. Three frightened men stood with hands behind their heads, staring at rifles pointed at their throats. She spotted the major's tall shadow near a workbench. He beckoned her with a closing-palm gesture.

"You say drugs," he said, in accented but passable English. He pointed a flashlight. "See."

Heavy black plastic, pulled back, revealed brown bricks she recognized, even before bending to sniff the sweetish-sick odor, as hashish. At least twenty keys, professionally shrink-wrapped the way smugglers tried to foil drug-sniffing dogs.

One of the captives suddenly broke free, shouting in a high voice. A trooper cracked him in the face with a truncheon. The others were shouting too, gesticulating at the truck, at the hashish. They were denying the stash was theirs, disclaiming any knowledge of it. Right, she thought. Sailors did that too, when they were caught.

One of the troopers called from the truck. When she

looked that way he was holding something up. A long tube with a thick blunt head, like some great spermatozoon.

"Rocket-propelled grenade," Erculiano breathed.

She was headed over to examine it when shots cracked outside. The troops crouched as Assad spoke into a cell phone, coordinating backup, she guessed. Erculiano grabbed her shoulder. She shrugged his hand off. "Let go, Paul. I've been in raids before."

"We shouldn't be here."

"This is *exactly* where we should be. Drugs *and* weapons; these people have a bigger problem than they're admitting."

More shots outside. The troops were emptying through a back door, checking their rifles. The agents were suddenly alone. She frowned. Where had Assad gone? The captives the troops had been guarding?

"Where are you going?" Erculiano hissed.

"Just follow me." She moved toward the only other exit, a linteled doorway wider than usual, as if to allow the passage of large parts. A black curtain separated it from whatever lay beyond. She stood to one side, then whipped it back with one hand, pistol in the other.

Then caught her breath, unable to make sense of what lay tumbled in the light of a hissing gasoline lantern. For a moment they seemed nothing more than bales of oil-smeared rags.

But the smears weren't oil.

Bodies sprawled across a concrete floor. Not just of men, either. Women in abaya, the small brown feet of a child—

And the soldier who'd shouted back at the woman, the one with the scraggly mustache. He lay staring up at something invisible, bloody fingers digging into his stomach.

She recoiled even before the sergeant pushed in front of her, blocking her view with his wide chest. He motioned her back, grunting. She obeyed, but couldn't stop a horrified flutter in her throat. Then realized: She couldn't leave. She had to find out what had happened. Had the rebels executed these people? Were they hostages? Captives? Why was there a dead soldier as well? Atop the other bodies, which meant he'd been killed after them?

Or had the *police* executed them? No, the firing she'd heard had been farther away. But maybe they hadn't been shot. Maybe those were slashes, not gunshot wounds.

She blinked furiously, trying to recall exactly what she'd just seen, but it was already blurring. She started forward again, but the sergeant shoved her back so hard she staggered.

"Aisha? What is it?"

"Bodies, Paul . . . I think." She took a deep breath. More troops were joining the noncom, shooing them out. Erculiano pulled her back as she stood irresolute. It was hardly possible Ashaaran security troops were executing civilians. But if they were . . . American special agents did not belong within a million light-years of the scene.

Assad had to know that: that if things like this were taking place, they must be hidden. It would be an enormous loss of legitimacy for the Ashaaran government, already widely regarded as corrupt and repressive, to be implicated in mass murder too.

But if that was what this was, why ask her along?

Why *invite* witnesses?

Or were they less there as witnesses, than . . . to be *implicated*?

No, it didn't make sense, the rebels had to have killed them, the soldier too. She put it aside for later and backed out into the alley again, into the soft brilliance of a moon just clearing the rooftops. She leaned against a wall, coaxing her slamming heart to slow. The image of the bodies came back, clear this time, the way it hadn't been a few seconds earlier.

She became aware of more shooting, a firefight in fact, on the far side of the block. She looked back to the alley entrance, where the trucks must still be waiting.

Then turned, and began jogging along a side court parallel to the road they'd come in on, hoping it would get her up closer to the firing.

Erculiano yanked her back. She rounded on him. "Let *go*, Paul. Stop *touching* me."

"This isn't our bust. These are rebels, not criminals—"

"Just cover me. Or stay here, if you don't want to come." She drew the SIG again but held it close to her chest. Slipping from shadow to shadow, she went down the alley. She heard nothing behind her. Then Erculiano's reluctant steps.

Bullets snapped overhead and cracked into the walls, knocking sprays of mud and plaster down around her. They were high, though, as if the assault was at the second story. She came to a corner and halted, screwing her courage up. Then went low, thighs protesting as she crouched, and peered around it.

Movement! She froze. Then rotated her trunk to face the wider alley-mouth in that direction. Her dark blue silk would be black in the starlight. She doubted anyone could see her. She pointed the SIG, level in her locked arms.

A slim figure hesitated, peering around. It carried a rifle. An AK, by the outline. Other shapes swam in the dim behind it. The silhouette's head foreshortened, searching the shadows, but didn't steady on her.

She shook the shielding cloth away and steadied the pistol, picking up the tritium-illuminated sights. The blue-green dots centered on his chest. Her breathing slowed as she took the slack out of the trigger. An escaping smuggler. An escaping rebel.

He lifted his face to the moon.

The face of an angel. His features were noble, his large dark eyes weary. So young, but he carried himself proudly. Like an East African David. The young and comely king. She held the extended pistol, trembling, on the verge of firing.

But at last did not, only held her aim, in case they turned her way. But they didn't, only paused to listen and then followed the young man as he ran swiftly, sandals scuffing in the urine-smelling mud, under the moonlight, running away.

6

THE RED SEA, PATROL AREA
"CRS"

Teddy Oberg was standing in the RHIB arguing with the big Hawaiian, how he was going to rerig the releasing gear, when the petty officer in charge screamed, "Helmet!" pointing at Teddy.

Midmorning, two days after they'd gotten under way. Hot and sunny, like every day so far, occasional patches of haze, a few knots of wind kicking up some chop. The wake was a freeway of whirling, jostling turquoise, a tan tint just discernible above it. Submerged exhaust, bleeding up out of the wake, the same color as the russet haze before sunset. And far off in the distance the black mass of a containership headed for the Canal and Europe.

Teddy and the other SEALs in the rigid-hulled inflatable had manned up on the fantail an hour early to run through everything again before they were in hailing distance of the contact. Nobody seemed to know what it was, this ship; just that the drill originally scheduled for this morning had been called off, and *Shamal* ordered to intercept.

They wore standard boarding gear: desert battle dress uniforms, knee protectors, assault vests with ballistic armor under climbing harnesses under orange Navy flotation gear, fastrope gloves, flashlight, flare kit, handcuffs, and so forth on and on for thirty pounds of additional equipment. Their weapons were secured inside the boat with bungee cords. They had MX-300s, the "bone phone" with the ear mikes, for intrasquad use and VHF in the boat for comms with the ship. They had plastic-sheathed knives and an M60 machine gun on a mount but with a bipod too so they could board with it if they had to, plus extra magazines for their HKs and SIGs. Basically, loaded for bear.

Only you were never ready for anything, he thought. Even a routine board and search could throw you a curve, usually one that meant blood, sweat, and shit to catch up. "What the fuck?" he muttered to Kaulukukui. He and his swim buddy stared at each other.

"He's poppin' a safety violation, Obie. Wants you to put a hard hat on, like every other swinging dick in the fuckin' boat."

"No shit! What I'm askin' you, when that tending line twists around like that on the release hook—"

Their heads whipped around, and the first class's too, at the blare of the long-range acoustic device, a flat-panel loudspeaker capable of breaking eardrums at a hundred yards. "VESSEL ON MY PORT QUARTER, YOU ARE CROSSING AN INTERNATIONAL EXCLUSION ZONE. STOP ENGINES AND HEAVE TO IMMEDIATELY. STAND BY FOR BOARDING. IF YOU DO NOT COMPLY YOU MAY BE SUBJECT TO USE OF DEADLY FORCE."

He caught the first class's swing back toward him, grabbed the hard hat, clapped it on over his BDU cap, and jumped on top of the gunwale, balancing on the round thick rubber with a hand to the center console windshield. The inflatable rocked in its cradle as on the other side the Hawaiian's not inconsiderable weight bore down as well. On tiptoe, they could just see the ship that had crossed within the thirty-mile reach of the slowly cruising *Shamal*'s surface radar.

So far, it didn't look as if whoever was on the bridge was impressed with the warship bellowing orders at it across the calm flat sea. Standard operating procedure was for *Shamal*'s bridge team to radio them as soon as they were in sight, passing the order to identify by Channel 16. But obviously this guy hadn't gotten the word. Like so many others Teddy'd had to hold wakeup calls on over the last few years.

Looking inboard again, he caught a familiar face gazing from the catwalk. Teddy had about shit, recognizing Lenson the day they got under way. Wasn't that he didn't respect the guy. He had notches in his gun, the operational kind the team could recognize. But their last op had had its unpleasant moments. He'd mustered a grudging smile as Lenson slid down the ladder. "Commander. What you doing in the Red Sea, sir?"

He'd seemed glad to see them, pumped their hands, asked what brought them there. "We're deployed, sir. Do it a lot," Kaulukukui had said, as if any fool should have known. Teddy had almost choked.

"I know you deploy—"

"Ah, what Main Meal means, sir . . . Team Eight deploys a platoon to each of the fleet commanders. Most of our guys are with the ARG in the NAG, but we're TAD'd to the TF for MIO."

Translation: most of the platoon was with the amphibious ready group in the North Arabian Gulf, but they'd been temporarily assigned with this task force to do maritime interdiction operations. "Uh-huh." Lenson had nodded, as if that was interesting but not what he cared about. "Still doing that mudhole driving?"

"Every chance, sir. Get dirty with us sometime?"

"First opportunity." Lenson looked back to the bridge, where, Teddy noted, the black CO was watching them. Jelly Man, Kaulukukui had named him.

"So, what you doing aboard a PC, sir? Still at TAG?"

"Right." He'd explained: some kind of study about where the Navy was going. Teddy nodded, letting it go by. Os always obsessed on big-picture stuff that had nothing to do with real life. "Well, good to see you, sir. Get together for cards later, okay?"

But whenever he saw Lenson after that the guy was huddled with the chief engineer or with the little analyst, Monty Henrickson. Teddy knew him too; he'd been aboard *K-79* when they'd stolen it from the Iranians.

"VESSEL ON MY PORT QUARTER, STOP ENGINES AND HEAVE TO IMMEDIATELY. . . ." The LRUS was blasting out again, more bullshit lawyerspeak no raghead could make sense of even if he understood English. Teddy craned again.

Their target was a black-hulled merchant twice the displacement of the patrol craft. Not one of the little cargo dhows you saw here and in the Gulf, packed tight with oil drums and camels and dusty wedges of pilgrims. Geller had mentioned pirate activity up here, but it didn't look like that. This was a trading dhow, long-hulled, steel—there weren't as many wooden dhows in the Red Sea as there were in the PG. A Yemeni flag. That could be tricky. They were supposed to make nice to the fucking Yemenis. But any craft transiting the central Red Sea was obligated to heave to on demand.

Which this guy wasn't. He was plowing up a big bow wave, smoke blasting out of his stack, hammering along. No one was visible on deck. Teddy watched as the CO and Lenson confabbed on the wing. Then the barrel of one of the bridge M60s swung out. The wing team covered their ears.

Spray leapt from the centers of eight circles, all in a line, from fifty yards ahead of *Shamal*'s bow to a hundred yards in front of the trawler's.

"That'll get his attention," said the boat handler.

But it didn't. Both ships plowed on, a hundred yards apart. Then eighty. Seventy-five. *Shamal* was slowly closing, but a second stutter of fire brought no more acknowledgment than the first.

"Time for the firecrackers," the handler said.

On the catwalk, crewmen loaded shotguns. They waited, watching the captain. *Shamal* and the stranger rolled in sync, sixty yards apart. Geller nodded. The Mossbergs recoiled. The firecracker rounds popped bursts of white smoke ahead and abeam of the other's bridge.

A crewman came running lickety-split from somewhere on the bow. A moment later the bridge wing door cracked and a startled face gaped out. "HEAVE TO NOW OR I WILL SHOOT TO DISABLE," Geller boomed on the LRUS. He didn't sound happy.

A pause, as Teddy noted the other ship seemed to be growing shorter.

The bridge team must have realized what was happening at the same instant he did, because suddenly there was shouting, then the solid-sounding clunk deep underfoot as the PC's engines slammed to full astern. The trawler kept coming around, though, the river between the two hulls narrowing. Sumo grabbed for a handhold, missed, and toppled off the gunwale like a falling tupelo as everything in the RHIB got pulled forward and to port. *Shamal* leaned in a decelerating turn. "TURN PORT. PUT YOUR WHEEL TO PORT!" the LRUS boomed out, without the slightest response from opposite.

Just as Obie braced for the collision somebody did something that grabbed the whole ship and twisted its tail far enough to starboard so that, combined with the reversed engines, it let the trawler pass clear, missing them by yards. Then they were jamming ahead again, the engines snarling like charging Panzers. Volumes of choking white smoke sheeted up, setting everyone hacking. In the middle of all this came the *blam, blam, blam* of the .50 cal. The cases, big as ladyfinger bananas, arced and clattered down through the catwalk forward of the doghouse. Teddy watched the bright tracers, like orange comets, burn past the trawler's pilothouse. No way anybody could miss *them.* And apparently he didn't, because the welter of wake lessened at last.

"Stand by, the RHIB," shouted the petty officer. Teddy jumped back down, ducking as the crewman in the bow swung the long metal-tipped boat hook into position forward. He braced, gripping a line looped along the gunwale—an inflatable could catch a wave and flip, or nose under like a diving dolphin, converting its occupants into projectiles—and concentrated on what came next.

The PCs launched boats differently than any other ship, a legacy of their original mission. Instead of hanging on davits, the RHIB squatted on a ramp slanting downward and aft. The advantage was, you could launch and recover in much heavier seas, since the ship could roll as much as it liked and the boat could still make up on her in the smoothed patch of the wake and drive straight into the stern and up the ramp. Now the petty officer twitched a knob on a hand-held control box. Salt-eroded bearings squealed as large gates slowly unlocked, letting the foam-pale sea swirl in. Beyond it the wake jetted and tumbled like a Jacuzzi as *Shamal* accelerated again after the trawler, which still had way on. Kaulukukui squatted in the stern, eyes on the port tending line. Vic Cooper and Mickey Dooley hunkered on the starboard side, and Petty Officer Lazaresky, the coxswain, pumped the choke and hit the start button. Blue smoke burst out, joining the murk *Shamal* was still sucking along after herself, though she had enough speed on now that the underwater exhausts had cut in.

His Motorola beeped. "MIB Team, Alleycat."

"Alleycat" was *Shamal*'s in-the-clear call sign. "MIB, over."

"Cast off and inspect. Carry out three-sixty eval before boarding. Do not board if hostile intent is manifested. Comm check every mike five."

Teddy rogered, and flashed the petty officer a thumbs-up. "Deploy," he shouted. The crewman in the bow yanked a line. The quick-release hook clacked, the cable snaked back into the massive block arrangement that would bring them back aboard later, and the inflatable began a heart-stopping backward toboggan slide that while it lasted fully satisfied what Teddy admitted was his addiction to risk. Out in a strengthening chop, weapons at the ready, to board a guy who obviously didn't want to stop. What could be better?

Going back to LA? Making more money, sure. Having all the pussy and drugs you wanted. But as they hit the water with a rocking splash, got a faceful of diesel exhaust and the sun shone down as if through whipped buttermilk and the coxswain swore horrible oaths while wrestling the wheel to keep the wake from sucking them into the stern, Teddy thought: You really ready to give this up?

"Enjoyin' yourself?" Cooper yelled, stubble shading his jaw. Even close up the guy could pass for Iranian, with that dark skin and heavy eyebrows. He spent his time listening to the team's Farsi tapes, and went around muttering in it.

"Havin' a great SEAL day, Crabmeat. How 'bout you?"

The coxswain finished lowering the motor—you'd break the blades if you tried that before you launched—and gunned it. The bowhook and four SEALs hung on as it porpoised over the wake, jerking and slamming, the M60 on its flexible mount nodding in agreement it was indeed a fine Navy day. The radar hummed atop the framework over the center console. The engine blatted each time they leapt clear of the sea, then resumed its powerful burble as they squatted deep. The coxswain looked to Teddy, who fingered a circle in the air. "Check her out first," he yelled.

Their first surprise was a stocky bearded guy in a hunting orange knit cap pointing a rifle over the side. An old long-barreled bolt-action Mauser. Cooper and Teddy had him covered before he even got the barrel around. Kaulukukui had the M60 on him too. Cooper yelled, "Drop your gun," then repeated it in Farsi.

"Fuck you," the guy yelled down. No interpreter needed, Teddy thought, tracking him over the sights of his HK. But the guy didn't shoot. Didn't drop the rifle, either. Just moved back, so they couldn't see him from where they continued to circle the trawler.

"Is this a hostile boarding?"

"I'd say so."

"What about that?" Kaulukukui pointed to where the orange-hatted man and another, younger crewman in coveralls were kicking a boarding ladder over the side. It was too long and trailed in the water, but the rifle was gone. "Looks like an engraved invite to me."

"Stassy, cover us with the sixty, okay?" Teddy asked the bowhook. "Anybody shoots, plaster 'em. But try not to hit us, okay? Let's get this over with."

He kept a sharp eye on the whole length of the dhow as it loomed, in case somebody else leaned out for a potshot, but didn't see anyone. He slung the HK and pulled up his fastropers, getting ready to climb. Better than hooking aboard with a bamboo pole, that time in the South China Sea. The RHIB curled in. He crouched, ready to jump to the ladder.

Instead an unexpected wave peaked, maybe the chop and *Shamal*'s wake—the ship had just passed and was putting her helm over to come back—and the inflatable lofted suddenly and slammed into the hull. The flash hider on the machine gun's muzzle caught between the doubled rungs of the boarding ladder, and as the inflatable dropped, the wave passing, the heavy long weapon levered itself up out of its pintles. Before anyone could do anything other than gape it executed a somersault, bounced off the steel hull, fitted itself like a key in a keyhole into the foot-wide slot that opened between the ship and the RHIB's gunwale, and vanished, despite the bowhook's instinctive plunging of his ash pole in after it.

"Oh, my *fuck*!" Sumo yelled. The other SEALs cursed too. Teddy clutched his head, staring down at an innocent ring of bubbles. His rage wasn't helped by the crewmen above, who were leaning over the lifeline and guffawing.

The dhow's skipper looked more Peruvian than Middle Eastern. His huge-nosed, narrow face sported teeth so horrible Teddy avoided looking at them. He kept playing with a set of wooden beads, looking alternately pissed off and surrendered to fate. "Captain, sorry to have to pull you over," Teddy said, abandoning the effort to remember who he reminded him of. "But why didn't you stop when we requested you to heave to?"

The guy mumbled that he didn't see them.

"Pretty hard to miss a ship right off your beam, Skipper. I see your radar head going around. Anybody up here ever look at the screen?"

The guy said he'd punish his officer, but there wasn't anyone else on the bridge, leaving Teddy to wonder who he was talking about. "Okay, second sticky, one of your boys pointed a weapon when we came up. The fat dude in the Halloween hat. That standard procedure?"

He said it wasn't, that man would be punished too, but there were pirates in these waters, that was why they had the rifle. Teddy let that pass. "So, where you registered, last port, where bound, Captain?"

The guy's gaze skated around the pilothouse and came to rest on his beads. "We are Yemeni register. Trade in parts, food, dates, and wheat. Bound to Al-Hudaydah."

Down south. Not the direction he'd been heading when *Shamal* had picked him up, but Teddy let that pass too. "Last port?"

"Ashaara City."

"Name of ship?"

"Al-Sambuk."

"Owner?" He kept pitching the standard questions while thumbing through the paperwork. " 'Farm products.' What, exactly? Oilseed? Cowpeas? Sorghum?"

The guy took too long answering, and Teddy held up a glove. "I'm gonna talk to my ship now. Then we'll go down and see what you got."

Outside the pilothouse, for better reception, he brought the bridge up to date. "What paperwork there is checks out, but I want to throw an eyeball in his hold and make sure. Oh, and we lost some gear overboard, coming alongside."

Fortunately they didn't ask what, and Teddy didn't intend to be the first to bring it up. With any luck the coxswain would report it, and get blamed. Actually, hadn't Lazaresky been in charge, as long as they were still in the RHIB? It was the ship's 7.62 anyway, not the team's.

Yeah, he'd let them handle the loss report. He left Cooper on the bridge and headed down and forward with Sumo Man, collecting the two crewmen (maybe there were only two after all) and motioning for them to get the hatch cover off.

The baking-grass stench met them halfway down the ladder. An eye-watering cross between marijuana, pipe tobacco, and nerve agent. Kaulukukui gagged. "What *is* this shit? Ever smell anything like this?"

"Smells like a fucking pot party."

"That's right, you're from Hollywood."

"I'm not from fucking *Hollywood.* I'm from Laurel Canyon. And this ain't pot."

"Want me to go back on deck?"

"Sure. Fuck, no, I want you here to carry me back up if I pass out."

"I could lower a line."

"What good's that gonna do me, I'm passed out?"

"I can put a hook on it."

"Get down here." Obie dropped to the deck and pulled his Streamlight.

"Here's something interesting," he said a minute later, trying to breathe shallow. "Look at this."

His light picked out the corner of a wooden box. The stinky stuff was bits of broken leafy stems, still green though the leaves were wilting in the heat. Someone had hacked it into four-inch chunks, bagged it in burlap, and laid it in the boxes. But that wasn't what he thought was interesting. Nor was it the boxes. Those were just heavy, roughly finished softwood, many with broken sides or slats, as if someone had wrenched them open with a sharp tool ten minutes before quitting time. No, what he found fascinating was the stenciling.

"*Ver*-y interesting. Type 69. Sumo. Know what that is?"

"Rocket-propelled grenade."

"You got it, Jeopardy Man. Let's see there's any live ones here, okay?" They began tossing sacks around, pulling boxes out from beneath them. A strobe flared as Kaulukukui took a photo.

Twenty minutes later Teddy staggered off the ladder, on deck again. Behind him Kaulukukui lurched like a broken robot. The big Hawaiian had started muttering something that sounded like "kwoo, kwoo, kwoo," and didn't seem able to stop. Teddy squinted in the sunlight, hacking and spitting. He felt like when you took too many of the amphetamines that were part of every SEAL kit, except worse. His brain was a popcorn kernel in a microwave, about to blast out the top of his skull. His heart was racing like a Yugo with a busted engine mount, and he kept jerking and flinching. "You feel okay?" he muttered to Kaulukukui.

"My mouth is as dry as fifty-year-old pussy."

The crewmen stared so deadpan it was obvious they were this close to bursting out in guffaws again. Oberg scowled, gripping his MP5, to make sure they didn't.

Someone on *Shamal* was watching through the Big Eyes, because they were on the radio right away. "Boarding Party, Alleycat. What you got over there?"

Teddy clicked the radio, still trying to breathe and stand up at the same time. For some reason he wanted to do high kicks, like a Rockette. "One here. Ah, it's qat. Tons of it. Which explains why he was in such a hurry. Shit loses its kick three days after it's picked."

"Copy qat, correct? That's his prime cargo?"

"His *whole* cargo. Question is, where's it from? He says Ashaara City, but I thought it was closed down. And what's he running on the back end? 'Cause from his logs, he's making this trip two, three times a month."

"Say again, One. You're talking too fast to copy."

"Uh, yeah." He glanced at Kaulukukui. "Ah, Sumo's not feeling too good. Those fumes were toxic, man. We're gonna take a break here . . . short break. Yeah. But first. What the qat's packed in. Wooden crates stenciled NORINCO. China North Industries Corporation. With model and lot numbers for one hell of a shitload of rocket-propelled grenades."

He faintly heard Geller and Lenson discussing it. Finally the CO came on. "Oberg, *empty* boxes?"

"Check. Empty. Turned over about a quarter of the cargo, no joy. Then we had to get out of there or we were gonna start drooling."

"All right. Get ready to retro."

He stared at Sumo. *What the fuck*, the Hawaiian mouthed. Teddy clicked the Motorola. "Say retro, Skipper? Evidence of arms smuggling here."

"Empty boxes aren't a violation, Petty Officer Oberg. Unfortunately, neither is qat. Not by Yemeni law, and that's a Yemeni-flagged vessel. We have no standing to hang on to this guy. Lawful commerce in international waters."

He started to protest, then shrugged. "You're good to go, Driftwood," he told the skipper.

"Good to go? You mean, free to go?"

"Right, free to go. Go on, di-di the fuck out of here."

The guy grew a big grin, as if he'd just crapped in his

worn black polyester pants. Those teeth looked even worse now that the qat fumes were magnifying every crevice and pore of whatever Teddy looked at. The captain threw a lever and took station behind the wheel. The engines cranked wearily, then built to a pounding roar.

"I can't believe this," Teddy's partner muttered.

"Me neither. Say qat's legal here, and the crates aren't evidence."

"Legal. So, how about we bring some back? Chew it when we're off watch?"

"Shit, all I did was breathe the fumes and I've got a worse hangover than I got off that Kahlua and schnapps shit you made up for us at Jillian's."

"Kahlua's rich in vitamin K."

"Yeah, and you're rich in vitamin B, Sumo. B for big-assed Hawaiian bull cookies."

They were hitching their trou, patting down to make sure they had their gear, getting ready to go aft to the boarding ladder, when the radio crackled again. "MIB, Alleycat."

"Go ahead. Over."

"Team leader, step outside pilothouse."

He raised his eyebrows at Sumo. "Say again, ah . . . all right, got it, Skipper. Stepping out." He eased the door to the wheelhouse closed. Through it the captain watched. "Go ahead."

"Teddy, we've got a closing contact. He's in that haze off to the southeast, but his track, we ran it back, it's on a converging course with your boy. They might have had an exchange planned."

He grinned and double-clicked the send button. *Fun,* he mouthed to Sumo through the grimy window. "Could be interesting, sir. What's the plan? Over."

"I'll fade south four, five miles. Low as we are, we'll be out of sight. Heave to and pretend to be fishing, if they're watching their radar. Run your RHIB over to the port side, under cover of the hull. Have your skipper resume previous course and speed. Maybe we can nab two birds with one stone."

"Especially since we can't touch this one legally."

"Affirmative, but gun up. Pull your sixty out of the RHIB, get it on deck. Just in case."

He didn't answer this, so he could say later he hadn't heard it. Their machine gun was on the bottom of the Red Sea, but if he told Geller that, he'd pull them back aboard and stand by with the PC, and the other ship would turn tail as soon as it saw their silhouette. If it really was a smuggler.

His eyes met Kaulukukui's.

No need to say a word.

The little guy with the bad teeth didn't like it, but given the circumstances, he couldn't protest. What was he going to say—"You messed up my drug rendezvous"? Teddy yelled down to Lazaresky to run around and tie up on the port side, and to load his shotgun. The bowhook looked up, eyes wide.

Back inside, to pass the word to Cooper and Dooley. The 60 would've helped, but four SEALs with MP5s should be enough, and if they needed more, they had the two combat shotguns in the RHIB. Neither Lazaresky nor the bowhook, whose name Teddy had forgotten, were probably exceptional marksmen, but that was what shotguns were for. "I'll make it quick. Everybody out of sight until we see what this new guy at the party's gonna do. Geller thinks he might be here for the qat."

"I'm here for the beer."

"Fuck's wrong with you two?" Dooley frowned. "Who punched your fast forward? You're actin' like a couple of fifteen-year-old girls."

"Fuckin' hold's solid with that joy weed they chew. Contact high."

"Contact high, huh? You guys kill me. Beavis and Butthead. Prob'ly snorted half of what's down there. Where the hell's Lazaresky going?"

Teddy explained, looking at the trawler's captain. Whose smile had been replaced by a sick look, and whose worry beads rattled like dice in a cup. "So, ship's headed off to the south. Us, we'll stay out of sight until he's alongside. Then see if this's the other half of the deal, maybe nab some arms smugglers. Any questions?"

There weren't, and he told Mickey and Vic to head aft, keep an eye on the crew but stay low, out of sight, and leave the channel clear on the bone mike. "Oh, and get Lazaresky and the bowhook midships with shotguns and full bandoliers." He squinted into the glare and caught a speck far out in the brilliance that must be the incoming contact. They had to get out of sight. A uniform would be a dead giveaway.

A scuffle and squeak behind him. He turned, to see the skipper floating in midair like a scruffy angel halted in midflight.

"Fucker was going for the horn," Sumo said. His biceps bulged, but he didn't seem to be straining to hold him up. The skipper's toes kicked for the deck.

"Who are these guys?" Teddy asked him. Going by the old saw: Ask 'em when they're in pain. "What you meeting them for? They your customers for the qat?"

The Hawaiian's grip must have tightened, because the guy's face started to go purple. *"Bass,"* he whispered. *"Bass."* Enough.

"Make it simple for him," Sumo suggested.

"Listen to me, Driftwood. These your customers out there?"

"*Aiwa. Aiwa.* Yes."

"Now we're talkin'. Not so bad, is it? They buy your qat?"

"Is not mine. But they buy. Yes."

"For what? Cash? Weapons?"

He didn't answer. Teddy looked out the starboard side window, to see the other ship gaining detail. Maybe a mile now. "Your arm getting tired yet?" he asked his swim buddy. Sumo shook his head. "They trade what, Jack? Work with me here. Things can get a lot worse for you."

"Trade guns. Yes."

"Kind of guns?"

"Don't know words."

"Machine guns? Grenades? Stinger missiles?"

"Grenades."

"Chinese?"

He nodded and Teddy winked at Sumo. A double thump as the guy's shoes hit the deck, followed by his ass as he collapsed. "Get up, you ain't fuckin' hurt," Teddy told him. He pulled the throttle back to what he figured was dead slow. The engine-beat fell to a putter.

He'd been thinking about how to deploy, and come to the conclusion the wheelhouse gave the best field of fire, field of view, and control of the situation. He removed his cap and took a knee at the starboard door, where he could see the approaching ship but not be made even with glasses. Kaulukukui took the port side. The skipper sat whimpering and wiping his nose with the back of one hand, kneading his neck with the other. "Suck it up, you ain't hurt," Teddy told him again.

"Charlie Babbitt twisted and hurt his neck. Serious injury," Kaulukukui said.

"What's that from?"

"*Rain Man.* Don't you think he looks like—"

Teddy grinned. "He does look kinda like Dustin."

"Lose ship. Lose cargo," the captain moaned.

"Ain't a thing we can do to the cargo, Jack. It's yours, free and clear. All we want's whoever's pushing the RPGs. Now *that's* contraband, anybody's book."

"Kill family," the guy whined. "Al-Sheekh, he will kill family. Those his grenades."

"Well, whoever Al-Sheekh is, he's gonna have to write it off. Maybe he can get a tax break, huh?"

"Here." Sumo was holding out something to the guy. Teddy blinked. "Want a Slim Jim?"

Kaulukukui got back a look of disgust, fear, and revulsion. "He doesn't want your Slim Jim," Teddy told him. "Put it back in your pants." He raised up a little and checked the other ship. "Nearer."

"*Definitely* nearer," Kaulukukui said.

"Try to warn these assholes again, you're the first one I shoot," Teddy told the skipper. "You transfer cargo out here? At sea?"

"At sea. *Aiwa*."

"At sea, *definitely*," Kaulukukui said.

"Shut up, Rain Man. Christ."

They waited, then Teddy peeped again. The other was a coaster, longer than the dhow, with a container lashed down on deck. Maybe that was where they stowed the ordnance. Easier to dump, if they had to. On the other hand, you wanted to keep your explosives cool. Out on deck in this sun the inside of a container could hit two hundred easy. Hot enough to bleed the binder out of a shaped charge. Heads were moving around on the foredeck. He cleared his throat, trying to slow his heart down. Excitement, but probably still some of the effects of the fucking qat. Man, the stuff had an unpleasant high.

The skipper got up and stood at the wheel watching the other ship, panting like an overheated dog.

Sumo. "Man, wish we had Jelly Man and *Shamal* back of us."

"We do."

"Four miles away. What if these dudes resort to violence?"

"Like always. Take the fight to the enemy, man."

"Wish we had that sixty. Lay down some covering fire."

"Well, we ain't got it. Can get you that guy in the ghetto hat, get you his bolt action, though."

"Fuck you."

Yeah, it'd have been nice, but he wasn't worried. They had six-shooters. More than enough to take a merchant.

Gradually the coaster neared. It sheered off for a time, as if waiting for a signal, but the skipper insisted there was no signal. Even a headlock in Sumo's beefy arm failed to dislodge that insistence. Teddy did a comm check with *Shamal* and thank God got them. Geller asked if he wanted them to come in. "No sir, they haven't committed themselves yet. Soon's they do, we're gonna need you here in seconds."

"Well, maybe not in seconds, One. We can go to flank emergency and get to you in about eight, ten minutes, though. Just pass the word. Over."

"He's got his helm over," Kaulukukui murmured. "Coming alongside, starboard side."

"Good, he won't see the RHIB."

"We may need that fucker."

Teddy didn't answer. He was studying the faces on the bridge opposite as it closed. The other ship had tires over the side for fenders. Not many crew on deck, three or four, moping around in that half-assed way you got around noon when it was this hot. No weapons in sight. Good.

Then other men filed out of a little after-structure stretched with canvas like a tent, and he sucked breath. Four, five, six . . . eight. Each on one end of a wooden box like the ones, empty now, down in the hold.

All gun-heavy with AKs and PKMs, the sniper variant. The men carrying them weren't black. Arabs or Iranians. Middle Eastern rather than African.

Weapons for qat. Nobody had mentioned this in the team's predeployment brief. Smuggling, yeah. Cigarettes. Booze. Somali emigrants. But not this.

The coaster was drifting in, the last few feet vanishing, the coaster's side five, eight feet higher than the dhow's low midships. He pulled the VHF over. Murmured, "Alleycat: Alleycat One. Target's alongside. Guys on deck with AKs, carrying crates of RPGs. I ah, I think we need that backup now."

As he let up on the button a long blast of airhorn ripped out above their heads. He snapped around to see the skipper, baring rotten incisors at them, knuckles white on the horn lever.

Kaulukukui loomed over him from behind. Only for a second. Then the captain was slumping again, head twisted over his shoulder, like an owl's.

Teddy cracked the door to see not what he expected, guys taking cover. Somebody'd taught these dudes to take the fight to the enemy too, because half of them had dropped their crates and were rushing to the side.

As he watched, from above deck level and twenty yards away, the two ships drifted together. Heavy worn rubber tires compressed with a squirt of reddish dust. A jar shivered though steel. And with a concerted yell four shooters from the other ship jumped the five feet down to the dhow's deck and split up. Ice touched Teddy's spine as he realized each carried his weapon *the exact same way.* They weren't facing ragtag crewmen, but something more dangerous.

"Fuck," he was muttering, when the first burst cracked out, followed by the booms of shotguns. One of the boarders looked startled. He straightened, then deflated like a cheap balloon.

Score one for Lazaresky. Unfortunately, the men left on the coaster had dropped to their bellies and were starting to shoot too. Within seconds a truly impressive volume of fire was clattering across the deck, most focused on a little sternhouse Teddy assumed was where Cooper had taken his guys.

"We got to take the pressure off Crabmeat and Skunk," Sumo shouted. Teddy nodded, trying to figure out how. If he went out on the wing he'd be exposed. There was no splinter shield or bulwark. But he'd have a rest on the life rail, and a perfect enfilade down the line of prone shooters below. He went to the bone mike. "Crabmeat, y'there?"

No answer. Not good, but he couldn't wait. Time to earn that combat-zone pay. He eased back the bolt to check the load, checked that the rear sight had the biggest aperture dialed in, wiggled the front sight to make sure it was secure, loosened the second mag in the pouch, and gestured *covering fire* to Kaulukukui.

Rolling out the door, he took a knee, thumbed the selector to semiautomatic, and put the front sight on the closest shooter.

He got three rounds off, all head shots, before they realized they were being fired on from above. The third he called low, the guy was still kicking on the deck, but he'd let go his rifle and Teddy didn't think he needed another tap. Especially since the others were jerking their heads around, yelling, reorienting on him. He double-tapped a torso shot and the target went limp. But by then the last guy was up in a crouch, aiming at him, and he was late, late . . . time went gluey as he waited for the flash and impact of the bullet . . . then Kaulukukui's MP barked from the other side of the bridge and the guy wavered and went down.

Teddy whipped left, covering the pilothouse opposite, and shot a man in a white shirt with blue piping who was trying to quick-draw a pistol out of a holster. The guy behind him, eyes huge, stuck his hands into the air. Teddy shot him too, two rounds center chest, just so he wouldn't get any ideas.

He swiveled right again, thumbed to full auto, and walked a burst up the sprawled bodies till the mag went dry. He stepped back into the wheelhouse and speed-reloaded without taking his eyes off the other deck. He pulled the mag and checked that the top round had fed. "Clear," he yelled.

"Going aft," Sumo shouted from the far side.

They went down port and starboard simultaneously, running the short ladders from the wheelhouse to the deck as shotgun blasts boomed below. Teddy ran in a crouch, reminding himself Cooper and the two RHIB crewmen were back here too, he not only had to not shoot them but to make sure any misses on the bad guys wouldn't hit them. Absolute control of every round was the only way to prevent blue on blue aboard ship. He hoped the coxswain and bowhook had the same idea.

He rounded the corner to run full tilt into a wiry little guy coming the other way. Their weapons clattered together and the other's fired. Teddy smelled burnt powder and sweat and tobacco. He felt a jerk on his sling and brought his MP around into the guy's face and pulled the trigger.

Not even the dead click of a pin on a dud round. The trigger didn't even move as he stared into the guy's eyes. Who apparently had some problem with his AK as well, because he suddenly gave up trying to shoot and backed up a step, jerking at the front of it. The glint of a short bayonet unfolding.

Ah, fuck, Teddy's mind said.

He started to go for his sidearm, then remembered: he hadn't brought one. He'd always thought carrying another full mag for the HK made more sense. But just now, looking down at the dished-out white-metal scar where the bullet had struck the receiver, he had to admit: maybe not the best idea he'd ever had.

The guy charged. Teddy did too, trying for a hand on the barrel so he could twist it up and go under with the knife already in his hand. Funny, he hadn't thought of drawing it, but there it was. But he missed his grip and the bayonet with the guy's weight behind it drove right into his solar plexus.

A textbook bayonet attack, but he felt the point snap as it hit the trauma plate in the vest at the same moment the sharper-than-a-razor thin-bladed Glock filleted up the inside of the guy's thigh. It snicked through the femoral and he curved the blade left, heard it ripping through cloth and flesh, felt another light resistance as the guy's eyes widened. His lips drew back and he screamed. The blade grated into the pubic bone.

Out and in again, slicing upward. His boy had forgotten about bayoneting anybody—he just wanted to get away. But Teddy had his head with his left hand, pulling him in, tight sweaty embrace, grappling, the guy clawing to fight free. He kept forcing the blade up, the guy going to tiptoe, trying to rise off his blade like a worm off the hook you were threading into its pith. But Teddy had his arm under it now, angling the point upward, trying for the heart or the big arteries beneath. Then gave a final twist and pulled it out.

He shoved with all his strength and the guy stumbled back, opened up like a chicken, everything falling out, till his heels hit the edge of a coaming and he toppled backward.

"You won't be much good to those forty virgins now," Teddy told him, wiping the Glock on his trousers and stooping for the Kalashnikov. He cleared the jam as two more booms from inside the deckhouse blew out a window and sent another boarder over the side.

Then it was over and his ears were ringing and his whole front was bloody, but he kept going. It was when you thought it was over that you made sure it was over. He tested each body with the Glock and found one wounded man who'd do for intel. Sumo was working the coaster's deck. As they passed, Teddy going aft, Kaulukukui forward, the Hawaiian said, "Skunk caught one."

"Bad?"

"He's not in good shape."

"Fuck. Fuck."

"That was why he wasn't answering up on the bone."

"Fuck. Boat crew?"

"Lazaresky got nicked. Took half his ear off. Got the guy who shot him, though. Orange Hat. Even did a combat reload on the Mossberg."

"These assholes fought. We had to kill 'em all."

"I thought ragheads didn't do that."

Teddy squinted up at him. The combat chill was gone and he felt angry now. Dooley, hard down. A perfectly good guy. "Oh, they do, Sumo. You get the right ones, they do."

"AHOY BOAT ONE."

He waved acknowledgment as *Shamal* came alongside, fenders out. Both 25mms were pointed at him, and three other MGs from the bridge and afterdeck. "Eight minutes," Sumo said, looking at his watch. "Seemed like longer."

The PC came alongside with a bump and lurch. Geller and Lenson stood on the port wing in armor vests and helmets. They looked down with startled expressions.

Teddy became aware that several of the sailors topside were aiming cameras. And that he was dripping with blood, surrounded by motionless bodies and empty brass, brandishing a bayoneted AK. He lowered it, snapped the safety on, and considered. Then shouted up, "You ever take a really good shit, and look down in the toilet and say, Hey! Good job?"

Their shocked stares told him he'd said exactly the right thing. The SEAL thing. "Tell them, put those fucking cameras away!" he added. "Right now!"

"NOW ON USS *SHAMAL*: PHOTOGRAPHY IS SECURED TOPSIDE. PHOTOGRAPHY IS SECURED TOPSIDE."

“Guys got any cold water?”

“I’ll send a case with the boarding party,” Geller shouted down. “All secure?”

“Not sure yet. Send the medic. Dooley’s hurt. Send everybody armed, might be more below.”

“Enemy casualties?”

“Saved one to interrogate. You bet.”

Geller and Lenson exchanged looks. “What?” Teddy said.

“We need you back aboard ASAP,” Lenson said. “We’ll send the corpsman for Dooley. Leave the bodies aboard for whoever follows up this, uh, event. Just got a message.”

“What’d it say?” Teddy asked. Saw him frown, like he should have said, “sir,” and nearly laughed in his face. Blackshoes. You hadda love ’em.

“Proceed to MODLOC off Ashaara City.”

“Off Asshair City? What for?”

Lenson glanced into the pilothouse as a radio crackled. “The embassy’s surrounded and under attack. Centcom’s considering how to evacuate it. They want us inshore as soon as possible. I need to go over some things with you. As soon as you get cleaned up.”

FOOD

7

USS *MOUNT WHITNEY*

Dan stepped over the knee-knocker, still shaky from a violent helicopter flight. The Combined Arms Coordination Center was enormous compared to the one he'd once worked in aboard USS *Guam,* as a lowly lieutenant (jg). Its tiered seats sloped down to electronic displays instead of enlisted men wielding grease pencils on Plexiglas. Before them were twin brown-leather-covered reclining chairs, for the Navy overall commander of landing operations and the Marine commander of the troops once ashore. The Marine chair was empty, the Navy one occupied.

By Commodore Goya, who looked up from a notebook computer locked between upthrust knees. "Lenson. How your men doing? The wounded?"

How had they become "his"? "Two are minor, torn ear and a defensive cut on the hand. The other's serious, but the surgeon says he'll make it."

"You left *Shamal* off Ashaara City?"

"Yes sir. Dr. Henrickson and I helo'd back."

"Where is she? Pierside?"

"No sir, but within visual range. Captain Geller's standing off to observe, pending orders. I told him to try to establish comms with the embassy. Serve as a relay, or a backup comm channel. Even VHF or a cell phone would put us ahead of the game."

"Okay, great. Question. Are you familiar with caps in geeks?"

That was what it sounded like, but Dan heard CAPS—the Crisis Action Planning System—in GCCS—the Global Command and Control System. "Yessir. At the Joint Staff College, then on the NSC staff."

Goya's eyebrows rose. "You worked at the White House?"

"Yes sir."

"Done any real-world crisis action planning?"

"The incursion into Syria after the embassy takeover in Cyprus. Arroyo Gold, the strike on Libya. Signal Mirror, in Iraq. Then in the Sit Room, for Eritrea."

Goya reached above his head. "Mr. Wurtz there? I'd like to see him, if he has a moment."

A short commander in sweat-stained khakis came in one of the lower doors, Kim McCall and Monty Henrickson a couple of steps behind. As he climbed toward them Goya said, "Commander Lenson, Commander Wurtz. Goes by Rocky, my N-3, Operations. He's new in the billet."

"Good to meet you, Rocky."

Dan stuck out a hand, but Wurtz's flinched back. "You don't want what I got," he said.

"See the doc?"

"Yes I did, Commodore."

"Well, we have a possible NEO downrange, Rocky. Can you brief Dan? I'm thinking of having him help with the planning."

Wurtz looked put out, then resigned. "Could use the help, sir. Miz McCall here's already getting sucked into the whirlpool."

"Whatever we can do," Dan said. "This is a noncombatant evacuation from Ashaara City?"

The operations officer outlined the situation. The president of Ashaara had fled the night before without bothering to officially abdicate. He'd simply left, in a chartered Air

Tanzania jet, along with his ministers and what remained of the treasury. Police and troops had evaporated. Al-Jazeera and CNN were reporting looting of foodstuffs and reprisal killings. "The ambassador's Jedidiah Dalton. You might remember him from *That Dalton Bunch*," Wurtz finished. "He was the youngest, who held his breath to get what he wanted."

"The cute one? With the pet bat?" McCall said. Dan was surprised she was old enough to remember it.

"That's him. Anyway, he's requested military assistance. As of 07 today."

"Requested a NEO?"

"Not specifically," Goya put in. "That's part of the problem. Apparently the Chiefs can't issue a warning order for an embassy evacuation until State officially requests one. Some interdepartmental thing."

"I thought we could plan, but not execute," Dan said.

"My understanding too, Commodore," Wurtz said.

"Then why's Centcom holding on to the order?" Goya frowned. "If I'm reading this right. And if it's not a reflection of what's happening in Tampa."

Dan nodded. Goya was referring to Commander, Central Command's recently being charged with sexual harassment, threatening his confirmation for a fourth star. "Think he's tied up with this suit, the woman who worked for him when he was Seventh Army?"

"That, or things are getting worse in Iraq."

"He's not in Florida," Henrickson put in. They looked at the analyst. "He's at the temporary command center in Qatar. So it could be Iraq."

"Sir," Dan said, "it's not labeled as a warning order? It's informational?"

"Correct."

"And you're an info addressee? It's from JCS to Centcom?" Goya nodded. "Who are the other addees?"

"COMUSNAVCENT, *Tarawa, Duluth, Anchorage, Oldendorf*, Comphibron Eight, CTG—that's me—and One-Five MEU."

Dan squared his shoulders, feeling a vacancy amidships that had nothing to do with nutrition. "Well, Commodore, I'd say they're working it inside the Beltway, the Chiefs and the NSC and the SecDef's office, but somebody in the Concrete Snowflake's trying to give us as much of a heads-up as he can. My guess is you won't be the final on-scene commander. Nothing personal—the amphib guys are trained for that job. Chain of command will probably go from NAVCENT to Comphibron on *Tarawa*. But we should start planning now. See if we can get those units started in our direction. Then everybody'll be up on step when the warning message hits the street."

"Concur, sir," Wurtz snapped.

"All right, pull your team together. Keep the chief of staff informed. I'm going to make some calls on the red phone, see if I can get any better sense of the situation."

"And get the amphibs moving, sir."

"I'll do what I can," Goya said, and for a moment Dan was afraid he might've pushed too hard. For a guy who wasn't even on Goya's staff and, though a senior commander, wasn't an 0-6. And might never be. But the commodore just hit the bitch box and began talking to the commo about covered HF.

Wurtz convened his Three Shop guys in the ops office for orientation. Dan didn't say much. It was the ops officer's show. He tried to keep his mind off Kimberly McCall's perfume. She sat next to him, legs crossed. He admired the curves of her calves. When she caught him looking he cleared his throat and glanced away.

"Dan? I said, anything you'd like to add?"

"Uh—I like most of what you've said. Using the MEU (SOC) and so forth. Running the helo routes around the populated areas, that's smart. But, uh, what comms have we got with the embassy? It'd be good to get them to confirm these information packages. Sometimes those run two, three years behind. And 'enemy capabilities'—I wouldn't assume permissive entry just because somebody says the army's dissolved. One hardcore in an old MiG strafing a landing craft and we've got a hundred dead marines."

He went down the notes he'd jotted, watching Wurtz getting steamed but not caring.

Ashore, the Marines were as close to unbeatable as a military force got. Afloat, the U.S. Navy's woven layers of sensors and defenses could deal with any imaginable threat. It was when they had to project force inland that both became vulnerable. The ships, because they were close to shore, constrained by hydrography and the obligation to support the landing force. The troops were shorn of heavy weapons, without cover, exposed and vulnerable on open beaches.

Those who'd studied the bloodbaths at Dieppe and Gallipoli, Salerno and Tarawa, had evolved a list of lessons that troops bent under rucks and rifles realized existed only when everything went horribly wrong. Dan had seen it done well and done badly, and he'd stepped up because he knew how deadly a beach could get. The grunts liked to sneer at the staffers, the pogues, the rear-echelon motherfuckers. But it was the words and times and numbers in the operations plans that preserved or expended their lives, and sometimes determined victory or defeat before the first boot sole stamped a print on wet sand.

Ignoring his hosts' frowns, he took Wurtz's concept of operations apart. He rotated this piece seventy degrees and machined a roughness off that one, then put them back together into a plan that now emphasized overlapping fields of fire, quickly available fire support, comm channels better tuned to what the forces would need if surprised, more precisely delineated areas of responsibility, and less time-critical phase and objective lines. When he finished there was silence.

Wurtz cleared his throat. "You've done this before."

McCall gave him a smile and a lifted eyebrow. "Commander Lenson here's high speed, low drag."

She couldn't be coming on to him. Could she? His head

hurt like a sonofabitch. The air-conditioning was ramming icicles up his sinuses, after doing without it aboard *Shamal.*

Wurtz cleared his throat again. "Well, here's what I think. You should take the lead on the overall plan, uh, Dan. Tell us what to do here."

"I'll need SIPRNET and JWICS accounts, and access to your workstations. But it's still your plan," Dan told him. "I mean, Commodore Goya's. All we're going to do is tweak it a little bit."

0200, back in the CACC.

Thanks to the development tools in *Mount Whitney*'s computers, including several matrix documents, they were able to generate a reasonably workable plan. Meanwhile, intel trickled in from Centcom J7 and various other codes at DIA and State, along with a cable from the embassy, responding to questions Wurtz had sent.

The plan opened with a time-critical reinforcement of the embassy's organic security force. A SEAL detachment would land by inflatable from *Shamal* and *Cyclone*, while marines from *Tarawa* carried out a helicopter assault. The marines would overwatch the embassy by securing an apartment building and a water tower. Security established, the 115 compound personnel, plus whatever local staff the ambassador cleared for evacuation, would be airlifted out by CH-46s staged from *Duluth.* Meanwhile the SEALs would fall back between the compound and the beach, holding the back door open if for any reason the on-scene commander judged air evacuation too risky.

Goya had asked to be briefed as soon as they had a product, so here they were, Dan and Wurtz presenting, the rest in the seats to answer questions. The commodore fidgeted through it, asking whether they'd included an amphibious option, and built in excess capacity in case of additional evacuees from the other embassies or UN and nongovernmental agencies. Dan let Wurtz take both questions. The commodore thought awhile, then asked to review the supporting-arms piece in more detail.

Dan reluctantly took that, having written that tab, and put up a PowerPoint slide showing support available if things turned ugly. *Tarawa* would cover the force with Cobra attack helicopters for close-in support and Harrier jets in case the aged MiGs of the Ashaaran air force were flyable. "We'll also have force-protection missile cover and five-inch guns available from *Oldendorf*, including semiactive laser-guided projectiles, and direct fire from her and the PCs if there's a situation on the beach."

Goya said, "We're counting on *Tarawa* for a lot. Are we sure she'll be here on time? No flight-deck casualties or equipment down?"

Dan looked to McCall, who handed over the helicopter landing ship's last readiness report and confirmed the movement order that had gotten her under way. She brought up a slide showing tracks and speeds of advance for the ships en route from the Gulf of Oman, and toggled to the GCCS display. *Duluth*, in the lead since she'd already been in the Gulf of Aden, would reach CH-53 launch range shortly before noon the next day. Since Duluth had no CH-53s, the plan recommended launching them from *Tarawa* at 1000, doing a hot refuel aboard the closer ship, then hopscotching in to Ashaara City.

"All right, that looks good," Goya said at last, swinging down from the chair. "Let's put it on the street and see what happens."

Dan borrowed a stateroom, showered, and turned in. For a few minutes his mind whirled in dizzying circles, like a defective DVD player, then went blank like a snapped-off screen.

He was deep in REM sleep, dreaming he was in his grandfather's house with his daughter, though the two had never met—his father's father had died long before his daughter was born—when the bulkhead phone buzzed. He folded his pillow over his ears, figuring the call was for whoever usually slept here, but it went on and on. Finally he got up and groped around the unfamiliar darkness, slamming a toe so hard lights flashed even in the dark. Found the phone and snarled, "Lenson."

"McCall. You might want to come down."

"Why?"

"Significant developments. Some, you may not like."

Was it A.M. or P.M.? From the dimmed passageways, the snoring from the other staterooms, it was 0400 rather than 1600. He made a wrong turn and got lost, but followed the smell of coffee to a cubby where two storekeepers were working late, nodding to Def Jam. They looked surprised when he knocked, and told him to help himself. When he let himself into CACC he was functioning above rudimentary brainstem activity.

McCall and Henrickson and Wurtz and his subordinates were at the workstations. "What's up, Kim?" Dan asked.

She pushed back and knuckled her eyes. "First off, you were right. The phibron on *Tarawa*'s been designated commander for the extract. But Commodore Goya talked to COMNAVFORCENT. The administration's been making noises about taking a more proactive role in addressing famine in East Africa. So Ashaara might go bigger than a quickie NEO."

"I'm not surprised yet. What about our plan?"

"NAVCENT forwarded it to the phibron recommending they consider it."

"All right . . . what else?"

"Message from the ambassador, Dalton. He okayed extracting nonessential personnel, but *he* doesn't want to evacuate. In fact he implied he wouldn't even if Secretary Revell ordered him out."

Dan nodded, thinking that over. "Things must be cooling off."

"Actually it sounds worse. Everything's walking out of the government buildings, the Interior Ministry's occupied by armed men, looting and shooting out in town. People getting even for things the president's clan did over the years. Somebody set fire to the prison, and most of his political prisoners burned to death. But he—"

"Who?"

"Dalton—says abandoning the embassy means looters will destroy the compound, the American school, the water-treatment plant, everything we've built. And our local staff: if we evacuate them, everybody thinks of them as cowards from then on. Worst of all, we lose street cred. Evac helicopters, the flag coming down. Saigon and Mogadishu."

"We looked limp-dick in Somalia, all right," Wurtz said. "Better to stay than to leave and try to come back again."

"The army's disintegrated. So has the police. That's ominous, but it means nobody's around to coordinate action against foreigners. At least not yet."

Dan said, "That's not a bad analysis. But we don't want this Dalton to end up like Chinese Gordon."

"Who?" said Wurtz.

"British general, got himself surrounded in Sudan. Ended up speared to death. Anything from the Chiefs, the White House?"

"Just back-channel e-mail on a coordination net, but it sounds like the secretary of state's studying the recommendations."

"Oh . . . great." "Mokey" Revell was a political general who'd served four presidents with steadily decreasing competence, a Marion Barry look-alike infamous for verbal gaffes and cluelessness. "If *he's* studying it, we'll just plow circles in the ocean until we get low on fuel, then go home. Anything from the Chiefs?"

"Actually yes. SIPRNET'd a girl I know on the J-3 staff. They're recommending we pull everyone out and let things settle. Iraq's too hot and Iran's too sticky to get tar-babied in Ashaara too. But Melinda Gates and Mia Farrow are getting a lot of publicity about the drought and the massacres on the western border. Anyway, we got an attaboy on the plan. They wanted to know who generated it. We said you did."

"It was us, not me."

"We're PC types, not amphibious planners," Wurtz said. "You pulled it together."

Dan shrugged and asked where their surface units were now. The GCCS showed *Tarawa*, *Duluth*, and *Oldendorf* approaching the Bab el Mandeb, the entrance to the Red Sea. The two faster ships were catching up with *Duluth*, which meant hot-refueling the birds aboard her might be more trouble than it was worth. They'd be in launch range in eighteen hours.

"Where's *Anchorage*?"

"Recalled. They decided they needed her in the NAG more."

The Northern Arabian Gulf, Navy-ese for what the rest of the world called the Persian Gulf. Dan rubbed his face, looking at the screen. Pinpoints scattered across it were U.S. ships. Thanks to radar, satellites, data uplinks, they could surveil the entire surface of the earth. The Air Force could drop special-delivery metal and explosives here and there. But control Africa, the Horn, the Middle East, not to mention the folded abysses of inland Asia, Pakistan, Afghanistan? There just weren't enough forces.

Goya let himself in through the lower door. They rose, but he motioned them down and climbed the aisle. "Just got off the horn to Oman."

"General Leache?"

"His deputy. Said the phibron commander junked his plan and is reworking yours. He'll send a draft so we're all on the same page." The commodore hitched up his trousers and smoothed his mustache. "So we're on the sidelines now, except for any involvement our PCs may have. *Cyclone* and *Firebolt* are under way to link up with *Shamal*. Anything else we should be doing?"

Dan couldn't think of anything. The approaching amphibious squadron commander would take charge now, carrying out the assault. The assault . . . he flashed on Oberg standing on the deck of the trawler, covered in blood, shaking a rifle and comparing the dead around him to fresh shit. There'd be more now, and they might include Oberg's team, and marines, and embassy personnel.

He hoped he hadn't missed anything, in the plan that was

now only hours from launching men and metal at high velocity toward an inexorable execution.

He and Monty and Kim hung in CACC, drinking coffee and watching the satellite feeds the Mountain's antennas pulled in. Finally he told them to chow down, clean up, get their heads down if possible. He shaved, then took his uniforms to the laundry to see if he could get service even though he wasn't embarked staff or ship's company. They said dry cleaning was no problem, but they washed only once a day.

Back in the CACC, smelling bad. Forcing himself to stay awake. Hour after hour went by with no word. Finally, late in the morning, he went back to his stateroom. Changed into PT gear and took his net bag down to the self-service washing machines.

While they were churning he jogged the flight deck, sweating in the dry heat, looking out over the blue-green basin. Past it sprawled the flat ocher and tan of the city, and beyond that the Martian wastes of the backcountry fading to distant hills backlighted as the sun reached its zenith. The flight deck radiated heat like a solar oven. At last he shambled to a stop, sweating rivers.

A seaman waxing the passageway stared. "You went *outside*, sir?" he said, as if Dan had just taken a space walk. He leaned against the bulkhead, waiting for the dizziness to pass.

Back at his stateroom a messenger from Radio stood at the door. Dan flipped open the aluminum clipboard with weary detachment. The icy conditioned air was a cold martini down the back of his sweat-soaked cotton T. He scanned the pages, absorbing acronyms and abbreviations that took years in the joint world to interpret.

It was from the Joint Chiefs, coordinated with State and approved by the secretary of defense. Navy and Marine forces currently en route to Ashaara would secure the U.S. embassy and evacuate nonessential personnel. But the core of the staff would remain, though the scene commander was directed to make preparations to evacuate them as well if conditions worsened.

A one-star Marine general would arrive shortly to stand up CTF 156, Joint Task Force Red Sea.

CTG 156.4—Goya—was assigned as Commander Maritime Security Group. He'd break his flag aboard *Oldendorf* and secure Ashaara's sea boundaries with the destroyer and his PCs, working with any remaining elements of the Ashaaran Coastal Defense Force.

The amphibious ready group commander aboard *Tarawa* was assigned as Commander, Amphibious Task Force, CTG 156.5. The marine colonel commanding her detachment would be the Commander, Landing Force, CTG 156.6. Eight paragraphs detailed the mission and rules of engagement, and attached a company of Army Guard civil affairs personnel, the only mention of any non-Navy forces, though by definition a "joint" task force integrated elements from several services.

Dan and his TAG staffers were assigned as special advisers to help stand up the task force.

CTF 156 was to support a humanitarian assistance mission to relieve famine in the city and backcountry, Operation Collateral Gratitude. Several paragraphs detailed the JTF's relationships with the other services and the interagency aspect—State, nongovernmental organizations, and a UN skeleton staff Dan assumed would fly in from New York.

He was rubbing his face, looking through blank eyes at a remembered map of Ashaara, when heels tapped in the passageway.

McCall looked exhausted; the collar of her khaki shirt was grimy. "Read it?"

"Just finished." He initialed it. "I need a copy of that," he told the radioman. "No, four. Bring 'em to CACC. I have to talk to the watch supervisor. We need to reconfigure to host a task force staff, right away."

When he left, McCall said, "We're assigned to help stand up a task force. Unfortunately I don't have a good idea exactly how to go about that."

"It means we have two hundred things to do somebody else should've done last week. Set up a teleconference with *Tarawa.* We sent them our plan; they sent us theirs; we need to smooth out any hard spots between the two and get this initial incursion rolling. Takeoff'll be soon—"

"Two hours."

"We need *Cyclone* and *Firebolt* positioned as helo guards, in case of trouble en route. See if Geller got backup comms with the beach. Wurtz knows Building Twenty's complement and capabilities. He can take charge of reconfiguring the command and control setup here to support the JTF. I want you and Monty looking farther out. After the embassy's secure we've got to occupy the port, airfield, communications, water, power generation, hospitals. Control the infrastructure. Get somebody here from Treasury to find out where the governnment's money went. Find what leadership's left now the president and his cronies have decamped—"

He grimaced, mind outracing speech as he thought of all that had to be done, immediately, before a country descended into chaos. McCall rubbed her palms down her thighs.

The 1MC hissed. "COMMANDER LENSON, YOUR PRESENCE IS REQUESTED IN THE COMMODORE'S CABIN."

"That's for you," she said, smiling wanly. He smelled ginger perfume and perspiration and apple shampoo. Even grimy, she belonged on the big screen, not at a computer workstation. They were alone in the passageway. He fought a sudden impulse to take her in his arms.

He put his hands behind his back. "Ever worked hard before?"

"Now and then."

"It won't hold a candle to this."

She put out a hand, and he sucked in a breath, unsure where she'd touch him. She patted his arm. "A chance to make a difference."

"Or wreck your career. This'll be the big time, Kim. The real deal."

She pinched a fold of his soaked T between finger and thumb, held it out, then let it snap back. Said in that oh-so-soft Savannah drawl, "Commodore wants you."

He took the hint, and ducked inside to change.

ZEYNAAB

For a long time she thinks she's in Paradise. Hauled up the cliff in a basket, she discovers a different world high on the mountain. She spends timeless days in an infirmary with rows of beds, empty except for her and a wrinkled granny who never stops talking, in a language Zeynaab doesn't know a word of. A woman in a cowled habit and leather belt with crosses plaited into it brings her meals but rarely speaks, and when she does her words sound twisted. Zeynaab understands but it's not how people speak in her village. The food's so good, milk and cream and cheese, that she eats too much and has to throw up into a brass basin the woman patiently holds, saying *"Bi-ism as-Salib"* each time Zeynaab retches. But then she eats more.

One day when her feet don't bleed anymore a girl comes for her. She's a few years older than Zeynaab. She tells her to be quiet and follow. As they leave they pass the woman who took care of her, and Zeynaab runs and hugs her legs through the robe. The woman smiles down sadly. She takes a cross on a chain from a shelf and fastens it around Zeynaab's neck. The girl pulls at Zeynaab again and she goes off, looking back with her thumb in her mouth.

She lives in a stone dormitory with bare wood floors. Thirty-three other girls live there too. Each morning, before dawn, a wooden bell rings. Everyone gets up in the dark and goes out under the stars or the fog to the assembly hall. They sit on benches along the walls while a very old woman in black prays for a very long time in that language Zeynaab doesn't understand. Then they go back to their dormitory and eat bread and milk. The smaller children are allowed to play then. At midday the bell rings again and they go to the hall for more long prayers. This time they eat there, at a children's table lower than everyone else's. This happens again in the evening, and then everyone has to go to bed.

She pieces together a vague idea of Saint Shenouda. That's what this place above the clouds is called. It was his picture on the pavement where she was lifted into the sky. There's another in the church where they go twice a week for long prayers. He lived centuries ago. The older girls say there are two places on the mountain, one for men, the other—the *deir*, the convent—for women. A lofty stone wall separates them. This explains why she never sees the boys from the truck. Another, even taller wall far down the mountain has protected the monastery from attack for a thousand years. The head of the nunnery is called Sister Abbess. Everyone, child or grown-up, has to do exactly as she says. The grown-up *ummina*, the nuns, live in cells. During the day everyone prays or weaves, or tends the vegetable plots around the buildings.

It's cooler than she's ever known, with low clouds that turn to mist as they approach the mountain, and different plants than she grew up with. Her village now seems more like a story someone told her than what life used to be.

Gradually as the months pass she understands more, but then all her understandings fall apart. The older girls tell her the *ummina* are Christians. That's why they have crosses tattooed on their wrists, and wear plaited leather, and make three hundred prostrations every day. Yet all the children are Muslim, except for a few who wear the crosses around their necks. Zeynaab loved her cross, but the girls say it's a sin for a Muslim to wear one. They take her to the outhouse and make her throw it into the hole. She weeps that night and when she wakes up and goes to the assembly hall and the nun from the infirmary sees her she smiles sadly and looks disappointed, but says nothing. Aside from blessing her when she threw up, Zeynaab's never actually heard her speak.

Zeynaab washes dishes in the kitchen. She's examined again in the infirmary, where they make her spread her legs and open her mouth, and poke things into her ears. There's a bakery, a printing press, a place where the nuns write and read, a place where they weave, a laundry. Outside the walls are more gardens, apple orchards, but not like those in her village. There are apples and pears and grapes. Barns with pigs—animals she's never seen before—and chickens, and cows that give the milk and cream and cheese. A few goats, not nearly as many as in the village. There are cats but no dogs.

One day the headmistress of the dormitory tells her she's old enough to go to school. Now she doesn't get to play. She sits at a long bench with the others and learns to write. She doesn't like to do this and one day she breaks her slate and throws it out the window.

The *ummina ra'isa* calls her in. Zeynaab sits straight, hands folded in her lap. She's frightened of this woman, who's holy and eats little and wears the great *skema* over her shoulders and wrapped around her waist. But the abbess speaks gently. She says if Zeynaab can't read she will not understand the *qanun* or the Bible. Zeynaab says she doesn't care.

The abbess asks, Do you ever feel the presence of the Holy Spirit? She says no, *Tamauf.* The abbess asks if she wants to marry Christ one day and give her life to Him, like Saint Demiana? Zeynaab says no again. The abbess asks, then does she want to leave the mountain, when she's grown, and go out into the World? Zeynaab's thought about this. Bandits kill people down below. Governments burn villages and shoot mothers. So she says, No.

The abbess says she need not give her life to Christ, but if she stays, she must serve the *deir* by tending the cattle. These are placid creatures who spend most of their time in the long low shed. There are five cows and a rather unaggressive bull. She feeds and brushes them. Learns to milk and make butter and cheese. She shovels tons of manure. She works hard and says nothing. They tell her when she dies she'll be buried in the graveyard behind the church, whether she wears the cross or not.

More years pass, and she grows into a young woman.

Then one day she hears a noise she's never heard before. It's like thunder down below the mountain. Then another noise, distant, somehow familiar, but it's some time before she remembers there are such things as motors.

The women come out of the weavery and the gardens to stand watching as—for the first time ever—a truck grinds up the mule trail that's the only other way up besides the basket. How did it get through the wall? Few of them have ever seen such a thing, but Zeynaab breaks into a sweat the moment she sees it. The men who jump down carry guns and she remembers. She runs to the cowshed. Trembling, she crawls into the hay.

They find her there hours later. By then the men are tired. They're covered with soot and blood. With wearied violence one drags her out. "Time to die, Christian," he says. "All the others are dead, now you."

"No. Not Christian! I'm Muslim!"

He seizes her arm, looks at her wrist. Her crossless wrist. "Then what are you doing here?" he snarls, and savagely twists her arm behind her. It's so painful she'd scream if his hand wasn't over her mouth. If his body wasn't against hers. If she had enough breath to struggle as the others jerk her skirts over her head and push her down into the straw.

When they're done they leave her for dead, but don't make sure of it, as they have with every other woman on the mountain, and all the monks too. When much later she staggers into the sunlight she doesn't know who she is, or where. The buildings are burning. The gentle bull lies stretched out dead. She looks at the bodies of women, children. Does she know them? What's the meaning of all this smoke?

She shuffles to the infirmary. The woman who welcomed her years before lies on a bed, the cord with the plaited crosses knotted around her throat. The men have done other cruel things to her too. Zeynaab kneels by her, wanting to pray, but not knowing who to. Where will she go now? At last she enters the burning refectory. She stuffs a basket with bread and cheese, then goes into the Sister Abbess's room.

Then she sets off down the mountain.

8

ASHAARA CITY

The crackle woke Aisha before dawn in the low-ceilinged cubicle she shared with one of the translators. The embassy's housing coordinator had looked horrified when she'd asked to room with another Muslim woman. The only others were Ashaarans, maintenance and cleaning employees. Most lived in town, and the rooms for those who slept on-compound were small and shabby: a row of curtained-off broom closets in a shedlike building huddled out back.

Not that different from the slave quarters, behind some Big House.

Her roommate, a small, quiet woman named Nuura, wasn't in bed. The sheets were thrown back, but she wasn't there.

Aisha rose, dressed, quickly did *wudhu* in the sink, then took her rug out for morning *salat*, orienting by the sun through a dirty window. The past day or so she'd listened for muezzins out in town but hadn't heard them. Strange that there were no calls to prayer.

She stood and recited the intention to pray, then the *takbir* and the other dawn prayers, prostrating, saluting the angels to her right and left. She did this in the Arabic she'd learned as a child in Harlem. Then muttered in English, "Forgive, bless, and protect me this day, and let all my work be done in your name." She strapped on her SIG, checked that her badge and other walking-around gear was in her purse, and let herself out.

Dawn in East Africa broke as she hesitated in the doorway. The sky held a hot blush scented with burning. An uncertain breeze stirred the dust and flapped the flag above the chancery. She scuffed toward the administration building, the backs of her sandals flipping up powdery gouts. Someone had tried to grow grass here, unsuccessfully. There were trees, though, the local acacia. She looked across the open area always left at the heart of every American embassy in these mercurial lands.

Jolene Ridbout, the attaché, had given her and Erculiano a tour the day they arrived. The compound was enclosed by a rose brick wall less carefully mortared from the inside; its finished surface faced out. Beyond it was Ashaara; inside, the United States, with its own laws and customs and extraterritoriality.

Uh-huh . . . to her left as she trudged, the heat building as light flooded pale dust like weightless lava, lay a gated extension with tennis court and swimming pool and picnic benches. Close by huddled Conex boxes, one her makeshift office. Ahead rose the two-story GSA Building, where vehicles were repaired, laundry was done, supplies were taken in, and garbage was sorted to go out. A generator droned, and blue mercury-vapor security lights still burned over pickups and SUVs on neatly painted asphalt. To her right the ambassador's residence, a white-pillared neo-Victorian, shimmered like a bad dream.

West, toward the main gate, was the chancery. Glass and aluminum, with slanted louvers set to cut the sun and "pay homage" to local architecture. An inner barrier of chain link was topped with razor wire and anchored by a concrete structure styled to resemble a minaret but all too obviously a guard tower. It looked like a keep, a last redoubt; the chancery, like a very expensive prison.

She came to a deserted playground under one of the acacias and after a moment's hesitation lifted the hem of her abaya and began climbing a welded jungle gym painted in faded reds and yellows. She was sorry halfway up but kept clambering, and perched at last, teetering and panting, where she could peer over the wall.

The crackling was growing louder, a grinding like an

icebound river giving way. Smoke columns pillared to the north. She wasn't sure enough of her bearings to know what neighborhood they came from. The crackling ebbed and waxed, as if the miles of baking buildings were frying under the rising sun.

She wondered if little Bahdoon and Major Assad and the old secretary who spoke perfect Italian were out there.

She squeezed her eyes, balancing on the hand-worn steel. Remembering the raid Assad had taken them on. The frightened faces of the smugglers as his security troops had beaten them, bound them, thrown them into the trucks. Rebels? Possibly.

Where had they gone from there?

She remembered the tumbled bodies of the dead. Women. Children.

She saw again the angelic young man who'd sprinted past in the alley. Whom she'd held in her sights long enough to end his life. But hadn't.

What was happening out there? Who else was dying?

Perched there, she said a *du'a* for God to be merciful. Knowing that all too often, it seemed, the best He could do for those who suffered was death.

They called everyone together in the chancery lobby. A chandelier of polished brass and aluminum shards hung like a massive scimitar from a ceiling speckled with stainless eight-pointed stars. Ridbout stood with the ambassador as the white-haired former child star explained the situation. The president and his cabinet had fled. The embassy guards the Ashaaran army usually posted hadn't reported for duty that morning. Nevertheless, no grounds for panic. The Marines were on their way from Oman. Nonemergency personnel would be evacuated when they arrived. Essential personnel would stay, with U.S. military protection.

If conditions degenerated, he'd evacuate everyone, haul down the flag, and wait for peace to return to the Ashaara they loved. Until then he was staying. Feeble applause followed, barely rising to those watching stars.

Aisha noted Nuura squatting on the pale marble floor. Her roommate glanced past her, as if she didn't recognize her.

The DCM—deputy chief of mission—took over, reviewing the emergency action plan, making sure everyone knew his assignment. Ridbout came over when the meeting broke. A tall, deeply tanned, crew-cut marine in dark glasses followed her. "We've got a problem," she began, no preamble. "No more Ashaaran security—you heard. Gunnery Sergeant Kaszyk here's in command of our Marine security det."

"Gunnery sergeant."

"Just call me 'Gunny,' ma'am."

"Unfortunately, we don't have a fully Inman-ized compound here. And I've only got a one-and-six detachment, seven men total, to defend it. I need you and your assistant to help Gunny out," Ridbout told her. "Unless you object. Gunny, this is Special Agent Aisha Ar-Rahim, Naval Criminal Investigative Service."

"Any problem with that, uh, ma'am? Till we can get a patch over this situation?"

"None at all. But call me Special Agent, please."

"How many with you, Special Agent?"

"Myself and one other."

"Can you shoot? Any CQB training?"

"We trained with shotguns and M16s at Glynco. Not to your standards, maybe, but we can take down a building."

He seemed to notice her abaya and headscarf then. Opened his mouth, looking her up and down; then closed it. "We'll put you on our Goalkeeper team. Come with me, please?"

Being a Goalkeeper seemed to consist of sitting in a burnt-coffee-smelling "React Room" in the tower next to the USIS Library, just outside the concertina and inside the main gate. Kaszyk signed out rifles and vests festooned with magazine pouches to her, Erculiano, and two staff civilians who said they were Vietnam or Gulf War veterans. They took their weapons like young knights receiving their first swords. Aisha held hers on her lap, fingertips tapping metal and plastic.

"D' it go out?" Erculiano murmured, leaning toward her.

The message to the Bahrain Field Office. She nodded. They might be trapped, but it was on record: the NCIS team at Ashaara City was officially part of the defense.

Kaszyk unsnapped a binder. "Listen up. Defensive plan. We have twelve riflemen, including volunteers, and two light MGs. Not enough to defend a two-mile perimeter. These walls, any dirtbag with a ladder can scale them. So, we double-team the main gate and put two rapid reaction teams in the vans. Isolated incursions, trespassers, we send one and hold the other in reserve. When we have to send both, that's when we secure the gate and fall back to the chancery.

"If that happens, both fire teams fall back on the Goalkeepers. From there on we hold. I think we can, unless they come through that wire with something like a truck, vehicle-borne explosives."

Erculiano lifted a finger. "The ambassador said a task force was on its way."

"We hold out, sure, they can evacuate us." The gunny's face seamed; suddenly he looked older. "But I saw what they did to the Kuwaitis in Desert Storm. You can't liberate the dead. Holding till they get here, that's up to us."

The radio crackled. "Post One, beachside overwatch. Movement along the fences of the tennis court."

"Fire team one, deploy," Kaszyk said, and the long afternoon began.

Standing at the front gate, which was being rapidly sandbagged by marines and staffers wheeling the bags out on dollies from a side shed, she watched refugees stream past. Fleeing the city, thronging the road south toward Asmara. Occasionally a truck snorted by, or a Mercedes, but most went on foot, toting bundles and chests, pushing carts piled with children and old people, rolled-up rugs, brass and aluminum cookware, wall hangings. One cart, pulled by a donkey the size of a large Labrador, penned an electric water heater, its white bulk rolling back and forth like a disturbed whale.

A slight black marine with a scar from a repaired harelip asked, "Where you from, ma'am? You new here, right?"

"I'm with the NCIS. A special agent."

"You Moslem? Way you dressed—"

"I'm from New York. Who are these people? Do you have any idea?"

"These the president's clan. Getting out of Dodge."

She surveyed the passing crowd. "*These* are Xaasha? They don't look like they've done too well out of it." When he didn't say anything she added, "And the rebels? Who are they?"

"Rebels is what the government says. Ain't seen any yet. May not even be any."

"What do you mean? Might not *be* any?"

But he didn't say, just stuck out his lip and pulled a grenade out of a pouch and fiddled with the pin.

After lunch, with the air outside like a hot towel over her face, the crackling started again. The portable radios beeped and chattered as the officers and the gunny discussed it. She waited with the vets and Erculiano and the marines who were neither on the gate nor in the vans at the moment. Finally word came to take position in the tower.

They climbed the steel steps and came out into something like an airport control tower, but without glass. Heat broiled down from the green steel roof like a toaster oven. A lance corporal said the shooting was coming from the National Museum. He sited a machine gun to cover the gate. He positioned her and Erculiano where they could watch the wall, and the two veterans the chancery. The Gulf War vet clanged a green metal can down and handed out ammo. Aisha filled three magazines, forcing the cartridges down until her wrists hurt, then aligned them fussily on the concrete floor. They weren't to load their rifles until ordered to. She had her pistol ready under her abaya, too, but she had serious misgivings about firing at starving people. She returned a look from Erculiano. It was quiet up here, except for the shooting. Which was getting closer.

"Tower, Post One, gate; crowd headed our way."

Gunny Kaszyk came up the stairs two at a time, boots ringing on metal treads. He looked around without letting go the handrails. Said a few words to the corporal, who went down with him and came back up with a case of bottled water. He passed the radio from his left hand to his right, then back, whistling through his teeth. The other marines leaned over the edge of the tower to spit the snuff they'd dipped before leaving the guardroom. The Vietnam vet sat on the ammo box, turning his tasseled loafers this way and that. He asked a marine if he could have a dip.

A distant murmur became shouting. She stood and tried to see. The corporal focused binoculars. He spoke into the radio, then listened.

"Looters," he said. "Don't seem armed."

"Will we shoot unarmed people?"

"Anyone comes over this wall, we shoot," the corporal said. "Ma'am."

"Call me Aisha." It seemed silly for him to call her "Special Agent," and "ma'am" was what she'd called her grandmother in Detroit.

"Okay, Aisha. You can call me 'Lance Corporal.' "

The column came into view up the road. It looked like a procession of multicolored army ants. They came to a compound with high white walls and slowly sucked in through the gates. When the corporal handed her the binoculars she saw them in the second-story windows, then the third.

"Chinese embassy," the Viet vet said. "They hauled ass last week."

Things began arcing out through the windows, which weren't always opened first. She heard glass breaking, sharp thuds on concrete or asphalt, accompanied by shouting. Cascades of paper drifted like square white leaves through the heated air. Figures passed to and fro behind the windows. She lowered the field of view and saw them staggering out, heavily laden. Computer keyboards. Monitors. Whole filing cabinets, presumably empty—hence the shower of paper.

Window air conditioners. A painted screen that must have been the delight of some bored bureaucrat.

"Water," said the corporal, more order than offer. She accepted a tepid bottle and drank it down.

The radio crackled. "Intruders, south wall. Reaction One, respond." The van gunned away, circled the roundabout past the chancery, and sped off.

She aimed the binoculars and saw, wavering magnified in the mirage, tiny figures silhouetted atop the wall before jumping down. The van stopped and a popping came. The figures hesitated, then vanished, either falling or jumping. She couldn't see, in the violent shimmer of hot air over dry ground, what exactly had happened.

Shouting and shoving at the outer gate. The marines had closed and locked it, a massive portcullis of chrome-plated steel. They stood back a few yards, weapons at port arms, stifflegged as guard dogs. Something flew between the bars and shattered.

"I'm going down there," she said to the corporal.

"That's not a good idea," he said. Then, as if recognizing his inability to actually order her to stay, held out another bottle of water.

The interior of the tower felt like the belly of an incinerator. Outside, in the open, was even hotter. The breeze burned her skin. Abayas and headscarves weren't just for modesty. In a climate like this they made sense. She passed three employees in colorful local dress, squatting in the dust inside the wall. They glanced up fearfully. Then their gazes turned inward, but they never stopped speaking, engaged in what sounded like an agitated argument.

A gate guard turned as she approached. His gaze fastened on her rifle, then looked her up and down. *"You!"* he shouted. "What're you doing with that?"

"The gunny issued it to me," she said, and handed it to him. The belated recognition on his face made her even more angry.

"Sorry. Didn't know you were one of . . . I mean, I thought you were—"

"Just shut up," she said, and went around him, up to the gate.

Hands and arms were thrust through, groping like the tentacles of an anemone. The smell hit her like a slap. Children pleaded to come in. On impulse, she held out the water. It was snatched away, and instantly two dozen other hands waved for more.

She was about to speak when the crowd parted, revealing trucks braking in clouds of exhaust and dust. The troops who jumped down wore drab, threadbare fatigues like the Ashaaran military, but not one wore a helmet. Some were bareheaded; others had cloth tied in sweatbands; most wore garish headgear from various sources: stocking caps, ball caps, hats of woven grass, even a green Tyrolean with a red feather, incongruously stylish on one strutting bantam of a man. They carried other things, too. Radios. Shiny tape or CD players. As they formed a line she thought, Thank Allah. They'll protect us until the Marines arrive.

Then she saw the golf balls embedded in their cheeks, their saffron-yellow eyes.

A hulking apparition in starched camouflage strode to the gate, hurling aside civilians slow in moving away. Sweat glistened on his stubbly, broad visage, and with him wafted a sweet stink of whiskey. At first she thought he was white. Then saw the mottling of vitiligo, melanin deficiency. She'd known a barber in Harlem with the same condition, but not nearly so extreme. This man's neck and hands were black, but it looked as if a white man's face had been torn off and pasted over his countenance.

With his huge size and the gangster-style shortened Kalashnikov he carried like a pistol, the effect was disorienting and terrifying. He stomped up to the gate, and for a moment she feared he might tear it apart with his bare hands. She gripped her pistol underneath her clothing. Even the marines took a step back.

The man shouted something long, involved, and angry. He shook his rifle at her. She tried to make sense of his words, but failed. She tried Arabic. He waited till she finished, then commenced roaring again.

"Get a translator," she told the marine still awkwardly holding her rifle. He hesitated, then trotted off.

Nuura came, looking as if she was about to faint. Watching her walk, Aisha realized for the first time that her roommate was pregnant. The huge man roared again. Nuura falteringly came out with English. "He wants the ones inside. Demands you give them to him."

"Who? Americans?"

"Us," Nuura whispered. When Aisha frowned, puzzled, she added, "Those who work for the foreigners."

Aisha caught her breath, remembering the frightened women arguing in the dust. When she looked back they were gone.

"They were made rich in place of those more deserving," shouted a fierce-faced young woman in a man's shirt. "Look at me! I speak English! Am I employed? My brother was shot. Give them to us! We'll decide which are traitors."

The translator shrank back. Aisha caught her arm and pushed her forward again. It felt light as a wren's wing, her bones thinner than a human's should be. Aisha smelled urine and swallowed, suddenly sick of the heat, the smells, the fear. "We're *not* giving you up," she told her. "Or anybody else. Right, everybody?"

"Fuckin' ay," said one of the marines. He lifted his radio. "Post One, I say again: need the Big Bird down here, *right now.* Main gate."

Aisha squeezed the thin arm again. "Now, ask his name."

"He says he is Sergeant Major Olowe."

"Sergeant Major Olowe. All right. Now ask if he knows Major Assad. Of the Interior Ministry."

The man thrust out his lips, glaring at Aisha. She went on, "Tell him the major will not be happy to see him annoying us, instead of providing protection as agreed. Does he know your troops are out here looting? Threatening people?"

Ridbout said, behind her, "Get away from the gate. Don't get so close to them."

"I'm talking to—"

"I'll do the talking. Get back." She watched, arms akimbo, as Kaszyk and two other marines set up a machine gun. The crowd murmured. "That one officer, or whatever he is. Sergeant major? Fine. Let him in."

Olowe had to lower his head to fit through. The marines aimed at the woman, who tried to come in too. She backed away, scowling, as they relocked the gate. Olowe didn't object as a marine took his AK. He expanded his chest, looking around the compound. "Very pretty," he said in heavily accented English. "Nice cars. Pretty."

"I'm Colonel Ridbout, military attaché to the People's Government of Ashaara," Ridbout told him. "What can we do for you, Sergeant Major?"

Olowe spoke rapidly; Nuura tried to keep up. "He says . . . there is no more People's Government. Open these gates and let his friends in."

"This is the U.S. embassy," Ridbout said. "Anyone who enters without permission, we have the right to kill. Tell him that."

Nuura's voice shook; she clutched her stomach. "He says, give up Ashaarans and he will not kill Americans."

"No deal." Ridbout nodded to a civilian who'd come quietly up from the chancery, a young man in a light gray suit and open-collared shirt, carrying a briefcase, whom up to now Aisha had not seen. "You may want to speak to our RSO, though."

The giant eyed her narrowly, then stalked toward the State employee. "What's going on, Jolene?" Aisha murmured to Ridbout.

"We're making him an offer. Hopefully, one he can't refuse."

Taking him out of sight of the gate, the regional security officer opened the briefcase. Olowe stiffened, as if insulted. Then bent to examine what lay within.

* * *

The streets were quiet for a few hours after Olowe left. Those who'd clamored for admittance trickled away, though a few, hunted-looking families of local employees, were admitted after lengthy checks. Gradually the shadows lengthened, but the air didn't cool. She was called down several times to carry out body searches. She did them in a restroom behind the gate shack, seating the women on the toilet and asking them to lift their dresses while she ran her hands over them. She felt ashamed, but couldn't help washing her hands after each search. She was climbing the tower again when shouts came from above.

"They're coming over the walls," the corporal yelled as she emerged from the stairwell. He charged his weapon and aimed over the parapet.

"Troops? Or more looters?" she panted, trying to catch her breath. Maybe she'd lose weight on this assignment, for a change.

"Looters, I guess, but armed. Some of them."

Someone handed her her rifle. A flashback to Glynco, where they'd told her she had to name "her" rifle, and it had to be female. She felt doomed. Twice in her career she'd had to kill, but both times she'd been facing an armed and dangerous criminal.

And both times, white men. She wasn't shooting any women. Not unless they fired first.

"Miz Rahim," the corporal said. "Your magazine. It was on the deck?"

"Sorry. Thank you."

"We'll fire over their heads first. A warning."

She wanted to ask how, if they were firing downward, but only nodded.

The first face showed above the wall. A young man, but not the angelic one. A narrow-faced, pinch-jawed individual with wild eyes and cheek bulging with the local herb. He threw a carpet scrap over the jagged glass, then followed with a leg. He held a machete, rusty, but no doubt sharp enough to kill.

"Off the wall, man!" the corporal yelled.

The Ashaaran looked up. His eyes met hers as the corporal's rifle cracked and brick split and flew. The man's hands flew up to protect his eyes. He lost his balance and tumbled backward.

"That'll make 'em think twice," said the Gulf War vet.

She lowered her weapon, wondering how much longer it would keep them pondering.

Two miles offshore, Teddy Oberg crouched in the RHIB. The others were crowded around him, all four men exposed in the waning afternoon light. SEALs hated going in in daylight. In fact, this was the first time he'd done it, other than in exercises. But *Firebolt* hadn't gotten to Ashaara till noon, and then there'd been disagreement about whether they should go in over the beach to the embassy, as planned, or secure the port area instead. For three hours they'd sat in the boats, until finally word had come to execute the original plan; looters were coming over the walls. Now they crouched in two inflatables as the PCs turned as one and ran at flank speed toward the beach.

"Stand by to launch," the petty office yelled. Teddy braced. The POIC's hand chopped down, the bowhook yanked the line, and they slid back and down in the dizzying release the SEALs referred to as being shit out of the boat. Behind him one man yee-haa'd, others gave rebel yells, as the engine gunned and the boat spun into a turn so hard she nearly went over, then headed for putty-colored dunes below the ruby ball of the setting sun.

Geller had taken them in until his keel had scraped sand. Teddy fingered the night vision goggles pushed up under his helmet. He didn't like the sun in his face, but couldn't object to the insertion. The PCs had roared over the horizon on diverging courses, to confuse any radar, before suddenly echeloning and spitting out the RHIBs. Even a well-honed coastal defense would find it hard to get a reaction force to the landing point before the team would be dug so deep into those dunes it would cost heavy casualties to dig them out. Especially with the direct fire of the PCs' guns on call.

The hard spot would be if they got stuck short of the embassy. It'd be only eight men and their rifles, grenades, and a single light antitank weapon. If they met determined resistance, they'd just have to haul ass back and try to swim out before they got rolled up.

He checked the men. They were goggled and black-uniformed, strapped with gear, fins lashed over their shoulders. Their eyes met his, then slid back to the beach. They'd all made insertions before. The one thing you could count on, it wouldn't be what you expected.

Smoke off to their right. Black, which probably meant either vehicles or fuel. Two hundred more yards, no time to change the plan now. The surf lifted the boat, the motor changing pitch as they planed. Two-foot seas a mile out, but bulging now as the bottom climbed to three-, four-foot waves. RHIBs weren't great surf boats, not great beaching boats either, but they were a hell of a lot faster than swimming.

The boat lifted again, coasted forward, and the coxswain yelled something. The motor whirred as it pivoted up. Teddy gave the signal and bailed out over the side. His boots hit bottom four feet down. The water was warmer than blood, the bottom hard sand and pebbles.

He glanced up, and his heart slammed to a stop.

Not at the danger; at the sheer fucking beauty. He'd never seen water so clear, sand so bright, a sky dimming so ravishingly toward dusk. To the east Venus glowed bright as a smaller moon. Tiny fish darted around his boots, pale as the sand. He stared, lost in the shimmering loveliness.

"You gone fucking tourist?" Kaulukukui grunted. Obie flinched and began wading shoreward, kicking up fine powdery white that swirled under the surface. He squinted through his Oakleys, tracing the tops of the dunes with the sight of his M4. They'd be easy meat from up there. Just lie in the dunes and take them down one by one, not a thing to do about it . . . He caught a stir, jerked the barrel around, but found only the wind-tossed sway of beach grass, the furtive flurry of some small creature making its escape.

Enough *thinking*, asshole, he told himself. Pulling the hot weightless air into his lungs, he burst out of the sea, sprinting with all his might.

The sergeant came up a little after six, bringing corned beef sandwiches and more water—they'd gone through the crate, and she wasn't peeing, it was sweat. She'd long ago given up on keeping halal, and bit into her sandwich with relish. No one else had tried to scale the wall. Erculiano complained bitterly about the heat and asked why they couldn't take a stint at the gate, or even in the chancery. The generator was still running over at the GSA Building. She kept thinking of the air-conditioning there. She felt dizzy from time to time, but bending over for a few seconds helped.

The sun dropped fast. The sky turned dusty salmon and hazy tan. So weary she could barely keep her eyes open, she slumped in a plastic lawn chair someone had carried up from the chancery.

As the sky dimmed, the breeze rose again. She'd yearned for that all day, but when it came it was scorching, the air like sandpaper rubbed fast against her skin. She laid her head back and closed her eyes.

She started awake with someone shaking her. "Better listen up," the Viet vet muttered.

The corporal was on the radio. "Right, down the southern avenue," he was saying, holding the binoculars steady with one hand. "These guys are armed. . . . Yeah, could be . . . big crowd tagging along behind. Over."

He set the radio aside, lips grim. "Could be it," he said to the Desert Storm vet, who he seemed to resonate with.

"More looters?" Aisha rubbed her face.

He nodded, slinging up. "Same as before. I fire a warning shot. If that doesn't stop them, a volley over their heads. Then shoot to kill. On my order, understand? Nobody thinks for himself."

The crowd noise swelled, as did the smoky pall. Shots began cracking out. She hugged her knees in the chair, fear warring with fatigue. She didn't care anymore. Except when she recalled how bravely her roommate had translated the huge soldier's threats.

She picked up her rifle. They stood looking down. Past their section of wall she saw only part of the road. For a time it lay empty. Then dogs raced by, raising puffs of dust, the starved mangy pariahs she'd glimpsed on the ride in from the airport.

Then men, many men, in colorful shirts or bare-chested, marching with fists raised, chanting. Some carried large sticks she realized after a moment were unlit torches. The light was going, the stars coming out. Some wore green trousers beneath civilian shirts. These were the ones who carried rifles.

Warning shots snapped from the gate. The radio spoke. The lance corporal rested his elbows on the parapet, checking his sights.

A shattering double crack echoed from below, followed by screams, yells, a burst of automatic fire. Then the growing surf roar of a chanting crowd.

"Say again, over," said the Viet vet, manning the radio as the corporal kept his sights on the wall.

When he set the radio down he looked shocked. "Explosion at the front gate. Two jarheads down."

"You, Agent, and you"—the corporal pointed—"reinforce the gate."

The concrete stairwell echoed as they hurried down. She lagged, her legs shorter than the others', and broke into a run as she emerged to try to catch up. At the gate embassy staff were lifting the wounded onto litters. The nurse knelt by one, shaking her head.

Aisha stared. The chest was torn open. Blood spattered the gate, the concrete arch above, to either side. Dark pools soaked into the dusty ground. It was the young marine who'd doubted she was American. Another sat propped against the guardhouse, face a bloody gristle, still gripping his carbine. His helmet lay beside him, Kevlar cracked open in a white star. "I'm okay, I'm okay," he kept saying. He tried to stand, but Kaszyk eased him back down.

"Where'd it come from?" the gunny asked, but the marine just wagged his head. "Sounded like a grenade or a LAW. But there wasn't anybody near the gate."

A flash lit the scene. She was astonished to realize it was from the evidence camera in her shaking hand. No one looked up. They were staring down the street, to where the mob shouted, waving lengths of cloth spiraling in the air.

"Hand me that bullhorn," Kaszyk said, straightening.

"STOP WHERE YOU ARE," the bullhorn echoed. The gunny muttered, "Take a knee. We're through fucking around. Take the ones with the AKs first." He spotted Aisha and his gaze narrowed. He pushed her into the gatehouse. "Put that camera away. Stay here. 240 crew, above their heads, *fire*."

The machine gun let rip between the gate bars. Through the plate glass window of the gatehouse she saw the marchers duck away. The crowd scattered, screaming.

A tremendous bang. Something racketed smoke and fire over the gatehouse, over the compound, and burst with a plume of dust near the school. "RPG!" a marine yelled.

She followed the smoke trail back to a man bending down on a rooftop across the avenue. He straightened holding a tapered tube with a bulging head. She yelled to the gunny, but realized they couldn't see him from their angle.

Just like the drills at Glynco, and she smashed the muzzle of the rifle through the window, breaking the glass out so it couldn't deflect the bullet, and got the butt to her shoulder as the man leveled the tube. He was looking along it directly at her, but then the shooting and yelling seemed to stop. Her vision tunneled in as if she were a telescope and at the end of it was that dark face, fitting itself to the sight. She put her front post on his nose and pressed the trigger. The gun jolted and sproinged and he whirled and went down. The tube fell into the street and bounced, but didn't go off. She put her sights back on the rooftop, waiting for someone else to stand. Within seconds another man did, but she lowered her sights this time and shot him in the legs.

All the marines were firing but the sergeant was pulling them back. Incoming blew craters out of the brick walls. Bullets clanged off the gate. She stepped back, fighting panic. Muzzle flashes lined every alleyway across the street.

A rough hand on her shoulder. "Falling back. Can't hold here."

"These aren't looters," she yelled. "They're troops."

"Can't hold the perimeter," Kaszyk yelled back. "Not with the bodies we've got left. Fall back on the chancery."

He propelled her across the yard. It blazed with blinding light. The generator throbbed at full speed. Flashes darted from atop the tower. Return fire hissed and snapped, blowing saucers out of the stuccoed concrete. She panted, throat dry as the dust she ran through. The fence loomed, the brilliant lights rose above. She staggered through the inner gate like a marathon runner finishing, and collapsed into Nuura's arms.

Behind her the marines leapfrogged back. Another tremendous explosion sent a jet of fire right through the outer wall. Bricks flew. The shooting built to a deafening clamor. Through it the gunny wheeled, pointing here and there as he positioned his remaining shooters.

A bottle of something pressed her lips and she gulped at it, choking as the soft drink welled into hot foam. She pushed it away, then pulled it back.

"You keep us safe?"

"We'll protect you," she said, hugging the slight woman. "But get inside."

"Agent! Behind the barrier. Anybody comes through that gate, take 'em down."

But solid masses were already streaming in. She saw with a sinking heart that those in front were women. The troops were behind, driving them with gun butts. She fired a burst over their heads but still they came.

"Light 'em up," the gunny said, behind her. He leveled his rifle and a woman screamed, gripping her shoulder.

"What are you doing? Stop. Stop!"

"If they get in here they'll kill us all." Kaszyk reloaded, face smeared with soot. "It's a lynch mob. Understand? We warned them."

Beside her Erculiano was on a knee, firing. Someone shouted by the gate, and the women broke into a run. They hit the chancery fence and swarmed it. AKs cracked behind them. Another woman fell, but Aisha couldn't tell if it was from an American bullet or an Ashaaran one.

Bursts walked up the tower and rattled on the steel roofing. The higher-pitched cracks of the 5.56s snapped above the deeper barks of the Kalashnikovs as the overwatchers fired down. She glimpsed a man with a pistol and fired, but wasn't sure she hit him. The lance corporal turned astounded to her. A hole pocked his forehead. He toppled into the dust, legs jerking like a galvanized frog's.

They were at the top of the fence, tearing at the razor wire with bare hands. Battering with a bench from the waiting area at the chain-link gate that was the last barrier around the chancery. An Ashaaran fired a burst into the lock, then staggered as someone in the tower shot him. Grenades lobbed out from the tower, exploding with cherry-bomb flashes and cracks that sounded puny amid the noise, but Ashaarans reeled and dropped. Another RPG's launch motor banged outside the compound. It flew over her head, wobbling in its ridiculous slow motion, and exploded below the parapet of the tower, blowing out chunks of concrete block and shrouding the chancery in choking smoke and dust. Steel sections slid down from its roof.

A man stood by the outer gate, pointing at the chancery. Two more ran in with RPGs. They squatted and rocked back on their heels, aiming up. She screamed, "Gunny!" but he wasn't there. She aimed and pulled the trigger but nothing happened. Her magazine was empty. She stared frozen as the conical noses of the rocket-propelled grenades searched, then steadied.

A sudden bursting-out of dust and smoke walked across the men from left to right. The hailstorm of metal chewed apart the bricks behind them, making them hop and wriggle before collapsing. The storm of impacts kept on, mowing down women and men alike. She crouched, squinting, to see men in black uniforms and blackened faces run from behind the generator building. They fanned out into a line and swept forward, a steady flashing and roaring from weapons held to their cheeks sweeping across the dusty field into the crowd.

At the same moment a deeper beat sounded under the rattle of gunfire, the cracks of grenades. Slapping her clothes for another magazine, she looked up only when Kaszyk and Erculiano lifted their faces. "Here we go," the other agent said, voice raspy but relieved.

From a black form swimming through the dimness above the lights poured a great howling and a brilliant light, turbulent wind and the stench of combusting kerosene. Dust and leaves exploded from the ground and tarantellaed through the air. The chain link shook and bodies rained from it. A thin screaming came from outside. Forms staggered through the roaring dust, visible to her only now and then in the seethe, under the pinning light.

The helicopters slid down beams of glaring brilliance. The night became murky clouds as they descended between the chancery and the shed she'd woken in that morning. Blazing lights grounded and began strobing, illuminating everything. Through the murk the crouched shapes of the uniformed men who'd appeared from seaward closed remorselessly on the gate. The lead figure motioned briskly with one hand, gripping a short weapon with the other. Two split off and made for the chancery. They wove among dead and wounded like broken-field runners, pointing weapons at each as they passed. One bent for an AK, smashed it against a wall, threw the parts spinning into the dark.

Kaszyk opened the inner gate and they sprinted through. The lead one spotted her as she rose clutching her rifle, and whipped his weapon around. Light speared through the darkness at her. Then darted upward, as the gunny knocked the barrel up, mouth open in an explanation that did not reach her through the roar of turbines but must've made sense because the man turned away.

Out of the whirling dust trotted more bulky figures, bent under heavy-looking packs and the Waffenamt helmets of the U.S. military. They jogged past toward the walls and she felt relieved, but also sad, as if what she'd just lived through had violated her in some worse way than death.

Kaszyk, holding out a filthy hand. She opened the bolt to check it was empty, and handled him the rifle. "Good job," he shouted into her ear. "Couldn't have held 'em without the two of you's help."

She doubted that but ducked her head, not speaking. Behind him was a white man in blackface with bright blue eyes and scars radiating across his cheeks like the rays of a crater on the moon. "Sorry I keyed on you," he shouted. "You didn't look like ours. With the head rag and all."

She didn't respond. He shouted to the gunny, "Nonemergency personnel on these birds. Twenty pounds personal gear each. Pass the word."

"We closing the embassy? You evac'ing us?"

"No. Nonessentials only, like I said. We got enough troops and ammo to hold until the task force gets here. Which way to your security officer?"

She sank to her knees, close to fainting from the terrible weakness that came from being so afraid for so long, as the sergeant pointed and the soldier ran past and out the gate, to become one more seeking shadow in the whirling murk.

NABIL

The boy stands alertly next to the table, holding the steel bowl that from time to time the white man reaches down to dabble his shining knife or rubber-gloved fingers in. Each time blood uncoils in lazy spirals, until the clear fluid's red. The boy clears his throat and lifts the bowl like an offering. The surgeon nods curtly. "Throw it out," he says, and the boy drags a foot as he ducks through the tent flap, into the insect-buzzing night.

The ten-year-old looks both ways. Satisfied he isn't watched, he squats. A plastic bleach bottle sloshes as he pulls it from its hiding place, pours the liquid into it, spins the top closed. In eight seconds he's back inside, blinking in the light, holding out the empty bowl to the aide. An exchange of glances, and the jug tilts a fresh dose of two-hundred-proof disinfectant.

Two hours later, Nabil stands behind the latrines. A girl holds a lantern while another trickles the fluid through layers of sanitary napkins. It comes out clear. Men and women fidget in line, waiting to trade coins and bills for a paper cupful. Everything—alcohol, charcoal, napkins, lantern, paper cups—comes from the medical stores that, along with a little food, are all the regime allots to the orphan camps.

The camp hones every resident into a skilled thief, an expert at dissimulation, begging, strategic lying. With his boyish charm, round, innocent face, his dragging foot, Nabil's among the best, though not the largest or most powerful.

As he's reminded by a sudden dazzling slap on the back of the head. He scrambles up from the ground with stones in his fists. That too the camp teaches: to fight with whatever you have. You might lose, but drawing blood on the way down is the only way to keep your ration. In a camp of orphans, the meek inherit only the earth.

The shadow's larger than he is and carries a flexible hose. Before he can react the hose slashes out of the dark again and bursts across his face so hard his eyes scream in his skull. Down again, he rolls, hands over his head. But the blows keep coming, hollow thwocks of rubber on flesh. Between blows the squat man shouts. "No selling without Eyobed's cut!'

Eyobed's Habesha, like a lot of others in the camp. The Habesha kids stick together. Their older ones run the smuggling, the girls who suck town men through the wire, the games, and the burial insurance every adult in camp pays for—there's no worse shame than to die and not have proper burial. Eyobed's squat and ugly and his breath stinks, but up to now he hasn't interfered with Nabil and the old aide's sideline.

Now that they're making significant money, their exemption seems to be up. Nabil covers his stomach as the hose descends again, but it slashes his face once more. He screams into the night as his customers scatter, a woman scooping up the liquor on her way into the anonymous dark. This too the camp teaches: anything left unguarded's yours.

"Learned your lesson, dog turd? Stinking mouse? Half what you get belongs to Eyobed. *Say it.* Half."

"Half my profit belongs to—"

The hose slashes again, across his stomach now he's covered his face. "Half the *gross*, licker of old men's dicks. *The gross.* Say it."

"Half the gross to Eyobed," he screams, loud enough the whole camp might hear, if screams in the night were rare.

The beating stops. Peering through his fingers he sees the figure tucking the hose under its arm. Its fingers fumble at its pants.

"Now you take a young, strong man in your mouth."

He crawls into the tent he shares with the aides, snuffling snot and tears and blood.

"He beat you?" comes a cracked whisper.

The old man who showed him the pleasures, when he first came to the camp. Who took him into the clinic, brought him food, held him when he raved in fever. He's very old now and shakes continuously, as if an off-balance motor runs inside him. They don't share pleasure anymore, but there's still respect and maybe even something like love. Nabil crawls over and presses against him, weeping softly, because it hurts, but not loud enough anyone else might hear. To be heard weeping is not good. Little by little, he tells him. The old man sighs.

Then he whispers, "Tomorrow the white doctor operates again. When he does, he gives me the key to the cabinet."

The next night Nabil waits behind the latrine, plastic bottle between his feet, a smaller, glass bottle behind it. The line forms. The women filter. Coughing men hand their cups to the next in line. The raw alcohol whets the air. The youth choir's practicing across the camp.

When the squat shadow approaches, Nabil bends, then

backs away. "Need another lesson?" the Habesha grates. "Where are you? I can't see you."

"Over here."

"Got my money? Half. Now."

"I have it," Nabil says. He comes to the wooden box behind the latrine and climbs onto it. He lifts the small bottle and unscrews the top. "Here it is," he says. "Up here."

Eyobed looks up as Nabil tilts the glass. It gurgles and for a moment that's the only sound, the acid gulping as it comes out. Then the night's shattered by a horrifying scream.

He and the old man have discussed it. He can't stay, after blinding Eyobed. The other Habesha will kill him. Nabil's old enough now to leave the camp. Those who don't shape their lives are already dead. He must go to the city, where in the stories clever orphans become rich, make fortunes, marry princesses. The old man cried, holding him, last night. Then blessed him and bade him go with God.

There's water and food in a plastic bag by the gate. The guard's left the gate unlocked. The old man bribed him, with his burial money. The gate squeals as it swings open. The desert night's dark, but the stars pour down light.

His breath catching in his throat, dragging his crippled foot, Nabil runs.

9

THE ASSAULT

The thunder began before dawn, shaking windows, bringing those barricaded in their homes out onto rooftops. The rumble came from all around the seaward horizon. No one in the city had heard anything like it before.

The machines hurtled out of the darkness.

They weighed 150 tons fully loaded and were ninety feet long. They flew two feet above the water, lifted by gas turbines on rubber skirts filled with air, propelled by giant pusher fans. At sixty miles an hour they trailed a fifty-foot-high roostertail, their fanfare a full orchestra playing Wagner on nothing but kettledrums. They came from forty miles out, launched from the cavernous bays of vast ships. Their decks were packed with Humvees, tanks, light armor, trucks, artillery, weapons, and troops; combat ambulances, fuel, ammunition, water, repair parts, and food.

The machines were landing craft, air cushion. Instead of dropping ramps at the beach for troops to wade ashore, their pilots nudged back on throttles. They double-checked their positions on screens in cockpits wrapped in shatterproof glass. Then increased the pitch rate on their lift fans, and drove in over the surf line and up between the dunes, out onto the dry mudflats south of the city.

In the dark they flew across dried-out fields, rutted roads, and wadis filled with the smoothed pebbles of ancient watercourses. They blew down the tents of panicked nomads, crushed homes, crossed ditches, uprooted and blew away small trees, leaving an emptiness as if a janitor's broom many meters wide had been pulled across the land.

From the guard tower Aisha Ar-Rahim heard the thunder and said a short *du'a* that all would go well, for American and Ashaaran alike. The embassy's reinforcements had stopped two more attacks by looters, but anarchy rocked the city. More asylum seekers had been allowed in. Their stories made her shudder: home invasion, rape, torture to extort money. Hundreds more had been turned away.

Lying atop a rise overlooking an intersection to the south, heads and M249s wrapped in dull-colored *shemaghs*, Teddy Oberg and Sumo Kaulukukui were trying to make radio contact with the lead LCAC. Teddy had thought the point was still miles away when suddenly the terrain lit up. Something enormous thundered toward them, lights like the landing lamps of a 747 blinding them before they could duck, clawing at their night vision goggles.

"Holy *fuck*!" the Hawaiian shouted over the annihilating roar of sixteen thousand horsepower as a wall of sand, wind, and noise rolled over them, tearing at their clothes. "Son of a bitch is like *Close Encounters*. And they go *uphill*?"

Even far out in the foothills of the Western Mountains, nomads woke to the airborne rumble, wondering what new thing had invaded their land.

The machines roared inland, ponderous beasts romping free at last. Each cost millions and burned fuel in torrents, but moved too fast for an enemy to stop. Occasionally as they swept by an Ashaaran emptied his rifle in unreflecting terror, but they never bothered to return fire. The bullets caromed off armor. The machines swept on.

Aboard *Mount Whitney*, Dan watched bright pips cross a pulsating line representing the mean low-tide mark. They sped up, drawing together to wheel northward in an immense hook, covering in minutes distances exhausted dogfaces had taken weeks to fight their way across at Anzio and Normandy.

Behind and above him in the darkened theater of the CACC brooded a spectacled, scholarly looking one-star marine general with six fingers, named Cornelius DeRoberts Ahearn. The task force commander had flown in with his senior staffers while the main amphibious element was three hundred miles distant. He'd merged Dan, McCall, Henrickson, Goya's people, and the One-Five MEU staff, when it arrived, into a forward element of a joint task force—a standard way of dealing with an emergent crisis, until the other supporting elements could be stood up—and immediately begun planning the follow-on to the embassy relief.

News from the city was limited to cables via Washington and Bahrain from the embassy and what one wire service stringer holed up in the Hotel des Vacances reported. A drone from *Tarawa* had sent back video of parts of the city burning, but its lens didn't reveal who led the mobs roaming the streets.

The Joint Chiefs had phrased Joint Task Force Red Sea's mission as "establish and promote peace, stability, and the efficient and fair distribution of humanitarian assistance to the People's Republic of Ashaara, in cooperation with United Nations agencies, nongovernmental organizations, and such elements of government as shall remain or be reconstituted." Centcom interpreted that as "As rapidly and peacefully as possible, relieve and reinforce the U.S. Embassy in Ashaara, disarm or neutralize such forces as may prove hostile, and secure ports, airfields, and roads to facilitate humanitarian assistance operations."

Over two days the combined staff of JTF Red Sea and CTG 156.4 had translated this into Operation Collateral Gratitude. It began with a seaborne feint around midnight north of the port, while special operations forces moved to overwatch positions near both bridges over the Durmani to detect any repositioning by the Ashaaran army. It then landed the Fifteenth Marine Amphibious Expeditionary Unit by LCAC over the beaches south of the port. The MEU's first objective was the Ashaaran Twenty-first Armored's camp at Darew. After either confirming the Twenty-first wasn't a threat or neutralizing it, the marines would continue across the downstream bridge, hook right again in a shallow envelopment, and link up with a helicopter-borne assault at the international airfield.

If this went well the feint force would land in a second assault, taking the port area of Ashaara City to handle the relief supplies Dan had requested in a message for COMJTF's signature. Once the airfield and the port were in his hands, Ahearn would fly in to meet with the ambassador and discuss what remained of the government and whether it could help distribute food aid.

Dan felt uneasy. The plan depended on rapid movement and no interference from any Ashaaran force. The LCACs were fast, but if the lift fans got damaged there was no way to tow them; they'd have to be repaired where they sat down, left under guard, or blown in place. Once they debarked vehicles—tanks, light armor, amphibious assault vehicles, fuel and ammo trucks—he wasn't sure what speed of advance to expect over unimproved roads.

But the big question was how they'd be received. They were trying to take over a whole country with two thousand marines and limited combat support. Even if the Ashaarans cooperated, the JTF would be stretched thin. If they fought, things could turn ugly indeed.

Dan got up as Ahearn lifted a little finger, all that remained on the right hand. Ahearn had lost the rest at Hue City to a 106 recoilless. He wore a heavy gold ring with the palm tree of The Citadel on his left hand. "General?"

"Hard to believe there's no air activity."

The Ashaaran air force had one fighter ground attack squadron and one counterinsurgency squadron. Dan massaged a tension headache. "We keep pulsing the AWACs and surveillance people, but there's no sign of activity, either from the aircraft or that SA-7 battery at the airfield."

"Nothing yet about the Twenty-first?"

According to CIA studies and attaché's reports, the Ashaaran army had five regiments. The president garrisoned two near the capital. The others were posted north, west, and south, covering invasion routes from Eritrea and Sudan. Ahearn was asking about the Twenty-first Armored Brigade, with surplus Egyptian and Polish tanks. The DIA called it an elite unit devoted to the president. Its camp was south of the international airfield. The Seventeenth Mechanized was north of the river, less worrisome, since Dan had surveillance on the only two bridges, Oberg's SEALs on one and a Marine recon team to the north, at Fenteni.

"No movement from their laager, General," Dan told him.

"Last update?"

"Imagery two hours ago, sir. We'll have the UAV refueled and back at dawn to confirm."

The general's screen showed the disposition off the beaches. Ashaara had no navy, but *Shamal* and *Cyclone* were on station off the main port and *Firebolt* off the delta at R'as Zalurah, to intercept any speedboats or dhows that might interfere. *Oldendorf* was covering the amphibs—*Tarawa* south of the islands and shoals of the Ashaaran delta, *Duluth* and *Anchorage* to the north, all under way at bare steerageway—from air attack.

Three huge screens constituted the display area. The leftmost showed operations ashore; the middle, the amphibious operating area proper—the one Ahearn was toggled to at his chair—and the right, the air picture from the Nile deep into Saudi, a fused display from AWACs, *Oldendorf*, and Centcom. An unidentified air contact to the north showed 420 knots at twelve thousand feet on course 167. As he watched, the symbol blinked from unidentified to friendly. A B-52 with IFF turned off, headed for the secret but hard-to-disguise U.S. air base in Saudi.

He thought they were doing it right. For a moment he let himself hope this might work out as planned.

The general picked up a phone and a light colonel rose from his terminal. The J-2, the task force's intel officer. Ahearn sucked on his glasses' earpiece. "So, why are they not moving? Did we miss a dispersal? A redeployment, before we got eyes on them?"

The J-2 said, "We saw some movement of light units yesterday, General. Jeep size, trucks. Consistent with troops loading up what they can steal and deserting. No value in a tank to a looter."

"The next decision's at Point Y," Ahearn said. Y was the remote wadi where the LCACs would turn off their fans and drop ramps for the tanks to trundle into assault formation. "We've got better night fighting capability. But if those T-55s get hull down behind a ridgeline, with infrared spotlights, they can cream us. I don't like these ROEs."

"They're definitely restrictive, sir," said the J-2.

"How's it go again?"

"Return fire only in the event of armed resistence. Fire will not be initiated; no interdiction or prep fires authorized."

"If we see movement to contact, we can do an air strike?"

"That'd stretch the ROEs, sir, but I don't see how anyone can reasonably object."

"Lenson, you worked in the West Wing. Can they reasonably object?"

Dan rubbed his face. Coffee wasn't working anymore. "Sir, without meaning to be cynical, from the point of view of the president's people, all those ROEs are for is to absolve them of responsibility if you drop a laser-guided bomb on a school. Failing that, the op order clearly gives you own-force self-protection. If interdicting an armored column en route contact isn't force protection, I don't know what is."

"But those could be dummies, or target hulks. Hal, you sure they haven't already redeployed? Waiting to kick the shit out of us when we drop ramps?"

The intel officer wiped his palms. "Based on the best recon available, it's our opinion the Twenty-first never left laager. But since we don't have before and after photos—"

"Then it's possible."

"Yessir. Not probable, but . . . possible."

"Which is one step above vomiting in a bucket." Ahearn waved impatiently and they moved off as the general reached for his phone again.

"I remember where I saw you before," the intel officer muttered. Dan lifted his eyebrows. "In Eritrea. With the briefcase, the nuclear codes, behind the president. Wasn't that you?"

"The emergency satchel. Yeah, that was me."

"I saw you in that video of the shoving match with the troops. In the mess tent? The Secret Service using you for a battering ram. Didn't take, huh?"

"Sorry, I'm a little slow right now. What do you mean?"

"Well, you're back in the field, right?"

Dan shrugged, unwilling to explain how protecting the president had gotten him exiled. "Can we check if those tanks are still there? Send that UAV back at low altitude, take a look infrared? Or get some recon-type eyes out there? Right now all we're doing is guessing."

The lieutenant colonel said he'd find out, and headed off. Dan stopped at the coffee mess in the back of the space and just stood, aching back pressed to the black-painted bulkhead. Ahearn was getting bent out of shape over nothing. Everything he'd heard about Ashaara portrayed poverty and social disintegration from decades of revolution, war, and misgovernment. If the president had flown, why should the army fight?

But the Twenty-first was an elite formation. If the whole army crumbled, evaporated, that might be convenient for Collateral Gratitude. But what about the follow-on relief effort? How did you maintain security with no host nation army? A hell of a lot easier to use troops people were at least used to, one they shared a language with, than try to rivet down order with a foreign force. Especially in a largely Muslim country.

He valved another hit of bad coffee, and headed back to his terminal. Eighteen messages glowed on his screen, and Henrickson and two other staffers waited, looking impatient.

Forty miles west of Ashaara City, in the dead dark of night, Dr. Gráinne O'Shea lay facedown in a ditch, digging her fingernails into dry earth as above her diesels roared and steel treads earthquaked down clods and dust as if to bury her alive. She'd forgotten her bloody toes inside her boots, her thirst, the fear that had hiked beside her since the afternoon before. Her mind felt like a bucket of dirty water.

The longest day and night of her life had begun the morning before, at the compound, when she'd answered her cell's chime to find her administrator from the Hydrological Programme on the line. "Tell me you're not still at Fenteni" were his first words.

"Ah—I am. Why?"

"Didn't you get my e-mail?"

"Down since yesterday, Derek."

"You've not seen the news? Right . . . there's been a coup."

"Oh God."

"At least that's what it sounds like. You haven't heard?"

She bent to look out the dusty window at the ravine, where nothing had changed for several million years. "Hinterlands here, Derek. If we don't hear it from the villagers, we don't hear. But a coup—"

"New York pulled its people out three days ago. We thought you'd gone with them."

"Never got that. Sorry." She bent again, catching a figure

outside, looking toward the road. Her assistant *had* acted strangely since Major Assad's visit. Outside for long periods, or when he was in, keeping a lookout at the window. Once he'd asked where she kept her passport.

So when she said thanks for the warning, she'd act on it right away, and went outside, she didn't like his evasive glance. "Abdiwali, I just had a disturbing call. The president's fled. There's rioting. You knew?"

A tight smile, averted eyes. "Yes, Doctor."

"Were you going to tell me? Or just let me find out on my own?"

"You always know what to do, Dr. O'Shea."

Sodding hell, it was like talking to some sly boyfriend. She pushed damp hair off her face—even newly risen, the sun was a torch—and tried for calm. An Irish temper didn't help with Ashaarans. "Stockholm says we should leave. The other agencies have already pulled out. Should we call the police compound? For an escort?"

"They have already gone."

"The *police*?"

He only looked toward the horizon. She huffed. "All right, we're leaving. The truck's fueled?"

"We have three-quarters of a tank."

"Is that enough?"

"To go where?"

"Well . . . the evac plan's always been the International Airport. If it's closed or occupied, then south toward Malakat. The Quarleses; we can stay with Howard and Michele."

"Will they still be there?"

"I don't know. I tried to ring but no one answers. If they're gone we can carry on south to Eritrea."

Her assistant grimaced. "Then you shall go. But what will happen to me?"

"What d'you mean? If I pull out, you go too."

He looked more hopeful, and followed her inside to pack.

Every INGO in Africa planned against this very situation. She stuffed the latest tomograms into a briefcase, jimmied the hard drive out of her machine, and found the padlock for the trailer door. She looked at the water-versus-population graph on the wall. Take it? She decided to leave it.

They loaded the seismograph and her luggage, then hitched up the trailer with the sound source and geophones. With one Blunnie planted in the Rover, she stopped to gaze at the compound. Her office was locked, but she doubted it'd be intact when she returned.

If she ever did. Everyone knew researchers who'd been exiled from the lands they studied, some for decades, others forever. For a moment the dusty bare earth, the muddle of sheds and prefabs against the backdrop of mountains, seemed unimaginably dear. Then, squalid as a vacant lot in Derry. She got in and twisted the key.

The hitch groaned as the trailer twisted on the uneven roads. They'd never been good, but over the past few years they'd really degenerated. Since the famine began, the government had become invisible, except for the police. Now they'd vanished too. She and Abdiwali rocked and grated over gravel and sand and broken stone, seldom at over twenty kilometers per hour; breaking an axle in Africa could be a death sentence. Here and there the tracks of previous vehicles left the road entirely to travel on flat desert. She always followed. The rebels were known to mine the roads. Staying on them when others didn't wasn't a smart move.

A dry dusty breeze made it hard to see, made progress even slower. They reached the first village around noon. At first she thought it deserted. Then people crept out of the shadows.

She caught her breath. Dusty skeletons, feebly lifting begging hands as the Rover ground past. She'd decided to take the back roads south of the river, rather than crossing to the highway. The river was dry now, of course, but she'd reasoned that if there was rioting when they reached the city, they might not be able to get through. The southern route would let her bypass it if she had to. The terrain was rougher, but it was the best chance of making it to the home of the Quarleses, who ran a school for AIDS-orphaned girls. But now she realized she'd immured herself too long. It'd been a fortnight since she'd left the compound, months since she'd come this way.

So when she saw the roadblock ahead she did the worst possible thing: simply drove up, halted, and lowered the window, smiling at ragged men who stared at her with disbelief, then at each other with glee.

It cost her two hundred pounds, all the cash she carried. They'd eyed Abdiwali as he sat rigid, but hadn't spoken to him, only her.

As soon as she was past the village she pulled off, bumped over a shallow ditch into a cracked-open field, and snapped, "Dump the bloody Bison. Pull the pin and leave it. I could have turned off and bypassed that village if I hadn't been pulling the fucking thing."

They could replace computers and trailers, but without the sound source—the only one in Ashaara—her days as a hydrologist were over. She watched it shrink in the rearview with a sharper pang than she'd felt leaving the compound.

Lightened, the Rover rattled more but went faster. This part of the country looked featureless to an eye new to it, but gradually revealed folds and slants. What she didn't like was the bodies. Some lay along the road, beside burned-out cars; others were just bright cloth in the dead fields. Abdiwali sat as if mummified in the passenger seat, staring through the sand-dulled windscreen, gripping a worn gray bag he carried his kit in.

They killed him that afternoon. There wasn't any way around the second roadblock, in a broken region furrowed by pebble-strewn gullies that had been a side channel of the Durmani back in the middle Holocene. The gullies made the road, never paved or even graded since colonial times, twist and writhe so that spare parts and jerricans in back slid and banged from one side to the other. This time when she stopped two men stood by her door pointing guns while six others went to the passenger side. Abdiwali threw her one terrified glance before they pulled him out. They questioned him briefly—two, three sentences—then the machetes rose and fell.

"Why thee travel with that northerner?" a gaunt man said in broken French, leaning into her side and looking around.

Her tongue and jaw felt as if injected with novocaine. "He was my assistant."

"And what are thee?"

"A water expert. With the UN."

This brought bitter laughter and jokes in a dialect she couldn't follow. "Thee came to the wrong place for water," the gaunt one said, leaning in again so his smell, like that of some carrion-eating bird, pushed into the vehicle. "But the right one for men."

As they laughed again her toe felt for the accelerator, ready to stamp it and hurl through the overturned carts and iron bedsteads; but they stepped back and waved her on lazily, as if whatever energy they owned had been expended on the killing.

At the next roadblock they took her car. She raged at them but they simply pulled her out and got in. She stood shaking, cupping her elbows in her palms. The sun stacked white cubes of radiant heat between her and them. They drove off, abandoning the roadblock as if it had served its purpose.

Leaving her standing in vibrating heat, in the middle of a planate wasteland strewn with baking rocks, baking rocks, and yet more baking rocks. And here and there, down any fissure or furrow, a few dusty thorn plants so sere and juiceless the starving goats of desperate nomads had turned their beards aside. She felt like a robot, though what robot would shake with terror? And turned and stumbled away, knowing instinctively now she had to leave the road. Without a car, that colored shell of steel, technology, and culture, she was nothing more than a pale grub of tasty prey.

She picked up a sharp stone and stuffed it into her jeans pocket.

She left not only the road but the Durmani Valley, stumbling cross-country as the sun blazed. She'd lost her bush hat with the car but had a kerchief as a sweat rag. She tied it over the back of her neck, rolled her shirtsleeves down, oriented by the sun, and marched.

Having no water felt like trudging naked across the desert. She was instantly thirsty, and after two hours began having walking dreams. At first of Ireland, a tumbling stream she'd played in as a child. Then the fountains in Cork, then a glassy lake where birds like none on earth stared at her, repeating nonsense phrases in the Gaelic she'd learned in grade school, with maddening repetition she knew even as she dreamed was tinged with delirium.

Sweat flaked from her skin, drying the moment it left her pores. She stumbled on scree, breaking the fall with palms that burned on the sun-heated ground. Got up, went on.

Then fell again, so heavily she lay full length, panting and moaning as the stones burned her face. She might not make it out. Too used to reaching for water whenever she wanted it. She was on her own now, in a land that tormented, then consumed whatever alien creature ventured out on it. She sat up and searched her pockets. Pens, coins, keys. She slipped a key off and put it in her mouth.

She lay down again, knees huddled to her chest, eyelids drooping like a lizard's. Conserving whatever moisture she had left.

With agonizing slowness the blazing sphere that tormented all life below it declined. It touched the mountains and ignited them like phosphorus. Then slipped into the evening's pocket, and the stars swung up out of the east. When the mountains glowed with backlight, far and intangible as a dream, she woke. "You must keep moving," she muttered. She forced herself erect and staggered on.

The desert was empty but not lifeless. With the cooling of dusk, creatures emerged from where they sheltered from the merciless radiation. Small leathery things scurried away from her bootscuffs. Geckos. A large spider, rearing crablike as she towered above it. She blinked at it as the light faded. A flash of yellow drew her eye. A thin plastic bag, the omnipresent detritus of Man. She plucked it up and stuffed it into a pocket.

A faint flapping lured her off her easterly course. A nomad tent of blackened skins, fly fluttering in the evening wind. She approached trembling and called out, clutching the rock-weapon in her pocket. No answer. She called again a stone's throw away. When she thrust the flap aside she saw the desiccated bodies.

Of course there was no water, though she tore the tatty rugs and stinking cloths aside, scrabbling down to the bare ground.

She walked and walked, feeling as if chicken wire were pressed against her toes and heels. Then they went numb as the skin wore away. She stood on a rise and from somewhere reason resurfaced. She looked left, then right, like a Muslim at prayer. Tens of thousands of years back this dry bed must've been yet another eastward-flowing stream. Stumbling on, she sensed a depression. Her boots clattered over rounded rocks.

A gully drew her eye, blacker than the surrounding dim. The blacknesses were low brush. Thornbushes, young tamarinds. Her feet drifted to where they clustered.

She fell to her knees and dug and dug as the light faded, breaking nails, scraping off skin, panting between clenched teeth. About a foot down she fell to her face and put her lips to the ground.

Dusty, powdery, millions-of-years-old dry. She gagged, then sobbed, losing it for a duration filled with agony and terror.

Then she got up again, and went on.

Sometime past midnight, lurching toward one particular bright star two hand-breadths above the horizon, she heard a waterfall. It faded as she staggered on, then returned. She was away with the fairies, surely, but where there was a waterfall there must be water, so she tottered on.

She went over a lip in the darkness and crashed into rocks and what felt like broken glass at the bottom. She lay dazed, drifting, as images wandered before her open eyes.

The sound came again, closer. Accompanied by a vanishingly brief flash.

Not a waterfall. Something more ominous.

Suddenly it was on her. She pressed herself like a filling into the cavity of the gully, clawing dry earth as the roar of diesels and the ground-shaking grating of steel treads broke loose dry clods and tried to bury her. She forgot thirst, the pain in her feet, even her terror, as the roaring thing reared, then clattered directly overhead while she crouched like a hunted fawn. The hot breath of a dragon blew down on her. Then it was past, gone. After hugging the ground against its return she wiped dirt from her face and raised her eyes over the edge of the depression.

Outlined by flames from their backs, the black monsters were rolling into a rough line. She stared unblinking as an insect must, neither comprehending nor trying to, only registering sensation.

The monsters were aligning themselves, three, four, six, when a lance of white fire burst from her right. It beamed with perfect impossible straightness across the black ground, sucking up dust and sand. The sound was like the tearing of the bedsheets of the gods. The flame impacted one of the monsters with a clang that shivered the night. By far the loudest sound she'd ever heard, and she clapped palms over agonized ears as more fireballs whipped across the desert, each lighting it like a fiery chunk of the sun launched in a perfect horizontal at supersonic speed. With each fireball a tremendous crack tolled over sand and rock, followed by a clang like a cathedral bell dropped from its tower onto granite pavement. Each clang made her teeth vibrate and sent a strange tingle through her legs. Which were, she barely noticed, suddenly and warmly wet.

A movement behind her, accompanied by a staccato clatter and whining growl even more threatening than that of the first monsters.

Surrounded by fire and machines, she dropped to her face like a desert eremite in the awesome presence of God. Her body felt enormous and not really hers, but she tried to hide it anyway, feeling distantly responsible, writhing wormlike into the soil. The clanging and brightness went on, perhaps for only seconds yet endless. Then at last, drew away.

When she lifted her head again intense fires blowtorched a mile away, white-hot, speckled by explosive pops and bangs.

She crouched, shaking, peering into the night. Then picked out her star once more, scrambled up from the ditch, and set out again.

She lay unseeing, face to the sky, until a vaporous iridescence gradually dawned. Then rose, knowing only she must move on or die. Staggering over stones amid which gleamed hundreds of small, bright metal cylinders, slightly sooted at their open mouths.

A mile on she stumbled over two men lying full length atop a rise. They were camouflaged so perfectly she hadn't seen them a pace away. They stared up, startled. One reached for a weapon, then stayed his hand. "Who's this?" he murmured.

The other, face scarred with radiating lines, said, "Hell, Sumo. Just one of them desert mirages. But I bet she'd say yes if you offered her a drink of water."

The ramps of the landing craft of the second prong of the offensive had been supposed to drop on Red Beach, two miles east of the marine terminal, precisely one minute after sunrise, when the rising sun, glaring over the heads of the men crouched in the wells, would dazzle any defenders. But they didn't fall until fifteen minutes later, due to coral heads in the shallow water. An LCM hit one so hard it bent a shaft. The wave leader ordered them to slow, and to post bow lookouts to steer between them on the way in.

This landing had the look of old newsreels: sluglike amtracs waddling out of the surf, then tipping upward to roll over the dunes; the slanted bows of landing craft, creaming wakes as they circled offshore. One by one they beached as helicopters passed overhead. Loudspeakers explained in recorded Asahaaran (unfortunately, the dialect of the former ruling clan) that the troops were there to help and feed the population.

In the midst of the noise LCM-25's ramp slammed down. The leader of the first fire team off—"Team," in Marine parlance—was a twenty-three-year-old lance corporal from Michigan.

Crunching on a homebrew mix of MRE powdered coffee, Copenhagen, and ephedrine-laced energy supplement, Caxi Spayer jumped down, relieved to find the water only a couple feet deep. "Follow me," he bellowed at the three others in his fire team, and waddled for the shore, the men so burdened with ruck and rations, armor vest, ceramic plate overvest, grenades, radio, rifle, and ammunition that they looked inhuman, inflated bulks capped by Kevlar.

Facing him was a white beach backed with villas. The tumbled granite of a breakwater. The square tower and the minaret, lined up, meant they were in position. In the distance, the blue cranes of the container port, their objective for the day.

Turning to check Ready, Fire, and Assist were still with him, he led them toward a two-story red house that dominated the beach. A helicopter scissored overhead, its gunner scanning the beach. He and Spayer exchanged thumbs-ups. The fire team on Spayer's flank was making for the same house, but he was ahead. He picked up the pace until his boots sank deep into soft sand above the high-tide mark. He lost his balance, toppled and fell. Trying to keep his rifle clear, he turned his head to spit sand and the gritty residue of powdered coffee.

He looked up to see a man so black he was like a hole in the light, wearing a pink straw hat, rubber flip-flops, and a lime green shirt, in his face with a camera. Behind him another camera strobed. A ripple of flashes alone the dune line above them made Caxi wince. He lurched to his feet facing a cameraman in blue flak jacket with a Fox logo. "Smile, Lance Corporal." A lieutenant slapped his back. "Gonna be on TV, my man."

The line of marines in battle dress went prone as they skylined the tops of the dunes. Then looked confused as they were swarmed by hundreds of kids, long-legged adolescent boys, grave older men in headwraps. Spayer waddle-charged slowly up his sandhill, heart knocking from ephedrine, caffeine, and his first beach assault.

Dozens of people milled at the red house. Kids pelted after a soccer ball. Women in saris waved from a balcony. A heavyset Indian in a tieless suit hurried over, hugging bottles of orange drink. "American? American! We prayed for you to come! Now we shall have peace, we are safe!" He shouted to the kids, who mustered into a ragged line at ragged attention. Veiled women advanced, dark eyes eloquent. They cupped filigree balls from which a blue smoke scented with lemon and sweet turpentine eddied. They circled the astonished fire team, waving fragrant haze toward them with hennaed palms as the children chanted, "Welcome to Ashaara! We are your friends!"

"We drink this orange shit, Team Leader?" said the assistant automatic weapons gunner.

"Take it and smile, but dump it when we're out of sight. Stay tactical, jarheads. Eyes on the swivel, watch those rooftops."

Spayer took his team downhill. The map showed broken dunes between them and the crane cabs that loomed ahead. The helicopter went over again, banking left.

"Raven Eight, Raven. Over."

He took a knee as he answered, reporting Raven Eight three hundred meters inland with no contact. They were exiting the dune line and in sight of the objective. As he spoke he caught the upperworks of one of the PCs gliding over the dunes, flying both the Stars and Stripes and the white, green, and black Ashaaran ensign. It was headed in to take a support station off the seawall, placing any hostiles between hammer and anvil.

He rose and went on. They came to paths winding amid brush. The wind from the sea languished and a buzzing cloud rose. The marines slapped and cursed as the flies bit and returned in hooking reattacks, concentrating on lips and eyes. The dunes grew lower, the bushes higher as the team pushed inland. The SAW gunner had his weapon tucked under an arm, ready if they took fire. He and the rifleman were discussing in low serious voices whether Indian women could be considered slut possibilities. The sand paths were littered with broken glass, turds, crispy-looking dried condoms.

Spayer was beginning to think this might be a walk-in. But then thought *ambush* and angrily gestured Fire and Assist into silence and vectored them farther to the right. This slid the two elements of the fire team forward parallel to each other but staggered by ten yards and separated by thirty. Closer than he liked, but he had to be able to signal to them above the brush. There were people all around, though he couldn't see them; their shouts and gay cries rang clear. He hawked and spat flies that bit as they died. Poor as hell, ragged, close to starving—at least the blacks, though the Indians looked pretty well off. They all sounded happy to see Americans, though.

He came around a bend in the trail and pivoted at a stir to the left. Then lowered his rifle. Just a piled-up nest of trash, crumpled boxes, wadded-up grass, greasy rags.

He turned away, but something caught at his arm. He whipped back, ready to take the rifleman's head off, only to see a small shaven head at the level of his belt. Gleaming black eyes above a big grin minus several teeth. The flies crawling around those eyes didn't seem to disturb their owner. *"B'jour,"* the boy said.

Spayer's gaze traced a trail of cardboard to realize the boy had emerged from the trash pile, apparently a nest. "Hey, guy."

"Hey." The grin grew. "Hey guy. *V' nom?*"

"What you trying to say, kid? Hey—where—"

"Nabil," the boy said, patting Spayer's side. All he wore was a torn, dirt-blackened T-shirt that read "Bofalo Bills." His legs were sticks. One foot dragged in the sand. His cheekbones were pushing through his skin. He'd been beaten recently; his face was bruised and cut to a degree that would've had an American kid in the emergency room for stitches. Spayer smelled strong by now, after the LCM, the heat, and the tension, but the boy's stink cut through his own, a possum-in-the-garbage stench that sent an American nose into overload. Holding his breath, he felt in his pocket for the Planters Peanut Bar he'd stuck there before loading. Held it out, expecting it to be snatched.

Instead Nabil—was that the kid's name?—smiled up into Spayer's face. He studied the colorful wrapper, the little peanut man with top hat and cane. Then tore it open, broke off a piece, and offered it back to Spayer.

"We movin', Team?" said Ready, looking at him quizzically. Spayer pushed the boy aside like a turnstile and advanced again, weaving through the rattling bushes, keeping his eyes roving. The radio was talking again, but not to him. He kept it low to hear the whisper and crackle of movement all around. Spooky, to be surrounded by civilians.

If they *were* civilians. But he hadn't seen anyone armed. They'd been warned to expect militia, but so far, nada. They were closing on the cranes. Beach recon showed a fence between the beach and the hardstand. He patted his belt to make sure he still had snips, but hoped they'd find a gate. They were to secure the container port, not destroy it. M16s and grenade launchers were authorized, but no heavy weapons unless absolutely necessary to dislodge resistance.

He glanced back, thinking the boy would've slipped away, but he was tagging along, exchanging that cheerful smile for the bemused regard of the scout-rifleman. One foot dragged as if the tendon had been cut, but he kept up, lurching and bobbing. He was carrying a bottle of orange drink. Fire looked abashed. "Sorry, dog. Couldn't see just tossin' it."

The scrub fell away; a parched, fallow field opened between them and stacks of rusty containers, motionless cranes. Close up the chain link was rusty too, and hung limp from its stanchions. Spayer studied it through a little pair of Kowas, making sure they weren't walking into anything. Then pointed his guys out left and right. The radio buzzed and crackled. Raven, urging them forward.

"Marine terminal looks abandoned. Being secured," a MEU staffer called.

Dan yawned, checking the screens again. Still no hostile contacts. The amphibious op area was isolated. The road south to Uri'yah and north to Nakar, the intersection southwest of the city at Darew, and the abandoned camp of the Twenty-first Armored had all been occupied.

The lead elements reported only one instance of resistance, a night tank battle northwest of Haramah, where lead elements of the Fifteenth MEU had clashed with fleeing elements of the Ashaaran Twenty-first Armored. The M1A1s had picked up the T-55s in their thermal sights and slaughtered them at long range. One-Five was across both bridges and digging in to defend.

The lack of resistance was spooky. The country's armed forces had evaporated like dew on a hot morning. The police barracks at Darew was an abandoned, smoking shell.

He rubbed his eyes, trying to concentrate on whatever Ahearn had just asked him.

The cranes were smaller than Spayer had thought, seen from a mile away. One looked as if it hadn't budged along its tracks in years. The PC lay in the basin, guns laid on an office building and a gate that led to the highway. The office's windows were smashed out. Scraps of insulation, charred like overdone chitlings, lay littered around circuit boxes and motor housings where someone had mined out the copper wiring. Trucks had been stripped of tires, radios, doors, then set afire. A pusher boat lay sunken, stern protruding above the oily surface. The place was silent except for flies and a dog pack that loped yelping away as he led his team along the concrete apron. The heat was a thick fluid they had to force aside as they jogged along, gazes jumping from one likely sniper position to the next. The wind stank of burning rubber, shit, rotting meat. Raven Six reported a body wedged between one of the fenders and the pier, apparently fallen from a crane.

What kind of people would destroy the only port they could get food through? He didn't get it, any more than he understood why there wasn't anyone here to protect it.

He and Fire were setting up the M249 atop one of the stacks of abandoned containers when a *zzip* penetrated the air and something jerked at his arm. He heard the crack of a shot. When he looked down his sleeve was torn.

"Sniper, right two hundred," the rifleman called. "Watch my tracer."

Spayer followed the burst to the paste-colored rooftops. Prone, he snarled into his radio, "Raven, Raven Eight; sniper fire from Old City. Returning fire." The SAW chattered. He fitted a grenade into his launcher and aimed at an open window. Over the radio the lieutenant was coordinating other teams, sending them to clear the building. To secure the terminal, they'd have to clear the whole area. He triggered another grenade, the recoil pulpy against the layers of cloth and Kevlar cushioning his shoulder. The gunner fired out another magazine. Spayer finally told him to hold fire. "We're just ratfucking, with nothing to aim at."

A helicopter beat overhead but saw nothing either. The city lay silent under black smoke from inland. Raven Four reported the house empty, the sniper gone. Spayer lowered his gaze to find the boy from the dunes dancing and singing at the foot of the container pile. Someone had given him a BDU cover. It was too big, but he wore it proudly. He danced harder when he saw them looking on. He shaded his eyes, squinting up. Smiling.

"Hey, guy," he called up.

10

IN THE OLD CITY

Even at midday the narrow alleyways and massive walls, angled to baffle and tame the sunlight, are bathed in shadow. The sky burns like white phosphorus above flat roofs, but its heat cannot penetrate. From above the city looks deserted, but hundreds of thousands carry on their lives all around the obscure walled house of mud brick in the northern part of the Old Town, home to the city's poor.

An old man sits in a windowless room. The scents of cumin and cinnamon enfold him like thin layer of precious tissue. Incense smoke curls from a brass holder that still, the young man notices, has a MADE IN INDIA sticker on the side. The old man's sparse beard's colorless against pitted skin. He wears dark-framed sunglasses, a turban, a white cotton robe. A sturdy hagarwood stick's propped in a corner. When he extends a palm a veiled woman hands him a bowl. He holds it beneath his face and inhales, then raises sightless eyes.

"They no longer oppress us. All praise to God, the Lord of the worlds."

Ghedi sits with long legs crossed at the ankles on a carpet so old and soft it feels like the secret skin of a woman. He and the two with him wait without speaking. A man of excess words is not respected. The old man pushes his fingers into his mouth, flicks away spittle. His gums pain him, but the old sheekh refuses to see Western-style dentists. That would be a betrayal of God's will for his aging body, which he seems closer to abandoning each time Ghedi sees him. Ghedi feels only contempt for the weak, but the sheekh's far from weak, frail though he appears.

"How is it with the Waleeli?" Sheekh Nassir murmurs.

The Waleeli—Brothers—follow Nassir's vision of an Ashaara returned to the Word of God as set forth in the Holy

Koran. Ghedi's followed the old man since he grew old enough to leave the bandits. The fact he's here, with these others, shows his value to his teacher. Or so he hopes.

"Faithful to you and to the Word, respected Sheekh." Mahdube bows, gaze averted from the master's infirmity.

Mahdube and Ikrane have been with Nassir for many years. Mahdube was his student when he taught at the madrassa, before the president closed it. He's thin, with weak eyes, and wears thick glasses just like the old man's. Ikrane's from the old man's clan, but Nassir says he loves him despite that, not because of it. Even when he was a simple imam, their master's sermons belittled blind loyalty to clan. Nassir Irrir Zumali is an Issa, one of the roving tribes that from time immemorial lorded it over the desert. He doesn't deny the genealogies, though he pokes fun at them, but he calls clan allegiance a colonial device to set those the Europeans want to exploit against each other.

The three disciples wear Western-style trousers and shirts, but each shirt has black in it. They don't wear beards, by the imam's dispensation, so they can move freely and hear and report. Ghedi's glad of this. He admits he's vain, too proud of his handsomeness. All gifts are God's, and in his prayers he's offered Him his comeliness along with his life.

"Tell me what you've seen."

Mahdube, the eldest, recounts in his high stilted voice the withdrawal of the police. They've walled themselves up in their clan neighborhoods. "The major now calls himself 'General' Assad. They don't patrol, but stop and interrogate anyone who enters their neighborhoods. I've heard they're short on fuel for trucks and ammunition for mortars. I sent two men in at night. Both were caught. The piebald dog returned their heads."

"The piebald dog" is a huge man with a frightening white face who serves as Assad's bodyguard and executioner.

"God's blessing upon them, they dwell in Paradise. And your answer?"

"Two heads from their men."

A silent nod, a lifted hand; then the sightless gaze turns

to the next. Ikrane's solidly built, with an impassive face and massive hands that move slowly, as if with great effort. Ghedi's seen those big fingers tear the tongue from a man caught spying. "My loved brother. What of the clan elders?"

"A Dr. Dobleh has returned. He's lived overseas with the foreigners and speaks their languages."

"What clan is he? Muslim, or not? Tell all you know of him."

"Zumali Dobleh. A Gilhir, but it's said his father was Tawahedo, a Christian. He grew up in Italy and speaks with their accent. The wealthy merchants, the Indians, the other exiles returning now that the Xaasha have lost power, all champion him."

"Such men are worms, glistening with the slime of the West. What are his plans, my strong brother?"

"He says the United Nations will feed those in need, if all unite under a new government. It will set up a new police, a new army. It must control all revenue. It will educate women and outlaw sharia punishment."

The old man sits bowed. Finally he murmurs, "What of those who defend their clans?"

"All militias must be disarmed."

"Including Assad's criminals? The so-called governing council?"

"All must surrender weapons to the occupiers. They will be given food and money. The roads will be rebuilt. We'll have electricity again. This is what Dobleh and the Americans say."

The old man lifts his head. "Surely the elders will not collaborate. The president was evil. May God burn him in a fiery Hell for ten thousand years. But at least he was Ashaaran."

The large hands lift and fall. "My father, not all agree, but many listen. They meet at the palace soon for discussions. To talk of elections so this foreigner may become president. Is it God's will he be killed? If it is, He has given me to know how to cause it to happen."

The old man works his fingers in his mouth before saying around them, softly, "Let us not speak of killing this one yet. But we cannot allow another evil ruler. And giving up weapons—no Ashaaran will like those orders. It may be time for the Waleeli to renew our country."

The three younger men sit pondering. Finally he stirs. "Ghedi, my youngest. Come sit by me. Tell me of our business dealings since the raid by the Assadites."

Since the police raid there've been no more shipments of weapons, but they have several hundred RPGs stockpiled, plus many grenades. He describes the attack he carried out in Malakat, at the police station. "Most had already left. The ones who remained seemed happy to be allowed to live."

"Their weapons?"

"I took them into the desert and buried them at a place only we know."

"No more ships with ammunition?"

"The Americans stop the ships, but with what we have, praise God, there is enough."

The old man's fingers tighten on his shoulder. "I know you do things for money that pain your heart. There will be reward in Heaven and perhaps too on Earth. Now tell me of the Americans. You have observed them, as I asked?"

"Yes, revered Sheekh. They come in machines that float above the ground. Even the tanks of the Xaasha were helpless against them. At the port they are building machines to unload ships without the labor of men. They occupy the airfield, constructing many buildings. Large aircraft land there every day. They carry conveniences and special foods without which the Americans cannot live. Our water sickens them. They must drink from bottles sent from Turkey and Jewish Israel."

The old man sits for a time lost in thought. The rattle of drums comes from another room, and Ghedi wonders that he lets the woman play Western music. Who is she? The sheekh never refers to her or addresses her in their presence. Surely he's too old to still desire women.

Ghedi blinks, ashamed to consider such a thought. This man's beyond lower things. They aren't the only ones who bring information. This blind imam knows more than any other in the city. Without stirring from this room, he may be the most powerful man in Ashaara.

Finally he speaks.

"My young brothers. You are of different clans. But Islam has no clans. To speak of one's family, when all Muslims are brothers, is to fall into a snare of Shaitan. What does the Devil want? For us to abandon God.

"That is why the Waleeli opposed the northerners: they embraced foreign ways. Those who do so are not worthy to live.

"Now the foreigners come to those in the south, and those to the north. Like locusts, they swarm over the lands of Islam. The holy kingdom. Palestine. The sheikdoms of the pearl. Somalia and Yemen. And now, Ashaara. You know what they bring: shamelessness, uncleanness, idolatry.

"How long will our people sit with arms crossed as the enemies of Islam torture and kill? Their soldiers shit and piss on us. They say they'll feed us. But America doesn't want more Muslims!

"America brings godlessness and sin. They make their women into men, their men into women, their machines into their gods. The martyrs are dying in Palestine, in Iraq, in Syria, in Lebanon and Afghanistan. Tell this to your brothers, that they are not taken in by lies."

The woman kneels by his side. She places a bowl of tea where he can reach it and touches his arm. Her gaze rises to Ghedi's. He stares until she turns away. She's veiled but he feels desire, then anger. How dare she, in the presence of this man? The imam feels for the bowl and sips, then works at his teeth for a while. Resumes, so softly his disciples must lean forward.

"Young brothers, God calls the Koran the 'Al-Dhikr Al-Hakim.' It is greater than any human doctor, even in the hospitals of the West. It prescribes the treatments for the illness of our hearts. Are we not all evil in our hearts?"

"Truly, yes," says Mahdube. The others murmur agreement.

"Then how can we become worthy? By obeying God's

precepts, trusting in His infinite mercy. The holy Prophet, peace be upon him, calls Him forgiving, merciful, wise, mighty, patient, and understanding. These are not empty words, like those from the West, where 'freedom' or 'peace' has one meaning for Jews and Crusaders, another for us.

"The Prophet, peace be upon him, said, 'Those who show mercy will be shown mercy by the All-Merciful. Be merciful to those on Earth, and God will be merciful to you.'

"Now, what does this mean? God is merciful, but not to those who deny Him and persecute His people. These invaders are worse than slavering hyenas. Is an animal equal to man? Not in the sight of God. But hyenas were created by God and do only what they were created to do. Likewise, He created men to worship Him. Instead the foreigners raise up images to worship, though God sent many Messengers to warn against this throughout the ages.

"Most blasphemous of all, they believe the world is theirs to know, theirs to shape. But this world is not ours; it is God's. It is not our will that determines it, but His.

"The Americans say they come to help. But no believer will take food from infidel hands. It's made from swine. The only way to cleanse it is to take it by force. This then is justified.

"Ghedi, you're very quiet," he says, and instantly the young man straightens, his heart accelerates. Surely the old man knows every thought in his mind. No one else is as kind as his master. Nor as utterly ruthless, when the Word tells what must be done.

"I listen to your wisdom, master."

The sheekh chuckles. "My wisdom, as you call it, is no more than the fart of the camel in the *shamal*. My son, I must ask a hard thing. I must ask you to leave us."

Ghedi sits motionless. The old man has schooled them to ponder before filling a foolish mouth with empty words. Finally he says, "I don't understand, my father. You wish me to leave you?"

"I do not *wish* it, my loved son." His hand's warm on

Ghedi's shoulder, his voice quavers in his ear. "You are the best of these and closest to my heart. Do you not understand, that is why I must put you from me? You must leave, bitter though it is for me to tell you so."

Ghedi sits confused, not so much at what the old man says, but by his emotions. His old life, as a child, is a distant dream. If he has a father, it's Nassir. He forces himself to say, "What must I do?"

"Help me up."

Supported between them, the sheekh's frail as a rotten basket. He totters as they half carry him into a larger room, then out into a courtyard filled with sunlight and the regard of three pure white cats with great blue eyes. The old man raises a hand, and they wait until the cats rise and drift away. He motions to a heap of old brooms and firewood. Ghedi pushes them aside, careless of scorpions, and uncovers a rifle.

Now that they're in the open under the flaring sun he hears wingbeats above, loud and nearing. The old man makes as if to take the weapon, then shakes his head. "I am too weak. Do what is necessary, my son."

"Here, master? Now?"

Mahdube's and Ikrane's envy shows in their eyes. He basks in it as in a father's praise.

He raises the rifle and waits. The sound increases.

It fills their ears, and a black wasp appears above them. He aims and pulls the trigger, blaced against the blast. The green tracer rises searching like the finger of the Angel of Death. The old man lifts his arms. He shakes his fists at the aircraft, inviting martyrdom. Ghedi fires until the magazine runs out. Surely he's hit it! But the machine only slightly deviates from its course. Then inclines, like a landing bird. He thinks for a heart-stopping instant he's killed it. But it passes from view, the whick of its strange wings fading.

"Thus do we declare jihad against the enemies of our faith and people," the sheekh says, patting his shoulder. "Go to the southern mountains. There, my young orchardsman, you will do your pruning. There you will find companions to do the will of God. You will report to us, and await our advice."

"I will do all you say, my master and father." Ghedi salaams to him, then to the other disciples. They nod back, supporting the old man, but hatred seethes in their eyes now.

He'll go to the mountains and lead men. So be it. It's God's will. Perhaps he'll even find his brother and sister, after whom he's asked and searched for years, yet never found. If they still live.

All will be as God wills. The thought brings peace in a world set on end. He salaams again as the blazing sun whitewashes spotless sky. Then kisses his master's wrinkled brow, smelling as he does so the mingled scents of cumin, and incense, and cinnamon.

11

ASHAARA CITY

Somehow he'd missed ever flying in a SuperCobra. There weren't many in the Navy-Marine complement, so no wonder, but as Dan walked toward tail number Four Two's low-contrast paint across *Tarawa*'s frying-hot nonskid he already regretted having so cavalierly volunteered for the lift ashore.

Cobras were smaller close up than in flight, when they assumed the larger-than-life presence of an angry hornet. But they still looked lethal crouched on skids, with bulging cockpit glass like an insect's eyes, the swelling shoulder pods of the turbines, stubby wing-mounts racked with drab-and-yellow Hellfire missiles. And not least, the triple barrels of the chin-mounted gatling tilted up like the stabbing proboscis of a predatory *Vespida*.

Skull wrapped in sweat-damp rubber and plastic, he set his boots where the crew chief pointed, swung up, and inserted legs and trunk down into a dauntingly cramped seat behind the pilot. Instruments, screens, and switches covered every surface. The crew chief strapped and plugged him in, with a running commentary on how to exit he knew he'd never remember. Curved glass sealed just above his head. They then squatted for long hot minutes with the turbines turning in a muted whistle-thunder as the pilot checked instruments.

"All set back there?"

He clicked the switch on the throat mike. "Ready when you are."

Before he'd finished they were skybound, the deck dropping away so fast vertigo and nausea struck simultaneously. He clenched his teeth and tried to focus on something other than being sick as the blue sea rolled up and nearly over the top of the cockpit. He grew heavy, then floated up till only woven nylon kept him from departing the aircraft headfirst.

Since Operation Collateral Gratitude had transitioned from Phase I, Insertion, into Phase II, Infrastructure and Governmental Reconstitution, he'd averaged three hours' sleep a night. The forward staff element had flown from *Mount Whitney* to *Tarawa* to prepare for Ahearn's arrival. The command ship would stay in Djibouti, since Ahearn was still dual-hatted at Centcom. The colonel commanding One-Five MEU would be in charge of most of the ground forces in theater.

The occupation had proceeded smoothly, with the exception of the armored clash west of Haramah, for which the U.S. had been criticized in Mideastern media. The marines had occupied the camps of the Ashaaran Twenty-first Armored and Seventeenth Mechanized, and were negotiating with the commanders of the other formations in their upcountry laagers. Ahearn had declared a cease-fire pending the outcome, and sent parties to meet with the tribal elders and with the last government representative in the capital, a General Abdullahi Assad.

Meanwhile, helicopterborne marines were securing road junctions and bridges. Armor and amtracs were moving up the MSRs, the main east-west and north-south highways. They brought small amounts of humanitarian supplies to grease the way, but their main function would be providing security for the distribution of food and medical aid by the Red Cross, UNICEF, and other relief agencies.

Dan was headed to what was fast becoming the curse of running a humanitarian intervention: meetings. Ahearn didn't micromanage. He laid out what he wanted done in a terse message each morning, and wanted briefbacks at noon and 1800. Beyond that, Dan scheduled his own movements. His status was grayish, though. He wasn't assigned to either Centcom or the JTF, but reported directly to Ahearn as a roving troubleshooter. He kept TAG as an info addee on his message traffic, and updated his commanding officer by e-mail. Mullaly didn't acknowledge most of what he sent but hadn't registered any objections. As for Admiral Contardi, Dan hadn't heard from him. Maybe his transformation assignment was OBE. Overtaken, in that wonderful Navy acronym, by events.

The AH-1W dived as it crossed the beach, hurtling over the labyrinthine streets of an ancient Red Sea city. He twisted to check out the terminal, wondering how the raising of the sunken tug was going, but it was past before his eyes could lock on.

The city was low, most buildings only one or two stories high. The walls were mud or concrete, with the typical East African flat roof. As they flashed over, women froze above clothes baskets, children pointed, men looked up from cards.

"Tracers," the intercom stated. "See 'em, from down by that minaret? Somebody don't like us. Hang on."

Dan braced himself as the Gs hit. Streaks of green light arced up from the maze of walls and roofs. Then curved away, falling astern.

"Not leading us enough. That's why I kept low. Give 'em less time to react. This ahead, with the gridwork streets, this is the colonial city."

Dan pressed his nose to the Perspex as the pilot rolled, giving a wide-angle view straight down. He recognized the Presidential Palace from overhead imagery. The streets were littered with overturned cars and the confetti glitter of shattered glass, the *Kristallnacht* aftermath of the breakdown of civil order. The ministries had been looted too, and their fallen roofs said they wouldn't be functioning again soon. Computers, files, equipment, were toast. The staffs—from the former president's clan—had fled. He was torn between astonishment at people looting their government, and a realization it hadn't been *their* government at all. The apparat of a cronyist tyrant was more like it. Unfortunately, one building down there—maybe the one with charred circles around it, the potholed street snowy with scattered paper—was the National Library; another, the National Museum.

The pilot jinked, and Dan swallowed. They flew over a wide space with stunted trees. The Champs Nationale. Among acacias and tamarinds his gaze snagged on rows of tents, military vehicles, the white-bordered outline of a hasty helo pad. Geometrical lanes of yellow tape channeled multicolored particles of humanity across the dead ground.

"Twenty-first CSH," the laconic voice-over noted. The Twenty-first Combat Support Hospital of the Thirty-sixth Medical Evac Battalion had been the first Army unit in country. This encampment would be the nucleus of an extensive health commitment. Treating the population, yes, but more important, getting local hospitals and clinics open again. Unfortunately, the limiter on both medical care and feeding was going to be transport. Since most Army and Air Force assets were tied up in Iraq, *Tarawa* was providing air support as well as most of the in-country logistics lift.

The city resumed after the park, but interspersed with homes now were small, lifeless fields. Once painstakingly irrigated by hand-dipped wells and motor pumps, now they were only baked dust. Here and there smoke spiraled. He hoped it was cooking fires. To his left lay the bed of the Durmani River. He saw no water, and the trees along the banks looked dead.

"Airfield, to your right."

The Cobra rose, then dipped in a corkscrew to throw off heat-seeking missiles. It went nose-up and dropped toward instant hangars whose fresh-minted aluminum roofs sparkled in the sun. Dozers and power diggers were excavating foundations and cable trenches. A star in the distance grew into the stubby wings and vortex tips of a C-17 on approach. The airlift route was arduous: C-5 Galaxies from Germany and the States to Incirlik, C-17s and C-130s for the final leg to the too-short strip at Ashaara. Graders were at work lengthening the tarmac.

Looking down, he locked building after building into the planning documents. Incredible what America could do. Like *Civilization* or *Age of Empire*, where each time you toggled back to the game screen your digital slaves had reared new monuments, bridges, cities. He wondered why it couldn't be done in the crumbling cities, the sucked-dry small towns, that paid the taxes Washington spent so lavishly.

The earth hurtled up, flattened, the rotors speeded up. Saliva sprang into his mouth. If only he could get the cockpit cracked before he had to spew . . .

The Joint Task Force's shore element was headquartered in the air terminal. He threaded construction tape past hardhatted contractors in coveralls. They maneuvered forklifts of prefab trusses through gaps in the walls of the waiting area, pushed cable reels on handcarts. Welding arcs glinted, and the smells of burning metal and fresh paint mixed with the limestone-cave draft of full-power air-conditioning. He checked in with a marine with a slung rifle and pinned on a security pass.

The next space was curtained off with canvas. Rows of metal chairs faced a plywood podium still being powernailed together as he found a seat, powered up his notebook, and checked for a wireless connection. No luck. Civilians in shirtsleeves trickled in. They made a beeline for the bug juice dispensers. Most of the chairs were occupied by men in BDUs and coveralls. A working meeting.

"Good morning," said a light colonel in battle dress. "Let me welcome everyone to Camp Matevenado, home of the Sixty-second Engineer Battalion, Thirty-sixth Engineer Brigade, Sixty-fourth Corps Support Group, Thirteenth Expeditionary Sustainment Command. Before anyone asks, the matevenado's a big mean mother of a desert spider native to the American Southwest. I'll be chairing this logistics meeting for General Cornelius Ahearn, U.S. Marine Corps. A special welcome to Joint Task Force Red Sea, the J4 transportation folks from Centcom, and our guests from State and other federal agencies.

"Our biggest problem's going to be transport, which our first speaker will address. Specifically, the fuel problem. Getting it in-country, distributing it, and paying for it . . ."

Dan leaned back. He forced himself to listen as, across the room, he noticed several men staring at him.

Aisha sniffed, shaking her dress out to let the GMC's air-conditioning underneath. She'd picked up some kind of respiratory bug. Her chest hurt when she breathed. The embassy van rolled as soon as the door slammed. Out the gate, past the sandbagged post that blocked half the street.

Led by a camo-painted Humvee with a rear-mounted machine gun, the convoy weaved and braked between wrecked trucks, half-collapsed buildings. The damage worsened after they crossed the Victory Bridge, a rusting, creaking monstrosity built by the British in 1944 in a futile attempt to create a Red Sea highway. Or so said an old book her roommate had given her. The building that housed the local help was now so crowded, Aisha was sleeping in an overflow women's berthing set up in the GSA Building. Her translator was growing huge; Aisha couldn't imagine even walking in that condition, but the little woman kept working.

Tanklike vehicles on wheels guarded both ends of the bridge. The New Quarter was deserted. Block after block were as gutted as if bombed. Vultures reluctantly hopped aside from dead things in the street. Those buildings not burned were barricaded, lower windows boarded up. Armed men glared as the convoy rumbled past. Only a few civilians haunted the streets, faces averted, as if they didn't want to see what their city had become.

"The Ashaaran national flower," Erculiano muttered.

"What?"

"Those plastic bags."

Yes, they were still there, drifting and tumbling; filmy pink, dark red, teal blue, thinner than American grocery bags. She knew now they were for qat, tossed aside once the chewer had his wad tucked.

A stonefaced contract guard with his assault bag occupied the front passenger seat, with her and Erculiano and Terry Peyster, the young man who'd paid off the sergeant major the night of the attack on the compound, in the rear. Peyster was the RSO, the regional security officer, from the Bureau of Diplomatic Security, Department of State.

The security detail had arrived two days after the embassy attack. They wore black shooting gloves and short jackets embroidered with a snarling wolf's head. They spent their off-duty time at the motor pool lifting concrete blocks and engine parts they'd put together into weight sets, but their bulkiness was also due to soft armor. They were polite, but she caught their evaluating and, it seemed, hostile looks. They patrolled the walls, and acted as bodyguards when embassy personnel ventured outside.

Not that they'd gone out much recently. The compound was an island, supplied by helicopter. They ate airlifted food, drank and showered with airlifted water; the GMC ran on airlifted gasoline. She stared out as deserted streets went by. Every tree had been cut down.

"No manhole covers," Erculiano murmured. She blinked at gaps in the buckled, potholed roadway. She met the gaze of a woman who'd stopped halfway across the road to let the convoy pass. Her reflection overlay the woman's in the tinted glass.

"Stand by to deploy," the driver said to the other contractor. "Watch your six."

"Nobody else is," the man said, as if it were a challenge and response. The lead Humvee turned suddenly, rocking, and scooted down a side street. The other vehicles followed, threading battered, overturned cars she realized were set as approach barriers.

They abruptly braked. Armed Ashaarans leapt up from around a small fire, angrily waving them to a halt, jerking cartridges into their weapons. They looked strung out on qat. Before the van was fully stopped their own guard was out, slipping a short weapon from the assault bag. More emerged from the other SUVs, each beelining for his assigned station. The two biggest jogged to the front and bulled up, confronting the Ashaarans chest to chest.

Aisha located her pistol under the abaya, her pucker factor rocketing. She reached for the door handle, but Peyster covered her hand with his. "Give 'em a few minutes." He had a boyish smile like some teen heartthrob. "They'll give us the all clear."

The last time she'd seen this man had been in a subbasement of the Palais de Sécurité, with dim flickering lighting and that strange smell from the cell blocks. Now, mysteriously promoted to general despite the flight of his government and dissolution of his ministry, Abdullahi Assad stood at a glass-topped table in a freshly pressed uniform and Sam Browne belt that made him look like the heavy in a 1940 Warner Brothers film. His uniform cap was set on the glass. The mirror behind him reflected his long neck and the dark skin at the crown of his head. The mansion had obviously belonged to someone wealthy, but there was no sign of him. Only the continual circulation of armed men from room to room, strolling from outside to inside. All were smoking or chewing qat, and some were doing both. She looked for the aged transcriptionist who'd bandied Italian with Erculiano but didn't see her. They were three on one with Assad, which might be difficult. The GrayWolf men stood in two corners, holding rifles. The other two were occupied by yellow-eyed Ashaarans with AKs. The bodyguards eyed each other like leashed Dobermans.

Assad bowed. Said in his deep, halting voice, but to her surprise in English: "American friends. Welcome to my new office."

Okay, she was used to that. Most cops in the Mideast

refused to speak the local language to Americans. Not because the Americans couldn't speak their tongue, though that was usually true, but because everybody wanted to practice his English. Even those who professed hatred for the West.

But the first time they'd met, he'd pretended he couldn't speak English at all. Or Arabic, for that matter. Would anything else he told them hold up in court?

But that too was the Mideast. If she had a dollar for every time she'd talked to someone who'd told her one thing one day and the opposite the next, contradicting both himself and what she'd seen with her own eyes, she could've retired long ago.

She pondered this as a very tall, very dark woman with a heavy mustache brought in a tray of soft drinks. The familiar bottle, but the contents were too pale to be Coca-Cola or its Mideastern imitators, Zam Zam or Mecca. She set the glasses out with faint clicks on the tabletop, poured, then left without a word or a glance.

Of course they each had to take one. Aisha hesitated—the bottles here were recycled without sterilization, so you risked hepatitis C and who knew what else—but felt the amused regard of the Ashaarans. To Jahannam with them. She drank off the warm sweet fluid and poured more.

Assad seemed unsure whom to address. He looked at Peyster, then at Erculiano. They nodded to her. He shrugged. "Agent Ar-Rahim. The first time we met, I did not ask about your family. You have family?"

"A mother and father in New York, yes."

"But you yourself, not married?"

"I'm not. You, General?"

"I am fortunate. Three sons."

"All in good health?"

He lifted his hands. "All praise and thanks be to Allah."

She let him play host. Sooner or later they'd get down to business. Perhaps she could steer it that way. "Congratulations."

He lowered his glass. "Excuse?"

"Major to General—a big jump. Your superiors must have great faith in you."

"Thank you," Assad said, face a study. "They do."

"Only—who *are* your superiors?"

She'd hoped the question would set him back, but it didn't seem to. "My superiors are the Governing Council."

She glanced at Peyster—shouldn't he be stepping in?—but he simply sat smiling. So she went on. "I'm sorry, I haven't heard of them. Did they replace the former government?"

"There is no 'former' government. It is the same, the legitimate government of the People's Republic."

"Please enlighten me. I'd understood the government had fled. I know the president's resigned."

"Mr. President has not fled. He is still president. Only in Switzerland for treatment."

"I didn't know he was ill. And the minister of security?"

"The minister of justice is also there for treatment."

"They're *both* in Switzerland for treatment?"

"This is correct. And I act for them."

"Um, very good. Well, General, as you know, the United Nations has tasked us to carry out relief operations. I've been assigned the force-protection mission. That means I work with you, badge to badge, to reduce any friction. We help you, you help us."

"I am very glad to hear this," Assad said deadpan. "What is it I do to help?"

She looked at Peyster again but got no clues this time either. Her throat itched and she took out her handkerchief. Coughing felt like her esophagus was being sawed open with a dull knife. Assad waited. She drank more juice or whatever it was.

"We have to protect the various relief agencies that'll be arriving. As well as our own medical, construction, and transportation people. First, we'd like your ministry to resume guarding our embassy. Second, we need locals to work with our security teams at the airport. Third, we need three to five SDI agents to help Mr. Erculiano work the antidrug and antiterror missions."

Assad was nodding, but wasn't making any notes. She decided he wouldn't appreciate having a woman point this out. It was tricky, trying to motivate local officials to cooperate when you had no real leverage. She'd gotten interview training in basic school, but liaison took skills of a higher order. She coughed, wincing again. "Finally, we need to sit down with your customs people, and discuss importation of weapons. We intercepted a shipment coming in from Iran a few days before—I mean, before the president left. For treatment."

"We also need to know how we can help him," Peyster put in.

Assad turned to him at once. "We need transport. Fuel. Food, and arms. How soon can you provide?"

But Peyster sat back smiling, fingers tented, leaving her to answer. "We can provide some food. And trucks. Arms . . . how would we know those who receive them can be trusted? There's a rebel movement—"

"Whatever comes to us will not go to the southerners, who are the rebels and looters. We have ways of identifying those we trust."

She frowned; she'd heard that before. Oh, yes. The little man who'd welcomed them. A local proverb? "By the way, how is Mr. Bahdoon? I trust he's well?"

One of the guards stirred. Did Assad glance at him? "Bahdoon we have not seen since the troubles. I'm sorry."

"Was Mr. Bahdoon a southerner?" She didn't use tribal names, since Assad hadn't, but Nuura had explained the "rebellion" more clearly than the CIA and State backgrounding.

Like most states in Africa, Ashaara's boundaries had been burned like a branding iron over a teem of mutually antagonistic tribes and ethnicities. Here that meant Cushitic-speaking Issas, Issaqs, Gadabursi, and Danakils. There were Bantus in the south and Ethiopian-dialect Tawahedo Christians in the west, and of course the Indians, into shopkeeping and import-export. Gilhirs from the high desert. The "northerners" were Diniyues, Jazirs, and the president's clan, the Xaashas, who'd dominated after the collapse of the Morgue.

She wondered how his world looked through Assad's dark, weary eyes. Did he really represent a rump government? Or even that? She said cautiously, "We'll have to discuss that in depth. Can you provide security to our embassy?"

"I will take that request to the Council."

"All right, and one final question. We saw armed men in the streets on the way here. Were they yours?"

He gave her the same smile she'd noted each time he'd lied. "Yes. They are reporting to the Governing Council."

"There are no other clan militias?"

" 'Other' militias?"

"I mean, besides your forces."

"The legitimate security forces of this country."

"That's what I meant."

Assad called, and the server came out again. Aisha had left a little in the heel of the glass, the custom in the Gulf to show she couldn't possibly finish it. The woman held out the bottle; Aisha wobbled her glass between thumb and index. That seemed to get the message across.

"There are renegade elements," the general admitted. "Responsible for the looting. They will be justified."

"Brought to justice?"

"That is what I said."

She decided to go in over the horns and see how the bull reacted. "General, we intend to put forward a policy of arms for food."

"Arms for food?" The phrase amused him. "An old concept in Ashaara. We use our arms to get our food."

"Not exactly. We'll supply food contingent on disarming the militias."

"Contingent?"

Peyster spoke a word she didn't catch. Assad said, to her, "Rebels and criminals, no problem. But government forces will not disarm."

“I see. Well. How would we contact these rebels? And the other—I mean, the clan militias? We’ll need to talk to them.”

“We will set that up. You will go through us.” Assad put his hands on the table and rose. The three Americans rose too. Assad bowed and left.

His qat-chewing bodyguards stayed. They watched the contractors and the contractors watched them as Aisha, musing on what had just passed, made her way down the steps toward the still-idling convoy. Anticipating, as she walked through the dense hot dusty morning, the air-conditioning there, once she was sealed inside.

AC would be nice, Dan thought. The dry stinking dust was reigniting his headache. He massaged his brow as the trucks ground toward the port area. Past its cranes rose the Old City, its hill still surrounded by remnants of the Portuguese-era wall.

He was riding in a five-ton dropside from the 100th Light-Medium Truck Company. Four more of the big 6×6s rumbled behind. One peeled off as they passed the exit for the park, loaded to twice the height of a man with palleted Meals, Ready to Eat. Some locals might find themselves eating pork with rice, but as he understood Islam, dietary restrictions could be set aside if you were starving. Others were stacked with lumber, welding equipment, prefab ramps, electric controllers, generators, coils of shining wire. They made a wrong turn, backed and maneuvered. Then came sandbagged revetments, alert faces under helmets. A glance at his ID, and he was through.

He picked up a sunshine yellow hard hat from a box inside the gate. The clatter and buzz of compressors and generators crowded the basin. A tug lay near the wreck by the jetty, hoses snaking over its side, as a landing craft warped beneath one of the cranes. Forklifts maneuvered between working parties. Cables and compressor hoses snaked across heatshimmering concrete.

A heavyset man with thinning reddish blond hair and

sagging, sunburned cheeks stood with hands on hips, directing a truck-mounted boom at full extension. It lifted rusty sections off the crane as cutters carved it apart with crackling arcs. His cheek bulged but it wasn't qat. He wore a cardinal scarlet hard hat and old-style green fatigues unbloused over Red Wing work boots. A portable radio, a Leatherman, and a canteen were clipped to his belt. His blue eyes photographed Dan as he came up.

"The harbormaster?"

"Parker Buntine." He stripped off a work glove to shake hands. Something had been burned off his nose and cheeks, leaving pink raw skin. "Lenson, right? Any questions before I tell you everything we need?"

"Looks like everybody's busy. When can you take the first ship?"

"Five days. Got to remove all this fucking debris, and I want to triple the staging area." Buntine swung and shouted, "No, you fucking moron! In the truck! *The truck!*" He swung back. "Weld up these fences and put concertina on top. These cranes are shit, faster to replace than repair. Them monkeys stole every fucking piece of electrical gear, every switch box, every motor. What kind of baboons would do that?"

"I guess, people who didn't think it made any difference to their lives."

"Absolute bullshit, Commander. People who do this aren't people, they're fucking animals. And I'm not letting 'em back through those gates."

Dan blinked. He didn't know what Buntine was: army warrant, civilian, contractor. But whatever he was, he'd have to get along with the locals. "We're going to need labor, Parker. And this *is* their country."

"I done this before, Commander. Da Nang, Haiti, Mogadishu. Let 'em in the gate, right away, your losses go to forty percent."

"Not *forty*—"

"You take in a hundred thousand tons, sixty thou gets on the road. You'll lose another half there. Everybody'll have his fucking hand out. Then they'll start fighting over it. I already had some big son of a bitch looked like a white-faced possum here trying to shake me down."

"Who?"

"Some asshole with a bunch of hired guns. Had the marines escort him out. Big black bastard, but his face white as mine. Give you the willies. . . . Keep the fucking skinnies out, that's my two cents."

"Parker, we've got a big job here. Nav aids, runways, power, water—the regime didn't spend a cent on infrastructure for ten years." Dan wondered what he was trying to say, then located it. "And there's *no jobs.* If we put people to work, we start money circulating. If the economy starts up, they can afford to import food. And even if we have losses en route, the aid's still getting to hungry people."

"So what. Just be twice as many of 'em, ten years from now."

"What's that?"

"Nothin', never mind. . . . Five days, that's what you wanted to know." Buntine scratched at a raw place on his nose, then jerked his hand away and spat and bawled at the men on the crane, "*No,* you fucking limpdicks! Who the fuck told you to splice? Everything out of the runs! Throw that shit in the scrap pile and pull me new wire, *new* wire!"

Next stop was the embassy, for Ahearn's first coordination meeting with the ambassador. He hitched a ride with Buntine, who was invited too, on a Humvee on a twice-daily run, stopping at the logistics headquarters at the airfield, the marine terminal, and the embassy. The gunner stood casually in his seat, leaning on the hatch rim as they crossed the bridge. The Humvee was old, its suspension worn. He barely noticed, deep in the daily sitsum on his notebook. When the gunner tapped his shoulder they were at the bullet-pocked walls of the chancery. He looked at the hole in the guard tower, wondering why it hadn't fallen. Apparently there'd been quite a battle here.

The enormous lobby felt empty. A modernistic chandelier, pale furniture set at wide intervals, an African-style tile floor. An elevator had an OUT OF ORDER sign, so they followed the other attendees up a staircase. One was a flaming redhead in tight jeans, Aussie boots, and a bush shirt, carrying a slung leather tote that looked as if it had traveled. He saw others he knew. McCall, turning heads as she tapped along in black uniform heels. Marines. Contractors in sport shirts and ball caps. A heavyset black woman in an embroidered dashiki and gold headwrap. He wondered where the other Ashaarans were.

At the door to the conference room two burly men in black battle dress, combat boots, gray jackets, slung rifles, baseball caps, and Oakleys were checking IDs. The caps carried a logo that grabbed his attention. Two more stood down the hallway. He was almost there when the biggest stepped forward, blocking the black woman in front of Dan. "You, stop!" he shouted. "Go back."

"I'm a presenter. I'm—"

She reached into her purse, and the guard shouted, "Gun!"

The team down the hall reacted immediately, one taking a knee and aiming, the other covering another door up the hall. Where the principals were meeting, Dan guessed. The others in line backed away. One stumbled, nearly falling down the steps but saving himself on the banister.

When Dan looked back they had the woman's arm behind her back and her cheek pressed to the wall as they patted her down, feeling around her waist, up her chest. Her eyes met Dan's. She didn't struggle, but a deeper hue suffused her chocolate skin.

"She's clean. Except for the gun."

"*Let me go.* Check the purse. My badge is in there."

Reluctantly, the guard searched the handbag. Came up with a black case. "What kind of badge is this?"

"NCIS. My photo ID's in there too."

"What's the trouble?" said a young white man in suit jacket, white turtleneck, and a gold chain from disco days. "That's my boss you got there. The NCIS agent in charge."

"It's all right, Paul," the woman said.

The guards looked at each other, and unhanded her. "Sorry, ma'am," one said. "Saw the pistol, had to check you out."

"It started before that." She sounded furious. "Just don't think that every—never mind. Never mind," and she smoothed her blouse, face still thunderous, and swept into the room beyond.

When it was his turn Dan said to the guard, "You were too rough with her."

"People die when we're polite, Commander."

"When did GrayWolf get in country?"

He didn't bother to answer.

Dan remembered the hills of western Virginia. Ranges, bunkers, barracks, training compounds with green steel-roofed shooting houses. Jet strips, helo pads, tank firing ranges miles long, and entire mock villages through which troops maneuvered to the crackle of small arms. Acres of concrete prefabs surrounded by new concertina, cornered by guard towers.

GrayWolf was a burgeoning empire. Torgild Schrade had been two classes ahead of him at the Naval Academy, so they hadn't had much contact there. But at their last meeting he'd offered Dan a job, even hinted at a vice presidency. "What are you people doing here?" he asked the guard again, not moving on.

"State Department contract. See Mr. Peyster, any questions . . . Commander Lenson."

That gave him a start—Schrade was known for tracking people of interest, by electronic and other means—before he realized the guard was just reading his name tag.

Inside he found the petty officer in charge and downloaded his slides. The military ran on PowerPoint these days. A laser printer was chuffing out takeaways.

A stir; everyone headed for gray metal chairs. He found himself next to the redhead, whose face was badly blistered. "Attention on deck," someone bellowed. The military folks stiffened; the civilians looked blank.

"Stand at ease," Ahearn said, ushering a white-haired man ahead of him who didn't look at all like the child star Dan remembered. The general and the ambassador took seats in front with advisers and staffers. Dan could have sat there but preferred the back. A handsome young marine took the stage as lights dimmed and the opening slide came up. OPERATION COLLATERAL GRATITUDE. BRINGING FOOD AND SECURITY TO ASHAARA. The briefer gave a quick overview of ops to date and the location and status of forces in-country and on the Time-Phased Force and Deployment List for arrival. He stepped down after introducing the next briefer, on internal security.

To Dan's surprise it was the black woman in the colorful dress. "The national police are disbanded," she began. "The closest entity to a government seems to be a Governing Council that claims to exercise sovereignty, but does it? Your guess is as good as mine. We've met with a group that calls itself the national police, headed by a 'general' who was a major before his bosses flew the coop. But it may actually be nothing more than a Dalangani clan militia.

"The other clans seem quiescent, but may be arming. Case in point: the shipload of weapons *Shamal* intercepted last month. So far animosities between the sects are muted, but this may be only a narrow window. We'll continue to broaden our circle of contacts, but my recommendation is to keep the Council at arm's length until a more representative group can be formed. Since they maintain they're the legitimate police, we may have to begin our disarmament program with another clan." She quickly covered the drug and weapon situation, then stepped down.

Before the next briefer could begin a rugged-looking Englishman in civilian clothes stood. "Howard Quarles, Save the Children. In-country six years. I agree Ashaara needs help. But are troops and occupation forces the way to do it?"

"That's beyond the scope of—"

"I'm interested in the gentleman's insights," Ahearn said, turning in his chair. "Can we meet after this brief, Mr. Quarles?"

The red-haired woman beside Dan raised her hand. "Dr. Gráinne O'Shea, International Hydrological Programme. Your efforts seem confined to the population hubs. But the real suffering's in the villages and mountains, and the nomads of the Quartier Vide."

"Right now we have to improve the transportation network, in order to handle shipments on the scale necessary to save more lives. But I'd like to sit down with you too, Dr. O'Shea. Any other representatives from local NGOs present?"

A nervous-sounding agricultural rep asked what the long-term intent was. Were they going to feed these people forever? "The ag sector has to be stimulated. There have to be markets, fertilizers. Above all, water. This country could be self-sufficient in grains, and the southwest was once a major citrus producer. The premium coffee market's taking off. Ethiopia's cashing in with Yegarcheff. That grows here too. There's another crop, teff, a gluten-free grain—"

"Well, that may be premature," the general said, sounding wary now, as if he'd let a cat out of a bag he should've kept laced. "I agree, we need to kick-start agriculture. But let's resume the briefing. I especially want to hear how our port reconstruction's going."

As a bluff-looking American spoke about cranes and wiring, Gráinne tried not to touch her sunburned face. Then she fell asleep. She woke with a start, her head on a tall naval officer's shoulder. "Sorry," she muttered, brushing drool off his shirt.

"Not a problem, Doctor." He plucked a hair off and dropped it to the floor. She looked away, cheeks prickling as blood rushed to burnt tender skin. His smell lingered. Exhaust and male sweat. Not a bad smell. She'd obviously been celibate too long.

The general closed the briefing with a forceful recap of his priorities and the necessity to get food and medical care out posthaste. She followed him and the others who'd been asked to remain into a smaller room next door. The embassy library, perhaps; it was lined with bookshelves, with terminals along one wall. The drapes were closed, all the lights on. He pointed at her, then at two chairs. "Tell me what I need to do first, Doctor. Have you been in touch with our medical people? We could use your experience with local diseases—"

"I'm not a medical doctor, General. I'm a hydrologist."

"Well, that can be useful, in a drought."

For a moment she was tempted to tell him. But she couldn't. He was military. Not just military, *American* military. He seemed well-disposed, if a bit simple, but she couldn't trust him, nor the predatory companies that would prowl in the wake of the invasion. If there was water beneath the sand, it belonged to the people of Ashaara, not multinational corporations.

But first, she had to prove it was there.

"Irish?" said Ahearn. She nodded. "Your face. What happened?"

"Bandits stole my car and shot my assistant at a roadblock."

"Why?"

"He was the wrong clan. I had to walk out. Cross-country."

"A survivor." Ahearn nodded approvingly. "Okay, tell me what I need to do."

"No doubt you have a scheme—"

"I'd like to hear your thoughts. See what we've missed."

"Set up stations in the backcountry. Supply them by air if you have to, but begin collecting the population. They'll need days to gather, but word will spread. By the time you're ready to feed them, they'll be there."

"And?"

She disciplined her voice. "The Quartier Vide's the most arid district. Even in good times the nomads walk twenty, thirty miles for water. Do you have any well-drilling teams?"

"Absolutely."

He was watching her, but what could he see? Not what she was thinking. She compressed burned, itching lips. "If we're gathering people into feeding camps, we'll need a supply of clean water. I can locate some—subsurface water deposits. I don't know how much."

He didn't seem suspicious. He opened a map and they discussed where to place feeding camps. She was able to help with the north, but didn't know the rest of the country. "Ask Quarles, and the other NGOs. Also, there was a Dr. Antwone Isdheeb at the Ministry of Interior Resources. If you could locate him, he'd be a wealth of information."

Ahearn made a note, gestured to an officer. "Find this man. Bring him in." He turned back to her. "This Hydrological Programme. UN affiliated, right? I've been in touch with New York. They're studying whether it's safe to return. I'm glad you stayed."

"It wasn't voluntary."

"Well. I'll give you a well crew. Just tell them where to drill. Thanks for speaking up, Dr. O'Shea."

She tried to feel guilty for tricking him, but couldn't. The military had more resources than any assistance agency. If she could use them for good, so much the better.

If it was there. As much as she suspected, not just a thin film, a few million gallons. With a drilling team, she could determine how thick the lens was. If it was worth exploiting, or if Nature was just teasing.

Ahearn was rising, shaking her hand. She winced—it was sunburnt too—and only then noticed there were just two fingers in hers. "Best of luck to you, Doctor. Report back on how you do, what you need. And may God bless your efforts and those of us all."

She almost laughed aloud, then stopped. Surely he wasn't serious? His seamed face gave her no hint at all.

12

THE PRESIDENTIAL PALACE

Aisha tried not to react to the smells. Those pressed close had traveled days to get here, many on foot. Even in the best of times, water was scanty. But she was too American not to notice stenches. To not feel intimidated by raised voices, angry gesticulations, the shoving, seething crowd. There were no other women, and frowns were directed her way. But no one protested aloud. She wore a flowered abaya. Her purse was at her feet, with the SIG and a cell programmed with the numbers for reinforcements. It was bread-oven hot in the vast room, with its arched ceiling and Moorish-style pillars. Only empty sockets remained where the air-conditioning units had been. She'd managed to get the broken tile swept up, and found tables for tea, cookies, sliced bread, and fruit.

The clan conference was meeting where the dictator had ruled only weeks before—of itself, a symbol of radical change. A loose confederation of intellectuals and returned exiles calling themselves the Alliance for a Democratic Ashaara had organized it. Beside her in one corner—carefully not occupying the dais—were Erculiano, Peyster, and Nuura. A beefy duo in GrayWolf uniforms scanned the crowd from behind their sunglasses like Secret Service guarding the president. She'd tried to persuade Peyster to leave them behind, or at least have them conceal their weapons. The Ashaarans had all had to check theirs on entering, and having them unarmed and the Americans armed didn't seem like the right signal. But got a flat no.

A short man in a black suit and open-collared Hawaiian shirt bent to a microphone. He said a few hesitant words with absolutely no effect on the babble. His round face glowed with sweat. Glancing at the inkjetted program she'd been handed moments before, Aisha saw this was the just-elected chairman of the ADA, a pediatrician from Rome. He tapped the mike again and heads turned reluctantly, carpets unrolled on the cracked tiles. She noted how as this happened groups drew apart, walkways of empty space appearing as gradually the assemblage sank and settled in a semicircle.

"He says welcome . . . wishes for peace . . . thanks all clans for coming."

"What's that one saying? Tall, with the beard?"

"He asks that there be prayer. To ask Allah for blessing."

Aisha couldn't follow the dialect most Ashaarans used, though she caught a word here and there, but could see the proposal wasn't universally popular. "The chairman asks for quiet. He says, to respect those among us who are not Muslim, there will be no prayer."

The bearded man sat amid a low buzz. Aisha frowned as she blew her nose into one of the paper towels she kept stuffed in her purse. Whatever was lodged in her chest, it hung on. She could barely sleep. Nuura said many white people got ill in Ashaara. Leaving Aisha to wonder if her translator saw *her* as white.

"What's he doing now? Why do they look confused?"

"He's proposing to not sit by clans. They are to mix up."

"Good luck," Peyster muttered. The Americans had folding chairs they'd brought along. "I'm going to check on the guards."

He got up, staying low so as not to attract attention, and left. True to his prediction, there was no mixing. The pediatrician shrugged and began speaking.

Proceedings slogged on. Most of the invitees were graybeards, though there was a sprinkling of middle-aged. Everyone had to have his say, often at cheek-numbing length. Nuura translated, but Aisha found it hard going. They sounded like campfire tales, endless litanies of who had descended from whom, interspersed with fulsome compliments to people she didn't recognize. By noon she'd never been so bored in her life. She and Nuura went into an antechamber for their prayers.

When they came back she noticed the men in suits hadn't prayed, had stayed by the microphone, arguing among themselves in Italian. "Secularists," she murmured to Erculiano.

"Our boys. I guess."

"Where's Assad? Did you see him?"

Peyster, who'd come back, muttered, "Governing Council's boycotting this meeting. These are the 'rebels' the president used to round up and shoot."

She swallowed, remembering the dead women and children she and Paul had seen during Assad's raid. "You mean, the northerners are all boycotting?"

"Not *all*. Some of 'em are here. But I couldn't give you a statistical breakdown. This is the ADA's ball game. We're just here to show our support."

By noon it hit 120 and she was soaking under the folds of cloth. Sweat was running down her legs, pooling in her shoes. At last the men stirred. Nuura said there'd be a recess, then a vote. She wasn't sure on what; the old man who'd proposed it had spoken very low, from the far end of the hall. The men straggled to their feet, headed for the back to relieve themselves or to the tables for tea and cookies. One ancient began expostulating to Aisha, waving at an empty platter. She stared until he noticed Erculiano and a GrayWolf behind her. He shut his mouth and melted away.

"Signora Ar-Rahim." The chairman, the guy in the Hawaiian print and sweat-stained jacket. Up close he looked done in, soaked and trembling. Not a confidence inspirer, she thought as she shook limp fingers. "I am Dr. Zumali Dahoud Dobleh. Very impressive, is it not? Issaqs, Issas, Gadabursi, Danakils. Bantus and Gilhirs. Christians and Hindus sitting down together. Even some Jazirs. The first step toward reinvigorating the national idea."

"And all so eloquent. I've learned so much about Ashaaran history."

He bowed as Peyster joined them. "Mr. Peyster. I am so glad you did not bring the military. That would send entirely the wrong message. Signora, we shall reconvene in committees. Will you do me the great favor of addressing our security committee?"

"Me?"

"You are the ranking American police agent. Not correct?"

"Federal agent. But—yes, I suppose you're right."

"We have a serious problem. You know General Assad." She nodded. "He and the Governing Council do not recognize these deliberations. They maintain sovereign continuity. Unfortunately he also controls what remains of the security forces."

"Isn't Assad a Xaasha? The former president's clan?"

"He is. There is much anger, but we would have seated them. If they will not join the provisional government, they'll be left out. Will you speak? Advise on how to reestablish the police? It would very much help us."

"I'd need to freshen up first. And, should I speak Arabic? Will they understand me?"

"Arabic would be good. Yes, you may speak Arabic."

Peyster made as if to say something, but she didn't look at him. "But I can't make any promises on behalf of the U.S. Make that plain before I speak. This will just be my personal advice on reestablishing a national force."

She looked at him now, and Peyster smiled back.

The committee met in the shade of a wing of the palace, a beaten open area that might once have been a garden. It was cooler in the wind, though now dust was a problem. Erculiano sat to her right; one GrayWolf stood a long pace to her left. She alternately shivered and panted. Was she running a fever? She gripped fistfuls of abaya before a pond of blank faces under a dead acacia. Intellectuals, returned exiles, but mainly, the fiercely traditional heads of age-old clans. Men who'd scorn to listen to a woman, but who'd accepted the challenge of rebuilding their society. Mutually distrustful, but sitting down together, if only to make sure they didn't get left out of the aid package.

The only jarring note was the steadily chomping jaws. At

least half were chewing qat. She hoped it didn't completely jam their mental processes.

How could she make them listen? Motivate them to work together? And what should she tell them to do?

"Assalaamu aleikum, shuyukh," she began, and waited for the ritual response. Enjoying their surprise as she continued, keeping her formal, *fusha* Arabic slow not just for herself but for them too. When she was uncertain, she used a formal circumlocution. The language worked that way, like Japanese. What you heard was a product of the listener's mind, as well as that of the speaker.

"'Allah, *azza wa jal*—mighty and majestic is He—has revealed to me that you should adopt humility, so no man oppresses another.' These are the golden words of the Prophet, peace be upon him, as given in the Riyadh as-Saaliheen.

"Amma baad." Dust spun up in a whirling wind. She coughed, and the dead leaves of the dead tree rattled above her. "These are the basis of the law. Not all here are Muslim, but all believe in law. Without law there is no civilization, no safety, no trade, no family, and no food.

"You have accepted the responsibility of caring for your nation, that it flourishes like the well-watered date palm. You have pledged to serve your families, clans, and all Ashaarans. A difficult road to caravan upon . . . but the right road. I praise you, and bow before you as your servant."

Narrowed gazes. But here and there, a nod. As if to say, *Speak on.*

"The president made an unjust law, and the police enforced it unjustly. Thus came double injustice. Now you will make just laws. But to enforce a just law requires just policemen.

"My name is Aisha Ar-Rahim and I am from New York City. I work for the United States, as what you would call a member of the national police.

"Dr. Dobleh asked me to speak today about a national police force. Some of you may doubt such a force is necessary, since you've suffered under the SDI. But the looting and killing since the government fled should convince you police must exist. It's up to you whether they'll act for the nation, or for only one clan."

Her lungs hurt. But they were listening. Trying not to cough, she went on.

"Ashaara's made up of citizens from many clans. My country is too. Perhaps you desire a law that favors your clan. But you have seen how a law that favored the northerners did not protect the northerners. It caused a rebellion, and they lost their power.

"A law that *favors* your clan will not *protect* it. All clans must be protected for any to be protected. This we eventually came to understand in my country, where there are many kinds of people, many religions."

Out of the corner of her eye she'd noticed Erculiano fidgeting. He rose. Hissed: "What are you telling them?"

"S'okay, Paul. Sit down."

"What language is that? What're you saying?"

She gestured him down, but he didn't sit. Only stood, arms folded, watching her.

"What does establishing just law require? Each one must advocate for all Ashaarans, not just of his family, clan, or region. This will require discipline: to keep each other in check if certain members lose sight of peace, security, and justice. And when they do so, instead of seeing this as confrontation, see it as honor—that it is noble to put your country above your own interests."

She glanced back at her assistant, but he wasn't there. She looked behind her, but he was gone. The door to the palace stood open. She coughed. She felt light-headed, her mouth dry.

"I suggest you name two members from each major clan to form a police committee. I recommend it be headed by a member of the ADA, one as neutral as possible in terms of clan alliance; perhaps a distinguished elder."

When she took a breath and looked again Erculiano was back, Peyster with him. "I'm instructing them on how to form a police committee," she asided. The RSO nodded slightly.

She sketched out what they should discuss at their first meeting. Identify mutual interests and common threats. Agree on which laws to enforce and what body would determine punishment. Determine their relationship to whatever representative body emerged.

"Then you must rebuild the force, establishing standards, regulations, and training. You must build confidence within their ranks, and identify and promote men—and yes, perhaps even a few women—as leaders. There's much to do, and it must be done soon.

"America will help, other countries too, but you must do this yourself. *You* are responsible for Ashaara's future.

"Remember above all the golden words of the Prophet, peace be upon him. 'Even as the fingers of the two hands are equal, so are human beings equal to one another. No one has any right, nor any preference to claim over another. You are brothers.' Thank you and *ma salama.*"

She bowed, feeling not only their eyes on her, but also the security officer's. She wasn't sure how much Arabic he had, or how quoting Qu'ran would go down with State, if they were backing the seculars.

In lilting English, the first question, from an Indian in a rumpled suit. "What about Assad's militia? They control the Italian Quarter. They are recruiting from clans that supported the old president. What will you do about them?"

She glanced at Peyster, but his expression hadn't changed. "Well, that will be decided above my level. However, I have spoken with General Assad. There may be ways to persuade him to cooperate. Before you assume he and the Governing Council are your enemies, why not formally invite them to join the ADA? A united government would make it much easier to provide significant aid, training, and equipment. To help all the clans survive this unseasonable drought and famine."

An old man hoisted one hand slowly as if it were growing.

She wasn't sure, but he might've been the one who'd scolded her for letting the cookies run short. In his other hand he held a bottle of water. She desired it intensely. "Speak, O Sheikh," she forced herself to say.

He did, at length, quoting poetry in an ancient dialect of which she could catch only a word here and there, like "camel" and "sword." Stopping him, once she'd given leave to speak, would be the worst possible discourtesy. The others shifted and scratched, but no one interrupted. At last the graybeard said gravely, "So it is I ask you: what is the first and most difficult thing we must do, to help you Americans feed and heal our suffering people?"

"Thank you for your insight, O Sheikh. And for your wise question. I will answer, though some will not like my words. The first thing and the hardest you must do is give up your weapons."

She heard the collective intake of breath. Several stood, and were pulled down by those around them. Even Erculiano looked at her sharply, and she was pretty sure he wasn't following this conversation. She went on, "I know this was the policy of the SDI: that tribes should not have their own weapons. And that many among you—not all—have taken weapons from the police stations and from the army, after it"—she couldn't come up with a word for "dissolve"—"went home. I understand your desire to defend yourselves. But those who distribute food will not give it to any who come armed."

The old one said, "Truly, our young men will dislike this. Already they want to make raids, to punish those who have oppressed us."

"Wise heads must temper burning youth. You must all realize, that if anyone"—she wanted to say "employs violence," but had to settle for—"unsheathes the sword, it will make it harder to distribute food. And harder to persuade other countries to send it."

Another oldster stroked his beard, looking cunning. "Is not a sword, bread? They will say: the American policewoman asks us to give up our weapons. Yet, the Americans come with tanks and helicopters. And she comes surrounded by men with weapons."

She glared at the guard. He worked his shoulders under the bulky ballistic vest, fingering his rifle as he became the focus of many eyes. "Go away," she told him. "They want you to go. And so do I."

"I'm assigned to—"

"Go away!"

He took one step back, then another. She kept glaring, and he retreated, to the palace, anyway. It'd have to do.

When she turned back many more hands were up. But this wasn't her meeting. The longer she stayed up here, the less time they'd have to horse-trade and hammer out their own leadership, their own agenda.

The wind gusted again, stinging her eyes. The dead branches rattled. "I thank you, noble *shuyukh*, for hearing me. Embrace wisdom. *Fi amanallah*." She lowered her head and walked away, scuffing the powdery dust. When she motioned Erculiano to follow, Peyster's gaze trailed her like the eyes of a painting, tracking her wherever she went.

13

IN THE *MAGAADA*

She's never seen a city before. Never seen *anything* so incredible. Lying in the back of the truck with eight other women, atop the huge bundles of leaves, sticks, and twigs bound with twisted grass that paid their passage, Zeynaab looks up amazed.

At towering houses, strange poles above the roads which one woman says *give light at night*. A bewildering crisscross of black strings from house to house that seem to have no function but to give birds a place to perch. Packs of honking, dangerous-looking cars. Men by the road vending qat, doughnuts, bread, even smoking meat braziers.

Lying wrapped in rags and blankets on top of the fascines, she gazes up in awe. At last, she has reached the *magaada.*

When she came down from the mountain she hadn't been this scared. She'd just walked, not even seeing anyone else. And like a ghost they'd let her pass, this strange girl wrapped in a bundle of motley garments, bent as if carrying pain itself in her abdomen.

The men who burned Saint Shenouda hadn't known about the money earned over many years selling cheese and skins and blessed shawls woven by nuns. But one of the girls had seen, years before. When the men left, Zeynaab had gone to the Sister Abbess's room and found the brass box under the bare floorboards, just as it had been whispered for so long. A rattle of money, many kinds, coins and bills and sheafs of old paper that smelled of hands long dead. She'd wrapped it and then herself in cloth, down where she bled, and set out.

As she'd staggered downward the heat had increased, the fogs vanished. This wasn't the world of the mountain. She remembered the desert, the heat, the dogs. She asked the way back to her village, but no one knew it. She only knew of one other place. "Go to the *magaada*, find *Abti* Jama," her mother had said. When she asked the way to the city, people pointed toward the new sun.

She trudged from village to village. Many women walked the road, some going east, others west, some with no destination. Each picked up sticks as she walked, and in the evenings they gathered in some sheltered place and built their fire. One by one each brought forth something for the pot: a handful of rice, a dried carrot, a blackened onion, a shred of meat no one asked the source of. They had no weapons, only sticks, but no man would dare attack twenty women. By the firelight they spoke of the famine and the fall of the government. Of the *khawayat*, the foreigners, who'd come bringing who knew what new curse to the land.

She walked for many days. Gradually the bleeding stopped. Then one day a military truck came down the road. She was frightened as the women parted to let it rumble through. But nothing bad happened, and a man shouted down to them where to turn off to be fed.

The distribution station was a field surrounded by long tin-roofed sheds. It had been some kind of machine station for the government. Now the sheds were empty and lines of people stood with buckets and bags. She joined a line. A man came down it with an ink pad, staining their thumbs red.

She stood for hours under the beating sun. Finally she was almost to where grain was being ladled out when another man walked the line asking what village they were from. He didn't ask men, just the women. When he got to her she began to explain, but he said angrily, "Where? Where? This isn't your village's day. You don't belong in this line. Go away."

"I've been on the road for days. I'm going to the city, to find my uncle."

"We don't care. There's only a little, enough for this village. Go back where you came from."

"Out of the line, whore. Out, beggar!" women behind her screamed. Hands thrust her out, tore her clothes. She almost offered money, but in a mob like this it would all be stolen. She stood a few paces off with the other rejected women, widows, mostly. After sobbing and wailing for a time they wandered off to squat and beg, but those who had grain hurried by with eyes averted. She tried another line and was forced out again.

She plodded back to the highway. Men passed her leading donkeys burdened with swollen bags. One was the man who'd made her leave the line. She trudged behind his donkey, watching food trickle out of the corner of a bag, a grain at a time. When he wasn't looking she stuck her little finger into the hole and yanked, letting it pour out, some into her cupped hands, the rest into the trodden dirt.

She watched it drain away as she crunched the dry grains. The nuns would have called this sin. But when he looked away again she tore another bag. The donkey's eye rolled back. For a moment she thought it would kick, but it seemed to realize what she was doing and agree. It snorted and kept on.

That night when the women gathered no one had anything to contribute. Those with blankets or rugs kept them to themselves. She'd lain with the hunger big in her belly, shivering, until she fell asleep.

The next day she met the fuelwood man.

Now she holds the side of the truck as it turns, turns again, and finally wheezes to a stop. The back thumps down and there's a whole street of people—children, women, men—more than lived in her whole village, the whole monastery, more than she could dream of counting. Her gaze darts from face to face, bewildered. And it's only one street out of hundreds. The hubbub dizzies her head.

The fuelwood man has the close-set eyes and furrowed upper lip of a Bantu. She knows to hate Bantu. But he called to her as she was walking and asked where she was going. When she said the city, he asked if she wanted to earn her way.

Again she thought of the money, and again sealed her mouth. It took four days to assemble the fascine of dried leaves and twigs and bark, gleaning far off the road into the hills. At night she shivered and listened to hyenas bark. But at last she had enough, a great heavy bale bound with grass rope she twisted herself, and waited at the roadside for the rattling truck trailing a cloud of dust like a stampede of cows. I'll pay you eighty cents, he told her. Or give you a ride to the city.

Now he helps them down, these women. He steadies an old one until she can lean on her stick. How had she carried her bundle? But when he holds out his hand to Zeynaab his expression changes. "Little sister. I'm glad you came along. Do you need a place to sleep tonight?"

She doesn't answer and he leans in and says in his broken speech things she's never heard before, shameful things that might once have interested her. But she knows now what he suggests means pain and blood. She places her stick on his bare foot and leans. He hollers and steps back.

She wanders the streets, at first asking for "*Abti* Jama," but the city people stare and laugh, as if she's got a demon. "Where's he live, this *abti* of yours?" one asks, and she doesn't know how to answer. Her mother said, but she can't remember. Must she sleep in a stinking alley tonight, with dogs? She's so hungry she has to stop every few steps and rest against a wall.

At last she's halted by the sizzle and smell of a stall that sells *fagasso*, sweet fried doughnuts. A light-skinned little man in a turban's making them, fingers quick over hot metal as the grease-smoke rises. She trembles, watching. Finally she goes into an alley and fumbles in her clothes.

When she drops one of the coins from the mountain in his tray his eyes widen. "Where did you get this?" he says, covering it with a hand. When he lifts his palm it's magic, the yellow coin's disappeared.

"What do you mean?"

"I mean, this is very old money. It's not good anymore. You owe me more."

"If it's not good, why do you want more?" she says. She's no city woman but she knows when she's being cheated. She snatches dough from where it hangs and crams it into her mouth, backing away as he begins to shout. Then turns and runs, runs, until she's lost in narrow, dark lanes.

She comes out panting, stomach twisting around fear and the raw dough, into a wide court filled with white and green tents, people, more people, and stall after stall of old things. Broken furniture, broken lamps, automobile parts, rusty bicycles, barrows of old broken Italian guns. Metal boxes a man says would make the air cold even when it is hot, if they worked.

"What is this place?" she asks a woman, who smiles as if she's very stupid.

"Why, this is the Suuqa Haqaaraba. Where one buys that which is broken."

She stops dead. Her hand covers her mouth.

That's what her mother said. Find *Abti* Jama. At the Suuqa Haqaaraba.

* * *

Yet even knowing this, it's hard to speak to strangers. There were none in her village, only family. None on the mountain, only sisters and brothers. She must harden her heart, as she did when she wasted the grain, drove the sharpened stick into the Bantu's foot, stole the dough and ran. They laugh at her, or turn away. But finally one grunts, "There was a Jama who sold clocks by the Chinese Gate. If that's who you mean, go ask there."

By the end of the day she knows her *abti*'s dead. She also knows a young man was asking for him too, a young man new to the city. He's a disciple of Sheikh Nassir, and his name is Ghedi.

14

THE RED SEA

Dan stepped back, snagging his scalp on a circuit box as the little harbor pilot, trailed by the captain, orbited like a dark comet from the port side of the pilothouse out to the starboard wing, then back. The sun was incandescent, the sky a milky smear, the wind light, barometer steady. Only one other vessel was visible, a dhow far off to the east.

Another blazing morning in the Red Sea. MV *Kirzen* was registered in the Grenadines, owned by a Kenyan company, manned by Sri Lankans. He'd boarded to evaluate the pilot. The guy had presented a pasteboard card printed in Italian and dated 1972. He never looked at the GPS, or even the radar. Just glared into the water as it passed, brow furrowed, and made angular comparisons with forefinger and thumb as the sunblasted silhouette of Jazirat Shâkir passed down the starboard side. Then snapped orders, jerking elbows and hunching shoulder blades like a chicken dreading the ax.

At sea, free of the complexities and minutiae of shore . . .

where all Dan had to do was make sure three thousand tons of steel, diesel fuel, rice, beans, and palm oil made it through the least-charted, worst-marked channel on the Red Sea.

Piece of cake.

He eased out a breath as a buoy passed down the side, fresh paint gleaming in the sun. The bow swung to port. Checked the fathometer, and his tension returned. Two meters under the keel. Ashaara was tight, shallow, shoal-fretted, but the only deepwater port in the country. Airlift made the news, but bulk food had to come by ship. He and Parker Buntine had buoyed from a landing craft, arguing over turn points, channel widths, and how the bottom had changed since a Royal Navy survey in 1943. The South Channel was deepest, but heavily silted after decades of neglect; they'd have to dredge to bring in anything larger.

The engine whumped. The coast slid by. A distant horn whonked, reverberating across miles of picric-hazed chop. *Kirzen*'s horn droned in stentorian answer. He lifted binoculars. Past the dunes the sun flashed bronze and scarlet from the windows of the chancery. Below it huddled abandoned beach houses. Ahead stretched a tumbled stone jetty, past which lay their destination.

Ashaara was a gravely crippled state, but not yet a failed one.

This might be the most significant mission he'd ever undertaken.

Half an hour later the first line went over. He leaned from the wing to sweep his gaze the length of the terminal. Sunken wrecks had been cleared, old cranes torched apart and trucked off, markings repainted, cracked concrete patched. *Kirzen* snugged her hull against new rubber Yokohama fenders. Gulls shrieked and wheeled. The Sri Lankans stared at contract line handlers, clothed in new dungarees and hard hats emblazoned with Falcon Football decals, Buntine's favorite team.

There was the harbormaster: boots braced wide, cheeks

scorched scarlet, mouth open as he bellowed commands and imprecations alternately at the hustling line handlers and into the radio he carried like a loaded pistol. The stern line went over and was manhandled to a bollard. Dan checked the wind. It hadn't shifted. He complimented the skipper, then looked for the pilot.

The Ashaaran was necking an icy-looking bottle of lemon pop, but lowered it as Dan came alongside. "America happy?"

"*Molto bene, signore.* But in case of bad visibility, you need to learn to read your electronic navigation."

The man shrugged. "Bad weather, do not go into South Channel. Anchor out and wait." A pale palm. "Bonus?"

Dan gave him a twenty-dollar bill. It all helped stimulate the economy. If they got that restarted, and the rains came, the country might recover. Buntine was right, the outside world couldn't feed them forever.

But at least they could for now. He stopped in the grimy passageway, hot and smoky as a burning building, and rubbed his face. Tired as he was, he couldn't help smiling.

The mood on the apron was "party." Behind fluttering yellow plastic DO NOT CROSS barriers waited factotums of the Relief Committee, one of the ad hoc bodies the exiles had stapled together. Here and there stood the marines and soldiers who'd cleared the basin and put the terminal back in shape. Generators hammered. Video lenses sparkled. A hand-painted banner rippled between brand-new light standards: WELCOME FIRST WORLD FOOD AID SHIP TO DOCK AT ASHAARA, with translations beneath in French, Italian, and Ashaari script.

A beeping of heavy equipment, and a boom truck fitted a brow into place. Dan followed the pilot and a World Food Aid representative onto the diesel-smelling concrete as a huge new Japanese-donated crane rumbled into position. Guided by a marine wielding batons, a truck rolled into position beneath a huge square steel funnel framed by bright green I-beams. Buntine screamed into the radio. The yellow tape fluttered down as the crowd broke across the apron.

Photographers and video crews fanned out like machine gunners seeking enfilade.

It took a good deal longer than the waiting dignitaries must have expected, but at last a clamshell dipped into the hold, deliberated, then rose again, trailing a veil of smoky chaff. It swung through the bright air, hesitated again, then descended.

A rattling roar resounded as a pale cascade plunged into the truck, briefly visible between funnel and bed. The wind brought the smell of starchy rice. The Ashaarans cheered, the younger ones breaking into a high-stepping dance. Dan shook hands with Buntine, who reluctantly extended a palm the size and texture of a boot sole. "How'd that fucking skinny pilot do?" the harbormaster grunted. "D'jou have to take the conn?"

"He's old-school. Never looked at the radar. Good work, Parker. And just in time."

"Damn slow way to offload."

"Better than labor gangs and burlap sacks."

"I want as few skinnies inside my gates as I can run this place with."

"I'd rather see us replaced by locals, Parker. As soon as possible, actually."

"Already had three of those suits over there ask for office jobs. Told 'em we didn't need 'em. We won't need much sweat labor, either, Commander. A couple boys to sweep up, but once we get those vacuators running we can suck the bulk out onto conveyor belts. Load four trucks at once. Cut turn-around to six hours."

Dan didn't like how he dismissed local involvement in what after all was the Ashaarans' terminal, but put it aside for now. Buntine groused that the military 6×6s were low capacity. If he had commercial tractor trailers he could move thirty tons out at a time. Had anyone load-tested the Victory Bridge, the two bridges across the Durmani, the bridges in the Western Mountains? Could the Coast Guard dredge the South Channel? And a higher light on the jetty might keep somebody from bashing into it some night. . . .

Dan entered everything in his PDA, not trusting his memory. Across the apron three marines, part of the security detail, were talking to a TV crew.

Spayer stood bemused as the woman spoke. New Zealand, she'd said. He could barely understand her. He stared at her chest. Attractive brunettes in boots, camo-fashion cargo pants, and vests were thin on the ground. Flanking him, Ready and Fire stood with weapons dangling off assault slings, staring at the same two points of interest like cats at a half-opened tuna can.

"Did you hear me, Sergeant?"

"What's the question? And it's lance corporal, ma'am."

"What d'you enjoy most about being in Ashaara?"

"Uh, having the chance to, uh, help people achieve dignity and freedom."

He watched the disappointment tremor her upper lip like a wind across a flawless pond. She was the most beautiful woman he'd ever seen.

"And that you enjoy least?"

"Not being able to take you out for a beer."

A too-high laugh, a quick turn away. The lens followed her. Then it paused in its swing as she furiously gestured. "And just *who* is *this* wee larrikin?"

Spayer looked down. "Why, our good friend and guide, Nabil."

"Nabil, eh?" Squatting, the reporter smiled into his entranced face. "What're you doing running about with these big chaps?"

"My main men."

"Where'd you find him? He's a love." To the cameraman: "Extreme close-up."

"He's our number five Raven Eight fire team member. Joined the day we hit the beach, hasn't left since." Spayer squatted to the boy's level. Kid smelled a lot better than that first day. Not as great as she did, though. He smiled hopefully but she was motioning to the cameraman, who was aiming at a stiffly-at-attention, saluting Nabil, the green plastic of an MRE peeking out from under his arm. "Position left, wide angle, get that ship in the background. Get the wheat or whatever muck it is coming off. Another close-up. Look at those cheeks! This ankle biter's going to get us airtime."

The crowds lined the streets of the Old City as the six-bys snorted uphill, negotiated a hairpin turn at the remains of the Portuguese fort, and headed north. Dan clung to the running board as above, from the open window, Dr. Zumali Dobleh's round foolish-looking face beamed out, acknowledging the cheers with wide smile and lifted hands. A SAW gunner scanned the crowd; other marines rolled a few yards ahead in a Humvee, rifle barrels tilted skyward.

It was like rolling through Sicily with Patton. Future convoys would avoid these narrow streets, circling the Old City via the autoroute before laboring west or north or south under their precious cargoes. But Dobleh had insisted the first shipment thread through the most heavily populated neighborhoods, showing food was on its way, at the same time associating the ADA with its providers. Maybe he wasn't as dumb as he looked. . . . Smiling faces, waving scarves . . . people were dancing, it was like Christmas and New Year's and beating Army all wrapped together. Women were throwing flowers, they were raining out of the sky. Where did they get *flowers*? He caught one and realized: they were plastic, made of colorful qat bags and wire.

The trucks descended into a saddle, then climbed between half-built, abandoned factories, tractor sheds, dusty dead fields. To either side stretched shoals of trash. Children pelted alongside, feet flashing, shrieking "Pay Day! Pay Day!" They rolled to a halt at the roundabout that led to the Seventeenth Division's former encampment, now rebuilt as a transfer point. After a parting word with Dobleh, Dan swung down into a Humvee. It peeled off and headed west, jolting as the asphalt of the autostrada ended abruptly, returning to rock-studded dirt.

* * *

"Your basic escort mission. Ten-truck convoy. Take two other fire teams. Order of march: Humvee in the lead, one in the middle, a tail end charlie. Make sure everyone sees your flag and you won't have any trouble," the sergeant had told him. "A phrog saw a couple technicals, but the Three Shop says the locals are friendly. No checkpoints observed. Remote possibility of Sudanese raiding across the border. Pansy ass. Milk run." Sure, okay, Spayer'd thought. Not the most challenging tasking, but a chance to see more than the beach, the terminal, and the airfield.

He sat in the lead truck, dipping Copie and trading in-country stories with the driver from the 100th Light-Medium as they clattered over a riverbed that was only mud and scattered mocha pools. Engineers waved them on over a creaking steel bridge that looked like it should've been torn down a long time ago. The driver was another WWF fan, and it turned out they'd both seen the last Tag Team Championship, Spayer on ESPN aboard ship in the Gulf, his new bud actually there, at the New Orleans Arena. Bitching about the Dudleys got them to the roundabout. The driver said they were setting up a big camp near there for skinnies streaming in from the delta. From Eritrea too, the drought was bad there too.

On the way to Darew white flashed ahead in the dust. A pickup, turning off the MSR onto a side trail that climbed parched hills. A technical? "That Assad could be one bad dude," the driver said, as if hearing Spayer's thoughts. "Him and his Governor's Council."

"Who're our skinnies?" He twisted to look back. They wore cutoff jeans, cheap printed T-shirts, and not one item of military issue. They perched on the canvas top as if riding a desert-tan elephant. Thin legs, bare feet like sofa cushions splayed out so that from his angle everything was visible; skivvies optional. The AKs hanging from their necks needed muzzle discipline. He got grins and waves when they saw him looking. He forced a half salute.

"Those are ADs. No idea what clan."

"What's an AD?"

"Fuck if I know, but they're s'posed to be our dudes."

"You figured out the difference?"

"Government used to be northerners. These are southerners. Hooray for Dixie."

Caxi doubted it was that simple, but even if the pickup had turned off, they'd better get tactical. He should call Fire on the intersquad and pull the convoy over. Climb into the lead Humvee and man up the sixty. But he put it off a few minutes, waiting for a better stretch. The road they were on now shook them like a cement mixer on high—you had to clench your jaw or chip a tooth.

A slap on his leg, teeth shining up. "Doin' okay, Big Team?"

"Doin' just great, Little Team." He gave the round stubbly head a quick rub. The kid beamed back another of those Energizer smiles that never failed to make Caxi's day.

After tagging along that first morning the kid had never been more than twenty yards away. He ate with them, tossed the blue foam Nerf football Assist carried stuffed in his battle rattle, and went along on perimeter. He picked up Marine Corps English at a dozen words a day, but faded whenever an O—an officer—got close, joining the gaggle of kids who came to gawk wherever they went. They'd gotten him a boot haircut and a shower. He ate everything and asked for more, and Spayer could swear he'd grown an inch since he'd joined up. The corpsman had treated his eyes, cuts, and diarrhea, though the dragging foot was beyond him. The ragged T-shirt, his only possession when they found him, Ready had soaked in lighter fluid and burned on the end of his bayonet. Nabil slept under Spayer's bunk in the choo at the terminal. Every troop who saw the kid had to get his picture taken with him, and one of the guys at company said he'd put his photo on the company blog.

"Let's have another MRE," the kid said, lying on his belly, feeling under the seat.

"Not now, Little Team. Big Team's gotta stay sharp. Hang loose and enjoy the view, ooh-rah?"

"Ooh-rah," Nabil said, already incisoring open the green

plastic as his eyes darted across a ragged copy of *Maxim* to the road. The pages were open to Angelina Jolie as Lara Croft. Spayer wondered what a ten-year-old Ashaari orphan made of Angelina with nipples erect in a wifebeater T, cunt-crack shorts, and her trademark nine-millimeter Heckler & Kochs. "Ratfuck me the coffee out of that, Little Team," he said, and without taking his eyes off the picture the boy flipped the envelope his way.

The instant crunched between his teeth like sand. The rising wind buffeted the armament carrier ahead nearly off the road. Something big and dark ahead. "What the hell are those?" he asked. The driver shrugged.

Nabil studied them through the glass. Finally he said through a full mouth, "Those are the mountains, Big Team."

When Caxi looked back up the ADs were pointing their weapons at each other, giggling and kickboxing with those big bare feet. He started to yell, then pulled his head back in. If they shot each other, maybe it'd teach 'em a lesson.

Dan had lunch at the airfield. Each time he arrived another steel building had gone up, another line of tents, a new messing facility. Fencing sketch-lined away into the desert, cutting across untended fields. Gunfire snapped from a rifle range as he ate penne pasta with chicken, pine nuts, and tomato sauce, fried squash, and only slightly wilted Caesar salad, watching television with a tableful of contractors, troops, aid workers, and flight crews.

He was discussing the load capacity of Globemasters with a twenty-year-old loadmaster from the Eighth Airlift Squadron when a familiar shape caught his eye on the screen. For a moment he felt disoriented, before he recognized the pale green angles of the new cranes. A truck moved into the picture; a zoom shot centered a Niagara of hulled rice. "Look at that," he said. "We made the news."

The puckish face of a small boy filled the screen, the clamshell of the crane trailing rice behind him. The boy's eyes crinkled. He glanced up at a tall marine and saluted as the table erupted. Dan grinned too. So perfect it was parody.

"The phones are ringing," one of the aid workers said. "Want this cookie? Oatmeal raisin."

"Sure," Dan said.

Outside the heat pressed down as he waited for a scoop loader with a Seabee logo to pass, then wended his way into a wilderness of modulars behind the terminal. Air conditioners whined beneath the rumble of arriving aircraft. Out of nowhere he remembered another airfield, another country, the chill nights of Bosnia. A dark-haired woman who'd called him *droozhe*. Friend.

But she'd died, shot at the order of a man who, last Dan had heard, was still barhopping in Belgrade.

He pushed that back, trying to recapture the morning's elation. He squeegeed his forehead and dragged off his cap as a door closed and cold air icepicked his sinuses. McCall looked up from a notebook from which a blue cable snaked. "LAN's up. Your password and user name's taped on the back of your monitor."

"Good job." He looked over her shoulder at the screen logo of a private company building an optimal routing system for aid deliveries. He'd asked her to validate their model, which it claimed had worked in Nepal. He wasn't enthusiastic about private contractors, but this one, staffed by former aid workers, had ideas like using local haulers from centralized distribution points, so cash went to locals rather than foreign contract movers, and involving the host country's tax officials in food allocation, so people associated paying taxes with getting a benefit.

He logged in and they sat back to back carrying on a sporadic conversation, mainly about the mechanics of routing downstream of the offload points. He checked his various sites and mailboxes, marveling at how many places the virtual Daniel V. Lenson resided. He was at TAG, he was still attached to Contardi's Transformational Task Force, he was getting mail from both CTG 156.4 and CJCS, Task Force Red Sea. The bulk of his traffic, though, carried the subject line COLLATERAL GRATITUDE. Certainly one was less isolated in the Web age than when naval message had been the only link to shore, but he couldn't say his level of global understanding was higher. Most of the time he was so far down in the weeds he had to look up at a centipede's belly.

Her computer chimed. "Mail," she said, clicking the icon while he admired the back of her neck. The Japanese thought the nape peculiarly erotic. He could buy into that.

"It's General Ahearn." She turned to catch him examining her and he dropped his eyes, clearing his throat. What did that look mean?

"Uh, what's he want?"

"Pin a medal on you, I think. No—I'm joking. He wants a brief on distribution. Sixteen hundred. *Nicht* PowerPoint."

"Got it," Dan said, back at the screen. He could update the daily logistics sitsum and be reasonably ready, he hoped, for any question the task force commander could throw. "Oh, just remembered. Got any bridge-inspection results?"

"Saw an Army message on that. Here it is . . . coming your way."

The information age. He had to love it. He only hoped all this data he was transmitting, reading, summarizing, had some vague resemblance to the reality, out there where the dust met the sky.

The convoy had climbed for an hour since Spayer had first glimpsed mountains through the mirage. According to the route map, one laser-printed sheet per vehicle, Refugee Camp Five was 175 miles from the city, 115 miles west of Haramah, and 8 miles west of Malaishu, on the south side of the road through the Malaishu Pass. At 20 miles an hour, a nine-hour trip. At 15, it'd take them into the darkness.

So far, though, they were holding 20 to 25, with bursts as high as 30. The road was arrow-straight between sparse, dead-looking bushes, but obviously hadn't been graded for years. It alternated between jagged rocks and sandy patches. Bare poles stood at intervals, wire missing, many hewed down to stumps. Buzzards watched from the crosspieces as the convoy neared, rising to flap a few times and then circle. The dust the point Humvee kicked up hung motionless, making it seem like they were driving through chocolate milk. They went through villages, mud walls crowding the road on either hand, shadowed alleys down which lay compounds, the occasional parked car, hanging laundry. Caxi blinked sleep away. They were pulling one in three at the port and nobody on the fire team was getting enough bivvy time. A weight slumped against him: the kid, out like a light. The ADs, lashed to the truck with their headcloths, were asleep too. The growl of the engine and the clatter of rocks in the wheelwells melted into a seamless black.

Caxi jerked awake to the radio crackling, the unmistakable rattle of fire. *"Motherfucker, we're takin' small-arms hits,"* Fire was yelling from the lead Humvee, voice gone high and fast. Something struck the truck's windshield, glancing like a rock flung up off the highway. It barely cracked the glass, but the snap, the sonics wiping off on the flat surface, said it was no rock. He ducked for his rifle, down by his boots on the floorboards.

The quarter of a second he had to make a decision stretched out like a quarter hour while his brain shifted into megaflop overdrive. He straightened and charged his weapon, peering out into the boiling cocoa.

Behind and above him the ADs were shouting, then shooting. Through the dust glimpses assembled themselves into a canted, broken surface that might once have been a road. A collapsed culvert, dry as dust. Past that, above, to the right, a rise. Rocks vibrated through the mirage. A human figure against the sky? Quick reaction drills, you turned into an ambush and charged through it. But it depended on your adversary, how well they knew marine tactics, how far ahead they thought. If you guessed wrong, you died.

Turn in? Away? Keep going? They were just escorting food, right? But *was* this an ambush, or just shepherds taking potshots?

Suddenly the radio was solid noise. Instead of molasses, time blurred. *"From the right, from the right,"* Fire was yelling from the point Humvee, which was accelerating, spewing dust. *"Hostiles at three o'clock, effectives four, five, six. Team, copy?"*

Spayer was on the channel, but broke transmission to shout at the driver, who'd let up on the accelerator and was drifting toward the roadside. "What the fuck . . . don't *slow down*, dude! We're in the kill zone!"

"Six motherfuckers in those rocks—"

The motor roared. He charged his rifle, jerked up his goggles, cranked down the passenger window, and craned out. "Over there. See? Past the washout. Pull off there and hairpin back."

"Off road?" The guy stared as if he were crazy.

"Fuck yeah! This is a six-by, right? Fuckin ay, get off the road."

"Truck three stalled out. Truck three stalled out! Team, you copying this?"

"Shit gaw-damn. Shit gaw-damn."

The shots merged into the clatter of AKs. As he talked Fire through the plan another hit clanged behind him. Their riders were firing nonstop, busting a lot of caps up there, but he doubted they were getting any just spraying and praying. Through the rolling dust a fraction of a second's glimpse of Assist standing in the lead vehicle, the muzzle flash of his SAW bending fiery sickles as he put out short bursts. *He* should be up there. He'd meant to go, but he'd put it off, doped off. Now his guys were up front and he was back here with the kid.

Who was standing up on the seat, staring through the cracked window. Caxi hauled him down and folded him under the dash. The wheels hammered over the culvert. Had the Ashaaran army stockpiled mines?

Dismounting didn't sound smart. Whoever was up there knew the terrain and he didn't. Keep pushing? Maybe, but taking fire and not returning it wasn't Semper Fi. They'd be safer off-road, and though the ground was rising, it ought to be flat enough for trucks.

The first rule of combat, shouted into his ear by an enraged DI at Parris Island: If you find yourself in a fair fight, your tactics suck.

"Go get 'em, I said," Spayer shouted, cuffing the driver to make sure he had his attention. He looked shocked, but obeyed, hauling the wheel over and downshifting as the big front wheels lurched down the bank. The load swayed, springs protesting as they hit bottom and then came through the stream bed and almost floated, but not quite, not with all those tons of rice weighing them down. The engine roared like a constipated dragon as the crest of the rise grew over the hood. Caxi caught the sparkle of muzzle flashes. Bushes snapped and flew as the bumper bulldozed them.

He should call this in, but through the seething dust and flying brush he caught Fire's Humvee pacing them on the left flank and the middle one pulling off to charge uphill on their right. It was the fucking Charge of the Light Brigade, motors roaring, spewing dust and the *brrp, brrp, brrp* of Fire's SAW ripping off six-inch bites of belted 5.56. The ADs' Kalashes went silent as they changed magazines. Then the heavier, slower note of the 7.62 got going, and mixed in with the rest of the noise the clatter of the hostile AKs. He slapped his magazine to seat it and leaned out the window, trying to aim.

This is my rifle. There are many like it, but this one is mine. . . .

But the dust blinded him and the truck was jouncing so much he'd put a bullet in the tires or the hood. Not to mention his militia blasting away above him. He'd be lucky if he didn't catch a bullet in the top of the skull. He pulled back inside.

"Breakin' out to the left—"

"Get some, baby. Get some."

"Cap the motherfuckers. Light 'em up."

"This is Team. Circle behind them, dismount your skinnies, and provide covering fire." He reached for the wheel and jammed it left. The driver fought him, cursing shrilly. Something snagged his boot. Caxi kicked something soft before remembering the kid was down there. Another bullet cracked into the windshield. If the glass hadn't stopped it he'd have taken it in the chest. Something black was sticking there. "The fucking bullet," the driver said as a lean form materialized from the dust. An armed man half turned, eyes widening as he took in six-wheeled Fate bearing down.

The front end jolted. Only the briefest glimpse but Spayer could replay it like it was on tape: a spindly stick-figure with a cloth around his head, the end whipping free as he vanished under the wheels.

He got the muzzle outboard again and searched the ocher murk vainly for a target. He'd lost his bearings. Had no idea where the road was, the top of the rise, anything.

Then the wedge of a Humvee with a roof weapon shadowed the dusk like a shark in murky water. The driver slewed to miss it as the M60 slammed out a long burst. Cases clattered across the hood. Spayer couldn't see what they were firing at but sent a half mag in the same direction.

Deafened, he pulled his head in as the truck burst out of the cloud. They were half a mile from the road. The driver locked the brakes and they skidded on gravel to a sloppy, rocking halt. He yelled up to the riders, pointing. They leapt off, hit and rolled, then gathered themselves and charged, yelling and spraying bullets wildly. They assaulted to the top of the slope, then slowed. On the far side, barely visible, he made out Assist and Fire dismounted, checking out something on the ground.

When he got there the guy was obviously about done breathing. The gravelly sand was dark scarlet. "Femoral," Fire said, keeping him covered. Spayer kept his rifle handy too, but this ambusher was past being dangerous. Nineteen or twenty, emaciated under a dirty white robe. He panted, eyes closed. They opened to look at the faces peering down, but didn't seem to register anything before the lids sank again. The ADs were shouting abuse, shaking their weapons. Spayer looked at them, then at Nabil, who'd come with him. "What're they saying, Little Team?"

"He's bad dude, Big Team."

"No shit. Where's he from?"

"They say, Sudan. Bad dude from Sudan." The boy kicked the dying man and the militiamen laughed. Spayer took his shoulder and eased him back.

Caxi halfheartedly got a battle dressing on him, just to be able to say he'd tried, but a few minutes later the wounded bandit stopped breathing. The other prisoner—the one they'd run over with the six-by—couldn't walk, but he wasn't bleeding, at least externally. Caxi put him in the back of the second Humvee with Ready to keep him away from the ADs, who seemed eager to put him out of his misery.

He walked over to the Humvee, feeling lightheaded. Its interior was acrid with sweat and dust and burnt powder. Sucking air, he got on the radio back to the Three Shop. Fire taken, fire returned, no friendly wounded or KIA. (A miracle, considering the DAs' frenzied barrage.) Fire hand-signaled from where the militia was policing up. Another dead hostile. The rest had scattered. He asked for disposition of the wounded man and got a *"Wait, out."* He hung up the handset and swapped magazines, in case Bad Dude had buddies on the way over the hill. But he didn't think so. These were random bandits, nothing more.

When he got out again Nabil was still hanging with the ADs, the boy chattering as they regarded him with bemused astonishment. "Thought these assholes was supposed to be friendly," the truck driver said, looking up from where he knelt beside the front wheel. "We're fuckin' bringin' 'em food, for Chrissake."

"Not all of 'em, I guess." Spayer flexed his fingers on the pistol grip. "You fucking totaled that one motherfucker, all right. Ran his ass down."

"Nah, I missed him," said the driver, but his voice shook and he was as white as a white guy could get.

"Raven Eight, Red Raider, over."

He jogged back to the Humvee. "Raven Eight, over."

"Confirm location and distance from offload point."

"Uh, not too fucking clear on that. Ten grid squares past that road, goes north to Fenteni? Stand by. Checking GPS." He read off the coordinates.

"Roger, copy, you're still sixty klicks out from Camp Five. On your prisoner: render first aid, load under guard, turn over to camp security element. Leave dead for local disposal. Over."

He copied and signed off. Cleared his throat and rinsed his mouth from a bottle of the crated water and spat the sick taste into the dirt. Held it out to the kid, whose bright black eyes tracked every movement.

"Let's get back on the road, Little Team."

Night at the airfield. Dan stood with other midgrade and senior officers, hands locked behind him. General Cornelius DeRoberts Ahearn didn't live in a modular. He had a tent behind the terminal. That was his bunk in the corner, with his ruck, camelback, and holstered Beretta on it. The only other furniture was a folding map table, field desk, folding chair, and computer. The tent was deathly hot, despite two huge fans that made it a canvas wind tunnel.

Ahearn conducted morning and evening briefs with everyone standing, to discourage long presentations. An Army captain was briefing on the convoy attack. "A counterambush was decided on. The escort element and one of the sixbys went off-road and flanked the snipers, then overran their position. No friendly casualties, two unidentified dead, possibly Sudanese, one wounded and captured. The convoy reached Camp Five and turned over cargo to WFO personnel on scene."

"ADs involved?"

"They made the final capture."

"Good. OIC convoy?"

"A Lance Corporal Spayer."

"Commend him. Interrogate the prisoner. I want the report in the morning. Hold him until we clarify his affiliation. Where's my JAGman?"

"Uh, not here, sir."

"I want him or a rep at the brief morning and evening. I don't want us accused of heavy-handed treatment." Ahearn turned to the rest of the attendees. "Gentlemen, our mission may be about to change."

He paused as jet engines screamed overhead and thundered down on the runway.

"The UN message, sir?" the N3 said.

"We're to organize a transition government based on the ADA. Disarm the militias and set up a police force. Distribute aid, run the camps, but number one, prepare for an early election. The Sudanese are just one hostile element out there. The Eritreans have always claimed the fertile land in the upper Tanagra."

Dan saw the map in his head. In the Darwinian environment of East Africa, without an army or functioning government Ashaara was prey. He wished they hadn't let the army disintegrate. It could've held the borders, while the JTF protected the relief distribution. He raised a hand and Ahearn nodded. "What about the Governing Council, sir? Have they come to an agreement with Dobleh? That's the main fault line, seems to me."

"Me too, Commander. The northerners resent losing power. But so far we've been able to buy them off. Not to put too fine a point on it . . . if we can get Dobleh to include Assad in a national unity party, maybe as chief of staff of a reconstituted army. . . ." He lifted his chin. "But for now, the camps are secure. We're getting wells drilled, generators installed. Food's on its way, thanks to Commander Lenson and his port team. Keep pushing and finish the job. That's all."

The ranks broke. Dan stayed in front of the fan, letting the hot but moving air dry the sweat. He'd pass on Ahearn's praise to Buntine. Maybe in not too long they'd have a functioning government, food distribution organized. They could start thinking about extracting.

He realized suddenly he was the last man in the tent, aside from the general, who was sitting at his computer. He put on his cap hastily and left.

THE CRISIS

15

DUBAI CITY, UNITED ARAB EMIRATES

This was Dan's first time, but everyone who visited the Mideast had heard about Dubai. The luxury hotels. The fantastic shopping. The desalinization plants that made the city a jeweled garden in a barren desert.

The stories were understated. He felt like a nineteenth-century time traveler as he followed his "butler" through the seven-hundred-foot-high atrium of the Burj al Arab, the world's most luxurious hotel.

He'd stared astonished as they approached over a causeway curving into the tranquil Gulf from a palm-dotted beach. The hotel bellied like a spinnaker, modeled on the mainsail of a dhow. Flickering lights gave its immense fabric the appearance of being on fire. It towered above bungalows, cottages, and fishing piers on the glowing white beach. It seemed less welcoming than out of scale, a titanic monument to unlimited money and unrestrained architects. And to judge by the construction sites along the coast, it was only the first of dozens in a city trying—literally—to build itself into nationhood.

The lobby was curved marble, deep carpets, gold leaf, and dramatic lighting, but the effect was less luxurious than nouveau riche kitsch. Still, no one in the JTF party said a word as the escalators glided upward between walls of gigantic aquaria teeming with reef fish.

Along with Ahearn and other military and State personnel, he'd left Ashaara on a C-17 direct to the Gulf. A separate aircraft had been dedicated to the new Provisional Government: Dr. Dobleh and eighteen other former exiles and tribal sheikhs deemed the most promising candidates to reestablish order.

The Dubai Conference on Red Sea Affairs had been convened by the United Nations' undersecretary-general for humanitarian affairs and emergency relief coordinator. Its goals were to "raise consciousness" of famine in Ashaara, Eritrea, Sudan, and throughout East Africa; raise funds; coordinate relief operations; and reduce tensions. The special representative, Shinichi Kazuma, would announce the "Hundred Day Program" of accelerated relief and recovery assistance.

Unstated, Dan had thought as he read the program, was that participating in a high-level conference would raise Dobleh's profile both internationally and in Ashaara. The diplomatic issues seemed obscure, but the meeting had been preceded by weeks of maneuvering about who would attend and who wouldn't. Also, whether JTF Red Sea would fund their trip, since prices in Dubai were beyond astronomical.

Finally orders had been cut, and State had reserved a block of rooms. But that wasn't why he kept checking his watch. In only a few hours Blair would be here, flying direct from DC.

Actually they'd met not far away. As the escalator ascended and the Gulf dropped away he could see far out to where he'd once gotten off a bicycle on a sandy deck so huge the crew used bicycles to get from one end of the ship to the other . . . and first seen her. Now in the falling dusk he counted eighteen tankers from horizon to horizon. To the east, cranes and dredgers were building new islands where open sea had stretched.

His room was jaw-dropping. Surely someone had screwed up. This wasn't just a "suite," but two stories high, with cream carpeting, damask wall coverings, green and rose marble, tilework, huge televisions, French colored-glass chandeliers, and enough gold that it no longer looked precious. Each of the four bathrooms was more outrageous than the next. Someone was busy in the kitchen; sizzling and good smells drifted out. He climbed a curved staircase to more white and scarlet, white and green. In the master suite he gaped up from a bed big as a tennis court to an enormous gold-framed ceiling mirror.

He grinned. When Blair got here . . . She looked passionless, but only till the doors closed. On that bed, under that mirror . . . tonight . . .

His per diem would cover about half an hour of this place. He walked from room to room, trying to enjoy it, apprehensive instead. At last he decided to say nothing. At least, he and Blair would have a time to remember.

Tonight's get-together was to coordinate the military message before the conference convened. Ahearn was to brief Centcom himself, General Leache. Dan had McCall confirm the meeting room was commercial secure. She reported back that it held twenty seats, shielded from external signal reception by wire mesh in the walls, with a separate cubby for guards with metal detectors.

But when they got there a technical security countermeasures team was finishing its own sweep to the accompaniment of rock music from a player. They had to be body-scanned and take their notebooks apart before they could go in.

Sweeping consisted of a frequency tracker/analyzer that picked up emissions from sending devices. A tech noticed his interest and pointed to the player. Some devices went active only when they heard room noise, he said, so they played music while they worked. Dan wasn't sure he bought that, but didn't voice his skepticism.

General Steven P. Leache was due at 2000. At 2015 McCall pointed out a window at the helipad atop the sail. Someone called "Attention" in the hallway.

Americas's viceroy from the Red Sea to Asia Minor wore BDUs and subdued stars. His hair was silver and his lean face ascetic as an aging pastor's. Two troopers with hip holsters preceded him. With Leache was a man Dan recognized with a shock as Brent Gelzinis. The deputy national security adviser was in sport coat and open-necked shirt. He wore rimless spectacles, and his jet-black hair was slicked back like Robert McNamara's, but his smile was more photogenic. If you considered hammerhead sharks photogenic. Dan had worked for Gelzinis, or more accurately, several layers below him, at the National Security Council.

Their relationship hadn't been friendly. Gelzinis stopped in front of him, not offering to shake hands. "Lenson. There you are."

"Mr. Gelzinis. How's Mrs. Clayton doing?" The national security adviser.

Gelzinis smiled but didn't answer. Leache nodded to the rest of the room and took his seat at the head of the table, pulling another chair over for the deputy.

"Cheerful faces. I like cheerful faces," Leache began, in sudden near darkness. His aide had dimmed the overheads at his end, leaving him in gloom, the rest in brightness. "I pulled in the deputy national security adviser to get his read on realities on the ground. I have only one question, Corny. Can you feed these people? That's the end state, from the highest level. Get them fed, hold an election, then extract. No lingering presence. No continuing mission. We're spending four million a day in Ashaara, but there's nothing we need there, and to be painfully frank, I have more strategically vital sore points. So tell me you have a road out, and how many weeks we are from it."

Dan couldn't help agreeing the long-term goal had to be to leave. The trouble was, once you started to help, in this part of the world, you became part of the problem.

"We can feed 'em," Ahearn said. "But only so long as we can maintain security."

"Local forces?"

"No army. No cops. When the president left, every man took his gun and went home, after he stole everything he could pull out of the wall. What's left's clan militias. At best."

Leache apologized if he hadn't given JTF Red Sea enough attention. "Things have been getting stickier with Iran. That hijacked sub"—he glanced at Dan—"triggered unpleasant consequences. Though it *has* kept my carriers safe. The *Nimitz* strike group carried the new anti-Shkval countermeasures when she transited Hormuz last month.

"Right now I'm pushing collective defense. Both the U.S.-GCC Cooperative Defense Initiative and NATO-GCC Istanbul Cooperation frameworks made clear their commitment to a WMD-free zone in the Gulf. I'd like to use this conference to explore extending that to the Red Sea area. Comments?"

"It's worth pursuing," Ahearn said. "But my feeling is none of the states in the area are in the running, either technologically or in terms of budget, to present that level of threat."

"Maybe, but we keep hearing about al Qaeda coopting local Islamicists. Trying to knit them into a cohesive framework, addressing the command-control challenge in an asymmetrical environment."

Like most very senior officers, Dan noticed, Ahearn spoke in a pabulumized shorthand that might make sense to people at his level but didn't convey much to those below. Which was probably exactly why they talked that way, but it seemed to have a very low sense-to-words ratio.

"We have a very good NCIS team keeping tabs on them."

"The locals need to do that. They can plant informers, take them down when the time's right. Also, I'm going to have to pull your agents back to the Gulf. Too many emergent needs here."

"That wouldn't help. If we didn't have—"

Leache didn't pause. "When will you have local security stood up? We need to depend on them, not our own counterintel assets. And I'm getting reports of pirate activity. So far they haven't taken down anything important, but they might. Anything like marine police, a coast guard?"

Ahearn explained what had happened in the aftermath of the collapse. The CINC seemed to listen, but Dan found his shaded, unblinking gaze unsettling, as if he was thinking about more important issues than the fate of one small, poverty-stricken country.

When he tuned back in Leache was talking for the benefit of the deputy adviser. "The difficulty's in integrating, aligning, and prioritizing our initiatives with the right bureaus at State. The lateral relationship's inefficient. We have to liase through two choke points: me to the ambassador, and the JIACG and my political adviser to the country teams. Both are problematic—especially since State and I have different geographic AORs."

"Is your JIACG effective?" Ahearn asked.

"Oh, I have a very effective Joint Interagency Coordination Group. I'll send you a team. Make sure you're not overlooking anything, or doing things we shouldn't be doing. If that's all right—you're the commander on the ground."

"I don't have staff to nursemaid visiting firemen," Ahearn said, and Dan sat up. This wasn't how a one-star talked to the commander of a unified command, who was Almighty God Incarnate to anyone in uniform.

Leache must have thought so too, because he leaned forward a millimeter, and the darkness at his end of the table got blacker. "I'd *appreciate* it. Let's get to the meat. Is this Dobleh a contender?"

Ahearn looked at Dan, who cleared his throat. "The situation's tricky, General. He has no official status yet, no forces, and no budget. The ADA's not clan-aligned. That's good, but it also means they don't control a traditional militia as a force core.

"Essentially, they're depending on us and on the private contractors State's providing through an emergency security assistance grant. For some reason, it's easier to get thirty million to hire GrayWolf than it is to get three million for an Ashaaran police force."

No one responded, so he went on. "We do have the so-called Governing Council offering their militia for security in the capital and port area."

"Any security's better than none," Gelzinis said breezily. "And weren't they part of the national police—"

"They were an oppressive operation," Dan said. "Actually not so long ago they had KGB advisers. Outside of the clans that backed the old regime, everyone in the country hates them."

"Still, they could serve as a nucleus. Do they have heavy weapons?" Leache asked.

"No sir, General. We seized their artillery, and destroyed the armored regiment at Darew."

"Aircraft? Battle helos?"

"MiGs and MI-8s. Inoperable junk."

"With no heavy weapons and no air force, they can't be much of a threat," Gelzinis said. "Let's at least try this Governing Council. Assir, right?"

"Assad, sir," Ahearn said.

"We can't wait around for some ideal solution. A country without security—that's like mayonnaise left out of the refrigerator, in this corner of the world."

Chuckles around the table. Dan said, "Yessir, but I don't think this General Assad—"

"Let's give him a chance," Leache said. Dan started to speak again, but caught Ahearn's glance. He closed his mouth, then winced. What was he doing? He lifted his hand.

"Dan," Gelzinis said. "I see you still just have to speak up."

"Yes sir, I do. The general needs to be told he's making a bad decision."

"According to some, the only kind I make," Leache said. "What's this one? Commander?"

Gelzinis said, "Let's move on. We don't really need to—"

"Take it easy, Brent. We've got a Medal of Honor winner

here. And I was on Schwarzkopf's staff; I remember how he got it." Leache nodded at Dan. "To us military types, he's a warrior god come down out of the sky, okay? Go ahead, Commander."

"Sir, um, thanks for the—but I didn't—well, never mind." He wondered if his face was as flaming as it felt. "Warrior god out of the sky." But it had been nice watching Gelzinis's face as Leache shoved Dan's pointy star up his behind. "Uh, I strongly recommend not supporting Abdullahi Assad. He's a warlord, plain and simple."

"Corny?"

"I agree."

"Okay, I withdraw the suggestion. Deal with it as you see fit. But get 'em armed. Don't leave it till our boy's elected, that'll be too late." Leache pushed his chair back, paused, looking at Gelzinis. "Brent?"

"Dobleh's speaking tomorrow. Is he presentable?"

Ahearn said, "He'll make a good impression. Guy speaks six languages."

"One'll be enough. How about the subcommittee? Who's your briefer?"

"Lenson will present. He's been doing a lot of my planning. I'll take questions. And I have one for the deputy."

"Shoot, General."

"Can we get any security help from the international community? Outside my purview, but it might lie in yours. NATO allies. The New Europe."

"I'll take it for action," Gelzinis said. Ahearn nodded, but Dan knew that was NSC-speak for "Forget it, asshole." Or at least, Gelzinis-speak.

"Thank you, gentlemen." Leache rose, shook hands with Ahearn, then with Dan as well.

Then he stepped back a pace and saluted. Dan was startled—it was in the regulations, that all ranks saluted the ribbon he wore—but you didn't often see generals doing it. His estimate of Leache went up another notch. Not for knowing the reg, but for not considering himself above it.

As they filed for the door his heart suddenly lifted as he remembered: Blair. She might even now be in their room.

Even now, in the bed, looking up at that enormous mirror. . . .

But when he got there, a light blinked on the phone in the study. The message was her from butchy Marine aide. "Margaret here. Blair's been delayed. She should be there tomorrow, around noon. Call if you have questions." Then the rattle of the phone going down, a dial tone.

There were two bidets, side by side, in the bathroom. The Jacuzzi, with hand-set glass tile and a wraparound painting on the wall, was big enough for two. He stripped, took a thirty-second Navy shower, and climbed into the bed. He stared down at himself from the mirror.

Was this what it felt like, looking down on your body when you were dead?

Next morning, 0830, in the Burj al Arab's palatial conference center. After the welcome coffee Shinichi Kazuma spoke for an hour, outlining the Hundred Day Program and its requirements in donor commitments. Hundreds of attendees in white *thobes* and dark business suits applauded when he finished.

He introduced Dr. Dobleh. Dan leaned back, registering only the first few sentences before drifting off to daydream about Blair.

He jerked back, flinching. Dobleh's face looked less round and foolish than it had at the port, when they'd paraded through the streets in trucks of rice. Rumor said he'd put himself on the same ration as those in the refugee camps. If so, it showed: his cheeks were thinner, and his jacket hung on him.

Dobleh spoke slowly, first in Italian, then Arabic, so Dan couldn't really follow the whole speech, except for some of the Italian. He caught the word "America" but couldn't tell what the ADA leader was saying. Something good, he hoped.

His peroration had the tone of Martin Luther King's "I Have a Dream," followed by a storm of applause. Dan stood with the rest, clapping, smiling. It looked like Ashaara would get its aid.

Lunchtime. The Burj's prizewinning staff was lined up abreast in chef's hats, serving with theatrical flourishes as attendees inched along with plates. Dan browsed the descriptions of dishes posted in French, English, and Arabic at each station. The baked hallwayo fish was marinated in a masala of local spices, crusted with sambal oelek, and served with coriander and tomato sesame. Aromatic yellow rice with pickled lemon, spicy red sauce, and a baby cos herb salad. Australian strip loin with blue cheese crust and braised Mulwarra lamb parcels. Dessert was a chocolate shell filled with milk chocolate mousse and a baked crumble of macadamia nuts and cherries, topped with a dollop of smoking-hot butterscotch sauce. Waiters served coffees, teas, juices, and sparkling waters from carts.

He caught sight of Dobleh across the room. The pediatrician-turned-savior fingered his lips as he watched diners at the damask-linened tables. The Ashaarans with him looked hungry too. A few steps away stood the NGO reps Dan had met at the embassy. Quarles, from Save the Children. O'Shea, the hydrogeologist. The ag expert who'd criticized food aid, arguing they'd be better off helping local farmers. He wondered if they'd joined the ADA leadership on its self-enforced diet.

He looked at his plate. One piece of fish, a little rice, some broccoli. Parsimonious, but he took it to his table anyway.

Two P.M.: the working group sessions. He was on a panel with three other invitees to discuss Operational Considerations and Physical Security, with four subheads that made only slightly more sense than sambal oelek, whatever that was. He was the opening presenter. He got his notes out and adjusted the microphone, fighting deja vu that this time he recognized: the counterproliferation conference in St. Petersburg, the last time he'd faked it on a panel. The other panelists were from USAID, Action Contre la Faim, and Oxfam. A waiter set a tumbler beside him, condensation beading on the chilled glass.

"Good afternoon," he began. To his astonishment, the mike worked.

He started with the facts of operating in Ashaara: famine, bad roads, desert, lack of water. Deaths had dropped due to food deliveries, but tensions were rising. "Targeted executions have occurred as clans struggle for resources and territory. The primary source of conflict is food aid resources in transit to distribution points," he read aloud, trying to keep his tone passionless, as if he weren't speaking about murders, beatings, the theft of food from helpless refugees.

"It's hard to tell which militia responds to whom, but General Assad's seems to be supported by a significant portion of those who were aligned with the former president and presumably were his most uh, affluent associates. In plain words, those who profited from his regime. Another troublesome group, the so-called Waleeli—or Brotherhood—has ties to Wahhabist Islam. It may have received arms from Iran and China.

"Currently JTF Red Sea's working to arrange the earliest possible elections. What's urgently needed is for the competing factions to back off, for their sponsors to withhold arms, and for others to make concrete commitments in food, money, and troops. I hope those attending this conference will help Ashaara rebuild itself as a functioning state."

He figured that was enough and sat back as the Oxfam woman took over.

Seven P.M., after a sumptuous dinner: the evening pledge session. The special representative spoke for another hour. As a result of increased transport costs, the World Food Organization was unable to respond as generously as it would like. He thanked those countries which had made a special effort to increase their cash pledge. Such funds now represented 24 percent of all pledges for the biennium to date.

That biennium still had another year to run, however, and he appealed for a special response to the situation in Ashaara. The Hundred Day Program could ship a round million tons of emergency and development aid through the end of the year. The UN was acting as overall coordinator, but Kazuma thanked various entities managing demanding logistic arrangements on behalf of bilateral donors.

Dan, sitting in back, noticed he never mentioned the U.S. At first it irritated him. Then he decided it made sense. If the Americans were handling things, why should anyone else give?

Dr. Dobleh spoke next. Again, his appeal was noisily applauded. Then the pledging began. One after another, men in *thobes* and headdresses stood to deliver flowery declamations. Most spoke in Arabic, but beside Dan, the ag guy was totting up sums on a calculator.

This was the guy who'd spoken up back at the embassy. Who'd seemed like a pain in the ass, a non–team player. But Dan Lenson had that rep himself in certain circles. He'd always wondered what he was being paid for, if he agreed with whatever his seniors proposed. Fortunately, there was still room for an attitude like that in the United States Navy.

Finally he leaned over. "How's it going? The pledging?"

"Biggest was the Saudis. A million dollars."

Dan thought he'd misheard. "Doesn't sound like much."

"It isn't, and that lets the rest of the Gulf off the hook. Who's going to pledge more than the House of Saud?"

"Who else is in?"

"Oh, everybody's *in*. Nobody actually says no, even if they have no intention of following through. So far we've got Bahrain, Kuwait, Oman, Qatar, and the United Arab Emirates. The British, of course, and the Italians. The Japanese and the Dutch haven't stepped up yet, but they usually do."

"The Iranians?"

"Not invited."

"Chinese?"

"Couldn't make it. Heartfelt regrets."

"Meanwhile, they're buying oil leases in Khartoum," Dan muttered, remembering that dismal city, the thugs struggling over that blasted land. Sometimes he thought the greatest curse that could come to Ashaara would be to discover something valuable there, diamonds, gold, oil. Her very poverty protected her from the worst scavengers. "How about security? Anybody volunteer troops or police?"

The tech eyed him as if he'd said something peculiarly fatuous. "No."

No question, this was a poisonous guy. "You know, I heard what you said to Ahearn at the conference. You really think we shouldn't be feeding starving people?"

"You heard that? 'Cause I never said don't feed them if they're starving. But one reason, maybe even the main reason they're starving now, is because we fed them before."

Dan couldn't believe the guy's cynicism. "Because they're still alive?"

"No. No! Because every time we ship in millions of tons of aid, their agricultural sector crashes. Nobody buys local, and the farmer has to go to the camp with everybody else. Pretty soon he figures, why bother. Ashaara fed itself once. The south was covered with orchards, truck farms, vineyards."

"Yeah, but the drought—"

"There's always been drought. It's cyclical. You see those canals they dug? The ones that are blowing away? You need to realize a couple things about this 'food aid' business."

The man was hissing, he was so agitated. "First off, only half the food aid budget actually buys food. The rest goes to transport it, because we can only buy U.S. We can't purchase in Thailand when they have a good crop, and ship it to Burma; has to be American rice. And the big one: almost everything we buy comes from the Big Four agribusinesses. They own USDA and the farm state congressmen."

"People are still getting fed."

"Yeah, they eat, but we could be doing it a lot cheaper. Or feeding a lot more. And if we actually helped them farm, we could get out of the aid business eventually. But that wouldn't be so good for Archer Daniels Midland, would it?"

Dan sat back. The guy sounded like a conspiracy Web site. Some of the NGO people were way out there.

He was checking his watch again, thinking Blair should be on her way from the airport, when his cell vibrated. The German representative was speaking; Dan went into the hallway before flipping it open. "Lenson."

"Dan? I'm in Lisbon. I'm sorry, I won't be able to make it."

"What's wrong? You said you could—"

"I have to go to Budapest. Trouble with the NATO accession. We have to be responsive or the European Union could look like a better bet. Szábo's got us in to see the defense minister. I'm sorry, I thought I could break out a day in Dubai."

He leaned against a marble column barnacled with gold leaf. "Actually, you said three days."

"That was probably never going to work, but I got overexcited."

"Can't you stop on the way back?"

"I have more commitments on the way back, Dan. We'll just have to keep trying to connect. How's your conference going? Are the Saudis ponying up? The emirs? The Kuwaitis?"

"The Saudis committed for a million. That's the most so far."

"Be lucky if you get half that. They love jet-setting to conferences, making bighearted gestures, then not coming through."

"We can't point fingers." He sucked a breath, suddenly angry. "We've got trillions to fight wars, but we can't spend a few million to prevent them."

Her voice grew careful, slightly distant. "But you know why that is, right, Dan?"

"Because we'd rather buy weapons?"

"And that's because?"

"Because . . . foreigners don't contribute to reelection campaigns?"

"Simmer down, Dan. Deep breath, okay? Are you saying

America's become . . . what? Some kind of military-industrial dictatorship?"

"Not really. I'm just tired and kind of pissed off. Were you?"

"No. Not really . . . but, back to the emirs. To be fair, the GCC's never considered the Red Sea part of the family."

"Maybe not, but we need help. Centcom's hardly got time to read our sitreps. We don't have the forces to maintain security. So far the militias haven't realized that, but sooner or later they'll wise up."

"Are we overreaching? Should we pull out?"

"The mission's worth doing. I'm just saying, we're accepting risk."

"Is there a national interest at stake?"

"Is keeping people from starving a national interest? If it isn't, then I guess not. But the civilian government's about to stand up. We've got the elders working together. If we let another country go down the tubes, nothing good's going to happen."

"I hear that, but we can't redeem the world. Not the way our economy's going, and not with November so close. This one's going to be a cliffhanger. But I could talk to the SecDef. Do you want me to try to—"

"No, Blair. No. His office gets our reports. But thanks for the offer."

"Gotta go, calling the flight. Love you."

Just two words, but they made the difference. "Love you," he said. "Love you a lot."

He hung up and stood looking down at the figures woven into the luxurious carpet, up at the golden chandeliers. Well-dressed men in suits and robes moved past, murmuring and chuckling. He rubbed his face. Which was the dream? And which, the nightmare?

This, or the horrific camps of Ashaara?

16

IN THE SOUTHERN MOUNTAINS

The trucks roar and rattle as they jolt over rocks and gravel. A miles-long cloud of tangerine dust drifts shadows across slopes dotted with the tormented yearning of acacias. The very sky's orange, the glaring sun a brilliant bronze.

Standing erect in a mufflerless cut-down Land Cruiser, gripping the windshield frame, Ghedi sweeps his arm in the signal to advance. His bare chest is coated with dust like bright rust. He wears goggles and camouflage pants and a Chinese tanker's helmet with earflaps. He carries a shortened AK over his shoulder and wears boots taken from an Eritrean soldier after a skirmish thirty miles south.

From that border to the southern river, the Waleeli hold sway.

His men have cleared the mountains of anyone who opposes them, all but one village to the west, which had enough rifles to drive them off. The rest have fled to the camps. The few families left offer water and what little food they have. Ghedi accepts the water, but executes any man who accepts food. He executes any man who offers insult to a daughter, disrespects an elder, doesn't pray five times a day, or is found drunk. Smoking he overlooks, since men are men, but he's told the foreigner who travels with them not to point the video camera at any Brother when he's smoking or he'll be killed.

He stands erect, scowl pasted to his lips, but trembles within. Who is he to lead these warriors? A farmer. An orchard tender. What if he fails, and they're defeated? Yes, he'll take death before that.

Death, in the name of God; he'll take that.

The voice of the blind sheekh whispers in his ear. *This world's not ours to determine. It's His.*

With that thought comes peace. Juulheed, his second in

command, wrenches the wheel to miss a termite mound twice the height of a man. There's the top of the hill. Ghedi signals to slow, waving the line of vehicles out in a hawk's wing.

His force is larger than ever, twenty-two trucks and two hundred men. More join every week. They arrive on foot, on horseback, in rattling wrecks. Juulheed interviews them. He shoots those he doesn't trust. Ghedi and Juulheed were bandits together. He's very tall and very thin and talks incessantly. His thoughts go in circles. Some say he's possessed by a demon. Ghedi leans past him and points to the two trailing trucks, gesturing them to stay back, while he waves the heavies up. He works fast, sorting things out before the cloud of dust arrives.

Behind the Toyota is a Pegaso with a heavy machine gun mounted in the bed. There are Land Cruisers and Land Rovers taken at gunpoint from aid compounds or hijacked on the road. Most have had their roofs cut off after having been rolled. They're stacked with young men, weapons, spare barrels, food, water in jerricans, and ammunition. They're painted in complicated patterns that owe more to artistic improvisation than uniformity. There's a Mercedes with drums of diesel and hand-powered pumps with hoses hanging from booms so vehicles can refuel even while they're rolling. The last truck is the "Tiger," a Russian behemoth stuffed with tanks of welding gas, parts, tow chains, jacks, and tools, taken in a cross-border raid targeted on an Eritrean motor pool. He doesn't want it or the fuel truck anywhere near the fighting.

Juulheed cranks the wheel, muttering so loud Ghedi can hear him even over the blasting muffler. They must know by now someone's coming. They've lost surprise. So there must be shock, force, overwhelming numbers.

When he looks up and down the line faces turn to him. He straightens his back, feeling their strength become his. Feels God's strength pouring into him too. Uncertainty departs. He points to the truck with the recoilless rifle. Inaccurate on the move, but their heaviest weapon. Then spins his hand in the air like a cavalry commander, and points over the hill.

Juulheed slams his sandal down. The worn engine barks, then yowls. The windshield jerks out of Ghedi's grip and he sits hard as the truck leaps off a shelf and lands with a rattling crash that makes the ammo boxes in back leap up and slam down again. The wheels dig in and they bound ahead. The crest rolls into them, and as they mount it the valley beyond comes into view, the riffled writhe of the desiccated riverbed, for all the world like the cast skin of some desert viper. The paler etch of the road.

And on it, copper dust staining the sky, the convoy.

The huge silver trucks are commercial, not military. Only the riflemen atop the trailers give any clue this is precious cargo. Chrome sparkles from bumpers. Blue flags ripple atop square radiators.

Ghedi hauls himself to his feet again, flexing his knees as the vehicle bangs over the desert, gathering speed downhill. Each time it leaps he's nearly thrown out. But he's got to see. He shades his eyes to one horizon, then the other. Below him both passengers are searching the sky too. "Nothing," says one.

"Sidna."

"Qufna."

On his wave Juulheed cranks the wheel over and the attacking rank opens up. The Toyota and every odd vehicle behind it turn right and race toward the column. The second vehicle back and every even vehicle back from it pivot in a buttonhook and in an immense cloud of ocher dust echelon to the left. After three hundred meters, when they cross the highway, they'll execute another turn to the right.

The outcome in sixty seconds is two flying columns of technicals, one on either side of the lumbering roadbound column. Ghedi and Juulheed have arrived at this over hours sipping coffee by campfires, arguing over rows of pebbles and sticks, the pebbles their vehicles, the sticks those of their prey. Now in the massed snarl of engines, the chatter of mistreated transmissions, the high-pitched battle shouts, masses of steel wheel across the desert like wolves behind trotting prey. And like panicked prey the enormous trucks accelerate, black smoke blasting from stacks, dust and grit whirling in their wake. One weaves from side to side, ludicrously ponderous, as if to throw off their aim. Ghedi shouts, filled with the glory of battle, the translucent joy of being one with the will of God.

The recoilless truck skids to a stop. A thud, thunderously loud, and a cloud of back-blast. Without haste a red-orange hibiscus flower of rock and dust erupts fifty yards ahead of the lead tractor-trailer. The Toyota tears past as sweating men reload, stripped to their waists, rags wrapped around their palms. The smells of burnt powder and dust and sweat thrill his heart. The smell of battle, where man reaches the border of Heaven. Had not the angels themselves, led by Jibril, fought at the battle of Badr long ago? The chamber clangs shut, the driver stomps the gas, and they're off again, loaders clinging for dear life as the tube sways crazily back and forth.

Then they're alongside the trucks, floating when they're not crashing through brush and hammering over rocks. The transmission whines as Juulheed screams without pause and hurls them back and forth. Ghedi nods to Hasheer. The boy stands, unstrapping the flag. Hasheer's his youngest deputy, a slim youth who reminds him of himself. Some say he's from the north, even a Xaasha. This Ghedi knows isn't true, the lad's a Diniyue, but he wouldn't care even if he were of the president's clan.

Jet-black, with a green fringe and the holy name of God inscribed in gold, the flag snaps in the breeze as it did for those warriors of the Prophet long ago, fighting against the idol worshippers and Jews who wished to kill him. The men in the cab stare. Ghedi gesticulates ferociously. This is the moment all turns on: whether they'll stop, or fire, whether they'll all live or die.

The gun slams again, deafening. This time the shell bursts so close the lead truck plunges instantly into the dust-cloud, as if sucked in.

When it emerges its wheels are locked. Gravel spits like bullets to rattle down far away. Ghedi slaps Juulheed's head and the driver pants, hauling the wheel around so they almost topple. He brakes to a steelscreeching halt beside the cab.

Ghedi points his rifle into an open window, into an astonished face. "Weapons out of the truck! In the name of God and the Waleeli!" Behind him come more shouts as each pair of vehicles closes on its target. Bursts stutter as some of his boys give vent to their excitement. "Who's the convoy leader?"

An astonishingly fat man squirms from the back of the cab. Ghedi grins. It's easy to deal with those who wrap their souls in lard. The man blusters, "What do you want? We're on World Food Organization business. Don't molest us."

" 'Don't molest us.' I would not be here if you'd paid your taxes."

"Taxes? What taxes?" But Ghedi sees he knows. Before the trucks ever loaded, an agent of the Waleeli approached him. Money, arms, food, he could have paid in any coin, save the worn worthless notes with the hawknosed profile of the former president. They're for lighting cookfires now, or cleaning oneself after sex with a prostitute. Using money for this, it's well known, prevents the wasting disease.

"What taxes? The ones you didn't pay! Now you've lost your trucks and cargos. Out of the cab! On the ground, salaam to God for your worthless necks!"

As they're scrambling down firing bursts out at the rear of the column. Ghedi whirls. Sometimes one man resists, then his clanmates begin shooting. These don't look aggressive, though. He calls to the ones atop the truck, "Throw down your rifles, O my brothers."

"We'll keep these rifles, brother."

"It's because you're my brother I don't kill you." He points to the gun truck and a clamor of heavy bullets stitches the air. "Throw them down. Now!"

The largest rider holds out his Kalashnikov and releases it. One after the other, the rest hit the ground in puffs of dust.

"Now descend."

He eyes the lookouts. Their only duty during a raid is scanning the sky. If American helicopters approach he'll take hostages. Scattering's not a viable tactic. One band tried that and was nearly wiped out. But so far, the sky's clear.

His men are climbing into the trucks. Each is a treasure trove. Not only do they carry radios, money, guns, fuel, and food, but the crews' own duffels are full. Much of this Juulheed makes a great show of burning, but somehow the magazines with pictures of women always survive. "All weapons into the Tiger," Ghedi shouts to his men. To the fat one, whose face is running with sweat, he says, "You are in the hands of the Waleeli. Those who believe have nothing to fear, but they must give up that which is unclean. Where is this convoy bound?"

"The camp at Malakat, on orders of the UN and the Alliance."

"There is no camp at Malakat. There is no Alliance."

"A camp is there. As to the Alliance"–the fat one shrugs—"if you say there is none, it does not exist."

Ghedi shoots him, there in the cab. His blood sprays on the faces of the others, who recoil but don't try to shield him. "Push him out onto the ground," he orders, and the wounded man tumbles like a sack of offal to the sand, where he lies moaning and weeping. "Thus to those who speak with contempt," he shouts. "God is great. God is great. God is great." They repeat his words feebly, echoing the fierce shouts and upthrust weapons of his men. "Now tell me what your clan is, and where you are to meet them."

He isn't surprised when they hurry to tell him all he wants to know.

The tent's stifling but Ghedi makes no show of noticing. Flies buzz above the dates and candies the women set out before they left. Across from him and Juulheed the gray-bearded elders wait. No one's armed. The experience of centuries: all weapons, even knives, are left outside, jealously watched by guards from both sides. The youngest offers instant coffee, a mark of great respect. Ghedi sips, head bowed before the older men. But his attention's on those standing behind them, against the tent walls. Those crowded outside, listening. Some, those whose weapons he took when he stopped the convoy.

This is a subfamily of the Gilhirs, rife with pride and ferociously suspicious of outsiders. Above all, he must treat them with respect. One can honor a Gilhir, or kill him. There's no third way.

The elders he faces are southerners, like most of the ADA. But they're far from the city, from the Americans and their tame dogs. He bows to a shriveled shifty-looking man with a sparse beard. At last the compliments ebb.

The old man begins in the slow measured speech of the "pure" clans, descended from the ancient *geelhers*, the camel camps of the high desert. His tone's that of an old man to a young one. Ghedi grows angry. He will not bear insult either. These men must be pruned out, to build a new Ashaara. They cling to the past: old stories, old names, old legends, old lands.

For a moment he remembers orchards, a burning village. Orphaned children, stumbling through the corn. Then pushes the memory aside. His sisters and brother are dead. Those who ride with him are his family now.

"Your young men are brave warriors. But they behave like bandits," the old man mumbles.

He fights to sound respectful. "We serve God, honored one."

"The foreigners also serve God in sending food. This does not disgrace, to accept help in famine and drought."

"My master is the blind and holy Sheekh Nassir of Ashaara. He speaks wisdom from the Book."

The old man makes a complex gesture with his right hand. "We have heard of the holy and wise Sheekh Nassir, peace be with him. I am not his equal. Just an ignorant toothless one. But surely stealing food from the hungry is not the way of the Prophet."

Ghedi explains the food is unclean. It can be restored to acceptability only by being used for God's purpose. "Only in this way can God's people be fed in a way pleasing to Him. This my men do to strengthen us against those who would destroy us and take our land."

A reddish-bearded man beside the elder stirs. "Why should the infidels want our land? There's much rain where they live. 'Accept gifts when they are in the offerer's hand.' "

"What is the price of these gifts?" Ghedi asks him. But he's silent. "What is it, this price?" he asks them all. "Come, I do not hear an answer. We have the true faith, but Shaitan gives the foreigners cunning. What wise man buys a camel the price of which he does not know? Or purchases a wife from one who says, I will tell you the bride-price next year?"

The clearing of throats, the ruminative slurp of coffee. Again Ghedi glances not at the seated graybeards, but at those behind them.

"Your people hunger? Let us make a bargain. I have no wish for anything but peace with the fierce and renowned Gilhirs. Without the help of God, could I have captured the convoy, guarded by the best of your fighters? I think not."

The eldest strokes his beard. "What is your price for this food? Gold we have none, and the old money's worthless."

"Then say what you have."

The reddish-bearded one says, "Camels and a few sheep. But we will not let those go, or we cannot rebuild the flocks when the rain returns."

"What else?"

Grudgingly he says, "Cannon and explosives. From the regiment at Malakat." He nods at a younger man. "Those who guarded it were of our clan when the army dissolved."

"What sort of cannon?"

For answer the elder waves. The younger man comes forward with a book. Ghedi can't read foreign writing. Only a little Arabic, enough to puzzle out the Qu'uran. Still, the picture's clear enough. "How many like this do you have?"

"Five, hidden in the hills. Shells, too."

Ghedi considers. From the picture, they're very large. Artillery would make his force powerful, but could his men move it, over the mountains? And what a wonderful target it would make for the American airplanes.

Perhaps not. "You mentioned explosives."

"We have that too, a great deal."

He glances at Juulheed, gets a nod. He tells the old man, "We will take your explosives, in exchange for half the food."

A buzz. "This is partially our grain already," the red-bearded elder points out. "The Americans distribute it to all who come."

"It *was* theirs, honored one. Now it is the Waleeli's, glory to God." He raises his voice. "Truly God is generous to those who fight in His name. This is a new day, brothers. There's no more evil government. Only Ashaarans, and invaders.

"It is said: 'He who is truly weak finds a foreigner as a protector.' Do you know what's happening in the city? Foreigners search from house to house for weapons. They give those they find to their puppets. Soon they will come to ask for yours. What will you do? Turn your naked rumps to them, whimper and lick their hands? In our brotherhood there's no longer any reckoning of ancestors, to set man against man. Only those who believe and fight. Do you have brave fighters? We need them with us."

The air hangs still. No one moves. Neither the elders, nor the young men who stand like so many concrete pillars behind them.

Finally the redbeard uncoils. "We need these explosives to protect our clan," he says. Ghedi sees the man he thought was the elder is not. He is only the oldest. "I do not think we should make this bargain. Nor should our young men join you. Thus we will continue to receive food for our grandchildren." He does not look at them, but the other elders murmur concurrence. "This is the way of wisdom, of peace and milk. We will not hinder you, but we will not join you. The Gilhirs will stand apart."

There's a stir in the back. Ghedi raises his voice. "Stand apart, you say. Meaning, let the strangers rule?"

"If we wage war, they'll kill us with helicopters. And send no more food."

Ghedi considers killing the redbeard. There's a pistol inside his pants. But the man stares back with disdain.

"You're old," he tells them. "Old and afraid. But Ghedi

disciple of Nassir does not fear their machines. The great blind sheekh declares to you jihad, for your country and for God. The Waleeli will unite all Ashaarans and eject the foreigners. Then we will form a government. But this time, not of this clan against that. Nor will it teach evil to our children and women. A righteous government, enforcing the holy law."

The middle-aged men stir, but don't speak. The stubborn elder rises, gathers his robes. "This is what Sheekh Nassir says? Attack the foreigners?"

"Yes."

"Obey mullahs, not the *ergada*? The clan elders?"

"Sharia law is greater than clan law. Islam unites; kinship law divides."

"Then your sheekh is mad as well as blind. Clan law is the Ashaari way. You talk like an Arab. Wait till the rains return. Then, if the *khawayat* don't leave, we can make war when we have eaten and are strong. Our young men will not join you."

Ghedi reaches for his weapon, but Juulheed's hand stops him. He smiles, as he sees what he's expected outside. It's Hasheer, giving him the signal.

He stands, dusts off his clothing, bows. "As you say, honored one. I thank you for your hospitality." He backs toward the entrance. "But for your safety, stay within the tent."

The elders glance up. "What do you mean?"

"Only that I have no wish to kill you. Your young men are already mine. They'll come back heroes, to shame the cowards who tried to keep them from battle." Ghedi laughs in their faces and turns on his heel.

Outside the young men of the Gilhir are gathered in the blazing sun and eddying dust. Already they're mixed in with his men. "Make sure they bring their weapons," he snaps to Hasheer.

"Yes, Maahdi. Weapons and blankets."

"Don't call me Maahdi, and punish with rods those who do. Where are the explosives?"

"Hidden above the town. I've sent a truck and loading crew with guides. And they have armored cars."

None of the elders mentioned this, but it's welcome news. "Let those who cared for them drive the armored cars. Leave one truck of rice here. Drive the others as close to our camp as they can get, then unload and camouflage. We'll ransom them back to the Pakistanis for ammunition, like the last convoy."

"Yes, Orcharder."

He walks around a barefoot girl lazily switching a sheep and raises his hand to the recruits. "Greetings, warriors of Ashaara and God. Forget your mothers and fathers, and follow me. Ours is the God of Battles. God is great."

"God is great," they shout, waving their rifles. "God is great. God is great."

Their eyes are like the sun at dawn. The cheers are strong wine in his veins. Holding up a hand, he swings into the Land Cruiser. As the young men scramble into the trucks he sees the elders standing by the tent. The eldest stretches out his hands, but they ignore him. They're the clan's no longer. They're Waleeli now. They're his. Glory to God, the whole southern mountains are his.

He nods to Juulheed to start the engine.

17

USS *SHAMAL*

Teddy was cleaning his carbine in the hooch when the news came down. Parts and patches all over, the oil and burnt powder all over their hands after their range session that afternoon. "I don't use anything but CLP," he was saying to the big Hawaiian. "What the fucking manual says, that's what I fucking use."

"Man, got to run that bolt greasy. The recoil spring, too. Or you get that sproing, sounds like a fucking toy gun."

"You don't need all that fucking grease." Teddy pulled the bolt carrier out of the black weapon broken-backed on the table. He fingernailed out the retaining pin, shook out the firing pin, took out the cam pin. The bolt fell into his hand. "Just collects moon dust. Keep it clean, this fucker'll shoot."

The SEAL "hooch" was one of the prefabs at the international airport. The Marines had renamed it Camp Rowley, after the private killed at the embassy gate. The SEALs were part of an on-call reaction force, formed since someone had started raiding convoys. They'd gone out twice, but both times too late to do much but police up the dead. Fortunately or not, there hadn't been many. Oberg suspected that was because the skinnies riding shotgun had deserted to join the bandits.

A disturbing trend, but sooner or later they'd catch up to whoever was raiding the shipments. Running a last oil-soaked patch through the bore—it was chromed, but he never left a bore unoiled—he reflected on how nice it would be to pop a few primers on them. With the perfect excuse: they were stealing food from starving people.

Not that he gave a shit. The blade of his Glock grated as he scraped carbon off the bolt face. He pulled the extractor and cleaned it, looking for cracks and wear. Kaulukukui was going on about some gee-whiz dry lube the GrayWolf armorer had given him. Teddy grunted. Usually he was good for hours arguing about weapons, but right now he was thinking about the Offer.

A friend of his mom's wanted him in on an action picture. The guy was a schmuck and a liar, but who wasn't in LA. He'd sent Teddy the spec script. Silly shit, but it came cheap from a new screenwriter, and with Teddy on board, he could make "an authentic picture of SEALs in action." Teddy would get a cameo, shared credit, maybe even a point of gross.

Unspoken so far was that the guy expected him to put money in, too.

Oh, he had it. All it'd take was a call to his mom's lawyers. Cavanaugh, Sillinger & Sukkar, the firm she'd banked her A-list earnings with for twenty years. But he'd grown up in that scene. Gone round the world to get away from it. Did he want to go back?

He didn't think so. Still, it might be fun to make a picture. He reassembled the bolt, cleaned the buffer assembly, scrubbed down the locking lugs. Spritzed everything and wiped it dry. He snapped the charging handle in, ran the bolt in, pivoted upper and lower back together. Pushed the takedown pin in and snatched the bolt and snapped the trigger. Good.

Just in time. The speaker outside said, "REACTION TEAM ALFA, REACTION TEAM ALFA, MUSTER ON PAD SIX, ON THE DOUBLE."

Sumo steered the Humvee around two camels fucking in the road, like big tangled sawhorses. Bare-legged kids fished in tide pools. Each time he braked to let a convoy rumble by, the beggars closed in. "Sir! Sir!" they yelled, thrusting their deformities through the windows. "On the eighth day God said, 'Crap, I forgot' . . . and created Ashaara," Kaulukukui muttered.

Fat flies echeloned in like attacking Stukas as the team rolled out at the terminal. Two ships were discharging. The little pusher boats were butting another out of the basin. Trucks waited under the discharge chutes of silos. Drifts of chaff and broken rice lay crisscrossed with tire tracks. *Shamal*'s engines shook the air with the familiar school-bus rumble, venting an apricot cloudbank that drifted straight up. Teddy and Sumo Man and Arkin and Kowacki, two more Team Eight guys fresh in-country from ops in Yemen—the former, "Barkin' Arkin" or "Bitch Dog," the latter inevitably christened "Whacker"—humped lumpy duffels and soft-cased weapons up the brow, across the afterdeck, and down into the SEAL prep area. The twenty-by-thirty steel-walled compartment was studded with hydraulic tanks and compressors, its overhead v-indented by the launch ramp for the RHIB.

When he bumped his gear down the ladder the first thing that hit him was the smell. It was rank, raw piss and shit. The second was the heat. Had to be 130, maybe 140, so hot his eyes burned. The black CO, Geller, was standing in blue coveralls dark with sweat, fists on hips, a chief behind him, watching Kaulukukui and Arkin stow their gear in the aft magazine locker. Since the engines were clamoring a few feet away, Oberg had to shout. "Alleycat, how you doing?" he yelled, tossing a salute. Jesus, he'd almost called the guy Jelly Man, Sumo's nickname for him. "Ever find that machine gun, sir?"

Geller's eyes crimped. "The one you lost overboard?"

"Not *us*, Skipper. *Your* guys. Teddy Oberg, team leader, reporting aboard. You know Sumo. This is Whacker and Bitch Dog. Jesus, what's that stink? Like a sheep's asshole down here."

The chief enlightened them: the level switch in the contaminated holding tank had failed. The pump had run and run, burning out the motor. Meaning, the heads were shut down. "Until we get that pump swapped out, everybody uses those five-gallon buckets in the corners. Lug 'em topside and dump 'em, but don't wait till they're full or they'll slop all over the ladders. Then we'll really have a mess."

Geller said, "What's the word, Petty Officer Oberg? What've you heard about this hijacking?"

"Sir, all they told us, pirates took down one of the aid ships. Up the north coast, lookin' for ransom. You and me, we have to get up there and see can we spring 'em. That jibe with what you got?"

Geller said that was about right. A Malaysian chemical tanker had reported being shadowed by speedboats that morning. One had cut in front and thrown objects into the water. Fearing mines, the ship had stopped her engines, whereupon the second boat aimed a burst of machine-gun fire at the bridge. She'd hove to and the pirates had boarded.

The captain had gotten off Inmarsat calls to Ashaara Port Control and the Piracy Reporting Center before the boarders made it to the bridge. JTF immediately tightened security on other ships en route, requesting an S-3 to fly patrols and assigning *Firebolt* to join up two hundred miles out and accompany each incoming delivery to the sea buoy at Ashaara City. *Shamal* was tasked to rescue the hostages.

"We'll talk plan once we get under way. I'm looking at twelve hours transit, so we'll get there about 0200." Geller stared as if daring him to make another crack.

"We'll work something up, sir."

"Rescued hostages before?"

"Couple times, sir. Just need to get up there, see the setup. And go over whatever intel you've got, whatever they can shoot to us. Pictures and layout would be nice."

Geller nodded and went forward. The engines gunned, reversed, fell back to idle, gunned again. The shrill whistle of "under way" piped over the 1MC.

Teddy had them rig for swim-and-climb, though it was conceivable they could assault from RHIBs, backed by the ship's guns. It was also possible everything would be settled peacefully, but he preferred not to think about that. The engines were vibrating the bulkheads and hazing the air. He sent the team to the mess decks, except for Arkin, whom he left in the space in case the CO called down.

Spaghetti and meatballs and apple pie, shoulder to shoulder with *Shamal*'s crew in the tight little mess decks. Whacker was telling about a teammate in Bosnia who'd come across a Serbian truck filled with loot from local villages. A cluster bomb had perforated everybody in the cab. Along with furs and silver, he'd found a small, heavy leather bag filled, when he opened it, with gold. Watches, rings, bracelets, coins, irregular lumps he'd been afraid to examine too closely.

"D'he turn it in?" Kaulukukui asked.

"Who to?"

"I don't know. The Bosnians?"

"They were fucking dead. No names on those teeth. No, he got it out of the country and sold it in Istanbul. Opened a Swiss account."

"I heard this story before," Oberg said. "Dateline, Vietnam. Or, no—that George Clooney movie, something about kings—"

"*Three Kings*."

"Sharpe's Gold," a *Shamal* sailor put in. The other guys at the table were throwing in more titles when they looked up and quieted.

"XO?"

"Petty Officer Oberg? Captain'd like you on the bridge."

Topside sunset was salmon and carmine beyond low mountains. He stared out. Over there was a blank space on the map. The patrols came back with empty eyes and weathered skin. They said there was nothing there, which made him curious. How could a SEAL get himself sent into the Empty Quarter?

Shamal davened over a slowly undulating sea, throwing up a roostertail and a big white bow wave. Geller stood spread-legged at the chart table studying a clipboard. "Obie? Some hard info. Pictures, too, but the resolution sucks. We're not comm heavy. Most of this is CUDIXS and UHF satcom."

He studied them while the skipper summarized what the comm-oh had boiled out of the message traffic and chatter on the Red Sea airwaves. "They're taking it inside the twelve-mile limit."

Teddy bent over the chart. Still hours away even at full speed, the scattered islets of the Sawakin Group freckled the coast. Looking closer, he saw most weren't actually islands, but reefs, awash at low tide and submerged at high. "I'd anchor inside this largest shoal," Geller mused, fingering a horseshoe shape. It resembled an atoll, though Teddy hadn't thought there were any in the Red Sea. "That'd give me a lee against storms, and make it tougher to get in at me."

"They know we're coming?"

"They've got to figure somebody's on his way."

"Anything from the shipping company?"

"JTF's trying to get in touch. Owner's Malaysian, flag's Panamanian, charterer's Danish, crew's Russian and Filipino."

"The usual. Uh, you said it was a chemical tanker?"

"Correct. *Tahia.* But not *chemical* chemicals. Just cooking oil. Still flammable, though, I guess."

Teddy adjusted his balls, checking out the photos. They were grainy and didn't show much. Standard tanker layout: deckhouse aft, no booms, lots of piping on a long foredeck.

"Word is we gotta bounce these guys hard," Geller told him. "There's hundreds of fishermen along this coast who'll turn pirate if they see they can get away with it. Guns aren't hard to get. Nip this hard and it'll save trouble down the line."

"No problem," Teddy said. "We'll put 'em down."

Geller got that funny look again. "I think they meant take them into custody and free the hostages."

"I only got four dudes, Skipper. We gotta work close on this. If I call for thirty rounds from that twenty-five-mil of yours, I gotta have 'em right away. No fucking around asking for clearance."

Geller shook his head. "Can't promise, Petty Officer. Not till we get some kind of ROE. See, we'll be inside territorial waters, but we won't have host country authorization."

"This ship's under contract to the UN. Doesn't that give us the right to—"

"Not necessarily."

"I can't do business without you behind me," Teddy warned him. "Simple as that, Skipper. Can't put my guys in without you having our backs."

"I'll draft the message," Geller said at last.

He had the guys set up for a night assault, just in case. But after dark Geller called him back. Things might not be that hasty. The pirates had contacted the Danish, who'd passed their demands to the contractor, Dampskibselskabet Kiersted. They were responsible, since it was the crew, not the ship or cargo, that was being held for ransom.

They did get a list. Nine men, most of the names Filipino, as Geller had said. Those who weren't sounded Russian and one might be Scandinavian.

He stood topside aft watching the dark sea rocket by under stars like lit gunpowder. Then went below and turned in, figuring Geller would call if anything changed. Berthing was three bunks high, hot, and noisy, but he was out as soon as his head hit the pillow.

Teddy came awake sweating, realizing instantly the ship wasn't at full speed anymore. 0605. He rolled out and pulled on his BDUs from the night before, quick-laced his boots, and pounded up the ladder to the main deck.

He emerged into incandescent morning. *Shamal* rolled in a leisurely manner two miles off a low islet of blinding sand dotted with bushes and fringed with lime Jell-O reef and whipped-cream surf. He paced, inhaling baking bread, hot metal, grease, garbage left too long in the heat. The hum of the diesels cored every piece of metal. A vagrant wind sucked exhaust up from the waterline discharges. Past the aft deckhouse three smokers looked at him inquiringly. The stern gates worked with a tinny clunk. The islet lay like a barrier between them and the upperworks of another ship. How had it gotten in there? Then he remembered the chart. The entrance wasn't visible, but probably would be soon.

He should see Geller, find out what was happening. But no one had shaken him awake, so he lingered, sniffing the salt breeze gratefully after the shithouse stink below. Listening to the surf boom on the strand. The sky was flawless as if just created.

A morning like this, plus a chance of trading supersonic metal with desperate pirates. Did he really want to give this up for pool parties and casting meetings?

In the pilothouse Geller snored in his leather chair. The XO was there too. "Ready to head over?" he asked as soon as he saw Teddy.

"Over where? That ship?"

"Not in uniform. Didn't you bring civvies?"

"No, Lieutenant. Didn't know we'd have liberty call."

The exec told him to watch his mouth, and find something to wear that wouldn't give away he was military. The pirates had agreed to let two witnesses board, to prove their investments were still alive.

Teddy didn't like the idea of going unarmed. On the other

hand, he could scout out where the hostages were being kept, how best to board, maybe even count the bad guys. "All right," he said. "Anybody got a cane?"

The RHIB purred across water so clear it was black. Kaulukukui wouldn't look at him. Sumo was bitter, but to hell with him, Teddy thought, holding tight as the inflatable's blunt bow headed for the surf line. The aluminum cane, from sick bay stores, lay between them. The radio crackled. Sandy shores slid apart like stubbly shaved labia to reveal an inlet. Not his fault no one aboard had a shirt that fit the Hawaiian's bulging chest. He felt strange in Geller's black pants and flowing white shirt, himself. Too warm for it, but he'd added a Nautica jacket for concealment.

He tensed as they hit green water, but it was only a tide line, the rich warm water behind the islands streaming out. The sound inside looked even calmer than the sea, and that sea, today, was so calm it set his teeth on edge.

He leaned. The bow wave made a shallow cup, a curve, a lens of clear smooth water. Leaning farther, he peered down into the shallows. Sinuous dark forms wove among coral heads, silhouetted against crystalline sand.

Suddenly he caught his breath. It wasn't shallow, but deep. And those were sharks, dozens of them, big mothers too. A continuous line headed in, others headed out. Several big hammerheads slowly orbited, as if they had nothing on their appointment calendars today.

The shores on either side contracted, then fell away. Dunes and scrubby bushes in their lee and nothing more. A few bits of the Earth were still innocent. Beach like this was going for millions back in Santa Cruz County. His mother owned a lot of it.

The tanker was less lovely. Shoved deep into the sea's pocket by her cargo, her green sides streaked with corrosion like dried tomato paste below the maze of white-painted but rust-stained piping he'd noted in the photo. As they motored closer he checked off a haze above her stack, a dangling boarding ladder, two skinnies aft on deck with AKs. Another sat in a speedboat tethered to the stern by a green nylon line. All three were watching the approaching RHIB.

Chem tankers were always tough. The labyrinth of piping and valves was impossible for the boarding party to figure out. Their empty runs and deep, sealed tanks, stainless or epoxy-lined, could hide all manner of contraband.

The coxswain made a pass, pointing to the ladder. One of the guys on deck nodded violently, pointing at it. Dark, almost unnaturally elongated, in worn short-sleeve button-ups, T-shirts, and ragged shorts. Teddy stood, thinking again about the sharks. "Put us on that boat," he murmured. "Not on the ladder."

"On their speedboat?"

"You got it, Driftwood."

The coxswain cut the outboards. The inflatable drifted the last few feet and jostled into the motorboat. It leaned, then jostled again as Teddy and then Sumo stepped over. The skinny in the boat blinked at Kaulukukui in disbelief.

"Point that thing someplace else, okay?" said Oberg, smiling. He fished a pack of Marlboros from his pocket and held it out. The guy beamed, especially when Teddy added a flashy butane lighter with the NASCAR logo. *"Mahad seeneed, mahad seeneed,"* he said, turning the little race car over and over as if it were a giant ruby.

"Your new butt buddy," Sumo muttered.

"He'll never replace you."

"Get the fuck up that ladder."

"*You* get up it. If you can without breaking the rungs."

He pulled himself up after Sumo with a definite feeling of stepping into possible shit. When he got to the top he held up the ID holder hanging around his neck on a chain.

As expected, the reception committee barely glanced at it. This was good, not least because it was fake, cooked up on a color printer to read World Food Organization. The deck guards searched them, shook his cane and tried to pull it apart, but found nothing. He leaned on it, faking a limp as they threaded through passageways to the mess.

Nine men glanced up as they entered. They weren't

shackled or tied, but their slumped shoulders betrayed their helplessness. As did the ragged ruffians sitting in each corner, rifles on tables and a green stick of qat poking from each ruminating jaw. Teddy had a confab with the tanker captain, who spoke English. He said they were being treated well, no one hurt, though they'd been shoved around. Their own cook was still on duty.

"What do they want, Cap'n?"

"The short answer's money. Suleyman will tell you. A billion dollars in cash."

Teddy assumed he meant million, not billion. "Will your company pay? They got hijacking insurance?"

"Everybody does, these days. But there may be delays. Negotiation."

The guy looked so whipped, though, that Teddy whispered, "What's wrong? They fucking with you?"

His Adam's apple bobbed, and he glanced toward a guard. A scowler, Teddy saw. He gave him one back, until the guy looked away. Back to the captain. "Well?"

"They're not treating us badly. But, if the ransom is not paid—they make threats."

Teddy eyed Scowler again. "Hang tight, Skipper. We'll get you out of this. How many of 'em? You keep a count?"

He didn't answer, but the fingers of his right hand splayed out on the table as if he was working out a cramp. Twice.

One of their escorts came back and said something that ended in "Suleyman," so Teddy got up and went with him. Kaulukukui stayed, milking everything he could from the hostages.

On the bridge wing an even more elongated Ashaaran in sun-faded Castro cap and beach shorts patterned with ferns and frogs had his big rubber-thonged feet up on the pelorus stand. Horrible lesions puffed raw-hamburger ankles. It looked to Teddy like the beginning stages of elephantiasis. He showed his ID again. The guy said something to the guards and shoved a folding chair over with the other foot.

Teddy sat, squinting in the glare off the silver silk of the sound. From forward came the jangle of canned music, the falsetto wail of one of the androgynous male singers Ashaarans loved. They tried various languages to no avail. Teddy shook out a Marlboro. They lit up, leaned back, and regarded each other.

The pirate chief produced a calculator. Teddy blinked. Sure enough, the display read 1,000,000,000.

Did this dude know how much a billion was? Just for shits 'n' grins, Teddy punched in 10,000 and handed it back. The guy tilted it this way and that before getting an insulted look. He shook his head and pointed his finger gun-fashion. "Pan, pan, pan," he said. "Pan, pan, pan, pan pan pan. *Tue, muerte, geeri.*"

"Subtle, but I get you," Teddy told him. "Stay with the sticker price, huh?"

1,000,000,000.

100,000, he punched in. The guy took it back and added zeros.

1,000,000,000.

"We're done, Driftwood," he said, keeping his tone light. "Hope whatever you got on your leg spreads to your cock."

"Danyo?" the guy said, making a drinking motion. Teddy hesitated, then decided he was ahead of the game. Time to fold and head home with his winnings. He shook his head and got up. Held up the cane. "Shall I jam this up your ass, Captain Kidd?"

"Captain," the guy said, grinning. "Captain Keed. *Khayr, nabagelyo.*" He held out a limp hand, which Teddy avoiding looking at while he shook it. "Pan, pan pan," were his last words as Teddy retreated toward the ladder, keeping that salesman's smile pasted wide until he turned away.

He collected Sumo from the messroom and gestured to the guards that they wanted to leave. They seemed cool with that. He told the ship's skipper they'd be in touch and not to worry or try anything stupid, but if he heard firing, get his men down on deck. He got an anxious smile in return, and a slightly firmer handshake than on the bridge.

Out into the open air again, across the deck, over the rail. He let himself down the ladder and waved the boat in.

Not the RHIB, but the speedboat. The guy in it was still nursing his cigarette. He grinned and hauled in on the painter, bringing the bow up so they could step down into it. Teddy dropped the cane first, then followed it, stepping cautiously, as if his leg hurt.

The RHIB was making its approach. He judged its closing rate, then looked back up at the deck. The guards were still there, but they weren't visible over the swell of the hull.

He took another pack from his shirt and held it out.

Kaulukukui's big hand closed around the man's mouth at the same moment Oberg reached for his ID case. The next moment the Hawaiian had the guard's head under water and Teddy had sawed halfway through the nylon painter with the three-inch blade of his Cold Steel push knife, hidden in the concealed pocket of the badge case. When it parted he threw a bowline in it and leaped across to the RHIB as it coasted in. Kaulukukui let his guy snatch one breath, then zip-tied him and gagged him with the sling from a first aid kit.

They left him hooked thrashing on the boarding ladder as the RHIB peeled away, bowline fast to the towing cleat on the stern. The pirates on the tanker waved a cheerful farewell.

Until they saw the painter come taut and their motorboat following it out into the sound. Yelling followed but the only shot went so far wild Teddy didn't even see it hit the water.

"Totally," Kaulukukui said, racking the boat guard's AK, which he'd kept. Teddy covered his ears as he emptied the magazine at an inquisitive dorsal fin. "They got hostages, great. Now they're *our* hostages."

"Think you nicked him. You see those others? Waiting down deep?"

"Fucking ay. Place is Shark Heaven."

"Shark Hell, they try to swim for it." Teddy stretched, looking back to where the tanker rode at anchor, centerpiece of an idyllic vista of beach and sky. He leaned to spit into the dark water.

"*Now*, let's negotiate."

18

NORTH OF MALAKAT,
SOUTH OF URI'YAH:
WITH THE WALEELI ARMY

Before Ghedi the flat plain stretches to the horizon, boiling in the heat. A hundred-foot-high dust devil staggers amid dead thornbushes, over gravel pans and salt flats and toppled termite mounds. Above him snaps the green-and-black banner. He raises the binoculars, stolen from a Canadian unit laagered along the Tanagra by a new volunteer.

There they are. Low huts, the same drab as the rocks and the dust. Tethered camels. And here and there between him and the roadblock, the occasional vehicle, plumes of dust, but mainly the distant specks of men at desultory work. Flashes of sun on polished metal. Shovels? Bayonets? Fresh razor wire?

In two weeks the Waleeli have advanced a hundred miles up the coast. Behind them lies Malakat, a skirmish at the Tanagra Delta, and brushes with nomads and village militias that ended with peacemaking and more recruits. The sea lies over the dunes on his right flank, but he hasn't seen it yet. Every moment's occupied sorting out disputes, allocating ammunition and food, arranging repairs, praising and calming the disparate elements of his quarrelsome forces.

Now, at last, they face battle. No more raiding convoys, trading long-distance shots with nomads on camels, managing skirmishes that are more like preludes to parley. Every day brings in more men from the west and north. He's halted here, though, facing the forces gathered at the roadblock.

Someone's decided to stop him. But Ghedi hasn't attacked. Not yet. For four days he's halted here, while both forces slowly grow in size, scout the hills, and prepare.

He lifts his head, watching the dust devil. Noting another on the horizon. A dimness in the sky. He closes his eyes and tastes the wind. It streams and cracks the bullet-tattered banner. It blows from behind them, from his right hand.

Is this the day?

A small group waits for his attention. Juulheed's out scouting in the Fiat. Instead Hasheer stands with the new arrivals. Ghedi insists on meeting each man who joins. This is dangerous—the enemy could try to kill him, and some still whisper Hasheer's not to be trusted—but he relies now as much on the awe simple men feel at his presence, as on his bodyguards and their pat-downs.

He lowers the binoculars and beckons to a tribesman who stares in admiration. Face shining, the man advances, bowing to the dusty ground.

After greeting the morning's volunteers he retreats to his command tent as the heat increases. The tent came from a medical-aid camp near the Asmaran border. Foreign-made, it's cool inside, made of a stretchy fabric he's never seen before. He checks with his radio man.

A rumble and the snap of stones under massive tires. One of the Gelhirs' huge Fiat armored cars. The crews are still Gelhir and the cars have spearheaded the advance north. Unfortunately they fired their last cannon ammunition the week before and now are only good for carrying troops, but the enemy can't know that. Juulheed, with his mad genius for weapons, has festooned clusters of RPG launchers off the turrets. They still have plenty of RPGs, plenty of green plastic Chinese grenades. The Americans haven't intercepted all their shipments. When Juulheed swings down Ghedi wraps him in a hug. His cheek bulges. Where has he found fresh qat? No one else has any. Ghedi pounds his back, glad to see the tall crazy man. "We've got to talk," his deputy says rapidly. "We went all the way around, out to the pass, then in to the road. Reinforcements. Guns."

"Tanks?"

"Didn't see any, and those we captured say they haven't either." His eyes flick to the new men. "Where are these from?"

"Out near Malaishu. There are many coming from the Western Mountains now." Ghedi doesn't write well and can't multiply, but he retains numbers and never forgets a man once he's met him. "We have two thousand men and forty vehicles. What's your count on the other side?"

He has troops from all the southern clans and many northerners as well, though on paper they owe allegiance to Assad. Most of his men are young, eager for fighting. He and Juulheed have tried to train them, but there's a limit. They thirst to win glory, and it's God who gives them strength, not training. Anyway, there's not much to know other than to race ahead and kill as many of the enemy as you can.

But this time he's facing an entrenched enemy, twice, maybe three times his strength. They have artillery too. He strokes his new beard. Is this the day? He's worried about fuel. Worried about his right flank; there was a probe last night. "Let me talk to these you captured," he says abruptly.

"One we had to kill. The other's here." Juulheed barks an order, and his men unload a limp burden from the Fiat.

The staggering prisoner has obviously already been questioned. His ragged trousers are bloody, face beaten to meat with rifle butts. "Give him water," Ghedi snaps. "And some of that goat cheese. Who mistreated this Muslim brother?"

"It was I, General," a sublieutenant says, acting the part.

"You were wrong to do so. Peace be upon you, my brother, you are in the hands of friends. I have questions, if you will be kind enough to answer."

The man gapes. He guzzles the water until it flows down his lacerated chest. He looks around.

"You're democrats?" Ghedi asks him. The man frowns. "ADA?" He just stares.

"How many technicals?" The man doesn't answer. "How many tanks? Are there any tanks? Are there Americans with them?"

"No tanks." The prisoner can speak, at least. He seems either astonishingly ignorant or damaged in the brain. "You have . . . qat?"

Ghedi ignores this. "Who is your general?"

"Awsami Michel."

Ghedi looks at Juulheed, who shrugs. It sounds Tawahedo. "A Christian?" he asks, but gets only another gap-toothed gape.

Juulheed spits. "Shall I shoot him?"

"No. That would be a waste." He says to the man gently, "Will you join us, brother? It is said: 'Those who believe fight in the cause of God, while those who disbelieve fight for the cause of tyranny.' If you wish, you may return to your comrades. But I ask: Will you join us instead? Fight under the banner of God, and win eternal Paradise?"

The man hesitates, and Ghedi puts his hand on his shoulder. When he looks up there's a spark of hope in those battered eyes. He nods.

"Put him in the first rank to go forward," Gehdi says, stroking the man's hair. Juulheed smiles in understanding as the bloody man falls to his knees, kissing his hands, sobbing thanks. Men outside the tent murmur among themselves. They look astonished.

Ghedi's turning away when he thinks of another question. "Where are you from? Where do you call your home?"

"Ashaara City," the man murmurs. Juulheed waits a moment more, then has one of his men lead him away.

"The lieutenants from the west are here," Hasheer announces at the tent flap.

They're the ones who marveled at his action with the enemy soldier. Juulheed rises and searches them, laying their weapons on a side table. Ghedi embraces each as he comes forward. Most are older than he, late twenties or early thirties, but they greet him with honorifics, calling him General or Orcharder. They have no troops for this battle, but they're vital all the same. They're from other Islamic militias, from the backcountry tribes whose women and children have been herded into the camps. Nassir has sent imams into those camps to preach and recruit. Now there are small bands all across the country.

"There is chai," Ghedi says, "and rice, and bread and cold lamb. We Waleeli eat simply, but fight hard. As you'll see today, when we crush the dogs of the foreigners and take Uri'yah."

He's unrolling a map when a commotion starts at the tent flap. A woman's confronting Juulheed. "I will see him," she cries shrilly. The tall Waleeli stands nonplussed, unwilling either to touch her or to let her pass.

"What is it she wants?"

"She says she is of your family," one of the westerners says. "We found her on the road. When she heard we were coming to see you she insisted on accompanying us."

Ghedi sets the map aside. He comes forward, studying her face. It's been many years. She looks very different. She's taller.

But it's his sister. It's Zeynaab.

The others look on astonished until he explains. Then they congratulate him. He asks her if she's seen Nabil, if Nabil's with her. She says no, after they were separated she never saw him again. He presses her to him, then holds her away to search the hollows of her cheeks, the dark pain of her eyes. She's suffered. That much is plain.

But he has a battle to plan. He tells one of his lieutenants to take her to his tent and give her water and rice. Then pushes her from his mind and tells Juulheed to send a technical with a white flag to the roadblock.

But Michel refuses to meet. He sends the patrol back with the message that other attempts at communication will be fired on, unless they bring a surrender. Ghedi smiles. This general doesn't trust his men. He's heard how others have gone to fight the Waleeli and joined them instead. He keeps thinking how gaunt Zeynaab looks. He sends her back to his tent to make sure she eats and rests.

He stands in the wind, peering through his goggles, considering again if this is the time for battle. Is the darkness in the east taller? The wind stronger? He's still gaining recruits. But the enemy's reinforcing too. Juulheed stands behind him, voice a low gabble as he continues his endless conversation with himself.

He keeps coming back to that road. His force travels off-road. They've ditched every vehicle that won't stand up cross-country, and his scouts have donkeys and camels. But the enemy opposite came down the road. They're from the city, city soldiers.

"See what they're doing over there?" says one of his lieutenants, a still-unbearded boy. "Those are mines. They're laying mines."

Mines! He's not thought of this. He frowns. "We have no way of detecting mines."

"No, General."

"But, who knows where each mine is buried?"

"The enemy, General."

"Who else?"

The youngster searches for a moment before he has the answer. "God knows."

"That's right. And He will reveal them to us."

"That's so, General. You're right!" The boy gazes at him with adoration. For a moment Ghedi wonders: Is this idolatry? Blasphemy? Then dismisses it. All that he does is dedicated to His glory.

"We will attack," he announces. "Gather my lieutenants for *salat*."

He leads the prayer, half his lieutenants standing with weapons in hand, the other half praying; then taking turns. Just as the Book describes, and it's not lost on them. They bow and kneel, murmuring. He stands from the final prostration, dusting sand from his knees; his troops carry no prayer rugs.

He stands for an endless moment, watching the wind shape the green-fringed silk above his tent. Feeling, more than thinking, how each fold and snap and rustle has been predetermined since the creation of the world.

And suddenly he *experiences* a world filled to bursting

with *meaning*. Not one grain of dust exists without *infinite love*. Not one thought passes through his mind without being lovingly created by God Himself. The world's the mind of God, and he himself is His thought. He bows again, though they're done praying. God does what He wills through him, and all his heart says yes to that subjection. "Praise be to God, the All-Merciful," he murmurs. To God Himself, close as his heart, far above as the blinding sun that blazes through his closed lids.

"Did you see his face? It *shines*," he hears one man whisper to another. He opens his mouth to correct him, then closes it. If a story makes men brave, he will not take it from them.

He discusses the plan with Juulheed, who'll lead the armor. Examines the sky again, then says, "Farewell, and God be with you." He waves as his talkative deputy climbs into the Fiat, wishing he could ride with him. The armored cars bump awkwardly, gathering speed, then swerve off to the west, into the hills.

Two trucks with dead engines have been towed into position flanking the tent. They'll provide splinter protection. Out here there's no other cover, and they can't stop to dig in as the enemy has. Like a caravan between oases, they must go forward or die.

"Screen forward," he tells Hasheer, and goes inside. He does not want to watch this opening of the battle, when a hundred men and women, enemies, prisoners, those being punished for unchastity or impiety, are driven into the enemy's line. The soldier he forgave and welcomed this morning will be one. They'll be shot down, the enemy taking them for the first wave before seeing they're unarmed. Others will step on the deadly charges beneath the sand.

That's out of his hands. All will be as God wills.

Engines roar as a dozen technicals start up. He lifts the flap of the tent, ties it up. He won't be able to see the battlefield for long, but what there is to see, he must.

There's one radio, but not enough receivers to make it tactically useful. In front of him's a board with colored boxes, in each, a cell phone. Each phone connects him to a sector commander. They have flag signals too, but the phones are his main communications.

A crack, and the sky splits. Ocher dust erupts to his front. Artillery or mortars. He wishes he'd brought the Gelhirs' cannons. Then shakes his head and reaches for the next phone. They have gasoline for one attack. If the enemy realizes this, that they need only hold to win, he'll have to stagger back into the desert with whoever remains. He must spend fuel, ammunition, lives, like a wealthy merchant. If he loses, he'll be a beggar.

Three hundred yards in front of his lines the technicals pivot, spewing dust as they race across the desert. The dust plumes grow. They're caught by the growing wind, whirled into dust devils, blown downwind in a seething cloud the color of earth.

Into his enemies' eyes.

"Attack," he says over and over, laying down one phone, picking up the next. "Attack. Attack."

The towering darkness grows. It's almost on them.

Within minutes all visibility vanishes. The desert plunges into night, the sun replaced by a russet fog through which invisible things lunge. Mortar bursts erupt, and the clatter of machine guns. And far away, the screaming of men. Ghedi hunches over the map. Its traceries of lines and cross-hatchings suddenly seem unreal, its sheath of powdery sand its only truth. What can he say over these telephones? His men know what they must do. In the corner of the tent, Hasheer looks apprehensive.

Ghedi grabs his Kalashnikov and runs outside. Hasheer tries to stop him, but he shakes him off.

Outside the dust is choking, whipped into the air by wheels and the enormous breath of the storm. The wind sends it into his teeth. His men fight swathed to the eyes, their weapons wrapped to exclude the grit. The enemy, though, are city folk. This howling chaos is new to them. On the other hand, there are the mines. Many of his men will die. This he accepts as right, and the manifest will of one who determines from eternity the fate moment to moment of His every creature. He laughs aloud, a toy of God who wills all that He wills.

The technical's already rolling, a Toyota pickup in the green and tan tiger stripes of those who were first to join. The men reach to haul him aboard. They scream, waving rifles. Under their headscarves a glistening membrane is plastered over their eyes. Plastic wrap, looted from one of the WFO trucks. He stuffs his pockets with rounds from the open box stenciled in Chinese. A shell explodes so close the blast ripples the murky air, and he screams too, God is great, God is great. The engine snarls and the truck slams against something he can't see. Engines roar from all around him. Other shadows loom, tearing along with them. The enemy has trucks too, but from each of Ghedi's flutters a long banner of black-and-green fire.

The storm hits, bellowing like a thousand engines, and they plunge blind into darkness. Clinging with one hand, firing with the other when he glimpses a target. Bullets whine past and snap into the frame. Cartridge cases spew, flying, rolling underfoot. A glimpse of wire to one side, but somehow they've arrowed into a gap. An enormous bang; a truck flips, throwing off men and weapons like a bucking donkey as it cartwheels. A machine-gun team their driver swerves instantly to head for. The oversized tires bottoming in shallow trenches, the men hurl the plastic grenades in every direction. They crack savagely, spraying death in the form of hundreds of tiny steel balls. Ghedi and every other man in the truck fires as fast as he can, the machine gun slamming slugs right over their heads, deafening him. The taste of smoke and powder, the gritty dust clogging mouth and nose, the exhaust from worn-out engines. His Kalashnikov barrel so hot he lets go the handguard but keeps firing, ramming in magazine after magazine.

Then suddenly he's in the air, flying. He turns over and crashes to the sand. Tires grate past as he grips at the dry dirt, then spots a crater and rolls into it. A man stares at him stupidly. Ghedi tries to fire, fails, jerks the bayonet out and runs it into him. A crunching give. The man screams and drops his weapon, clawing at Ghedi. Someone else shoots him and his head splatters like a ripe pomegranate. Another truck tears by. The men in it fire at them but the bullets crack into the soil and the body that now sags lifeless.

Two of his men haul him up. They stagger into the murk, trailing the technicals. Screams and moans all around. Broken bodies, blood, a screaming camel dragging half its body across the sand. He's lost all orientation but the wind. He lets it drive him forward, stopping only to snatch up a new weapon when his grows too hot to hold. His hands are blistered claws. A man with gray in his beard kneels in the dust, clutching his belly. His eyes bulge as he stares at a pool of his own entrails. Past him trucks lurch, troops clinging to their sides as if to a bucking boat. They carry not the Waleeli banner, but the black, yellow, and green of the old national flag, before the president put the red star on it.

A shout. "Airplane! Airplane!" And a screeching louder even than the storm as a shape sweeps overhead. It's followed by a noise he's never heard before: a deep bellow that suddenly turns the whole inside of the storm yellow with flame.

He's both terrified and joyous. The terror's part of the joy, the joy's part of the wind, God's entering him as he fights for God. This is Paradise despite the screams as men burn alive, whirling like Sufis, lighting up the bloody murk. The planes tear over again and muffled *whoomphs* echo over the plain, the gasoline smell's suffocating, but he doesn't fear them. They can't see within the murk, the dust; all they can see is confused struggle. They're bombing both sides as they swirl in the demonic brew of battle.

Another explosion flings him through the air and he crashes into soft things, bodies. They push back, cursing: aim rifles; lower them at sight of his armband. The dead man at their feet wears a string of amulets, inscribed with a holy verse that deflects bullets. Another bends and strips it off the corpse and slides it onto his own arm.

Ghedi's in a secondary trench system. Ahead he makes

out the low buildings he saw that morning. Beyond them is the roadblock, then Uri'yah itself. An emaciated woman crawls through the dust as if swimming; she drags a dead child. One of the refugees driven into the minefield. There's no point feeding those who can't fight. But how has she gotten so far? And what grim determination drives her on, hauling her dead with her?

He's gathering his men when a yell comes from the direction of the huts. A line appears, wavering shadows dotted with pricks of light. Bullets whine and snap. Ghedi fires back until he's out of cartridges. The men search bodies, but find only a few rounds. The advancing line fall to their bellies and fire. Then a few rise and rush forward as the others lay down a hail of fire. His men hug the ground. One breaks and runs, throwing away his rifle. The attacking line rise and rush again.

A blow rocks his head back as something invisible strikes his mouth. When he puts his hand to it, it's numb and wet. Motors bawl in the murk. When he looks behind him men are scrambling down from trucks, aiming rifles. They're not Waleeli. His little party's surrounded and falling fast. A poppy-colored flame lights the murk again, and a wave of heat, smoke, and gasoline fumes rolls across the desert.

Ghedi looks forward, at the huts. He gets to his feet and rotates the stubby bayonet out again and locks it. "God is great!" he shouts. "Follow me!"

Lurching like a camel spider, he claws his way over the lip of the trench and charges into the gun flashes. And hears, behind him, the eager shouts of the men who charge with him, into the face of Death itself.

When tubby shapes snarl from the murk ahead and the charging line slow, twist to look behind them, then scatter in panic, he still lurches ahead. As lances of fire and smoke erupt from the bannered turrets and four, six, eight RPGs fly overhead and detonate on the trucks behind him, he screams and brandishes the rifle in the air.

The steel hulls of Juulheed's armored cars churn past from their great loop to the west and back, taking the enemy positions from behind, grinding over trenches and bodies and hastily discarded rifles, utterly shattering the enemy front. Ghedi stands erect, chanting into the sky through a smashed mouth filled with blood. The road to the capital's clear. No barrier remains between the Waleeli and their goal. "This is what God and His messenger have promised us.

"There is no god but Allah, and Muhammad is his prophet!"

The chanted refrain from all around on the battlefield is echoed, as by an inhuman choir, by a roar from the very sky.

19

THE EMPTY QUARTER

Gráinne stood watching the rig with hands on hips, ignoring glances from men in dirty uniform trousers, sweat-soaked T-shirts, green hard hats with names and rank insignia, muddy boots. Even through shades and a bush hat, the glare was like a hot lead helmet. Far off a mirage danced on a salt flat, wavering and jerking like a lure dangled by the Devil to tempt men to doom.

The soldiers were from Naval Mobile Construction Battalion 133, out of Gulfport, Louisiana. They called themselves "Seabees." They'd introduced themselves as steelworkers, equipment operators, electricians. There were even a few women. One had given her the camouflage pants she wore.

She'd met the lieutenant in charge, and they'd followed her Land Rover from their airport staging point up the road to Nakar, where she'd led them off-pavement. Minutes later his Humvee had pulled up as he waved her over. "Sure you know where you're going, Doctor?"

But here they were, all the same. He'd told her 133 had teams and equipment to drill not one, but five wells at once. After the meeting with Ahearn she'd explored her conscience and her maps, trying both to test her hypothesis about the paleowater lens and to actually provide fresh water to the nomad Nasaris.

She'd plotted five locations. Four were in already-known artesian formations, where she was fairly sure they'd find water close to the surface, though it might not recharge. Which would mean the wells would run out, maybe in a month, maybe a year. There was a reason this was desert.

Number Five wasn't going to hit water. At least, not for a long time. If it came up fresh, Ashaara's future would be different. If it came up brackish, or contaminated with salts or sulfates . . . no geologist could change what was under the ground.

Now that fifth rig, perched on the blasted side of what looked almost like some ancient volcanic crater, was roaring its way down into the dry dirt, sending fine blue smoke drifting on the desert wind.

The first day the Seabees had dug postholes and put up targets, then fired rifles for two hours, the cracks fading echoless into the desert. Some rite, perhaps, to remind them they were soldiers.

Then they'd put away their weapons and begun assembling equipment, and it quickly became evident they were also a good deal more.

The lieutenant had left a chief in charge. He'd immediately started preparing the site. A desert tan front-end loader had scraped away meters of gravel and sand, exposing bare rock. They'd leveled equipment, stacked pipes on wooden racks clear of the ground, and covered them with tarps. Unloaded barrels, electric lights, pumps, generators. Other teams dug pits and lined them with heavy green construction plastic, the edges carefully turned and buried to present a smooth surface to the wind. They bolted together a steel shed and positioned a satellite station and trucks for water, fuel, and maintenance.

By the end of the first shift everything was set up but the drill rig. They leveled the ground once more, then erected a steel tower. By the time the floodlights came on that evening drilling was under way. She'd sat out on the sand most of that day, keeping her sunscreen fresh and her hat pulled low, watching one man.

The Chief, they called him.

She'd known when Fletcher had stepped down out of his truck he was going to be significant in her life. His easygoing drawl was unlike any she'd ever heard. His muscles outlined under his damp T, the casual way he strolled among his troops, their obvious respect, all turned her on. He'd looked back, too. He wore a wedding ring. He chewed something, not qat, some kind of tobacco. *That* would have to go.

But they were both a long way from home.

He'd come to her tent that night. She'd already changed and dabbed on some Je Reviens. A heavy scent, but when water was scarce that was what you needed. She'd offered him a drink. It hadn't taken long after that.

His first name was Efrain. He said it was from his grandmother's family. She tried to feel guilty about her husband, but it seemed like so long since she'd cared. His chest hair felt like a wire strainer against her nipples. His mouth tasted of whatever he'd been chewing, but it wasn't unpleasant. Her first boyfriend had smoked.

None of this sounded romantic but it still felt very nice indeed to bring her legs back to her chest, in her sleeping bag, and take him in. It had been a long time and when she came it seemed to last for a month and a half while she hung on, making small sounds she hoped didn't carry to the other tents.

When she returned he was looking into her eyes. Dipping his head to kiss the silver symbol on her flushed chest, then her nipples, first one, then the other. "Oh. God," she said.

And he'd said, "My turn."

All the next week the drilling went on.

The diesels chugged or roared, depending on how hard the strata was. The mud pump gurgled and spat. Organized into teams, the Seabees drilled right through the dark hours. They averaged thirty to fifty meters a day, depending on what they were punching through. Every four hours they brought samples to her tent. She examined each core with a poker face, filing each in its own plastic sample box.

Fletcher spent the nights with her, but they treated each other with distant politeness on the rig. Did the others guess? There were probably a few discreet liaisons going on in the unit itself, the hardworking men and the sunburned, muscular women in sweaty T-shirts with navy-issue bras visible beneath. Those who wore them; not all did. As she passed she felt their gazes, men and women alike.

Efrain had frowned when she told him how deep this well would be. He'd never gone past nine hundred feet, and according to her estimate, the lens would be at least six hundred meters deep—more than twice as far. But he'd agreed, after saying he'd have to order more pipe.

The refugees had started coming the day after they began. She had no idea how they knew. The camp was fifteen kilometers away. Perhaps they'd heard the generators, in the night. They walked the entire way. They brought brightly colored water containers and left them in neat lines, weighed down by rocks in case the wind came up.

One day, bored, she climbed in the Rover and drove to Refugee Camp Three. Threw a scarf over her head; red hair had an unfortunate effect on the kids, and old women would scold her. She didn't understand their words, but she'd just as soon avoid spoiling anyone's day.

As they walked the camp the Swiss director explained the situation in French. "The coast road is our lifeline. We truck water in from the port and issue it with oral rehydration salts. Sometimes the bandits stop the convoys, or there are breakdowns. We keep a reserve for drinking but actually we're only ever three days away from being completely out."

"How much do you use?"

"Each family needs forty to fifty liters for cooking, washing, and drinking. At the moment, that's thirteen thousand liters a day."

"Chlorination?"

The woman looked at her proudly. "The water on the

trucks is treated to one and a half milligrams per liter. That gives us an adequate residual concentration by the time it gets into the pots in their tents. Unfortunately, if we don't receive enough, they have to walk half a mile to a wadi."

"What's that taste like?" Gráinne asked her.

"The treated water?"

"No, from the wadi. Is it bitter?"

The Swiss woman made a face. "I've not tasted it, Doctor. It's probably contaminated."

"I agree. Let me ask you something. If I had a message for New York—could I send it through you?"

"No e-mail, but I have a radio. We talk to the airport several times a day. If you have a message, we can forward it." She held her hand out.

"I don't yet. About your wadi source: it most likely is contaminated. Most surface water is. I could test it for you."

"It wouldn't matter. What else can I give them? And there's no fuel to boil it. I truly am worried, if we have to keep them here much longer. Of course, most of our residents have lived in near-drought conditions all their lives. They're Afar, after all. The desert has made them what they are. Do you know how they refer to this drought? As a blessing from Allah. I'm never sure if they're being mystical, or just ironic."

"I thought they were Nasaris . . . ?"

"That's a tribe of the Afar. They're a very clean people, so long as they're on the move. Unfortunately, they're not used to living in large, static groups." She blinked, hugging herself. "You're alone, out in the desert?"

Gráinne smiled. "I have a hundred and sixty-eight armed troops with me. I don't really worry."

"We all need to be careful." The Swiss woman glanced away. "I see people about the camp I don't know. When I ask, I learn nothing. When I look again, they're gone."

"I'll stay until we find you some water, anyway."

"Oil, you mean?"

She'd blinked, then grinned. "Is that what they're saying? Believe me. There's no oil here."

"Of course. Well. If you do find water, I have enough fuel to send a jeep twice a day. It would save many from dying."

Gráinne had wanted to tell her then, this small worrying woman with her hundreds of children. But she couldn't. No one must know until she was sure, and her own office must hear it first. So she'd just patted her arm. "I hope I can help. But only the drilling will tell for sure."

Another week passed. Now Efrain came every other night. He said he had to sleep sometime. She wondered where this was going. At first she hadn't. A fling, nothing more.

The trouble was, she'd miss him, when it was over. He always seemed to know what to do. She'd never met anyone like that. Reece had never seemed to know shite.

She couldn't go back to him. Nor to Ireland. Maybe Fletcher was just simpler, not better. He'd never said he wouldn't go back to his wife. And children. But whatever happened with him, her marriage was over.

Maybe he was her way of proving it to herself? She'd smiled wryly. "Overanalysis, O'Shea," Dr. Kyriazis would have said.

She wished he, Costa, were with her now. To see if his great suspicion was right.

Every day was the same. A hearty breakfast, with eggs. The diesels roared. The mud pump gurgled. The water truck refilled the pits. The men shouted, manhandling the collar into position to take the next length of pipe. Foamy brown mud bubbled up and ran down into its settling pit. The smell of burning diesel fuel and shit drifted over the camp in the evening. They had a latrine for women, *all plastic*, with a minute sink built in and even a soap dispenser. Ridiculous, but better than squatting in a ravine, or worse, on an open plain, while your driver pretended not to wonder if your hair was red there too. No showers, though. She kept to her liter a day for an evening wash.

Out on the sand, lines of colorful jugs waited.

Was it possible? Today she might find out. She paced rapidly around the compound. No fence, no wire or guard posts. It wasn't that kind of camp, and anyway, out here in the Quartier Vide, whom had they to fear?

Today they'd hit six hundred meters. Of course the depth of the upper lens was only a guess. It could happen tomorrow, or this morning. She stood by the rig, blotting sweat and sunblock off her forehead.

"We're ready, if it happens," Fletcher said behind her.

She turned, fingering the claddagh. He was smelly, hard hat shoved back, cheek smeared with mud. He looked absolutely cunning and she wanted to take him in her arms there and then.

But she didn't. A woman in a blond ponytail was greasing threads on the next section of pipe. So she just murmured, "When it does, let's take a shower together. I'll take you to the Cosmopolite. It's on the Champs Nationale, the best hotel in Ashaara City."

She got a grin, but he said nothing, neither yes nor that he couldn't, or that the Navy would probably send him somewhere else; just looked away. A blade twisted in her stomach. Don't do this to me, she thought. Not today.

"Do what?" he said, gaze back on her.

She must have spoken aloud. "Nothing," she said, feeling herself flush. Get a grip, O'Shea. You're not sixteen anymore. She rubbed at a burning where sunblock had run into her eyes. "I'm going to lie down in my tent. Call me if anything happens."

They didn't hit anything that day, though, and she sat up late trying to write a letter to her mother. They hadn't had e-mail contact for weeks, and her mother would be worried. Efrain had said that if she posted a letter with the fleet post office system, it'd get to Ireland eventually. He'd put his return address on it, so it'd go free. But everything she wrote sounded trivial.

She woke to the blond-ponytail trooper shaking her. "Water" was all she said.

All she needed to say. Gráinne squirmed out of her sleeping bag—it got cool in the evenings—and shook out her boots, shook out her smelly bush trousers, which she'd meant to wash but hadn't yet. She'd been stung by a scorpion in the Sudan, and ever after had inspected every item of clothing before putting it on. Her heart was beating faster than usual.

When she ducked out dawn was breaking. They were all standing around the rig. When she looked down the floodlights gleamed on a smooth jet of clear fluid, leaping from the drill collar to weep down into the sand. The dirt around it was dark with moisture.

She examined their faces as they handed her a plastic cup. Her hand shook. She brought the cup to her nose and sniffed, alert for the telltale stink of sulfur dioxide, the bite of dissolved CO_2. She didn't smell either. She held it to the floodlights, looking for turbidity or foaming. There was a bit, particulate too, but that could be from the drilling.

She took a sip delicately as a oenophile at a wine tasting. Tasted with the front of her palate, then tongued it back into the corners of her mouth. No salt, her biggest worry. Hints of calcium or magnesium compounds, but they wouldn't make the water undrinkable. In fact, just the opposite.

She'd have to test it, of course. But it tasted good. Rainwater from thirty thousand years ago, held down there in trust all this time.

"You have to keep drilling," she told them.

"Isn't it good? Tastes fine to me," Fletcher said, frowning. "All we need to do's the sanitary seal."

"It's excellent water. But I need data. How thick this sandstone is. How thick the aquifer is. So we can . . . so I know if it can support additional wells." She let herself smile, let excitement show. "It's wonderful water. You've done a fantastic job."

Efrain's hand was on her shoulder. "You led us here, Doc. It's your water more than mine."

Since everyone else was hugging her, she didn't think it would hurt if she let him kiss her cheek.

The sandstone was soft. The bit went through it much faster than it had the harder strata above. She tested at each string of pipe. They got to seven hundred meters before the lens ended.

There was a lot of water down there. A *lot* of water.

And the artesian seeps she'd mapped told her it ran west, and north, for nearly a hundred miles.

She tucked a little Skoal against her gum and held it while she wrote her report in longhand. There was no Ministry of Interior Resources anymore. No Dr. Isdheeb to report to. She was wary about telling the Americans, too. Fletch she trusted, but Ahearn and those above him she did not. She addressed it to her funders at the Hydrological Programme. They'd know what to do.

She told Efrain she was going to the city overnight; did he want to go? Take that shower at the Cosmopolite? He said he couldn't leave his people. She understood that, and the tone of his voice, too. He'd be moving on to the next job. Building a school. Repairing a road. Their time was over. She allowed herself a short cry on the dirt track down to the coast road, then cleaned her face with a desiccated wet wipe and concentrated on not blowing a tire.

The roadblock was set up on the reverse slope of a gravel ridge. The men had black headwraps over their faces. They were armed, of course. She slammed on the brakes, remembering suddenly, with a cold sweat, how Abdiwali had died.

How could she have driven out alone? Cursing her stupidity, she clutched the wheel as a dark man with a beard tapped on the glass. Politely, or it might have seemed polite, if he hadn't been tapping with the muzzle of a rifle.

She rolled the window down and held out the paper. "This is very important," she told him, and repeated it in French. "*Tres importante. C'est l'eau.* Water for everybody, for all Ashaara, for many years. Please let me pass. You have to let me pass."

The paper fluttered to the sand, torn into bits. Too late, as they pulled her out of the Rover, she realized she spoke no language they would recognize.

20

THE OLD QUARTER, ASHAARA CITY

They spend the night in an abandoned bakery filled with wrecked machinery. Every scrap of copper's been looted and the walls daubed with intertwined clan symbols, ADA slogans, obscenities from the Assad forces. Hasheer throws out several squatter families and posts guards before he waves Ghedi's driver in. And even then, has armed men running alongside, shielding him.

There are still those who say Hasheer's not loyal. But Ghedi's never seen any evidence of it.

This morning they eat lamb and rice from the common dish, drinking chai so thick with powdered milk and sugar it's almost pudding. Ghedi chews painfully, trying not to tear the roughly stitched flesh where the bullet tore apart his gums. Each man scoops and eats, wiping his lips after each rolled ball, left hand swathed in his robe or tucked under his haunch. Their weapons lie to hand. A buzzing echoes in the hot air. When he looks up Ghedi sees hornets' nests. The insects drift toward bullet holes in the metal roofing, clamber clumsily through them, then disappear on their errands.

The men around him are silent with anger. They lost many at Uri'yah, but were victorious. Juulheed's charge broke the enemy. They not only captured hundreds of prisoners, they gained hundreds of recruits among the soldiers. The captured officers, though, he did not welcome. He shot General Michel and all his staff, officers from the old army. Some begged for mercy, saying they sympathized with the Waleeli, or had sent information to Ikrane before the battle. These too he shot. Who can trust traitors not to turn again?

He says, "I'll go alone. As the sheekh asks."

"They stopped us after the victory. Why?"

They speculate quietly. Finally his deputy voices what's on all their minds. "What's to prevent them killing you?"

Juulheed may have a point. Ghedi rolls another bite and chews thoughtfully. "You think they'd kill me?"

"They founded the Waleeli, but you lead the great army. Can they let you live?"

Could God have spared him in battle, to have him die at the hands of assassins? It seems unlikely. Could his old teacher turn against him? Someone ordered him to stop fighting, on the verge of triumph. What can that be but treachery?

He holds out his cup for more chai as his bodyguards watch each other. He flicks glances at Hasheer, at the mumbling Juulheed. At Ini Fiammetta, who stopped his bleeding and sewed his mouth, a scarred intense nomad who despite his Italian name is Issa, who seems to carry in his throat a coiled snake he's forever swallowing.

"God will prevent them." Ghedi swallows the last of the tepid chai and rises, brushing off his camouflage trousers. American, taken from one of the officers he shot. A light fabric with many pockets. He likes them better than any other he's ever worn.

"God carries us only so far," Hasheer murmurs. "Then we must act for ourselves."

The others ignore him, too pointedly. Ghedi slaps his shoulder, then hugs him. He looks at his new watch, also a battlefield prize. He checks his AK and slings it. The others get up.

"We'll find out what is in their minds," he says. "And I will not go alone. Come, then. We will meet with the sheekh."

Through the alleys and cobbled streets of the Old City, one technical a block ahead and three more full of his men behind, he smells the difference. In the way shadows fall. How empty clotheslines hang where no woman tends them. The technicals lurch and whine. Dented with fragment scars, shocks and springs broken, they show hard use and the scars of battle. But the guns on their beds are greased and loaded, the breeches wrapped with black plastic against sand. The gunners swing from side to side, searching rooftops and cross streets as they pass. Women duck away, or stare from curtained balconies. The bright hot sky's visible between buildings, and now and then the black cross of a foreign helicopter passes to an echoing drumbeat. Pulled-up cobblestones are piled in barricades, reinforced with wrecked cars, staircases, shattered masonry, cannibalized machinery. He notes the clan markings on the walls, erased and defaced from block to block.

The city's changing, dividing. Families wheel carts piled with bedding. Neighborhood militia stand scowling at intersections. Juulheed calls greetings, his men wave the black-and-green pennant enthusiastically, but the sentries stand their ground, allowing passage to such a heavily armed column but not welcoming it. They glimpse an American vehicle, antenna bobbing as it jolts over the road. They slow until it passes from sight, turn left, then right again.

At last they pass a black-and-green banner, then another. The faces at the balconies turn friendly. Plastic flowers rain down. People come out, the street grows not thronged exactly, but not empty, either. Here the women wear burkas, though some still favor African cloth with loud patterns. With a screech the technicals halt at the shabby compound Ghedi knows so well.

He finds himself trembling. Remembering how he came here to learn, at the feet of the man who seemed to see more with no eyes than a hundred with perfect vision.

Armed men step forward to object, but Fiammetta and Hasheer ignore them. They jump out and set guards at overwatch points. The few men Sheekh Nassir keeps contemplate the bores of the technicals' machine guns and make no objection. For blocks in every direction boys with cheap radios are climbing roofs, watching for the helicopters. The technicals' crews angle muzzles skyward and arrange feed belts. A vehicle pulls around back, should the foreigners or their hired militia stage a raid.

The Orcharder swings his boots down to plant them on the cracked pavement of the capital. If they hadn't stopped him, he'd be here as a conqueror. The knowledge smolders. Why stop short of victory, when it was so close?

"Want me to come with you?" Juulheed, beside him. Ghedi considers, then tells him, only to the inner court. But he protests. Talking as if to his devils, Juulheed mumbles, "I won't let him go in alone, he won't go in alone." Ghedi gives up and says he can come.

In the inner court the air tastes more of danger than it did before Uri'yah. Chickens peck at a scorpion in the dust. Two men demand his rifle. They accompany him and Juulheed up the stair.

The old man sits in the darkened room before a bowl of fruit. The smells trigger Ghedi's memory, as if he exists in two times at once. Cinnamon and cumin, peppermint and incense. Nassir Irrir Zumali wears a black robe and a velvet cap like a Jew's. His beard glows against desiccated skin. He sits motionless as Ghedi pauses, surveying those who sit at either hand. The old man works his fingers at his gums.

"Greetings, honored master. Ghedi returns at your summons from our victory over the idolators at Uri'yah."

"I hear many things of my young son," the sheekh murmurs. "He is called Tiger of the Desert. Whip of God. Pruner of Dead Branches. Give him one of these mangoes, my brothers. Was he not born where they grew?"

Ghedi bows, though the eyes behind the dark lenses cannot see him. "We are faithful to you and the Holy Word, honored Sheekh."

The withered fingers beckon in a familiar gesture. Ghedi leans close, closing his eyes as they explore his cheeks, his eye sockets. He winces as they trace his swollen mouth, his truncated beard. "So," the old man mutters. "No longer our most beautiful son."

"He's wounded. Bring chai for our brothers," says Mahdube, at the master's right hand. He looks even thinner than before in a Western-style suit, black shoes, even a black tie. Ghedi blinks. Has he returned to teaching? On Nassir's other hand Ikrane sits motionless as stone, save for an inclination of his head as Ghedi greets him too. The Waleeli spymaster's not a man to be ignored.

He introduces Juulheed. For once his garrulous deputy's silent. "What is your clan, my brother?" Nassir asks.

"He's of the Berdaale," Ghedi answers for him, then wonders why, if there's no clan in the Waleeli, the old man asks.

The tea's served by a nervous-looking young boy in student's garments. Ghedi regards its dark surface. Then gathers his courage and takes a sip. Unable to resist their smell, he takes one of the mangoes. It's unutterably delicious, wet and rich and sweet. Its slick flesh and the scent of its juice take him back to being a child, far away, in a village that is no more.

Suddenly his anger takes command and he disregards politeness, courtesy, even the cunning he's vowed to bring into this room. "Your wisdom is great, your knowledge profound. I am glad to find you and my brothers in good health. But I do not understand. What is happening? I see clan militia, I see neighbor turning against neighbor, I see foreigners unresisted in the streets. Why have you agreed to this cease-fire? No army stands between me and the capital. I could have taken Ashaara, and recognized you as supreme judge."

The only answer's a whisper as incense ash topples. The lines on the old cleric's face grow deeper, as if pain torments. Perhaps so; it's said he was tortured long ago, in the time of British rule.

Ikrane sits forward. "You've built an army, my brother. Killed a general, and made yourself into one."

"We have no ranks. We are all fighters, all volunteers."

"You're not the leader?"

"God only is our leader, His name be praised."

"Indeed, praise be to His name. It is said you have fifty technicals. Can this be true?"

"I have nearly a hundred, and armored cars as well."

The assistants nod soberly. "It's true, the clans are arming. They're dividing the city, and no one ventures across their lines. Are you equal to them? And even their numbers are as nothing compared to the power of the foreigners, which increases every day."

"Their aircraft were helpless at Uri'yah. I can defeat them, and the clans as well."

"Your battle took place during a dust storm."

He smiles. "The storm was sent by God."

"All praise to His name," the old man puts in. "But we cannot count on His sending a storm each time we fight."

"Is this why you agreed to this cease-fire?" Ghedi asks him. The expression of pain deepens. The old man waves his fingers, then digs into his mouth again.

Ghedi feels something he's never felt for his teacher before. After a moment he realizes it's disgust. What is he but a blind old man with bad teeth and a habit of speaking in riddles? Yes, he's memorized the holy books. But has he built an army from the dry sticks of the desert? Now he sounds as if he doubts God's power.

Mahdube speaks. "Some call you the Maahdi, the Guided One, he who makes straight the way of Jesus when he returns at the end of days."

"I can't control what people say. Those who called me Maahdi were whipped." He shifts where he sits, growing impatient with this spectacled nobody's tone of accusation. This academic who's done nothing in the years he's sat beside the sheekh eating and drinking and counting shillings. Ikrane he respects; the older man sent him many recruits from the west. But how do they presume to question him? To tell him not to fight? He asks, "Again: Why have you ordered this cease-fire? Why have you cooperated with the foreigners' government?"

"Certainly the end of days must be near," mutters the old man, who seems to still be on the subject of the Maahdi. "The great battle that will end with Islam triumphant and all the saints returned."

"It's not yet a government," Mahdube says, ignoring him. It's the first time Ghedi has seen an utterance of the sheekh not treated with respect. "There have not yet been elections. We have spoken to a woman of the foreigners who speaks Arabic like an imam."

"A foreign woman?"

"An American, but a Muslim. She told us we must give up our weapons. If we do not, we will be outlawed. If we do, we will have a voice in the government."

"You *met* with an American woman?" He can't believe his ears, directs his question to the old man. *"You?"*

Mahdube says, "At the honored sheekh's command, I also met with representatives of Dr. Dobleh's party. Doing so made us part of the interim council. Also, it allowed us to contradict certain lies circulating about you."

"That I'm the Maahdi?"

"No, that you've killed hundreds of refugees. Taken their food and abandoned them to die. Driven them into minefields. Machine-gunned Jews and Christians who refuse Islam."

Juulheed leans close. He speaks breathily faint, within Ghedi's ear alone. "They're selling you to the foreigners. That's why they called you here."

Ghedi taps the soft carpet. He sees now deep within it bits of rotting food. "I killed only those God marked for death, who set themselves against Him. Is that not your will? If it changed, no one told me. Are we democrats now? What *murtadd* is this, that you're sitting on their councils?"

"No," says the old man, but again Mahdube speaks over him. "We seek righteousness, as always. But the Americans take killing Jews and Christians badly."

"The foreigners have strong weapons, but they are not gods."

"The fact is," Mahdube says, taking out a cheap lined school tablet, "you have been asked here to make clear certain things, that we can answer to the authorities."

"What things? What authorities?"

"You cannot question this man," Juulheed says, speaking aloud for the first time. He jiggles one knee as he sits. Glances at the concrete-still Ikrane. "Who are you to do so? He brings victory. He is our general, our lord of war."

"Now, now," the old man puts in, but the spectacled scholar goes on reading from his tablet. Ghedi's anger mounts till he can no longer sit still. Yet he does, as the little man in the suit and tie reads off lie after lie. Some incidents he recalls, but others are stories. If they happened, it was without his knowledge.

"You deny these crimes?" Mahdube says, and perhaps because of his disbelieving tone Juulheed suddenly leans and slaps him so hard his glasses fly off. The old man cries out. Ikrane seems not to have moved, but Ghedi sees he has a black pistol. He hasn't said a word, just taken out the pistol.

"Apologize to our brother," Ghedi says, and his deputy stammers reluctant words. Mahdube holds his face, the tablet shaking in his other hand.

"What is it you want?" Ghedi shouts. "Why did you call me here? Not to question me about worthless pagans, traitors, and backsliders. We could have taken the city. You call the foreigners evil, then you bargain with them."

"You've killed too many. Many Muslims—"

"To make them submit. Were not these deaths justified?"

"Not I," says the old man, making a rejecting gesture with his fingers. "Not I."

"It was not you?"

"It was at your word, O Sheekh," Mahdube bursts out, holding his face. "All is at your word, the talks, the agreement, all."

"So many deaths," Nassir whispers. "I see this! I see the war to come! Do you remember the war with Sudan? This will be a thousand times more terrible. The battle, yes. But the way of God is not altogether the way of blood." Behind the dark glasses he seems to be weeping.

"A *wahi*," Mahdube whispers in awe. "A prophecy of the Apocalypse."

Ghedi stares. "Were not these deaths by the will of God? Is not all that happens willed by Him? That's what you taught."

"Not so many," the old man mutters. "To say God blesses you when you kill, this is *haram*. You are not the Guided One. He will invite the created to the Creator. His nature is that of the angels." He catches his breath in a sob, and gropes out. For a moment Ghedi thinks it's for his hand, or to feel his face again, then realizes. It's for a mango.

Abruptly he's filled with loathing. An old man with bad teeth and bad breath, greedy for sweets, pretending to prophesy to get his way. Surrounded by flatterers and jackals. "Come," he says to Juulheed, and they get to their feet. "You will not judge me. I no longer acknowledge you as leader of the Waleeli. You are softhearted women. Tomorrow you will be the foreigners' tools. It is my soldiers who do God's will, not you."

"Come back," Mahdube says. "We agreed to the ceasefire only to gather strength. Once the foreigners leave, we'll strike." The old man sits with head drooping, fingers in his mouth. On his other side the spymaster sits unmoving.

Numb, Ghedi walks toward the door. A lizard hesitates as he nears, then darts for an open window.

"You were right," he mumurs as they reach the corridor. Together he and Juulheed pull the small green balls from their pockets.

The men on the carpet don't move as the grenades bounce across the figured rug. Mahdube stares like a goat about to be slaughtered. The old man's probing finger pauses at the double thump and roll. Only Ikrane flinches back and tries to aim.

Too late. When they crack open, jarring the air and shattering bowls and vases, the old man jerks but doesn't rise. He slumps as if falling asleep. The one in the suit starts to his feet, then collapses, white shirt stippled scarlet where scores of the tiny steel balls have sieved it. Only Ikrane manages to rise, spewing blood from his throat. His face is livid. He manages two steps forward, the pistol rising in his big hand. Then it droops, as if weighing more and more, until he can no longer support it. He wades as if through mud, blood pouring from his neck mixed with foam. Then he too topples to the spattered carpet.

Shots snap outside as his men deal with the guards. Ghedi closes his eyes, unable to erase the image of the old man sagging, shattered lenses dangling from one ear. A pulp of mangoes dripping down his knees.

He tries to speak, but words catch in his throat like stones. Juulheed darts him glances. As they step out into the sunlight at the top of the stairs, looking out over the courtyard at the crowd already gathering, Ghedi lifts his arms. Then cannot speak. He tries again, and again something closes in his throat.

It's faithful Juulheed who raises his nervous voice to carry beyond the walls, into the listening streets.

"The foreigners have killed our beloved sheekh and his trusted counselors. Listen, O ye faithful! His last words were a fatwa against them and their secularist puppets, worms in the body of the Faithful."

Lifting his rifle, his second in command screams, finally in the mad voice of the demon Ghedi has always known lives within him, "In the name of the foully murdered, we will avenge him. It is the call to jihad!"

21

IN THE SAWAKIN SOUND

The stink filled the ship now, so pervasive and inescapable they'd stopped smelling it, like medieval serfs their own stench. Only when Teddy went topside did the clean wind smell weird, after the shithole below. Which was why he'd insisted on going ashore.

Shamal had been anchored inside the sound for two weeks, between the anchored *Tahia* and the open sea. He'd read the message traffic with growing frustration.

Teddy had floated an assault plan relying on surprise and night combat expertise. They'd board and sweep from the stern forward, cutting electrical power to shut down lighting, then freeing the captives in a zero-light shootout. Unfortunately, the Malaysian government had "strongly advised" against an attack unless hostages were actually being killed. The Filipinos chimed in, insisting on negotiations. As a last straw, Dobleh's provisional minister of defense had refused to sign off on an attack inside territorial waters. Which left Oberg seething but helpless.

A negotiator from the shipping agency had come and gone with no agreement. The pirates either had no idea how much a billion was, or had nothing better to do than lie around, eat, and demand cigarettes from whoever came aboard. At any rate, they flatly refused to take less than nine zeroes. He'd been over every other day to keep the hostages' spirits up. Each time he came back angrier. Suleyman and his boys were playing the situation for all it was worth. Marooning them aboard hadn't helped. They acted like the lords of the earth, with Kalashnikovs as their scepters.

"I'm getting sick of this," he muttered to Sumo. They were in swim trunks, sprawled side by side on the seaward beach. A little time off, though he'd sold it to Geller as a training day. In fact they'd done some conditioning, starting at 0600 by paddling the RHIB a mile to the island, then running the dunes for an hour. Then sand drills on which compartments each team member would hit if they had to do a hasty entry, how they'd reorient if one of them got hit. Then running through it on the beach using rocks to mark doorways and hatches. At last, everyone reeling in the heat, he figured, enough. They'd cooled off with a swim, though he kept it short, recalling the sharks. Now they were just basking, though he had Arkin in a hide site atop the tallest dune with binoculars, a radio, and a carbine, just in case.

"Rather be back in Camp Crawley, polishing your dick?" Kaulukukui rolled over and blew like a papa walrus. "I'll take this. It all counts on thirty."

"I'm gonna start calling you Hakuna Matata. You're fat as a warthog, too."

"Call me whatever, gotta take it as it comes. For a California dude, your dope's dialed way too fucking tight."

"It's not me. Nobody can make up their fucking minds."

The Hawaiian jerked a thumb at the water. "The guy who counts, his mind's made up."

"Who's that?"

"Suleyman, that's who. He ain't gonna take a dollar less

than a billion, and the fucker's too dumb to know otherwise. Can't read, but he knows the numbers on his fucking calculator. He thinks every time we offer him a million we're trying to outwit him. Like rug merchants in some fucking bazaar."

Teddy slammed his fist into the sand. The pristine beauty of the beach enraged him. At the moment even the flies were gone, blown back into scrub and dunes by a sea breeze. No question, if somebody with cash and vision built a little airport, this'd be prime resort property.

As it was, he couldn't figure why they were even in Ashaara. Unless, like coffee mess scuttlebutt at Rowley had it, there was oil here and they were jockeying for access. He had no problem with that, but why waste time on two-bit pirates? "There's gotta be some way to pry this fucker off the dime," he muttered.

"Sixty-two grains of diplomacy through the head?"

Teddy spat. "We keep talking to him, we're encouraging every fisherman in the Red Sea to go rogue. What's the problem with taking 'em out? A couple hostages get killed. Tough titty for them, but it'll save dozens down the line."

"Hey, no argument. I think—"

Kowacki came running out of the surf. "Chopper," he yelled. Teddy and Kaulukukui scrambled up and grabbed rifles. They took a knee without a word, scanning the horizon while keeping one eye on the approaching mote.

The helicopter circled, its manner cautious too. A small bright yellow civilian model, unmarked. At last it flared out and drifted down like an unreeling spider. The SEALs shielded their eyes as sand stormed from the rotorwash.

When the skids hit, two men rolled out, in sunglasses, long trousers, chukka boots, and desert hats. Cases were handcuffed to their wrists. They trudged up to Teddy through the sand. "How's it, chummie? You're Oberg, nay?" said one, his accent maybe European but hard to place, facial structure hard, sunburned, dark hair combed straight back. A guy who'd spent a lot of time outdoors, someplace hot. "Tay-o-dore Oberg?"

He nodded and they shook hands. "This here, this muerse oek's Sumo?" the guy said to Kaulukukui.

"Only they china call 'oom that," the second man said. He was built heavier, but he wasn't fat. His accent was Dutchish. He had enormous hands. They carried no visible weapons, but the way they looked slowly around told Teddy these weren't office types. He felt them examining the scars radiating across his face, the team's sweat-stained Ts and trunks and combat boots. An invisible field formed between the new arrivals and the SEALs standing in a spaced circle around them.

"Koos," said the taller man. "This lattie here's Con."

Oberg introduced his guys. "What's in the suitcases, Driftwood?"

They looked down as if they'd just noticed them. "What, this? This's kroon, bru."

"It's what?"

"Money, chommie. What yay kakstamper Sooley wants. A befok billion."

Kowacki said, "A billion? *Dollars?* Get real. You couldn't lift it. What's it in, million-dollar bills?"

"Bloody near," said the stocky one. He unlocked one and the SEALs whistled as they caressed the stacks.

"I've never even seen a hundred-thousand-dollar bill," Arkin said.

"Still 'aven't." The tall one chuckled. "Look close at the picture."

They peered. "Who *is* that?" said Kowacki, but Teddy recognized him. He'd come to his mother's parties.

"It's Moses," he said. He touched the top bill again, stroked it. It felt real. "Charlton Heston. It's fake, guys. They printed up a billion fucking dollars in play money."

"Only way to deal with the domkop. Owners would have gone a million. Maybe even an' a half. But a milliard . . . They coom to us, says, 'Help out, 'ere.' So we brings the konkop." They looked toward the shoreline. "Gi' us a lift?"

Suleyman received them in the captain's cabin. He was bare-chested but still in the frog shorts, which didn't look like they'd been changed or laundered since the first visit. He smelled evil, but no more so than the run-of-the-mill *Shamal* crewman these days. Teddy felt uneasy, looking around the compartment. It was too much like another cabin, in another ship, where he'd had to kill a man who'd never done anything wrong.

He shoved that aside and put the old smile on. Patted his ID holder, feeling the hard weight within it. They still hadn't wised up to the knife. Hadn't found anything when they searched the South Africans, either. Teddy had caught a glance from the tall one as the pirates ran their hands over him. Like himself, though he looked disarmed, he probably wasn't.

"Marlboro?" The Ashaaran held out his hand. Teddy grunted and forked over. As the pirate lit up the Afrikaaners chuckled.

They made a show out of unlocking the handcuffs. They unsnapped the latches, swiveled them, and opened both at once, like impresarios at a Hollywood kids' party.

"One billion dollars," the tall one said. "As agreed."

Suleyman looked suspicious. He tapped out the requisite sum on the calculator. The South Africans nodded. The Ashaaran extracted a sheaf of bills and fanned them. Peered underneath, as if to make sure the others were the same denomination. To Teddy's relief he didn't look twice at the picture, just traced the zeros in the corner with a cracked fingernail.

He turned to the captain's bunk and began laying them out. "Fuck me, he's gonna count it," Kaulukukui muttered. Teddy shot him a *Shut up, asshole* look. Two other pirates leaned against the bulkhead, fingers on triggers. So far, he hadn't seen a single one of the RPGs these guys were supposed to have. But they could be below. Up close, an RPG could punch right through a PC's hull plating.

Suleyman was muttering, counting. Oberg stared at the horrible crusts on his legs. It *was* creeping upward. Maybe his curse was working? One of the guards sauntered over.

Teddy held his breath, but his boss sent him back to his post with a curt phrase.

The Ashaaran straightened, and Teddy let out his breath. He was chuckling. He handed a note to Kaulukukui, then one to Teddy. They took them, acting pleased. He held out two more to the South Africans, who bowed, just short of mocking. "Many thanks, you moffie kaffir," the heavyset one said. The tall one just smiled, but even Teddy found it intimidating.

"We'll be vaai then." The taller one nodded at the SEALs. "You'll see to getting our hostages off, nay, chommie?"

"We'll take care of it."

Suleyman snapped orders to a guard, who held the door. The Afrikaaners disappeared around the deckhouse without a word of good-bye. Teddy stepped out and keyed the radio. He'd brought Geller up to speed on the new arrivals and what they'd brought before they'd left the beach. "Alleycat, this is Goatrope. Ransom delivered and accepted. Stand by to come alongside for hostage extraction. Remember your manners. Over."

" 'Remember your manners' meant every mount manned and every crewman at general quarters, but without showing it. Sweat dripped down Teddy's ribs, down his leg. Could they get away with this? Boatless, he figured the pirates would slip the anchor, drift the tanker ashore, and paddle to the beach in life rafts. But considering how they'd been paid, he couldn't let even one escape. The Afrikaaners' trick could be pulled again, but only if no one ever heard about it. Which meant Suleyman and his bully boys had to go somewhere they'd tell no tales.

Across the water he heard the bark and moan of *Shamal*'s engines, the creak and grate as her anchor came up. "Let's go," he muttered to Sumo, and headed for the mess decks.

The hostages perked up as they came in. "Good news," Oberg announced. "Ransom's been turned over. We'll cross-deck as soon as our ship comes alongside."

The captain translated into Dutch, which seemed to be the working language. Chatter grew, but Teddy raised his palms. "Leave everything but your passports. Important thing's to get you all off, right now." He blotted his neck. The mess decks were stifling hot, but that wasn't why he was sweating.

Suleyman had come down the ladder, and was handing out packets of money. His men shifted their weapons to their left hands to accept the stiff new bills. Teddy tried to keep his expression businesslike. Across the compartment he caught Sumo's eye. The flicker of a lid, expressive as speech. *Keep your cool, haole boy.*

A Filipino stood to see better. He said something surprised. The other Filipinos' heads turned. A murmur passed between them.

"Everything's cool," Teddy announced. "You won't have to worry about these guys any more. They're *happy* with the ransom." The Filipino got the message; he sat down; the buzz died away. "Our ship's headed in to pick you up. Don't say anything to rile these guys, okay?" He couldn't help fingering his badge holder. Two steps and he could off the closest pirate. There were four more in the compartment, though, peering at their new bankrolls. He hoped they weren't NRA members.

Suleyman was finishing his Santa Claus rounds, making his way to the ladder. He lifted the suitcase—only one, Teddy noted—and made a long speech, with many gestures. He nodded to the guard who'd evidenced some faint command of English. "Talk," he said.

"You give am-mo," the man told Oberg. He pointed to the hostages. "Then we give back these."

Teddy tensed. "Not part of our deal."

"Part of deal now. Am-mo." He pointed his rifle at the captain, who was sitting white-faced.

"Fuck this, dude. I don't have ammunition that fits your weapons. We paid you your fucking ransom." He slapped a hand on the skipper's shoulder. Hauled him to his feet. "I'm taking these people out of here."

The muzzle of the AK stopped him. And the murmur from Kaulukukui. "Uh, better not, Obie."

"Tell Suleyman a man who doesn't keep his word's a piece of shit. Even a pirate."

The Ashaaran shrugged. "He does not care, your words. You bring ammo, we leave. Other, we stay."

All the AKs were pointing at the trembling hostages now. Teddy was shaking too, but with rage. He'd thought it was over. Now they wanted more. He took deep breaths, forcing himself not to reach for the knife. Had Suleyman seen through them? Was this his revenge? They were outnumbered. He couldn't do anything. He *couldn't do anything.*

"Let's go," Sumo murmured, big hand on his shoulder. Unwillingly, he let himself be led out.

"They're upping the ante," Geller said from his skipper's chair. They were watching the tanker, now only a couple hundred yards away. *Shamal* had dropped anchor at short stay, just enough chain to hold her. "But we can't meet it. Right? We don't have ammo for them."

Teddy felt as if his guts were made of lead. "We'd have to have it flown in. Plus, what's to say they won't ask for something else after that? Sooner or later, they're going to figure out that's funny money. One of the crew almost gave it away already. We're ready. All we need's the word."

But Geller shook his head. "Get approval, I'll back you to the hilt. But you're not assaulting without clearance."

"We've got to, Skipper."

"No." Geller pointed his finger. "Hear me, sailor? I'll radio for orders, but *you* stand the fuck down."

Dusk was falling. Teddy stood on the wing, watching the lights across the water. The other ship was quiet. Too quiet. Always before there'd been music. He felt minutes going by like steel wire being pulled out through his butthole. What would Suleyman do when he realized he'd been tricked?

He'd start killing.

A dark form stood on the main deck, looking in the same

direction. It was bigger than any man had a right to be. "Sumo?"

"Hear that?" the Hawaiian murmured. His head was turned, right ear toward the tanker.

"What?"

"Screams. Hear 'em?"

Teddy held his breath. He heard the wind, but nothing else.

Then he understood.

Ashaara had forbidden them to attack. So had Malaysia, and the Philippines. Their own chain of command had nixed it.

The sole exception being if the hostages were being harmed.

Warm as it was, the sea silked his skin with cold fingers as it infiltrated the wet suit. He let go the ladder and floated, checking gear. Ahead of him a faint splash sounded as Sumo and Bitch Dog oriented and began swimming.

The outboards on *Shamal*'s RHIBs were quiet, but not silent. Moreover, the pirates knew what they sounded like.

A swimmer made no noise.

Geller had listened, squinting, to the wind. He said he didn't hear any screams. If others thought they had, he had no choice but to launch a rescue. But he'd do it from the PC, bringing her alongside while sweeping the bridge and weather decks with suppressing fire.

Teddy had pointed out they'd heard screams, not shots. For shots, an immediate, all-out assault was the right response. As it was, they could reduce the risk. Let his men do it. Silently. In the dark. They were trained for it, they'd rock-drilled for two weeks, they'd even been inside the spaces, seen their enemies face-to-face.

At last, Geller had agreed.

Detaching one by one from the shadow of the stern, they slipped into the graceful SEAL sidestroke, kick and reach and pull, angling out into the dark. They could keep it up for hours, and know by their watches how far they'd gone.

Teddy sensed the sharks somewhere below. But if a SEAL didn't swim where there might be sharks, he wouldn't get out of BUD/S. In two hundred yards, the risk of getting hit was probably not great. The four swimmers stayed close, though, to be able to warn each other if one felt a nudge that wasn't from a swim buddy.

He breathed through his mouth. Whacker was noisy, splashing, a whispered curse. From *Shamal* came the throb of generators, the hum of ventilators, and the ululating rap-core of Linkin Park and Limp Bizkit. He'd asked the crew to bring their personal players on deck for aural cover.

His weapon was slung over his back, bolt wedged open so it would drain the moment it was out of the water. He remembered the last time he'd done this, in the Malacca Strait. Not from the water then, but from a small boat disguised as the same sort of pirate as the men he'd be knife to knife with in a few minutes.

It wasn't a question of right and wrong. A boy with a different name than Teddy Oberg had learned that years before, when a man he was supposed to trust had come into his room. Since then he'd known there was no right and no wrong. Only force, advantage, and action.

He thought again, but only fleetingly, about the producer's offer. But there were sharks in those waters too. All in all, he preferred the ones with gills.

An illuminated citadel rose from the sea. Every porthole blazed. Every deck light was on. They seemed to be slowly drifting to the right, as if the ship was under way. The swimmers were being set aft by a current that set toward the mouth of the sound. Teddy had anticipated this, and they slowly finned the last yards, black masks and snorkels invisible in the black water, and one by one reached up to rest a glove on the rough steel of the tanker's afterhull.

"Go," Oberg muttered.

Kowacki sucked thorough breaths, flushing carbon dioxide from his bloodstream, and submerged. Teddy felt his belt for the backup. A tapered pine plug from *Shamal*'s damage control stores. He doubled, pulling off his fins and lashing them over his back. A few yards forward, below the waterline, the other SEAL would be feeling across the underbody. Finding, at last, the intake for the ship's auxiliary generator.

A hoarse inhalation as Kowacki resurfaced. A wordless nod. Teddy pulled his carbine around and reseated the magazine. He torqued the suppressor to make sure it was tight. A little water in it actually made the suppressor work better. On the other hand, a team guy had once had one blow off the end of his rifle, pretty much finishing off staying covert. One of those lessons passed on in bars. The others busied themselves, hugging the shadows, avoiding the light from the portholes.

It dimmed. It flickered, then died. Even down here, they heard distant shouts of dismay.

Electricity perked in Teddy's blood. He pushed Kaulukukui's meaty shoulder. *Go.* An arm held aloft a device like the Statue of Liberty's torch. It recoiled, with the twang of a stout spring.

A thunk above them as the plastic-padded grapnel hit steel. Teddy was oriented, the green lit circle of his night sight steady on the line the deck made against the sky. If anyone heard the hook hit, and looked over the side, he wouldn't live to yell.

But no one came, and a black bulk heaved itself out of the water and began muscling up the line. Sumo always managed to talk himself into going first. Or if he couldn't, you'd find him there anyway, his big mitt gently maneuvering the man in front of him out of the way. Teddy had long since given up trying to get ahead of him, even when he was team leader.

Four minutes later, breathing harder than a thirty-foot climb in full gear should have warranted, Teddy crouched aft of the deckhouse. The starlight was bright enough to see by. The afterdeck was only big enough for the four of them and the piping of the stern manifold valves. A deck-mounted cargo pump occupied a semienclosed compartment to port. The deckhouse went all the way across the beam, which meant a cavernlike breaker to starboard was the only way forward and up.

He unleashed the team with a hand signal. Whacker and Bitch Dog would head around the main deck, taking out sentries, then do a quick, violent entry to the mess decks. He didn't need anyone in the engine spaces; *Tahia*'s own engineers were in charge down there; Suleyman's men had been content to let them provide power, fresh water, even air-conditioning.

He and Sumo were going after Suleyman. If something went wrong, if some of the pirates held out in an isolated compartment, their leader might be a bargaining chip.

So far they still had surprise. He'd been afraid a backup generator might kick in, but all the lights stayed off. Combat booties squishing, they stopped at an open door. Beyond lay blackness. Teddy indicated the high side; Kaulukukui pointed low. They sliced the pie, bulled in, and swept the dark.

"Night viz," Teddy whispered, so low he could barely hear his own voice. A crackle in the dark, though, showed Sumo had heard.

The goggles lit a green depthless world where stray gleams glared like lighthouses. The effect was uncanny. He could see, though only in a narrow cone, and only with his right eye. Fortunately it was his dominant one, so he kept it to his rifle.

They didn't meet anyone until the 02 level, where they found a body facedown in a pool of blood. He knelt. The blood was warm-fresh. He started to turn it over, then left it as Kaulukukui hissed, "Up here."

The cabin where Suleyman had held court was empty. The safe was open and another body lay on the floor here. Even in the green shadows Teddy recognized him.

It was the captain. Someone had been at him with a knife.

He couldn't help shivering. He turned for the door. "Mess deck," he muttered. "And we go in full auto."

But there was no one in the mess. At least, no one alive.

The hostages lay under the tables, atop them, wherever

their final moment had found them. No smell of powder, but lots of shit and blood, sprayed over the ice cream maker, the racks of cheap dishes, the serving line. Arms, hunks of flesh, severed heads.

"Machetes," Kowacki murmured as he crouched with finger carefully lifted from the carbine's trigger. "Like in Kenya."

"Anybody on deck, Whacker?"

"No sentries. Nobody."

"Nobody on the bridge either." Teddy saw a hand move, and went to the body. But it had been an involuntary spasm, the slow drawing up of an arm. He swallowed. "Okay, search this fucking ship."

They assembled fifteen minutes later on the main deck. *Shamal* swung to her anchor two hundred yards distant. The moon lofted over the silvery beach, glimmering in the sound. Teddy looked shoreward. Half a mile? He saw neither motion nor light. It was as if they'd never been here.

Except for the dead.

"Where the fuck did they go?" said Arkin. "They *swam*?"

"We did," said Kaulukukui, just as low. "Why'd we think they couldn't?"

Kowacki murmured, "Fuck. Fuck."

Teddy said nothing. Just stood with his shooting gloves on the rail and his head down, telling himself it hadn't been his fault. It was the Dutch, for trying to get cute with the ransom. Koos and Con's, for not staying to make sure the hostages were released. Geller's, for not letting him assault earlier.

But inside, he knew it wasn't.

The hostages would still be alive, if he'd been more aggressive.

22

IN THE SOUTHERN MOUNTAINS

Aisha had prepared for this meeting, but not well enough. She wasn't ready for ten sickening hours into the southern wastes, along the worst roads she'd ever driven. Nor for the dusty heat. Nor the slovenly, stinking men who avoided her eyes as they muttered things she couldn't make out, as they avoided her touch and even her shadow.

Nor above all for the emaciated, listless children who scrambled slowly to surround the white GMC and its Gray-Wolf escort vehicles, begging in soft hopeless voices whenever the caravan pulled over to debate the map or take a pee break.

They'd met the Waleeli escorts on a shell-crumbled corner in Uri'yah. The town might once have been pretty, with the remains of shops and houses, sagging fences around what once had been gardens, a large cemetery on its outskirts. Now it was a ghost, the houses dead sockets, the withered gardens cut with slit trenches, the few inhabitants staggering husks. It marked the farthest the Waleeli forces had gotten in the face of a U.S. ultimatum: Stay on their side of a line five kilometers to the north, or be bombed.

"Stay with the vehicle, please, Agent Ar-Rahim."

Whalen, the hard-ass GrayWolf squad leader, barking his requests like orders. Embassy personnel no longer had Marine escorts. The PMCs—private military contractors—accompanied them everywhere. She liked neither his presence nor his tone. But protesting had gotten her nowhere. Peyster insisted anyone on State business had to be accompanied by bodyguards outside the compound, and wear a vest. She snapped, "I'm taking a leak, all right?"

"Just stay in sight."

She thought an unpleasant image as she searched for a corner to lift her abaya. But one boy, with an enormous hole in his face that he presented shamelessly, kept trotting alongside, hands outstretched. At last a Waleeli smashed him aside with a buttstroke, after which she found privacy behind a wrecked truck.

Dust, everywhere. Her lungs hurt with each breath. She blew her nose and wiped reddened eyes. Coughed, until the choking passed. Then they climbed back into the vans for the last leg.

Trying not to fidget, she said a du'a to quell her nerves.

She was on her way to meet the mysterious man of the desert. General Al-Khasmi—which Nuura said meant "the Pruner" or "the Orcharder" in southern dialect—had emerged from obscurity to lead the mobile militia that'd defeated a small Governing Council force at Uri'yah. She'd tried a documentation build, but as happened so often here, there was no official paper, no computer hits, and verbal accounts conflicted. Some said he was a former imam, a madrassa student turned warrior. Others, a brigand and smuggler who'd made his bones in the qat trade. One summary suggested he had links to Iran. The one thing all agreed on was that he was no more than twenty-five.

None of which prepared her for the bare-chested man in camo trousers who sat under a blue UNHCR tarp stretched tent-style over a frame of thornbushes.

He *was* very young, with handsome features except for an ugly swelling that marred the lower jaw. The holes the thorns punched through the plastic sprayed beads of sunlight over his dark face. The GrayWolf uniforms—Whalen had insisted on clearing the area before letting her "exit the vehicle"—parted reluctantly as she advanced. They faced several ragged Ashaaran youths with the ubiquitous AK-47s.

Beside Al-Khasmi another young man, tall, nervous-looking, with eyes red as stoplights and a qat lump in his cheek big enough to choke a goat, handed him a faded shirt as she came up. Pulling it on, he motioned to the carpet before them.

Peyster had tried to make her use a male translator, but after trying him, she'd gone back to Nuura. Faced with a male, Ashaarans talked to him, ignoring her entirely. Nuura settled her swollen belly awkwardly. She was very close to term. Maybe she shouldn't have brought her. Flies buzzed in tight circles, undeterred by the OFF! Deep Woods she'd soaked her clothing in.

She was here to try to make a deal. The poorest quarter of the Old City had erupted into riots after the assassination of a local cleric. ADA forces, though grandiloquently titled the National Army of Ashaara, could keep order only within about a mile of the Palais du Président. Abdullahi Assad still defended his stronghold in the southern and eastern neighborhoods of Ashaara City, while Islamic elements, apparently allied with this young man, were gaining strength in the hinterlands.

She'd pushed back against State's assumption that an Islamist was automatically an enemy. Peyster had been dismissive when she'd suggested sounding out Al-Khasmi. "Another tinpot warlord," he'd snorted. "Cut off his supplies and he'll wither. If that doesn't work, Ahearn can take him out with an air strike."

He might be a warlord. But she wasn't so sure he was a "tinpot," whatever that was. A nobody months ago, he now controlled the southern mountains, and there were reports of banditry under green-and-black banners in the west, heretofore solid Assad territory. She wanted to give him a chance to come in from the cold.

She started in Arabic, but didn't offer her hand. *"Assalam aleikum."*

He half smiled. *"Tafuddal,"* he said, waving again at the carpet, and she settled herself, careful to stay modest as she shook out her skirts.

"Ismee Ar-Rahim. Ana min America."

He looked puzzled; shook his head. Nuura translated into lilting Ashaaran, and he spoke at length. When he was done she relayed, "He says he does not speak Arabic well. He is not educated. He has never met an American who wore abaya."

"Tell him I'm Muslim." She watched his frown.

"What is your lineage?"

This was the typical greeting in this part of Africa, and she made the best answer she could. His frown grew deeper, as if everything she told him pleased him less.

"He wants to know if you will have food."

"I'll have a bite with him."

He called and a woman emerged from a tent carrying a large copper pan. Aisha gave her a close examination, surprised to see another woman here. She was tall, perhaps even pretty under full *hijab.* Only her eyes showed, but in a microsecond's flash they seemed to take in everything. Then she was gone, back to the tent.

The pan was filled with a lumpy yellow paste, like her mother's corn muffin dough before it was baked. The first sweet taste told her what it was. World Food Organization corn-soya blend. Along with long-grain rice, cooking oil, and beans, CSB made up most of the aid distributed in the camps.

An insult, and not a subtle one. He was serving her the very food he'd stolen. Her jaws stopped. How to respond? He was waiting for her reaction. Yes, he'd have been handsome, before whatever had torn up the side of his face. For a moment his features tugged at her memory.

"He wants to know, do you enjoy it."

"It is excellent in taste and very nutritious. It would make a good meal for starving children."

"He says it builds strong soldiers as well."

She thought they came out of that exchange even. But obviously guilt wasn't going to work. She took another bite before he called again and the woman brought *injera* bread, dates, durra, and what Nuura whispered was camels' humps, a delicacy. Well, perhaps she ought to make allowances. He *was* sitting down with her. Treating her on an equal basis.

She wiped her mouth, remembering not to use her left hand. The dusty wind rattled the tarp with a sound like falling leaves. Suddenly she remembered Central Park, holding her father's hand as the white passersby stared. How she'd hated them . . . "Try to explain something to him. Tell him: The Americans are not necessarily your enemies."

The answer came lightning quick. "They are enemies of Islam and God. Therefore they are our enemies."

"I'm an enemy of Islam? How can that be? I am Muslim myself."

"Americans are Christians," he said with the complacency of the ignorant. She tried not to bristle. If only a closed mind came with a closed mouth!

"Americans are of many religions. There are those who say Americans are the most religious people on earth."

Al-Khasmi shrugged, popped meat into his mouth, but winced as he bit down. Nuura added something in an undertone and he looked at her, at Aisha, then back at the food. Finally he muttered something she translated as, "Let them practice what religion they like, so long as they don't do it here."

"If it's our presence you object to, we'll be gone as soon as the famine's over and you have a functioning government. If you want us out of Ashaara, join the ADA. There's room for your men in the new police force, the new army. Room for you too.

"The Prophet, blessings be upon him, always sought to make peace. He endured hunger, torture, his loved ones' murder by those who hated him, but he remained merciful. When he conquered Mecca only four died. Do you wish a name sweet in the mouths of the people? Then join in making peace."

Al-Khasmi had listened attentively, both to the English and the translation. He spoke at length, tapping the carpet with a fingertip. Nuura said, "He says: I do not know the Book as my old master did. But I do know this: 'To those against whom war is made, permission is given because they are wronged; and truly, God is powerful in their aid.' "

A voice in her left ear whispered, "You're going to have to move six inches to your left to give me a clear shot."

She leaned forward, making sure her head covering

concealed the earbud she'd tucked into her skull before getting out of the van. Behind her, behind the deeply tinted glass, Paul Erculiano would be focusing a telephoto. If nothing else, she'd return with photos of the elusive Tiger.

Who was still speaking, in that gentle, persuasive voice. "It has been revealed to me that what the foreigners present as help is really war against us and our religion. If some, even innocents, must die as we defend ourselves, that must be God's will; since to do otherwise would mean Islam itself perishes. If you are truly Muslim this must be clear to you as well."

She said more sharply than she'd intended, "That's superficially persuasive, but both your premises and conclusions are wrong."

Nuura hesitated. "I don't know those words," she muttered.

"Sorry, I'll use simpler ones. Tell him we're not here about religion—I mean, we're not here either to attack or to promote Islam. We're just here to feed the starving."

"He says that makes no sense. Why should those who have food give it to those who do not?"

The Ashaaran spoke on, wearily, as if he'd said all this many times before. "What wise man buys a camel the price of which he does not know? Or a wife from a father who says, 'I will tell you the price of your bride next year'? What is the fee for what you bring? Perhaps you can tell me. After all, you say you are an American."

Ah, she thought, sitting back. He talks Muslim, but thinks Ashaari. She'd noticed their callousness toward each other. The hardness toward even their own suffering. Like the boy with the hole in his face, who'd pointed to it, grinning, as he begged. Like the children she'd watched torture a kitten, pushing it into a fire with sticks, laughing as it screamed, until it lay down and smoldered and burst into flame.

Maybe they had to be that way, to survive. She wouldn't judge. But how to reach one whose view was so stark? So underpinned with the certitude that—like rainwater dipped from the hollow of a dune—something for you only meant less for me?

"Because we're all of the same family," she said. "You understand the obligation to family, don't you? It's the same. Those who starve must be fed."

Now it was his turn to lean forward, no longer smiling, as he gave his triumphant words to the slight trembling woman beside her.

" 'Those who starve must be fed.' This sounds well, yes. You foreigners have so much. Machines and radios and airplanes. But you do not say, 'If you are hungry, we will feed you.' What you say is, 'If you want your children to live, you must give up your weapons, give up your law that avenges injury, give up the purity of your women to our licentiousness.' Did you not propose that bargain to my martyred master, the revered Sheekh Nassir Irrir Zumali, peace be upon his memory? For so he told me the day he died."

She deliberated her answer. It was acceptable not to respond at once.

Who was "General" Al-Khasmi? The madman in the desert the intelligence agencies were portraying? The "menace to the fragile reconstruction of Ashaara" the *Economist* had called him? She had to admit, he looked the part. Wild-haired, with that terrible wound and far-off gaze. Again that familiarity tugged at her brain, and again, faded without bringing any association to the surface.

But he didn't seem clinically paranoid. (The jittery, mumbling guy next to him acted much more bizarre.) Only obsessed with narrow fundamentalism and dreadful suspicion of foreigners. The peace *was* fragile, but so far, it could still be called peace. The essential thing, Peyster had told her, was to drag the guy into the process. Once he was out from behind a machine gun, they could feel out leverage. Give him incentives to cooperate, and disincentives if he didn't.

"It's true, that's what I told Sheekh Nassir. And I believe he was considering what I said. I think he was murdered for it by elements of his own circle."

"This I do not believe," spat the jittery man, the one with the swollen eyes and the hockey puck in his cheek. "American lies. It is they who killed our revered sheekh."

"We were not involved in his death."

The man shouted, spittle flying. Nuura translated. "You want to disarm us so you can occupy us. You are colonialists like the Italians and French. Your election is a fraud, and your Dobleh is a toy."

"I have met Dr. Zumali Dobleh. He is the wise leader Ashaara needs. Not only is he a devout Muslim, he is a hajji, as am I. We have made the pilgrimage to Mecca. Have you?"

The red-eyed man didn't answer, just jittered his leg violently and glanced at Al-Khasmi.

"What about General Assad?" she asked them. "You don't like Dr. Dobleh. Do you like Assad better? The Diniyue, Jazir, Xaasha—do you want them back in power? That's what you'll get if the Governing Council have their way."

Al-Khasmi answered that. "Assad's our enemy, yes, but he's a patriot in his way. At least he's not uncovering himself for the foreigners. But they're not the true government, no matter what they say."

"What's the true government? If it's not Dobleh, and not Assad?"

"The only true government is of the ulama; sharia law. This is the policy of the Waleeli. The West lies with honeyed promises while they steal and kill. We tell the truth about our goals."

"That's not an option," she said flatly. "The United States won't back it. Nor the UN. What about the Christians? The Hindus? Muslims who don't care to stone women for adultery? You're talking about starting a civil war, a religious war."

They shrugged, both at once. "So America will be our enemy," the tall one said.

She felt any chance slipping away. But maybe she could leave him with something to think about. "Only if you choose. But yes, we'd be your enemies. Do you have any idea what that means? How fast we can put a precision-guided bomb on your encampment here?"

His wounded mouth twisted into a painful-looking smile. "Now we hear the true voice of America. Not food, but bombs. If what you say is so, why should I not take you hostage now? See what your people will pay for you." Nuura flattened her hands on the carpet, looking fearfully at Aisha as she translated. "He says: 'It seems to me, they will pay much.' "

"Tell him he forgets my guards." She nodded at the Gray-Wolf men, who stood facing her in a rough circle around their meeting place. Then she stiffened.

Behind each stood a Waleeli, cloth wrapping his feet. They must have crept up step by step, noiselessly. Each aimed a rifle at his target's head.

If one of the PMCs looked around, he'd start shooting.

A massacre was only a motion away.

Without thought, she was on her feet. Her SIG was out, muzzle pressed to Al-Khasmi's skull, which she cradled with her left arm. The nervous guy jerked back and scrabbled for his weapon, then froze at a glance from his chief.

"Call them off," she muttered. To Nuura: "He's not taking any hostages today. Or he'll be doing it without the side of his fucking head. *Tell him!*"

The bandit chief sat motionless. "You're a Muslim fighter," he murmured.

"No, I'm a fucking federal agent, with police powers through UN Resolution 610 to support humanitarian aid to this benighted shithole. Tell him that."

The tall one burst out with something violent, but his boss put out a weary hand. He called to his men, who began backing away. Whalen turned and saw them; he glanced at her but, to her relief, didn't go off the deep end. He patted the air, signaling his personnel to stay cool. Then nodded at the smooth-faced, very young man who'd been covering him, as if to say, one professional to another, Yeah, you got the drop on me; nice play. Next time it'll be the other way around.

Al-Khasmi waited till she took the pistol from his head.

Till she stowed it away inside her abaya. "Tell me something, Aisha Ar-Rahim. You say you are Muslim."

The voice in her ear said, "Jesus, Aisha. Don't know what just happened, but I got a terrific shot of it."

She wondered how he'd missed four terrorists taking aim at their protective team. "Yes. I am," she told the Ashaaran.

"A convert, or from your birth?"

"From my birth."

"But the true Muslim fights for victory of the faith and the restoration of the caliphate. Are you fighting for the faith?"

She saw the trap and didn't want to go there. Then steeled herself. "I *am* a good Muslim. But I won't force others into Islam. I try to be the most generous and compassionate human being I can. If all Muslims showed the compassion of God, all those who saw them would want to follow God too."

"Sharia? You don't believe in it?"

"It was God's way for us at that time in history. But He's given us more knowledge since the days of the Prophet, peace be upon him. I believe in what sharia was meant to accomplish. An Islam of justice, not violence. One with its women's faces uncovered, its daughters healthy, everyone educated and fed and at peace. That's what I believe in, General."

He plucked at the tarp, studying her with narrowed eyes. "You have lived too long with the Jews and Christians. You are not a true daughter of God."

"I believe I am."

"Be silent and learn. This is His land, this desert. Here He spoke to Musa and Issa and Muhammad, may their names be blessed. Here He speaks to me, the Pruner. There are those who call me the Maahdi, the announcer. God in His time will confirm or deny.

"Come back to Islam. It is not I who give you this chance. This is God himself stretching out His hand."

Nuura gasped and fell silent. Aisha nudged her. "What is it?" she hissed.

"I can't."

"You can't *what*? Tell me. It isn't your *water breaking*, is it?"

"He said . . . he wants you to marry him."

At the last instant she stifled her first reaction—to throw back her head and guffaw. An Ashaaran warlord was like a street punk in Harlem: One did not dis him in front of his men. She let her head covering fall forward to hide her eyes, as if deeply moved. At least, she hoped that was how he'd read it.

The first time anyone had ever asked. One to tell her grandchildren. If she ever had any. Proposed to in the African desert by a crazed terrorist.

One thing was for damned sure: She wasn't ever going to mention this to her mother. In no way, shape, or form. She nodded toward the woman who'd served them. "You have one wife already. At least."

"She's not my wife. She's my sister."

Enough. She cleared her throat and stood again, and he stood with her this time, still smiling. She remembered to step aside from the line of sight from the van, in case Erculiano hadn't gotten enough photos the first time around.

"He asks: You are leaving?"

"Yes. But the offer stands. About the police, the army. His men will be welcome. There'll be food and steady pay."

"And all we have to do is take the orders of the infidels."

"No. Of the democratic government of Ashaara, representing all the people."

Even as she said them the words tasted like cardboard. She believed them, but on another level, maybe she didn't. And he must have sensed that uncertainty, because he moved a step closer, till she could smell him again, as she had when she'd held his head against her chest. Nuura coughed. "He says: Perhaps he will attend one of these conferences. To see what it is you bring. Will you arrange that? If he sends a man to you?"

"I'll be happy to," she said, surprised.

"He also says: 'Sooner or later you will realize no one

can be Muslim, and fight against Islam. When you realize you are on the wrong side, come and join me.' "

"I'm on the right side already."

"Be silent. God knows you better than you know yourself. Join your Muslim brothers and sisters. Only then will you know true peace."

"It is Shaitan who lies," she told him, and turned and headed back to the van as the guards wheeled and pulled in.

She slid onto the hot leather seat as the engines started, the air-conditioning came on. As she returned to the metal electrical womb of America. She'd made her words loud, confident. He was a head case. A bandit with delusions of Apocalypse. But was she as confident as she'd pretended?

It would bear thinking about.

23

ASHAARA CITY

Dan swung down out of the white Suburban, bewildered. Who could have done this? He'd thought they were making progress with the population.

The Humvee had been traveling unescorted, but there'd been no trouble in the city. Tension, perhaps, in neighborhoods where the black flag flew. Disquieting preaching, in the mosques and new madrassas being set up with Saudi grants. That had been reported by the NCIS agent in her security updates. But the attack hadn't occurred in those neighborhoods, but at the Nakar roundabout, where the ring road—the route the Thunder Run used—branched off to points north.

As he circled it the vehicle was still on fire. The smell of burning diesel was varied by upholstery and insulation, cloth, the roast-pork odor of charred flesh. Blanketed bodies lay on the concrete. The response team had established a perimeter, and corpsmen were working on the survivors.

He lifted one of the blankets. A dark-skinned man, perhaps American but more likely Ashaaran. He dropped it, lifted the other. Stared at a familiar face, red-skinned, with blotches of sun freckles and incipient melanomas.

Buntine. The harbormaster.

"Come from that ghostville, sir," a lance corporal said, not saluting, which was SOP under fire. He pointed to an abandoned building surrounded by junked cars. His face was dirty but very young, raccoon-sunburned behind pushed-up ballistic goggles. He was chewing something crunchy. His name tape read Spayer. "Junkyard, far's I can tell. Blast marks on the back wall."

"Any trace of 'em?"

"Long gone, sir. Motherfuckers jerked that trigger and didi'd. Nabil here talked to the neighbors, but they didn't see anything."

Dan glanced at the kid. Black hair, buzz cut. Outfitted in size-small camo gear and women's combat boots, but they were still too big for him. He grinned up at Dan, favoring one foot.

"Your translator?"

"Translator, ambassador, gofer. We take care of him and he takes care of us." Spayer reached out to tousle the kid's hair. The boy submitted, then pushed his hand off. He ran off, limping, toward the garage. Spayer watched him go, shaking his head.

A chime; Dan's cell. They were depending more on cells than on VHF, at least around the city, where an overachieving Korean company had set up service. Dan was still wary of discussing movements on them, though it was hard to believe anyone in Ashaara had the equipment to break a call. "Lenson."

"Pride here. What's it look like?"

"Two dead, two wounded, sir. RPG from an abandoned junkyard west of the Nakar roundabout."

Colonel Pride—what a name for a marine—had arrived at the head of the Joint Interagency Coordination Group team Leache had promised/threatened them with in Dubai. Dan had had to submit to Pride's quickly famous interviewing technique, which consisted of long lists of questions asked in a monotone like that of a computerized Verizon operator, but less cheerful. It all came out of sleep time, which had been short even before Pride arrived. Now he asked in that same monotone, "What is the reaction of the local populace?"

"They say they didn't see anybody."

"What is the reaction of the engaged troops?"

"I don't know. They're either dead or being treated."

"What is your reaction, as first on the scene?"

"Well, I wasn't first on the scene," Dan said, then paused. What *was* his reaction? Seeing Buntine dead was like saying farewell to some force of nature, like the wind. "But my reaction is, uh—"

"Go ahead, Commander."

"I don't have one yet. I'll have to call you back, Colonel. Casevac's here."

Spayer was too. Beside him the kid panted, head down, gripping his ankles. "Look what L'il Team brought us. He talks to 'em and suddenly those folks remember seein' them throw this away, and where it went."

He held up a curiously grooved wood-and-metal tube Dan's tired brain took a moment to identify. "Great," he said, though unsure what good an empty RPG-7 launcher would do. He doubted whoever had fired it had his fingerprints on file. Still, he accepted it. Then felt in his pockets. "Would he take a PayDay?"

It was mashed flat and melted, but the kid had the wrapper off and most of it in his mouth in eight seconds.

The helo flared out above what might once have been a planned access ramp, kicking up a roiling cloud that when it reached them filled mouths and noses with the sick savor of pulverized dung and shrouded everything in a chaotic haze of flying sticks, smoke, and the ever-present filmy plastic bags. Dan waved the driver in the SUV off, and climbed in with the bodies.

At Rowley he walked into the JOC to find the noise level high and confusion level higher. The Joint Operations Center had opened adjoining the CACC. It wired highly secure, mission-tailored communications and intel modules into a common network linked by broadband to Centcom and intel sources. There were three dozen flat-panel displays with men and women in shirtsleeves and headsets, and a larger one up front for the commander. The watchstanders murmured into throat mikes at their keyboards. Dan found it creepy and unsettling. Were they here to feed people, or push the cutting edge of high tech?

General Ahearn, his deputy, and Colonel Pride were watching footage from security cameras on the ring road. A petty officer pointed out landmarks. A flare bloomed in the corner of a frame.

"That it?" said Ahearn, adjusting his glasses.

"That's the firing, General, affirmative," the petty officer said.

The general thanked her gravely and said she could leave. He swiveled, taking his glasses off, and saw Dan. "You were just there."

"Yes sir." He expanded on what he'd told Pride. Ahearn listened without expression.

"So we have no idea what faction they represented?"

Dan set the launcher on the table. They looked at it. Then Ahearn said, "The NCIS woman," and the deputy picked up a phone.

Pride was staring at Dan as they waited for the call to go through. "Commander, tell me again exactly who you are and what command you're from."

Dan did, but Pride didn't look satisfied. "What's a Navy tactician doing in Ashaara?"

"TAG doesn't only develop tactics. I was originally here on a transformation project for Admiral Contardi. From Naval Education and Training."

"He's made himself useful," Ahearn put in. "I asked for his attachment pending more personnel. Does Centcom intend to send me some staff reinforcement?"

Pride didn't pursue that, just picked the launch tube up and looked through the bore. "Did you have this checked by

EOD? In Vietnam they left ordnance items with grenades wired under them. It'd be easy to pack explosives in this and wire them to the trigger."

Dan had to admit that though he didn't much like the guy, and no one else seemed to either, he had a point. He shouldn't have just handed it to the joint force commander. He cleared his throat. "You're right. I should have done that."

From now on, they were going to have to question all their assumptions about Ashaara.

He had a bunk now, in a "choo" shared with three other men. The Containerized Housing Units were the size of a singlewide, with cheap vinyl tile floors, cots, and flimsy steel lockers the color of old vomit. No shower, no head, no air-conditioning, so it was uninhabitable during daylight hours, but it was only a short walk to the latrine area. It did come with power, light, and an office-sized fridge, so he could work at night, recharge his computer, and drink chilled water. The day before he'd scored a six-pack of soft drinks and a box of PayDays from an AAFES outlet in the terminal building.

He popped a Diet Coke and sat down at his notebook and logged on, first to the Rowley LAN, then through a portal back to his mailbox at TAG.

The first e-mail was from Monty Henrickson. The analyst was reporting on a project he'd been working on with one of their contractors. Best known as a supplier of financial-data-mining services, they'd come up with software that integrated gigabytes of data to pinpoint hidden investment opportunities. But the commercial fishing industry had picked it up to locate tuna, and both political parties were using it to spot clusters of swing voters for the November election. Marty's version integrated hydrographic conditions, electronic intercepts, passive listening arrays, and TAG's tactical database to locate submarines in shallow waters. Dan read through his notes, frowning over autonomic variable selection, nonnegative matrix factorization, orthogonal partitioning clustering. He wasn't stupid, but the analyst's mathematics left him feeling like a second-grader confronted with calculus.

Blair said she might have good news. The undersecretary of defense for acquisition, technology, and logistics had announced his retirement, and Jack Weatherfield's executive assistant had called her to schedule an appointment.

He stopped typing as the implication sank in. There were ten assistant secretaries, Blair's current position. But there were only four undersecretaries, with acquisition probably the most powerful. If the secretary promoted her, and the Senate approved, she'd essentially move up to number three at the Pentagon.

Great news for her. But would she have any time left for him at all? He sent her a long e-mail back saying he still wished she could've made it to Dubai, and how much he missed her.

But he was putting off what he knew he had to do. Finally his trailermate came in. "We made the news," he said, unbuttoning his BDUs as he went through the common area into his cube.

"What do you mean?"

"First U.S. fatalities in Ashaara. Big play."

Dan called up MSNBC and then ABC online. Both carried the story. One even had video of the burning Humvee. He wondered how, he hadn't seen a camera, but there was the junkyard behind it. "Thanks," he mumbled, but his roommate had already gotten whatever he'd come back for and Dan was alone in the trailer again.

He rubbed his eyes, wondering what this would mean. Remembering all Parker Buntine had done for the relief effort. He'd never seemed to like Ashaarans. He might even have been a racist. But he'd worked for them, fed them, and in the end, died for them. And for what reward?

But he was still putting it off. A commanding officer's toughest job. He hadn't been Buntine's CO, not directly. But the grizzled harbormaster had worked for, or at least with, him. Whatever family he had deserved something better than a form letter out of the Military Personnel Manual.

The final would be handwritten, of course. But he drafted his on the screen first, weighing each word for as much truth as could be tolerated, as much praise as could be justified. A compressor stuttered outside. Sweat ran down his face. The computer whined, its fan struggling in the heat. He opened a new file, took a deep breath—remembering a rugged, weatherbeaten face, a misanthropic snarl that had somehow helped bring hope to thousands—and started drafting the condolence letter.

24

THE PRESIDENTIAL PALACE, ASHAARA CITY

Ghedi catches the glances as they pull up in their battered trucks. The mufflerless engines make old men cover their ears. Even beggars cower against the walls, or duck away, averting their faces.

He clenches his remaining teeth and winces at a sensation like a hot iron skewer being pounded into his jaw. All his lower teeth have come out on that side and he feels something hot and hard forming where the bullet hit at Uri'yah. Fiammetta sewed the flesh together but something isn't right.

A man lives with pain. But when his hand goes to his shoulder and encounters an emptiness like the missing teeth he feels not like a man at all. He's gotten used to the gun's weight, the way a man's used to his legs. But Juulheed, who made the advance arrangements, made it clear: no weapons would be allowed into the *jirga*.

"I want our people outside, though," Ghedi had told his deputy.

Today Juulheed's even more on edge than usual. The night before, when they camped outside the city in a wadi, he didn't sleep, muttering to himself and then shouting until Ghedi had yelled at him to go away, they had a big day tomorrow. For answer he'd gotten a stare emotionless as that of a locust.

Sometimes he wonders if the Waleeli still need Juulheed. Each time he comes to the same answer: maybe not, but *he* does. What old Nassir said was true. People remember the deaths of innocents. The time may come when he'll need someone to blame for them. The splotch-faced, peanut-headed, strange-limbed man even his friends whisper is demon-possessed could be useful then.

The four of them walk slowly toward the entrance. He and Juulheed in front, carrying the rolled-up carpet. Hasheer and Zeynaab behind, their guards flung out to either wing, scanning roofline and street. One aims a rifle at an approaching sedan. It brakes and backs like a challenged ram, then turns tail and putt-putts away.

Ghedi's seen the palace during his studies with the old sheekh but never been inside. It was defended by the army, with fixed bayonets, when the president lived here. Now men in loose *maawis* and the close-fitting *gofe* guard the doors.

"God bless you, brother, you must halt. Do you have weapons? Guns, knives, grenades?"

He spreads his arms. Hands run up and down his sides. The other sentry eyes the carpet roll. "Put it down. Unroll it."

"Peace be to you, brother, there's nothing in it," Juulheed says, grinning his crazy grin.

"Unroll it." They unsling rifles and point them.

Ghedi kneels, setting one end on the pavement. Juulheed hesitates, then lays the other down too. Ghedi puts his hands on it, ready to roll it out. He hesitates, then suddenly pushes.

"Bang!" he shouts. The guards flinch. The carpet unrolls across the pavement and snaps open with a puff of dust. It holds nothing.

"We may pass?" Juulheed grins. They nod grumpily, motioning them in with the rifles. Hasheer and Zeynaab follow, the hem of her abaya swishing on the sand.

Inside a raucous crowd mills on red and white tile, nearly all in traditional dress. The huge room's so hot that even used to the desert as Ghedi is, sweat springs out all over his skin. The ceiling sparkles with bits of mirror and colored glass. Thin pillars meet it as it dips in graceful arches.

Hundreds of men are at the Second Clan Conference. Which means, apparently, there was one before, though he hadn't known about it. Most are graybeards. Everyone's talking, shouting over the din. Shaking fists at each other. He catches the accents of mountain speech, of northern, of every clan and family.

Hundreds of carpets cover the buckled antique tile. He heads for an open space, walking slowly. Men glance up as he passes, then blink, noticing his boots, his camouflage, and last, his face.

A murmur swells. It eddies out from where they bend to unroll their carpet. Zeynaab sits, spreading her dress around her, then adjusting her *hijab.* There are other women, but they're old and sit in the back. She's the only one sitting with the men. But once the murmur's spread to the walls of the great room and then rebounded, heads turning and hands raised to brows to study them, no one raises his voice to object. The talk resumes, not as loud as before.

"They have nothing to say." Juulheed grins. "Can it be they recognize the Orcharder?"

"Keep your voice down. Don't talk so much." Ghedi looks for foreigners but doesn't see any. Is this for Ashaarans only? But he doesn't see the one man he'd hoped for. Maybe he won't come.

An old man straightens and begins. His voice is weak and though he speaks first to respectful silence, soon there are calls to repeat what he's saying. Here and there men get to their feet, wandering toward restrooms or a table set with foreign bottled water. Ghedi sends Hasheer for some.

"These elections are false," the old one ends. "The Americans back those who think like they do. I'm not saying Dobleh's a bad man. But he's spent so long in other lands he doesn't know our ways anymore."

"Our ways are changing," another graybeard laments. "My young men will not obey. They follow others."

"If they follow others, it's your fault for not bringing them up right."

The two men scream at each other, but their neighbors laugh, as if they're old opponents. Ghedi smiles too, exchanging glances with his sister.

It's good having her back. If only he could have found Nabil as well . . . regather the family. . . . He tries to muster nostalgia about the village but can't. She's told him what happened. That she'd spent years with the Christians but never become one. That a group of bandits hurt her and burned her refuge, but she came away with gold. *That* he understands, the suffering the bandits are causing. It's one reason he's here today.

But only one.

This is traditional Ashaara, men who speak of God but whose hearts belong to the clan. Whose first question is "What's your lineage?" Who judge and are judged not by holiness or deeds, but solely by who is their cousin.

Like those who took him from his sister and brother, and made a bandit of him.

He reaches for God within himself, and hears Him speak. This assembly is unclean. There's hate. Corruption. Greed. These men are rotten limbs on the body of the ulama, the people of God.

They must be . . . lopped off. Pruned away. So beautiful fruit may grow.

At the front a heavyset man with a bullhorn voice—no, he actually holds a bullhorn—exhorts everyone to support his party. "If there's to be real democracy, the city people must be opposed. The Americans will install them no matter how we vote this time. We know that. But what about the next election? We represent the real strength of the country, the farmers. All must join our party. Except the Issa dogs."

Zeynaab leans, careful not to touch. "What are these men discussing?" she murmurs.

"Politics."

"They are very loud."

"The American elections," Juulheed snaps contemptuously.

A small man with a single white tuft atop his scalp stops at their carpet. "What clan?"

"We are beyond clan," Ghedi tells him.

"No one's beyond clan. What's your descent?"

"We're past that. We follow the Prophet and the Law."

He notices everyone around them's listening. Heads cocked, looking hostile.

"We all follow the Prophet, peace be upon him. But no one's beyond clan," the little man says again. "Your accent says you're from the south. You belong over there, not here. And women are not permitted at *jirga.* With respect, she must leave."

"She must leave." "Go with your clan," men shout. Ghedi bows his head. His pain probes down into his chest with a throbbing agony, as if he's being pierced by long needles from his jaw to his toes.

"So be it," he says to the man, who stands arms akimbo, staring them down. Like an old rooster in the yard.

"Old roosters can be plucked too," Juulheed tells him.

"What? What's that? Roosters?"

"Never mind." Ghedi stands, dusting off the Western trousers he's proud of. God forgive him, he shouldn't be proud of his clothes. He was proud of his looks too. Now he's disfigured. This is the will of God. He moves and lives now feeling that will in every word he utters, in the least sign that passes. He reaches a hand to Zeynaab. She shifts her legs, adjusts the black enveloping cloth, and rises awkwardly.

From either side Juulheed and Hasheer reach past her ankles, under her skirts. Ghedi, kneeling, reaches too.

When they rise they hold Kalashnikovs.

The old man's shout's blotted out by the chatter of Hasheer's rifle. He goes flying, nearly cut in half. Ghedi and Juulheed begin firing at the same moment, left and right. They shoot down those sitting closest first, in case one's smuggled in a weapon too. But none has. The wounded go down screaming, then try to crawl away. The three men change magazines, taking fresh ones as she hands them up.

She shivers at the noise, but her face shines as if, Ghedi thinks, she's gazing on Paradise.

The deafening noise is focused by the graceful arches of the ceiling. Where bullets hit plaster and tile a spray of chips and smoke flies. Amid the shots he hears more shouting from outside. Then a rattle, a stutter that becomes a shattering roar.

But he's not yet done in here. He drops the empty and fits another magazine in as old men link arms and stagger forward, screaming curses. He cuts them down like wheat before a hand scythe. Others cower, shielding boys with their withered arms. The women in back are screaming without cease. Ghedi aims a full magazine their way, holding the short rifle like a pistol as it recoils, the handguard smoking as it starts to char. Even in battle he's never fired so many rounds this fast. Blood sprays on fluted columns, antique tile.

His weapon falls silent. He holds out his hand, but his sister shouts, fists balled, "No more. There is no more." And there's only a moaning, a slow stirring all around the room. A river of blood runs toward the courtyard.

Shadows fill the sunlit rectangles of doors. Ghedi waves to make sure they see him.

Noise fills the room again. Guns flash as his men finish off those still crying out or trying to crawl. At close range the bullets tumble as they hit, tearing flesh into pieces.

He holds his jaw as the pain lances, so fierce he can scarcely see. If these are true Muslims God will reward them. But he doesn't think they are. They're rotten limbs, better burned. The light flares and jangles behind his eyes. A man grabs his arm and he jerks the weapon up, pulls the trigger before he recognizes Juulheed. Fortunately his rifle's empty.

"Just as you said, General. They were foolish enough to come unarmed."

He raises his gaze to the shattered glass embedded in the ceiling, reflecting the huddled corpses. His jaw flames. He regrets the deafness of those who wouldn't listen. But he's not to blame. Perhaps he truly is the Guided One, who will rid the world of injustice and tyranny. All that he's done has been written from time immemorial.

All, all is the will of God.

25

REFUGEE CAMP ONE

The penalty is death," he says. The man before him in his tent was caught naked with a young boy. The boy's been punished with two hundred lashes. The man doesn't weep or protest. He simply nods.

Ghedi understands. Each man has to die. No point making a fuss over it. He touches the knot in his jaw that seems to grow larger each day. Sometimes he can't think. His vision blurs. The pain's so intense he must pray himself from minute to minute, until God in His mercy makes it ebb.

"This punishment," the man says at last. "It is just, O Guided One. But may I choose my way of dying?"

Ghedi looks at the man in the Arab-style robes in the corner. Their chubby visitor wears his beard without a mustache. After a moment he nods.

"Perhaps," he tells the prisoner. He *was* one of the Waleeli. Until, of course, he was caught in uncleanness. "How do you wish to die?"

"May I not be martyred fighting the infidel?"

Ghedi hovers his fingers above his jaw, not touching it. Then rises and lifts the flap of his tent. Looks out.

In the months since it was set up the refugee camp's sprawled over the countryside. From a hundred acres of saltgrass flats it's exploded west across the foothills and down the Southern Road nearly to the coast. From here the Old City and the cranes the Americans have installed are visible fifteen miles away across the mud plain where the river flowed before the drought.

Nearly forty thousand live in Camp One now. All the acacias and even the thornbushes have been cut down. The dusty ground lifts into the air at the slightest wind. It smells of dried shit, since each family defecates outside its tent. Ruts lead from the road to a feeding compound the whites occupy in the mornings. Those who live here seldom leave their tents, inside the rusty wire. There are gaps in it now no one bothers to repair.

Still pondering the man's question, Ghedi sips the coffee his sister's brewed from beans she bought in the city. Outside a long queue of women, aluminum and plastic pots and buckets balanced atop their *hijabs,* wait for a few liters of dusty water. His men guard the pumps, decide who may approach the spigots.

Many of the women squat or even lie as they wait. It's dysentery. The foreigners announced an inoculation program, but Juulheed learned the real reason for the needles. They were to sterilize Muslim women. After that no one went for the shots, and after a time, the needles disappeared.

Ghedi's tent holds only a worn carpet where he sits, a field desk captured at Uri'yah, a box of MREs, and five rifles laid out on a blanket. Two are AKs, one is American, one Canadian, the last Iranian-manufactured. He watches dust filtering through the sunlight like silver smoke. The Arab's petting his beard like a mother her child's hair. When Ghedi looks over he smiles. His teeth are porcelain white, perfectly regular, as if they've been bleached and straightened. No one in Ashaara has such teeth.

He tells the prisoner, "Your wish does you honor, despite your crime. You may die fighting the infidel and invader."

"Thank you, Maahdi. God is great." The condemned man and his guards about-face to leave.

"It is wise?" he asks the Arab, whose name is Yousef. Yousef nods, showing again those incredible teeth.

One of Juulheed's lieutenants puts his head in. His eyes are red and his hands shake. "You called for me, O Maahdi."

"What time does the food arrive?"

"It is said, when the sun is so high."

"Guard it well. Food is life. Water is life. The Waleeli bring life to the people."

"The Waleeli bring life to the people," the lieutenant repeats. It's what the handlers shout each time they pitch a bag of corn mix, rice, or bulk flour from Ukraine off the trucks in village squares across the country. "The Waleeli bring life to the people," little girls shout as they play, stick legs flashing in the dust. Ghedi looks at Zeynaab's turned back, her spine curved as she adjusts the Chinese stove.

He pushes aside the tent flap and goes out. The air's so thick with the blowing powder it's like living in the center of a dust devil. His guards touch their headdresses, a black cloth worn pulled across their faces to breathe through.

Across the country that headdress is recognized, along with the black-and-green flags of the technicals that rumble over tracks only goats picked along before. From the Western Mountains to the Empty Quarter, the Waleeli steal from the foreigner and give to the people. When they work for the foreigners they don't wear the headdress, and shave their beards. The aid agencies pay them to guard the trucks, but food, medical supplies, water pipe, fertilizer, vanish all the same.

He looks across to where the foreigners work. He doesn't speak to them. There'll come a time to deal with them, but that time is not yet.

A commotion in line draws his attention. A woman's confronting a guard. She demands to know why there can't be another line, why only one at a time can fill her container. They spend hours getting water. The sentry looks at the ground. The woman sees Ghedi watching, wavers, then turns away. She rejoins the line, pushing her way back in, screaming at the women behind her.

Yousef comes out and side by side they walk through the camp. A beaten path leads around its edge, inside the rusty barbed wire.

Ghedi's been thinking about how to use the explosives he got from the Gelhirs. He ponders the man he's just condemned to death. Can he put the two together?

"You came to our attention when you eliminated the clan chiefs," Yousef says, strolling with hands locked behind him and the hem of his soft dishdasha brushing the path. His shoes are expensive braided leather with golden buckles. "We recognized a man we should make our friend."

"The elders were conspiring with the Americans."

"Oh, a bold act. When will you deal with the puppet government? And the foreigners themselves?"

"Soon."

Yousef runs a finger along the rusted wire, lifting it at each barb. "You are called Al-Khasmi, the Pruner. Yet that prisoner named you Maahdi. What do you say to those who call you these things?"

"I fight in God's name. It's for Him to say what I am."

"That is acceptable and pleasing. But be vigilant against those who would deceive you. There are imams who pretend to speak for some hidden Maahdi, infallible in all he says. This is not Islam. It is like the polytheists and their pope."

"This is beyond a simple soldier."

"Yes, it's not worth confusing people with hairsplitting, such as this one is Matridi or this one Ashari or this one Salafi. That's for the *Shura* that will govern once the Americans are expelled. Your mujahideen will be the refreshing pond around which will gather the tribes and elders, those merchants who are not sullied by cooperating with the occupation. But that can wait. The important point is to strike at the West. This is the aim of the Prince of Believers, our sheikh, Usama bin Laden, may God bless him."

From a sheekh to a sheikh, Ghedi thinks. From Ashaari to Arabic. And what is this Shura council? But aloud he says nothing. The longer he spends as a leader, the more he realizes the worth of silence.

Yousef kicks at pebbles. "You have a great opportunity in Ashaara. You can build an *imaamah* like that in Sudan, in Afghanistan. One day all will unite to fight the final battle with atheism, and restore the Great Caliphate. God will grant you victory over the idolators, the secular nationalists, the other traitorous apostates and deviants.

"We can send fighters and weapons, money and those who build bombs. You have heard of the bombs in Iran and Iraq that kill the *kufr* Shiites. Another was to destroy the Jews, but that went off too soon, though it destroyed an American warship."

Ghedi scuffs along as pain wraps his neck in red-hot wire. Children trail them but keep silent. Guards stay back from the strolling figures. He murmurs, "We have arms, and money. Outside fighters we don't need."

The Arab chuckles. "All men need money."

"To buy what?" Ghedi waves at the human skeletons around them. "You see how my people live. Should I eat off gold plate while they eat the crap the foreigners send? But, true, it is food. If we strike at them, it will stop."

"You see clearly. But let me ask this. What is the reason the foreigners give the world, for being in your country?"

Ghedi frowns. "To prevent starvation. It's a lie, but—"

"Of course it's a lie. They are like the Jews, they do nothing for pity. But let me ask this. How can they stay if they can no longer distribute that food?"

Ghedi halts. "I don't understand."

"Those who give the aid—who distribute it. What happens if you attack them?"

He catches his breath. "Then what will our people eat? Will you feed them?"

"You don't have to depend on the charity of infidels. Ponder this: To a land truly devoted to God, rain must come."

A boy pelts up. He gasps, "Respected General, the honored Hasheer Ali Wasami is here."

"Let's go back to the tent," Ghedi says, and they turn back along the footpath, along the rusty wire lined for a hundred yards with its silent, watching audience. And although he doesn't say it aloud, he wonders:

When did his lieutenant become "the honored"?

Hasheer looks fresh. He comes forward with arms spread and Ghedi embraces him tightly even though the pressure reignites the flames of Jahannam in his neck. This young fighter has finally admitted he owed loyalty elsewhere before he came to swear fealty to Ghedi. Perhaps this conversion is even how he feels, but can he ever be trusted again? They hug each other and then Ghedi seats him at his left hand, the Arab at his right, and Juulheed, who's come in too, across from them so all may feel honored but the guest most of all. "You have not met our new friend, one who comes to advise us from a country of high mountains."

The courtesies accomplished, Hasheer puts his palms on the worn carpet. Ghedi says, "You met with this former major of police?"

"General Abdullahi Assad compliments you on your victory at Uri'yah. He regrets having to fight you at the Tarkash oasis, but is displeased at your activities north of Malaishu. He says the Governing Council will resume power once the foreigners leave, whatever the result of the election."

"Who will then be president?"

"I believe it is in his mind he will be."

"You explained the Waleeli do the will of God?"

"He smiles at this. Assad calls himself Muslim, but he is not a man of God."

"No one but God is perfect," Yousef offers. "Still, he's not a creature of the Crusaders."

Hasheer nods. "He gets Western food to distribute to his clients. But he has hidden weapons from the old army, and is backed by the Indian merchants."

"He accepts gold from the idolators?" Yousef mutters.

Ghedi claps, as if making a bargain in a souk. "What did he say when you put our proposal to him?"

"First, there must be a line drawn. Your power to the south, his to the north. The clan lords who remain have lost all respect. It is now only the Waleeli, the Council, and the secularist traitors."

"Perhaps the traitors will be destroyed. Where to draw this line? The Durmani River?"

"Not acceptable. Don't forget, he says, much of the north is the Empty Quarter, which has no water." Hasheer unfolds a map. They lean over it as he explains various proposals.

"Each of the lines ends outside the city. There, no line is possible. You hold some neighborhoods and he others. Yet others are stubbornly obeying the Americans."

"Juulheed?" Ghedi asks his elder adviser. Then changes his mind and turns to the Arab. "But first, what is your advice, O my brother? As one who sees from afar."

Yousef frowns, knitting amber prayer beads into his fingers. "This poor servant has not yet heard that Assad Abdullahi will fight."

"This was not openly promised. But I believe, speaking with his second in command—"

"Tell us of this second in command," says Juulheed, and Ghedi nods. It's wise to know who's next in line.

"His name is Olowe, a terrible man with the hideous pale face of a European laid over that of an African. He was a sergeant in the army, much feared. He has killed many who were once set over him, but seems loyal to Assad."

"Is he a man of faith?" asks Yousef.

"He did not join me in prayer."

Ghedi sits unmoving as flies crawl over his face, though they seem to annoy the Arab. Does it matter where a line runs on a map? So long as the Waleeli flag is not openly flown, a village can be God's no matter where it lies. He murmurs, "I feel inclined to agree to the southernmost line."

"That's very far south," Juulheed says, blinking. "We lose fourteen villages."

"Ghost villages, abandoned. Who owns them isn't important. I will agree to this division. But only if his men join in the jihad." He watches Hasheer as he says this, but the boy betrays no flinch or blink he can detect. "Will they?"

"I believe he'll agree to this. Yes, my elder brother, I believe he will."

How long has Hasheer been working for the northern warlord? Reporting on the inner circles of the Waleeli? No doubt Hasheer, and through him Assad, believe they're using the Pruner for their own ends.

As he's using them. Because what's left unsaid, though he's sure all four are pondering it, is what happens once the

Americans leave. Ashaara may be divided, but it can't stay that way. Either he, the secularists, or Assad must rule. Ghedi holds more villages, but this will not determine who finally wins this deadly game. The key will be the *magaada*—Ashaara City. Whoever holds it will control the import of aid; whoever occupies the capital will be believable as a government. Whoever can eject the Crusaders and intimidate the other factions will rule.

Aloud he says, "Thank you, my brother. Take this agreement to the general, as my most trusted emissary." Hasheer puts his hand in Ghedi's, and they sit smiling at each other.

When he's gone Zeynaab comes in with fresh cups and a steaming pot. She leans, murmuring there's no more coffee, only tea. She's going into the city to buy more. Men arrive here day or night, from across the country and even from Eritrea and Sudan. There must be hospitality. He nods. Yousef glances at her, then drops his eyes. "Yes?" Ghedi says.

"This unworthy one did not congratulate you on taking a wife."

"I have no wife. I have a sister."

"I see. Well, about this relationship we offer. It's good sometimes to trust, and bargain. But it's also necessary to be hard in the face of evil."

"You don't believe I can be hard?"

"What we hear is good. But that's why I'm here. The Western media trick the faithful into seeing dusk as dawn. How can we know what we hear is true, unless we ask?"

Ghedi ponders, then looks to Juulheed. "You said you had someone to bring to me."

"Those working in the city captured him. They would have dealt with him there, but realized who he was, and brought him to me."

Ghedi takes a sip of the hot tea but it goes down wrong, and his throat blazes like hot metal poured into his mouth. It's all he can do not to groan aloud. He wipes sweat from his face. They're watching him.

"Bring him in," he says.

* * *

His sergeant of guards pushes a limping boy in. "Name," Ghedi demands, although he knows it.

Yes, it's Nabil. He recognizes his younger brother, from the dark eyes to the dragging foot. But his brother doesn't recognize him. Why should he? It's been years. They're neither what they were. The boy's been eating well, that's obvious. He's dressed in bits and pieces of American uniform. He even wears tan American boots.

"What is the charge against this Ashaaran?" he asks Juulheed.

Who hesitates, unsure what he's being called on to do. "The guard who captured him will report."

A bearded young man in a headwrap steps forward. "This one was taken aiding the infidels. Translating, and acting as guide."

"But this is only a lad," Yousef puts in.

The boy flinches and looks up, staring from one to the other.

Nabil stares at the man who sits. His face is savage. Hairy, swollen an angry red-purple. But the voice hasn't changed, and by his voice he knows. "Brother!"

"You were *once* my brother, yes," Ghedi says, and his tone stops the boy halfway across the tent. "But my brother would never help the infidel. Is this true? You guide those who invaded our country?"

"The marines aren't infidels."

The men chuckle. "Not infidels? How can you say this foolish thing?"

"They're warriors. They feed the people. That's why I helped them." He takes a breath and his face works, desperate to convince. "I saw the port, the rice. Floods of it! So much you can't believe!"

"Truly, this is only a child," Yousef murmurs. "He can be set on the right path. Your brother? Truly?"

Juulheed's gaze swings from whoever speaks to whoever speaks next. "But also truly, he helped the invaders."

Nabil trembles. His gaze returns to his brother's. "You won't let them hurt me, Ghedi," he mutters.

Ghedi's hand trembles too as he massages his neck. The heat streams into his head, clouding his thoughts like steam from a boiling kettle. The rule's his own, ruthlessly applied in the villages he controls. All who help the enemy military must die. But this is Nabil. A face distorted with tears wavers through the boiling mirage of pain.

"Is Zeynaab here? Have you seen Zeynaab?"

Thank God she's left; he can decide without a woman's softness. Though she has less in her than any other he's ever met. "This is your defense? That they bring in foreign grain, to buy the souls of the faithful?" he manages to get out. How could his own brother defy his word! Turn against him! He takes a deep breath. The words are irrevocable once pronounced. The agony's a sheet of lightning in his head.

When he opens his eyes they're all staring. Has he pronounced them? Apparently he has.

"In what manner?" Juulheed finally manages.

"Beheading," Ghedi says. He doesn't look at his brother.

The agony comes again. When it clears he's outside, in the sun and wind, and a crowd's gathered. The guards hold Nabil, but their grips seem tentative. They keep looking to him, as if for a counterorder. He finds this strange, that at times he's not himself, then is again. His head and neck feel enormous, taut, as if about to burst his skin. The knot of poison in his jaw's killing him.

The pain comes again and without his knowing it the thing's occurred. A corpse writhes on the ground. Dust is already blowing over it. As he watches, the blood soaks into the earth and the wind blows more dust and it's gone. He takes a stride and kicks sand over the thing's back. "What's it to you?" he shouts. "Don't complain. You're not hurt. You're not hurt!"

Behind him a woman screams. When he turns, it's Zeynaab. She's uncovered her face. She hurls herself onto the corpse.

Beside him Yousef sways, hand to his chest. "Was he truly your brother?"

Ghedi stares at the foreign boots. "This is how we deal with those who aid the Crusaders."

When Yousef looks up from the body respect shines in his eyes. And something like terror.

Ghedi sees the same amazement in the faces of the guards who surround and protect him every day. Of the men and women behind them, forming a witnessing circle. A whisper goes from mouth to mouth.

"What did you say?" he mumbles.

The Arab speaks, looking away from the sobbing woman. "Nothing, my brother. You have done justice here, nothing more. Behold how the Pruner deals with those who aid the Crusaders, even those of his very flesh. God is great indeed!" He turns, lifting up his hands, and a chorus echoes him, but not as loud as the gusting, whirling wind.

"Now, as God is the guarantor of every good thing, let us discuss among ourselves how we will achieve the victory of Islam."

26

CAMP ROWLEY

Watch your step," her aide said. "I told you not to wear heels."

The heat and the dust made her throat close and her eyes water. She'd been to the Mideast many times. But as Blair Titus came down the C-9's ramp it all began to swim. Too little sleep, too much travel. She reached for what she thought was a railing. Too late, she realized it was only a flimsy stand holding up a plastic dust barrier. It toppled, and down she went.

When they lifted her from the concrete, Margaret on one arm and a trooper from the back of the plane on the other, blood trickled down her shin. "I'm all right, let go," she said, shaking them off, furious. What if this had been some foreign capital instead of a military base? Maybe her aide, annoying as she was, was right. Heels weren't worth the trouble.

On the other hand, heels and a slit skirt, a button unbuttoned on a blouse, had paid off before.

When she tried her footing her knee held and she hadn't broken a heel. The sky was so bright she couldn't meet its gaze. The wind chapped her lips and dried her tongue. Margaret picked up Blair's briefcase and carried it along with her own. Twenty yards away a general and a colonel held a salute. She limped to them and made her handshake double firm.

"Ms. Titus? Cornelius Ahearn."

"Of course, General. Good to see you again." The colonel's name was Pride, apparently an eyeman for General Leache. She shook his hand too, introduced Colonel Margaret Shingler, USMC. Then looked around. "Did my husband make it?"

"Commander Lenson's out of cell range, but we got word to him and he'll be here in a couple hours." Ahearn bent to examine her knee. "I'm eager to get you briefed in. But let's see to this first."

They steered her into a noisy terminal, through plastic sheeting and steel construction scaffolding into an infirmary. A corpsman cleaned her knee, stanched the bleeding, taped on a dressing. "A bad scrape, but you don't need stitches," he said, handing her a tube of antibiotic and an extra dressing. Limping slightly, she followed the general into the JOC.

"I understand you're to be congratulated."

"It's not official. But thanks." She'd thought Force Management would step into the slot. And you could never count Policy out. There were the armed services secretaries and the CEOs of major defense corporations too. She actually wasn't sure how the secretary had decided the job was hers. It would be a challenge. Weatherfield was known for burning out subordinates, because he himself did so little actual work. Then he'd turn on them when they did something he didn't like. It might be a no-win situation, but not one you walked away from. For one thing, she'd be the first woman in the slot.

"We had a tour planned," Ahearn said with that courtly smile. "But if your injury precludes—"

"It's not an injury. Just a scrape. I'll change shoes, though—I can see Jimmy Choos aren't the best thing for a combat zone."

His smile froze. Too late she remembered this wasn't yet an actual combat zone. Or, at any rate, hovered between a permissive environment and one that might become dangerous very swiftly. She muttered an aside to Shingler, who winked, squeezed her arm, and disappeared. "What I meant is—the tour, yes, most definitely. I'm interested in transport, and of course, your relationship with the provisional government. Will we be able to meet with Dr. Dobleh?"

"All set up, later today, in town. But first let's show you our little operation here."

He took her through the JTF complex and mess hall, waved at prefab billeting and contractor-furnished cubic behind the terminal. She asked about power and water and the runway extension, about base security and what percentage of his construction went to Ashaaran contractors. He offered a drive along the perimeter but she said she'd rather see how things were going in the field. Soon they were climbing into an SH-60 and having earphones and a throat mike fitted. Then the escort ships lifted off and their own turbines chorused in heavensong and she was accelerating toward the angels.

Despite the glare through the Perspex the abrupt cold was a relief. So was Margaret's absence. She had to decide whether to keep her or return her to the Corps. She had nothing against her aide's sexual preference, but it would've been simpler without the woman having fallen for her.

Oh well. From two thousand feet she admired the city sprawled in a checkerboard of dun-colored fields. Coastal plain, but drier and more blasted-looking than any she'd ever seen. Ahearn pointed out the waterless writhe of the Durmani River, and beyond it, the blue marble of the Red Sea. Lateen sails, and a gray hull that must be one of Dan's PCs. He hadn't been on hand to meet her. But she hadn't given him or Ahearn much warning.

Weatherfield had asked her to look into Ashaara. "Can we do any good there?" had been the way he'd put it. "That's always bad, the first dead GIs. Those who don't say Vietnam say Somalia."

And she'd said, "The president wanted to make a difference in East Africa. He's got to support us when the tab comes due."

Weatherfield had looked incensed, as if she'd reminded him of something he was supposed to do and hadn't. As the first African-American secretary of defense, maybe it had to do with Africa. Or maybe not. But all he'd said was, "Find out if they can get the job done with what they've got. It's either that or pull out. And let me know before you talk to anyone else about it."

"That's the port, below," Ahearn's disembodied voice in her earphones. The pilot banked, aiming her gaze straight down on a teacup of muddy brown sea tucked under the battlements of an ancient-looking citadel. Cranes reached toward her. A black-hulled ship lay alongside, pallets rising from cavernous holds.

The general was reeling off statistics: offload rates, tonnage deliveries, the bottlenecks they'd reamed out one by one. "The shipping channel, off to our right. Your husband buoyed the shoals for us. He's been a big help." As she murmured a response the horizon scrolled up and precessed clockwise. Please God, not to hurl. "At your three o'clock, the road to Nakar. That dust cloud's the Thunder Run going out. I've had to cut the number since the ambush at the roundabout, and added light armor escort and air cover. That decreased wastage from bandit attacks, but hurt daily tonnage. Net's about the same, but the bad news is, we still have refugees streaming in."

She noted a Cobra, a speck hurtling in a weaving dance. The tubby hull of a light armored vehicle shook out a curtain of concrete-colored dust. "Meaning?"

"Meaning we have to cut the individual ration on folks who are already borderline. A hundred calories less a day, we'll see malnutrition diseases again."

The turn steadied and the nose pitched down. The pilot never kept the same course for more than five seconds. The intel on the Maahdist insurgents hadn't mentioned shoulder-fired missiles, but she and Ahearn would be high-value targets. Far ahead, miles away across terrain seamed with what looked like lava flows, rose mountains. She looked at her watch, wondering where Dan was and if there'd be time before the Dobleh meeting to spend with him. She did want to see the next item on her agenda, though.

"The Darew camp," Ahearn said. "We can skip this if you want—"

"I don't want to spend more than twenty minutes on the ground, but I definitely want to see a camp. That's why we're here, isn't it?"

"Absolutely right," the general said. But was there doubt in his tone? "That's why we're here."

She'd felt skittish, but how could she with four armed marines between her and people who gazed as inexpressively as if she were walking past in another dimension. She'd visited camps in Bosnia, but those had been vacation resorts compared to this sapping heat, this stink of dung, this smoky, eye-stinging, all-pervading grit. She watched listless children being treated for skin diseases. Old women squatting in the dust, shrouded in faded black, didn't look up as she passed. One of the feeding staff held out a bowl of corn mush. She had to gulp for all she was worth to get one spoonful down, but the moment she set it aside a bony hand flickered and it was gone.

She asked the Italian staff about disease. They said their main concern at the moment was TB. They had antibiotics, but were seeing more and more drug-resistant cases. Diarrheal diseases were already epidemic, and pneumonia, meningitis, and urinary tract infections—a minor annoyance in the West, but a major cause of death in Ashaaran women, with their butchered genitalia—were barely contained. Isolation was impossible. At any time there could be a disastrous outbreak of typhoid or cholera, and barbed wire wouldn't keep it in.

After half an hour they trudged toward the aircraft, the marines walking backward with them. She caught other sentries on a hill, scanning with binoculars while holding scoped rifles.

"No question, they need help," Ahearn said, looking at her.

She nodded. No, there was no question of that.

The question—as always—was, how badly did the United States want to give it?

Back at Rowley, she and the JTF commander conferred in his tent. The flap was closed and the fan was loud enough for privacy. She passed on Weatherfield's doubts. "That's what worries him, and the president just now," she told him. "Iraq has us tied down. If that develops badly, it'll suck in all our forces. Iran can make real trouble. And our reading is, they want very much to. Syria, Lebanon, Yemen—we have challenges all along the arc of crisis."

The general played with his glasses, flipping them as if the missing fingers weren't missing. With those moves, he could have earned a living as a card sharp. She waited for him to say something about Dan. About the submarine he'd hijacked from Iran the year before, ratcheting tension close to war. But he just sighed. "What I'm hearing, between the lines, is a pullout."

"We're not there yet. A little personal input, Corny. I came to DoD from the Hill, and maintained my contacts. Bankey and Telfair are responsive to our concerns about Ashaara. There's been a lot of coverage of the famine. We've been approached about having Angelina out here—"

Ahearn grimaced. "I can't act as a tour guide for superstars—"

"I'm not asking you to do a thing about her, General. What I'm saying is, both Hill and West Wing interest follows media coverage. We can deplore it, but that's how democracy works. Can you give us a peaceful transition to Dobleh with the forces you have? In the face of this Assad, and now this so-called Maahdi—"

"Calls himself Al-Khasmi—"

"—What*ever.* Look, I can sit out there in your JOC and have your staff brief me up the wazoo on metrics and prognostics, and I won't come out any the wiser except that we need to rebuild the Ashaaran army. State will tell me Ashaara needs more development aid. Ag will say we have to revive the agricultural sector. But it all costs money. I've got to tell Dobleh tonight to what extent we'll support his government after the elections—"

"Do you mean his elections? Or ours?"

"General, if we lose this November, the opposition'll write off East Africa so fast your boots'll be here while your ass is on a C-5." She bent to check the dressing. The scrape had stopped bleeding, so she pulled the old bandage off, taped on a new one. She caught him eyeing her thighs. Even him . . . "Can I level with Dobleh? That our commitment's paper-thin? Can he handle that?"

"He might. I wouldn't say it in front of anyone else, though."

"I'm not stupid, General. If you can't hold the lid on, we're going to have to leave Dobleh, Assad, and this al-Maahdi to duke it out. The UN and European Union can pay the warlords to protect whatever NGOs have the balls to stay, but we'll have to live with another failed state, and maybe, another haven for terrorists. Well? Can you?"

Ahearn took a deep breath. He flexed his remaining fingers. And for a long time, did not reply.

When the van braked Dan jerked awake, groping for his sidearm. The bulky vest made it hard to reach. Then he relaxed. They were back inside what the troops were calling the Blue Zone, the airfield and the administrative center of the city down to the terminal. In front of the Cosmopolite Hotel, and safe.

She was here. He couldn't help the excitement, as if someone had tromped the pedal on his heart. He cased the street, traded gazes with the GrayWolfer at the lobby entrance, and rolled out.

The Cosmopolite was a dump compared to the Burj al Arab, but it was the city's sole halfway-modern hotel. Five stories of reinforced concrete and bronze-tinted glass, most of it still intact. Twenty yards of fearsome heat, brick, and concrete radiating up even fiercer than the sun beating down, then the doors hissed shut. Overhead fans were turning, music was playing, lights glowed in the bar. After an expensive effort by a German engineering firm, power had come back on two days ago. From noon until midnight, life could be almost normal.

"Blair Titus's room?"

The desk clerk shrugged. "Don't know, *signore*."

A ten-dollar bill changed his attitude. "I'm her husband. There should be a key for me."

Instead there was a note: *C'mon up, sailor.* He was crossing the lobby to the stairway when he noticed the hum of elevator motors. Tempting, but one trusted the Ashaaran power-distribution system only so far. He ran up all five flights.

A black-uniformed guard leaned beside her door. He checked Dan's ID against an entry list, comparing him to the photo. Then nodded, and Dan knocked.

"That you, Dan?"

She stood before the window in a robe, holding back the curtain as she gazed down at the city center. She'd lost weight. Her collarbones were outlined. At the second look, nearer, he saw that the skin at the corners of her eyes had not escaped the passage of time. She'd cut her hair, too.

Then he was too close to see, and she'd never felt better in his arms.

She held on desperately, then seemed to come to and backed him away from the window, into the singing breeze of an electric fan. "Can you put the chain on? In case Margaret comes back? I was going to take a shower."

"Don't let me interrupt."

She tasted of sweat and dust and the familiar intensely exciting scent of aroused woman. His hands went under the robe, and she caught her breath. "Right . . . there. God, your hands are rough."

"Like sandpaper?"

"More like cheese graters. But that doesn't mean I don't like it."

"Do you like this too?"

Her closed eyes told him she did.

A minute later she struggled up from the bed, pulling her robe closed. "I know what you want, Dan. I do too. Problem is, in half an hour I meet with Dobleh and the ADA leadership to map election strategy. He'll stand for president—"

"You spend too much time with presidents. How about if he waits?"

"Hmm," she said. "Maybe it wouldn't hurt him that much."

"It would do him good." Dan pulled her down again. "Teach him to be patient."

"Maybe so." She let the robe go and lay back naked, hair a mess and breasts sweaty in the close air. Her pale body gleamed like wet ivory in the dim curtained room. "If he's patient, maybe good things will happen."

He ran his hand up her thighs and softly separated twin leaves that unkissed to a slick wetness. She put her hands on his shoulders. He buried his face in her belly, then ran his tongue down into the taste of the sea.

"Get that fucking uniform off, Commander," she murmured. "Right now."

With a sudden, violent heave the bed rose behind her and he was on the floor, the cheap carpet prickling his back, bewildered, ears ringing.

Before he could register what was happening the wall surrounding the entrance door blew in. The overhead light shattered into cloudy spray.

He rolled onto her just in time to take the toppling fan in

his back. Simultaneously the windows blew out with a sound so loud it struck him in the breastbone, the lamps in the room burst as if packed with dynamite, and the walls shook apart into plaster dust and fragments. The mattress came down on top of them just as part of the ceiling fell with a resounding crash mixed with a jarring, reverberating bang from outside, echoing from the dust-brown rock of the old citadel.

He gripped her tight, his right leg thrown over her naked ass, one arm flung out to clutch an electrical conduit which had appeared in a gap in the wall. She lay with head turned away. A thread of blood wormed her scalp, turning blond hair dark. He blinked; her hair was *glittering.*

The floor heaved again and sagged toward where the door had been. Screams came from outside, up from the street, amid the staccato trumpeting of car alarms, as if the Judgment had touched down in Ashaara. He lay with every muscle rigid, outstretched arm shaking. He didn't like gripping an electrical conduit, but the way the floor was popping beneath them it might go any minute. Which would drop them five floors, and the reinforced concrete ceiling on top of them. He remembered again how much he disliked prefabricated concrete buildings.

"Honey?" he said into her ear. To his enormous relief, she stirred. Half turned her head. "A bomb went off, or a gas main. Anyway this floor's about to give way." He coughed. "Can you move?"

Blair came back from the black to find herself pinned under something. She understood immediately what had happened. The embassy bombings in Kenya and Tanzania. Dan's voice in her ear. The necessity to escape. She flexed her toes in experiment and took a breath. Nothing seemed to be broken, though her scalp stung as if savaged by hornets. She cleared her throat. "Yeah."

"You okay?"

"Think so. Can you get off me?"

"That's the mattress and half the ceiling, not me. Crawl forward . . . that's right. I'll hold it up. There."

"My robe. My clothes."

"Forget about—"

"I'm not going out of here naked, Dan. And neither are you. God—"

"What?"

"Your back. It's bloody, all over." She bent and saw shards of glass twinkling in the blood. "None of them look deep, but—"

The floor sagged again and half the wall facing the corridor slid away with a crackling roar, leaving them staring at a smoking chaos of rubble and, even worse, empty air. "We've got to get out of here," he said.

She couldn't agree more. She found a corner of her robe and tugged it out from under the mattress. Found, thank God, her computer too. She shook plaster and glass out of the terry cloth and pulled it on. Handed him his pants, slipped her flats on, and handed him his boots. While he was lacing them she smelled something she'd hoped she wouldn't.

Dan lifted his chin, catching it too. "Smoke."

"Yeah." She stepped over him and swung the computer through the shattered window and followed it out onto the balcony. Caught her breath as it leaned under her weight, but it didn't go. Not yet. "Come on, come *on*."

He bent and stepped through.

And halted. Looking down a hundred feet to a street paved with a crystalline sparkle. Over it people staggered or ran or crawled. Humvees and trucks crunched and swerved between them. Dark and white ovals of upturned faces stippled the crowd. As they looked down a wave of choking smoke burst up through the shattered floor and billowed out through their windows, through other windows to left and right and below too. Other guests were out on their balconies, waving and calling to those below.

She caught her breath, wondering how many hadn't made it. If the bomb had gone off in front of the building . . .

"Dobleh," Dan said, looking down.

"Where? You see him?"

"That's who they were after. Or maybe both of you."

She sucked her breath, realizing the whole ADA leadership had been scheduled to meet in the conference room. On the street side . . .

Dan's cell went off in his pants pocket. He flinched and snatched it out. "Lenson."

"You all right, sir? We just got word of a bombing at the Cosmo."

"We're trapped on the fifth floor, Kim. Me and the undersecretary. Where are you?"

McCall was back at the JOC. He told her tersely they needed either a hook and ladder or, if there wasn't one, a line-throwing gun. "We can get down if I can drop a line. But there's a lot of smoke. Probably fire behind it. I don't know who's on-scene commander, but get help headed our way. We need oxygen, litters, extraction crews from the helo squadron. All the medics and quick response you can scramble. EOD too—there might be more than one bomb." It was a common terrorist tactic, to detonate one bomb, then use a delayed-action device to mow down mourners, rescuers, and just plain gawkers. She said she'd pass the word, then come herself. Dan told her no, to stay there and coordinate the relief effort.

He flipped the phone closed as the balcony next to them squealed and collapsed, dumping the shirtsleeved man on it a hundred screaming feet down into the street. He pulled Blair against the outer wall. "We can't stay here," he yelled.

"Don't go back in there."

"You stay here. Less weight, maybe it'll hold. I'll see if there's another way out."

She reached for his arm, but her hand slid off sweat and blood and grit. The next moment he was ducking again through the shattered doorway, then dropping to hands and knees. Keeping close to the wall, he crept toward the open sky at the far end. Came to the corner of a wall; hesitated; then curled around it like a cat, and out of her sight.

If he kept low, the smoke wasn't as bad. He still wouldn't be good for more than a few minutes. Still, he'd groped his way through torpedoed and burning ships, and knew that what looked solid could be a trap and what looked impenetrable could sometimes be wriggled through. If you moved fast, before the wreckage settled.

Above all, if you were lucky.

He found himself in what had been the corridor. Most of the roof was gone and the sun streamed through the smoke, making it look more crimson than black. The carpet tilted at an absurd angle, as if to spill him off into the smoke-obscured, wire-hung, rebar-studded cavern of smashed masonry below. Maybe that's what had happened to the GrayWolf. There was no sign or remnant of him.

A cold numbness had taken his hands. There was glass all over, but he didn't feel it in his palms as he crawled. His knee slipped on the carpet and his boot shot off into space. He clung with his nails, belly to the floor, panting plaster dust and smoke and, yes, explosive fumes. When he didn't slide off he pulled his boot back and crawled on.

The floor widened. Then became almost whole, though littered with chunks of concrete, asphaltum roofing material, twisted tin from air ducts. Some yards on he made out the stairwell. There was nothing left of the elevator. It was down in the volcano with the rest of the facade and central core of the hotel.

Including anyone who'd been there. He pushed that out of his mind—he had to focus on getting Blair out—and rose to a combat crouch and ran into the stairwell. Smoke was streaming just like up a chimney, so dense it would be impossible to breathe, but the concrete of the stairs was rock solid and there wasn't much debris on them. At least the two landings he could see. Someone was yelling below and the words, not in English, echoed as if from a cavern. He yelled down, "Up here," and was seized with a choking fit so intense he couldn't get air to cough with. He backed out and caught his breath in the corridor, but the smoke was heavier and the air hotter there now too.

His cell phone again, just as he was about to cross the

tilted bridge. He debated not answering, then realized he'd better. "Lenson."

"Colonel Shingler here. Are you with the undersecretary?"

Her aide, the one who didn't like him. "We're in the hotel, Colonel, trying to get out."

"I'd like to speak with her. Her cell doesn't seem to be—"

"She's busy," Dan told her, and punched END. He almost pitched the cell into the smoking crater, but didn't. "Blair!" he yelled. *"Blair!"*

No answer, and suddenly sweat broke over his back as he gagged. Either she couldn't hear or . . . an image of her tumbling as she fell, hitting pavement, bouncing . . .

He bent and ran on tiptoe across the narrow section, hugging the wall, realizing as he did he shouldn't, but made it to where their door had been. Started to slide around the broken wall, but stopped. Another ceiling-slab had come down, a solid expanse of stippled concrete. He couldn't see past it. "Blair!" he bawled, loud as he could over the clamor of sirens and the growing roar of fire.

"I'm here. Where are you?"

He breathed again, but the flame in his lungs was getting worse. He sprawled, but it was smoky near the floor too. It blew past him toward her, whirling to the right as it sucked through. A gap? . . . "Stairwell's clear. We can take the stairs down. If we hurry. Can you get to me?"

"You sure?"

"I got there and back. There's smoke but it's . . . navigable." He saw a towel and shook glass from it and mopped his face. It came away looking like the Shroud of Turin. "We don't have much time. The fire's taking hold."

"Coming."

He saw her hand first, groping through the fallen roof. Then her arm. But that was all. "I can't get through."

"Try to the right. No, to your left, your left."

She was hacking hard. "There's a lot of glass."

"See where the smoke's coming out? Is there a hole there?"

Her arm first again, then her head, hair blackened with

flakes of dark matter. Her face was charcoaled except where tears had gouged streaks. She still wore the robe, but it wasn't white anymore. He worked his way in, got an arm and pulled. Something snagged and she cursed. Cloth ripped but her torso came free. Then her legs, kicking and dirty. She'd slung her cased laptop over her back like a rifle. Her eyes looked boiled as she stared around. "Okay, fuck this, which way?"

She was so angry she could barely keep a civil tone even to Dan. Once she was out of here, let everybody just fucking *beware.*

Her husband's naked chest was streaked with blood and soot. So were his trousers. His face was black except for tear trails down his cheeks. His grip was very strong and she held it gratefully. She'd been terrified out on that balcony, waiting for it to give way. A chopper had circled but then flown away. Couldn't it lift them out? Maybe that one hadn't had the right equipment. She'd been tempted to stay, but if they could make it to the stairwell, it'd be a more dignified exit than dangling naked in some goggled aircrewman's embrace like Jane in Tarzan's arms.

Crawling was tough on the knees . . . but nothing hurt. Yet. They just had to get out. Nothing mattered but that. Her eyes burned, weeping so continually in the smoke she could barely see. A hand had the back of her robe. It tugged her along. The floor slanted and she started to slide. She twisted to look where she was going and caught her breath in a near scream. Yellow flames beckoned deep in a smoking pit of shattered rubble.

Far down in it, a human figure moved. Impossible, in that chaos, yet it moved. She blinked as it squirmed past a broken support column, across a cracked slab. It groped its way with dreadful slowness toward what once had been a lobby exit.

Then a third-floor wall collapsed. A cloud of dust and smoke drifted across the scene. When it cleared, the figure was still there, but broken. Motionless as a crushed bug on a pavement.

Dan kept tugging her along. Every few feet she'd stop in her tracks and stare down into the abyss to their right. But gradually they neared the bottleneck. It was shakier now than the first time he'd crossed. Like that bridge he'd read about, with Hell beneath for sinners who couldn't keep their footing. All too literally, here. He hoped she didn't freeze in the middle of it.

"Want me to lead, or follow you?" he yelled over the clamor of the flames.

"I'll go," he thought she said.

There wasn't room for two, side by side. She could see that. If she went over, she wanted him behind her. Then he could go back and wait on the balcony.

She felt it vibrating beneath her, like the floor of an aircraft in flight. Only there wasn't twenty thousand feet of air beneath them here. Just jagged steel and flames.

She coughed and coughed, then made herself creep out onto it. The carpet was slick and hot. Was it starting to melt? It was smoking. The smoke was choking. The bloke was croaking. The blond was broken. "Just fucking *stop it*," she muttered.

Dan followed her dirty rump, one hand on her ankle. She was crowding the ragged edge of the floor, where it was fraying like a worn rug. Cracking, pieces crumbling off as they put weight on it. Somewhere below another section gave way with a roar like a calving iceberg. Where were the rescuers?

Then he remembered, and it wasn't a good feeling: there was no such thing as a fire main or a fireman in all Ashaara. Except for whatever extinguishers the military had in their trucks, the flames below were going to have to burn themselves out. And except for a few soldiers, and maybe some foolhardy bystanders, anyone who wanted to survive would have to see to it himself.

Blair felt the black coming back. There wasn't any air, only asphyxiating fumes that felt like sucking lava. Her hands were burning. She didn't want to look down, but the drop and the slickness below kept pulling her eyes. Nietzsche and the abyss. For the first few minutes after the blast she'd felt superhuman. Now what little strength she had left was going fast.

Her knee skidded on the carpet, on something that was both slick and burning hot. Her hips twisted toward the drop. She clawed the carpet like a cat, feeling her fingernails tear, but still lost ground. She was going. Going . . . a scream burst from her throat, raw and savage.

A palm on her ass and a terrific shove sent her sprawling across the melting polyester. She clawed again, trying to use the momentum to carry her up onto the level section ahead.

She teetered, mass and energy balanced so precisely that for a second she didn't know if she was going to make it or not.

Behind her Dan was fighting just as grimly to recover from the shove he'd sent her skidding ahead with. A smoking black rain drooled and spattered around him. The melting tar was burning their hands, greasing away their traction. It scorched his legs, dripping from the melting roof. On the next floor down flame hissed and leaped where tar ran like molten lead poured by a hunchback from a cathedral's downspouts. At any moment the flames could climb that liquid ladder and ignite the very surface they crawled on. He squinted through streaming eyes. Had she made it? The round white blur that was her rear end, was it slipping backward?

The clawing fingers of his right hand found a patch of carpet without tar. His left boot, bent and pushing, got a grip. But he was still slipping. Still *slipping*—

Savage fingers closed on his hair and yanked hard enough to brake his slide. Then yanked again, and he scrabbled desperately, leg kicking at intangible air. With a breathless scramble he surged across the crack as it opened up, falling away into the flaming chasm, and slammed into her.

They collapsed wheezing and choking, unable to speak as sparks blew overhead. Black greasy patches ignited, some on the carpet, some on them, and he beat at her with his hands as she beat at him, locked in a strange embrace, grunting and panting.

They crawled up and onward, like creatures emerged from the deep, toward the black rectangle of the stairwell, outlined in the growing orange flicker from all around.

When they emerged soldiers in camouflage and black men in civilian clothes were carrying limp smoking bundles out of the building. "Over here," shouted a trooper. He draped a blanket over Blair. She tried to thank him, but couldn't force a word past whatever blocked her throat. Detached pieces of the world whirled around the bowl of her sight. A high tinnitus went on and on, making it hard to hear what people were saying, or formulate a response when she did.

The first thing those around them did was lead them an agonizingly long way off down the road. When she looked back she understood: the hotel was still yielding to gravity, wall by wall and floor by floor. Each collapse sent a gush of spark and flame out into the street, where the rescuers ducked and cried out, retreating; then, when it withdrew, darted in again. Windows were smashed. Walls lay toppled all along the street. Cars lay on their sides or thrown into buildings, gushing up greasy smoke. Cables lay in dangerous snarls, wrapping toppled power and phone standards. Women in the bright local clothing crouched wailing over clumps of scorched cloth and flesh.

Ashaaran and American stood in line together at a makeshift aid station. Dan was talking to a man in a ripped suit and no tie. She felt too apathetic to listen. Until something the Ashaaran said woke her. "What's that?" she said, forcing her attention through the ringing silence that kept threatening to seal her away from everything that could hurt.

"I saw it," the man said, keeping his voice low. "A welder's truck. Square like a box. A blue truck. The driver looks scared. He drive up to hotel. He sit there, until a guard go up to him. Then, the explosion."

"How'd you see this?" Dan asked.

"I was in other car, getting briefcase for the minister."

"What minister?"

He didn't answer, just kept on in a low insistent voice. "They are all there, in the front room. The doctor and the others, those to be ministers. They wait for an American woman."

"That was this lady," Dan said. The man stared.

"So what are you saying?" she asked more sharply than she'd intended. "I'm sorry—I meant—they were in the conference room when it went off?"

"The roof comes down." The Ashaaran spread his palms, then clapped them together. "Then walls fold in. Then, all the hotel above. And fire. All are dead, I think."

"Over here. Here she is." Heavyset GrayWolf PMCs in ponytails, beards, and bulky protective vests emerged from the smoke. The leader rasped, "Miz Titus? Ma'am, we can treat you elsewhere, no waiting. This your husband? We got to take you out of here. There's snipers reported on these rooftops."

She didn't object. Without her in line, those behind would get treated more quickly. One guard handed her a soft cloth dampened with what smelled like pure alcohol. She used it to mop her face, wincing as it stung. The contract guards scrummed around them and began to move, in a unit, like a Macedonian phalanx. Their rifles traced the rooflines until they reached an SUV two streets back. As soon as the doors slammed it pulled out, a Humvee in front, another behind, sandwiching it as machine guns swept the street.

Behind them sirens faded, the wails dropped away. They turned onto an open road and added speed. She leaned into Dan, drawing quavering breaths. The anger was gone, vanished. Only now was she really frightened, totally filled with breathless terror.

She'd never show it. Not to these men. Not to him. And never to the public that watched for any sign of weakness or frailty.

The anger would return, she was sure of that. Probably her confidence would, too. It always had before, after a bad fall from a horse.

But right now, she was very frightened indeed.

IV

THE SNIPER

27

JOINT OPERATIONS CENTER, CAMP ROWLEY

The JOC was icy in a hot land, bright in a dark night, murmurous with subdued speech and the gunfire crackle of keys. Dan snapped up from a doze, from exhausted dreaming to exhausted waking. He'd been trying to make formation but couldn't find some item of uniform. Did every academy grad have the same recurring dream? Everyone who'd ever worn a uniform? Silver islands had floated on a violet sea. He'd known them in some previous life, but where? If only he'd found the belt to his trop whites . . .

He massaged bristly cheeks and reached for coffee. Instead his fingers groped a mess of grounds and cigarette butts the previous JOC chief had left in the arm of the watch captain's chair. His face was haggard in the semireflective screen of an overhead monitor above. He had on smelly BDU trou worn for too long and the olive drab T-shirt that was all he could stand on his back since a corpsman had picked out thirty-one shards of glass. The bandages rasped when he moved. His throat was still raw from the smoke.

But he'd been lucky. None of the shards had gone deep enough to kill.

The truck bomb at the Cosmopolite three days before had killed forty Ashaarans, eight Americans, and one Briton, wounded scores more, and wiped out Dr. Dobleh and almost the entire leadership of the ADA. The explosion narrowly missed Ambassador Dalton and General Ahearn as well as Blair, all scheduled to be in the conference hall too, but who had for various reasons been delayed. Someone had known exactly when that meeting would take place. No one knew the bomber's identity, though the NCIS was investigating.

The foreign-educated professionals everyone had been depending on as a provisional government, to make a graceful handover possible, were either dead or so badly injured they'd be out of the game for months, if not permanently. A ton of Czech-made Semtex and a suicidal maniac with a push button had derailed every plan they'd made. And almost killed Blair.

For that alone, it was his personal mission to find whoever was behind it.

The SecDef had had Blair flown out as soon as she was treated. Dan had been with Ahearn; they'd had to say goodbye by cell. Since then he'd slept only in uneasy snatches.

Well, lost sleep wasn't new to anyone who'd been to sea. He slid out of the chair and wove between terminals to the coffee mess. Straining for some semblance of alertness, he stared at the map.

The country was staggering, bleeding, once more headless. Gripped by what seemed like insanity, but had obviously been cunningly planned.

First a respected religious leader had been killed. Then the tribal elders decimated. No one seemed sure who'd committed those outrages. But they'd crippled, if not destroyed, what little remained of the traditional conflict-resolution mechanisms—tribal courts, clan treaties, all the blood-money and bride-wealth arrangements that had once kept a wide-flung, nomadic population from endless war.

The truck bombing did the same thing to what nascent democratic institutions the country had evolved.

But worst of all, and revealing some mastermind at work: militias throughout the country had begun a Tet-style offensive against refugee camps, hospitals, water-drilling operations, feeding stations, transport garages. They'd assaulted a Seabee unit and nearly wiped it out before the survivors withdrew to a hilltop and called in air support. They'd taken over all the refugee camps, even the one within sight of the capital. They'd blown up the Victory Bridge and staged a dawn assault at the marine terminal. The security team had beaten it back, killing the attackers, but every handler, crane operator, and truck driver had deserted. Four ships lay offshore, unable to offload. Along with everyone else in JOC and on the ground, Dan had scrambled to get units out to the aid agencies, get their personnel loaded into trucks or helicopters, and pulled back to the airfield.

Reactive, not proactive. But at least he'd done it so fast that friendly forces had arrived at most of the posts ahead of the insurgents, who'd found only empty drilling sites, evacuated medical centers, unguarded piles of food and medicine. Sometimes the aid workers protested. The dispensary at Camp Two had been run by Caritas, the Catholic aid agency. The staff had refused to leave, putting mission before safety. The marines had unceremoniously flex-cuffed and hustled them onto the CH-46s. The nun in charge had buttonholed the first colonel she saw at the airfield, who happened to be Pride. Dan had overheard the exchange, along with everyone else in the terminal, so there was a new expletive in circulation: "Innemagott." That's how she'd blistered the speechless colonel: "In nema Gott, Colonel, in nema Gott, you are fulss, fulss."

Unfortunately so far that was their only strategy: react and pull back, to airfield and port. If the JTF had to evacuate, those were the only ways they could exit. Dan didn't think they'd have to—the insurgents weren't targeting the U.S. military per se, unless it was colocated with aid agencies—but no commander could let his forces be trapped.

Still, they couldn't react forever. They had to retake the initiative. Or the mission, and the whole country, was going down the tubes.

Fifty miles to the west, going two hundred knots in the dark a thousand feet off the deck, Teddy sat hunched over his rifle, chewing pineapple-flavored bubblegum Sumo's mother had sent from Hawaii. Trying not to think about where they were going.

It was too noisy to talk, to even think. They were all covered in a thick, buttery film of sweat. You'd think things would cool down at night but if anything it felt hotter. The stripped-down, metal-walled cabin felt like a microwave oven on high. It was pitch dark aside from an orientation strip down by their boots. He was so gear heavy, and they were packed so tight into the rear of the SH-60, his jaw was all he could move. But he had a knobber on; he did have that.

Him and Sumo and Whacker and Bitch Dog, on their third back-to-back mission today. Ever since the hotel bombing, the quick reaction force had been on nearly continuous call. Fly to a camp or distribution station, secure the high ground, stand by in case hostiles tried to obstruct the exfil. Once you set up lookouts you might catch a catnap on a protected roof. The night before he'd even gotten a couple solid hours in half watches in a night defensive position. Nothing like Hell Week at BUD/S, but it made you just that little bit slower, put some glue in your reactions. Eventually you started seeing things that weren't there, or not seeing things that were. He'd have to nitpick the guys tonight. Have to watch himself, too.

Only once in three days had he even taken his safety off, warning away four dudes with honest to God spears who'd objected to his taking away their U.S. government–funded free health care. Most times, the whack of helo blades and the sight of the QRF had been enough to make the insurgents disappear.

This time, though, the head shed guaranteed they'd take fire. The major had given it to them straight at the briefing.

Teddy had to admit, no one talked to that guy and came away confused. "Tonight's payback," he'd said. "These shitheads killed the Seabees at Hill 153. They're coordinating attacks all over the country. Killing doctors. People who came to help. If they don't surrender, Article 556 'em."

And the assembled marines and SEALs had given the deep grunting "Hooyah" that meant they'd taken the directive aboard.

The helicopter banked and he leaned into the webbing, eyes closed, chewing for all he was worth as it dropped a thousand feet in sixty seconds. Something broke free aft and rolled forward. He stuck out a boot and trapped the grenade. "Somebody lose something?" he yelled. Nobody answered, so he jammed it into his thigh pocket. A spare might come in handy.

Taking buildings wasn't your typical SEAL mission. Usually a team just spotted the bad guy, then sent in the direct-action dudes. But the major had asked if his guys could do it. There was only one answer.

More sweat broke as he contemplated it. They had the gear, hooleys and hammers and demo, but as far as he was concerned, the best way to clear a building was with a five-hundred-pound bomb. Except this BVIP's hide site was in the middle of Fenteni, the second-biggest city in the country. Guy had his own militia, and Russian-trained personal security with night vision equipment. They'd already gone after him once, in the city, but missed him by minutes.

The major had passed around a photo. Teddy had held it, burning it into his forever memory. Abdullahi Assad. A dark face, long-boned, in a Brit-style uniform blouse. The expression intellectual, calm, but the dark eyes burning. In any group, the major had said, Assad would stand out.

He might not be here, either. No point getting worked up before they knew. His hyperactive brain started to go over his gear again, but he stopped it. He'd checked every round in his mags, he was in full battle rattle from body armor to flex cuffs. He rubbed his crotch, visualizing the Air Force captain in Saudi, the tangled nest between her legs. The reddened, pouting, somehow surly-looking slit, as if it could eat anything and it'd never be enough—

"Minute out, frogs," said a bored voice in his ear. "Dude on the roof. Lookin' our way."

Obie made his voice weary too. "Roger dodger. Locked and cocked."

He pulled his night vision down and turned it on. The black interior became a green-and-white seethe, angles distorted by the short focal length lens on the imaging tube. Across from him Sumo grimaced under his own goggles, snarling like a Maori war god crossed with a cyborg techwarrior. Teddy put his game face on and snarled back. Arkin demonstrated his trademark pit-bull bark-and-growl. Kowacki was rapping his mag against the seat frame, shoving it back in, hitting it with the heel of his hand. "Concentrate and live!" he shouted at them. "Fuck up and die! Hooyah!"

"Hooyah!"

"Forty seconds," the voice said in his ear. "Gunship engaging."

Tick tick tick tick tick, not far distant. The Cobra, taking out that rooftop lookout with IR sights and twenty-millimeter shells. *Tick tick tick.*

"Thirty seconds. HLZ hot. Marines going in."

They were hitting the buildings overlooking the compound, to overwatch and suppress so no one could fire down on the team as it went in. He hoped nobody got confused. They had reflective patches on their backs, but from the front, in a narrow hallway, one shooter looked like any other.

He tripped the seat belt. Stood awkwardly and braced his boots, got his gloves on the door handle. The fast rope at his feet, ready to kick out so they could drop into the dust and murk to whatever awaited. His heart squeezed beat after beat like a sniper squeezing out rounds. He panted, salting away oxygen. No fear. Let them fear him. Fear the Navy SEALs and American vengeance.

"Ten seconds . . . five . . ."

The howl of turbines. The slam of his heart.

"Assault team: Go! Go! Go!"

The door hauled open over a pit of black sparkling with flame. Muzzle flashes. The disorienting pulse of an IR strobe through a seethe of dust. *This* was why he was alive, while he was alive. Not to make deals, or movies. Savage joy filled his heart. He kicked out the rope, positioned it so nothing would hang up on the way down. Then grabbed it and dove through.

Back at the JOC, Dan slid from his chair as Ahearn appeared in the doorway. Peyster was with him, the guy from State security. So was Pride, and the JTF J-3, an Army bird colonel named Dickinson. His shaved head was pebbled like an orange, and he wore wraparound sunglasses even indoors. Ahearn looked tired but recently shaven, in fresh BDUs, cap pulled low. He tossed it on a terminal. His gaze moved past Dan, then back. "What's the status on Viper, Commander?"

Viper was a truck convoy evacuating all World Food personnel and as much equipment as possible from camps and feeding stations in the southwest. The pullback had been rendered more difficult by the sudden vanishing of all the hired Ashaaran security. Dan was trying to protect it, but aside from a Spectre gunship from the Air Force's Sixteenth Special Operations Squadron, he had no way to defend a convoy of fifty-seven trucks with 270 aid personnel and transport staff. And right now, the Spectre was over Fenteni, backing up the QRT assault on General Assad's hide site.

On the other hand, he *did* have imagery. "Sir, the convoy's ten klicks north of Tarkash."

"What in fuck's name are they doing there? That's way south of the river." Ahearn sounded angry but Dan knew now this was his battle persona. His own was detached rather than enraged, but either worked, as long as you kept your brain engaged.

"I rerouted them off the main road." Dan went to the main screen up front and bent to the keyboard. The scene zoomed, superimposing tactical map and overhead imagery. A road junction, a village, ragged folds of difficult land.

He explained the rerouting, then toggled another video source. This moved jerkily, ten frames a second, with bright streaks that wiped out the picture from time to time. It was in the green-tinted monochrome of night vision. Grid, altitude, and other reference numbers flickered at the edges of the frame. "Real time, sir. Downloading from a Pioneer."

Pioneer was the Navy's and Marine Corps' go-to unmanned aerial vehicle, a four-hundred-pound drone that looked like a downsized Piper Cub. The Marines used it for over-the-horizon recon, targeting, and damage assessment. The control station was west of Haramah, but the output from onboard electro-opticals went to a satellite via a C-band datalink, then down again to both the control van and the JOC.

"What's he got in mind?" Ahearn muttered.

Meaning Assad. The leader of the Governing Council had vanished after the bombing. No one claimed credit, but the consensus was he was responsible. The QRT had assaulted his compound in Ashaara City. They got aides and a mass of security ministry files, some dating into the rule of the Morgue. But Assad was long gone.

If the raid went right, they might have him in custody tonight.

"It's an ambush," Dan told him. "The Night Owls picked up these guys in the valley and tracked them into two villages. Our reading is they're still there. But we'd need troops to go in."

"We're fully committed, sir," the J-3 said. "As you know. Did Centcom forward our request for follow-on forces?"

Ahearn had requested another MEU and a light infantry battalion, an armor task force and a battery of self-propelled artillery. Also a corps engineer battalion and a lot more aviation. And a special operations task force to take some of the strain off the SEALs, who were getting worn down with back-to-back missions getting the civilians out of the field.

Ahearn chewed the inside of his mouth, blinking.

"They don't pony up, we need to start thinking about a

withdrawal timetable," Pride said. "I know you don't want to. That's why you need to start your planners on it."

"I'd rather have them thinking about how to hold," Ahearn said, not angrily now, but as if he'd lost the energy to invest emotionally. He squinted at Dan. "How far from contact's our lead vehicle? What do you have on tap?"

"About half an hour," Dan told him. "I've got two Humvees with the force itself. Fifties. That's about it."

"Ma Deuce. Always nice to have her, but where's the Spectre?"

"Over Fenteni, sir. Supporting the raid."

"Cobras? Same-same?"

"Yessir."

"Can they do without one, Jim?" Ahearn asked the J-3, who looked dismayed. "Never mind. Forget I asked. There are times when you really wish for fast movers."

"Yes sir, General," Dan agreed. Fast movers were fighters, attack aircraft.

This was one of those times.

The fast rope was fast. It burned Teddy's hands despite the gloves as the pop-pop-pop of blades and howl of the turbines scrambled his ears. Every second you were on the line you were a target.

And he was in somebody's sights, despite the marines overwatching this rooftop. Not close enough, because bullets were zowing past him, punching through the helo above. He hoped the team was out of the box, because the box was getting shot up pretty bad.

Whoever put out the burst only nine-ringed him all around, but the second his boots hit rooftop somebody *else* started firing too, the tracers floating by just overhead. *Over* his head, even though they should've hit him, because he'd gone right through the roof.

"Holy fuck," he muttered, slapping at something crackly corseting his waist. He was so heavy with gear and water and ammo that, despite scorching his hands on the fast line, his boots had punched right through what felt like layers of tar paper. Or maybe, leaves glued together with what stunk like dried dung. He was kicking his feet in the air while the rest of him stuck out of the roof like a heavily armed mushroom.

His whole body convulsed at an image of his legs sticking out of the ceiling below, balls wide open. He rolled, jackknifed his knees, and kept rolling, over hard things that didn't move. He came up with the sights to his face and triggered two quick bursts full auto toward where he figured the shooter was. Whoever the Cobra had seen on the rooftop, either they hadn't gotten him, or somebody else was up here too.

Then Sumo charged past, bounding and covering. Teddy got to his knees, then his feet, and cut left to cover the Hawaiian with another burst as he bounded again. Until the flash and crack of a grenade stilled whoever was firing.

When he spun, his IR beam lit up reflectors like bright billboards jerking against the still-triggering strobe the marines had put down. A lot of light, too much for the AN/PVS's tube. He pushed it up but still couldn't see anything, dazzled from the lightning flashes of the screen. You were supposed to keep your left eye closed to retain night vision but that didn't work when some asshole was shooting tracer at you.

"Fireinahole!" yelled Bitch Dog. He and Whacker crouched on either side of a rooftop doorway. Another grenade crack, and both SEALs went down the black gap of the stairway.

When Obie caught up they were in a downstairs hallway, stacked against the first doorway on the left. Standard clearing procedure—they'd done it ad nauseam back at the Kill House. Drilled it again and again waiting to assault *Tahia*. A flash of Suleyman's contemptuous grin. Just let him come face-to-face with that asshole here. . . .

He took low position, left of the door. Bitch Dog crimped his shoulder. He grunted, "Go," and Sumo jerked it open.

Teddy went through with carbine at low ready, sticking to the left wall, sweeping right as Kaulukukui went right and swept left. Still dark as shit, and the fucking night viz had zero peripheral vision. Anybody with a flashlight taped to an AK could mow them down. But he saw only empty bunks. Shouts from the hallway: "Clear left."

"Clear right."

"Coming out!" he yelled, but overlaid with his shout was the flash and stutter of a burst from down the hallway, a turn in the corridor.

Four carbines chattered as one, chewing through the corner somebody had taken for cover and knocking the guy sprawling back into the opposite wall. Oberg held the aim point for a second, in case there was someone behind, then hugged the wall as Whacker caromed a grenade around the corner.

But when they rounded it, it was empty, except for blood on one wall. The smear was still hot, glowing in the IR image. Dots across the floor glowed too, cooling and darkening even as he moved past, covering the looming emptiness of another door down. He hesitated, not knowing why, just that something about the glowing blood didn't seem . . . "Hooley it. Hooley it!" Bitch Dog was grunting behind him, followed by a splintering crack as the pry-bar destroyed the lock.

Sumo's big hand slammed onto his shoulder as the other fire team yelled, "All clear," from the other room, and "Coming out." Teddy eyed the stairway, not liking it. He pulled the grenade out of his cargo pocket. Dropped the carbine to hang by its assault sling, pulled the pin, and crammed into the left wall, folding up small as he could. "Frag out!" he screamed, coughing in the dust and smoke. He hated clearing buildings. Still, it pushed buttons he liked having pushed.

The crack dented his eardrums in the narrow space, the blast focused upward by the stairwell. He went down it fast and low and double-tapped a skinny coming out of a hide behind some large console thing. In the weird green looming of night vision he recognized a pachinko machine. Skinnies played pachinko?

A burst flared from the far end. Bullets whacked and whined off concrete and metal. They traded bursts, ducking, and Sumo fired from behind and above him. The Hawaiian yelled, "Frag," and Teddy went down on his face. When he scrambled up a glowing blur lay in the doorway.

"Lights," he yelled. Enough of this, he couldn't see shit. He tore the goggles off and stuffed them—you didn't want to leave them behind—and hit his Surefire. The whole room and two doorways illuminated. The body lay in one; the other was closed. He checked behind where the guy had fired from. Pantry. A stir, and he aimed, but it was too small to be human. Probably a rat.

Whacker and Bitch Dog took the door. Looked at each other, leaned to the wall. Oberg frowned, then put his ear against it too. Through the pitch-pipe whalesong of fire tinnitus came the babble of many voices, raised in frenzied shouts of . . . defiance? Disagreement? Insult? He couldn't tell, but that many people meant Mister Big's personal bodyguard. Maybe the Main Man himself.

"Demo," he said, but Sumo was already on it. The Hawaiian loved making things go bang. He folded the clayey brick and stuck in the detonator. Pasted it to the center of the door panel. Yeah, they were in there waiting for them to crash through, so they could AK them. Great, see how they liked a door coming at them at the velocity of a pistol bullet.

"Fire in the hole," Sumo grunted, not too loud, in case they spoke English on the other side. The SEALs ducked and covered, Teddy vising his gloves over ringing ears. Much more of this and he wouldn't be able to hear a fucking thing. The door blew in a blast of smoke and splinters. He and Sumo took the opening, high and low, carbines at high ready, following probing beams of brilliant light.

Ahearn stood, turning toward the door of the JOC. So did the others. Dan glanced that way, then rose.

The ambassador was in cream slacks and a sweat-mooned golf shirt with a Whiskey Creek logo. His white hair was rumpled and sweaty, as if he'd just taken off a cranial. He looked smaller, more worn, than at the coordination meeting at the embassy. When they'd beaten off a few looters and considered themselves invulnerable. Sure, they'd feed Ashaara. Stand up a democratic government. Fix a country run into the ground since colonial days, and save seven million people from drought and famine that had plagued them for generations.

Right. Piece of cake.

Jedidiah Dalton wrung Ahearn's hand as if being rescued after many days adrift. "General. The convoy?"

"Being watched. And the raid's going in on our friend." The marine waved to a seat in front of the main screen. "Colonel Dickinson's got the big picture. Where we go from here, what our options are. Should we let him start?"

Over the next few minutes the J-3 outlined the status of current operations, then blocked out a four-phase campaign plan. He recommended a strategic withdrawal, while maintaining the tactical offensive, to what he called the "country core." Phase Two was Consolidation and Search for Allies. Phase Three was Stabilization; Phase Four, Withdrawal.

Ahearn sat contemplating the final slide. Dalton didn't speak. Finally the general said, "What if I want to go firm earlier than Haramah?"

"We accept more risk," the J-3 said.

"Have to secure the force first," Pride pointed out. "Before we make some of these decisions. And really, they're Centcom decisions."

"I know that, goddamn it, Colonel," snapped Ahearn. "But we couldn't leave these NGO people out there. And whoever the enemy is, he'll need an operational pause too. At some point."

"Search for allies," Dalton muttered, trying to smooth his hair but making it look worse. "That means internal allies, right? We've got all those weapons your people collected. I mean, you've gotta have a shitload of guns there. Mr. Peyster, can you organize that?"

The security officer said carefully, "The question is, who we could give them to, Mr. Ambassador, without in effect turning them over to the insurgents. Without the elders and the ADA, we have few links left to the population."

"The key to everything's going to be mobility. And frankly, our mobility planning so far has sucked," the J-3 said. He seemed on a different wavelength, even given the fact he was still wearing his wraparounds. "Not due to any shortcoming on our part, but this whole idea of combining the JTF J-4 with the Centcom transportation people—"

"Let's not revisit that," Ahearn said. "Concentrate on what we can do, not what we can't. And I don't want to hear that fucking word 'frankly' again in this discussion. What *about* withdrawing, Ambassador? If it gets to be a bloodbath."

Peyster argued fiercely that withdrawal wasn't an option. It would leave the whole west bank of the Red Sea ungoverned, threaten energy traffic through the Suez Canal, and irretrievably injure U.S. prestige. "We can't withdraw until the NGOs and camps are secure. At least that. And we can't make them secure unless we can hand over to someone at least sort of representing the will of the people. But if we had someone like that, there'd be no need to withdraw."

"Or as close as we can come, someplace like this."

"Right, I don't—I don't think we can be too fucking selective. But the ADA looked good."

"They were weak sisters," Pride said. "Talk, talk, talk."

"So did the tribal elders," Dan said. "So does Congress, for that matter."

They looked over as if he was too junior to speak, but didn't object. He mustered his thoughts. "Both the elders and the ADA are gone. At least, radically weakened. We can kill all the insurgents we want, hold any phase line forever, if we get political support. That's not what's at issue. We have to have *somebody* to hand over to." He gave it a beat. "Who's it going to be?"

Dalton was staring at his name tape. "Blair's husband?"

"Yes sir."

"I play golf with Childrey."

Her father. Dan shook his hand, managing not to say anything stupid, such as "Who won." Dalton's hand was wet and tremulous. Well, it hadn't been a good three days for anyone.

Ahearn got up. "Lenson's right. It's not a military question. Mr. Ambassador, I've got to kick that up to you and Higher, up both our chains of command. Till it gets to somebody who can make a decision and make it stick."

"Are you recommending it?" Dalton asked, sweat running down his face into his shirt.

"Pulling out? No sir, Mr. Ambassador. Not yet."

"Fair enough. Long as we don't have to do helicopters at the last minute, like—well, you know."

A corporal cleared his throat from a console. Dan rolled back, the wheels of his brand-new chair whispering. "Viper Convoy's coming up on the village," the operator murmured. "And we've got hostiles."

Pride leaned. "Sounds like you got a job to be doing, Commander," he muttered. "If you can spare the time from hobnobbin' with the State Department, that is."

The beam reached into smoke, into whirling dust. All that was left of the door, atomized by the two-ounce charge. A body writhed on the floor, clothes shredded by splinters and the grenades he and Kaulukukui had hurled in. The floor was dirt, hard under their boots.

Past thought into conditioned reflex, Obie Oberg crouched, sights sweeping a deadly arc. A human form filled them and he tapped off two rounds, high chest, the kick of the carbine not even taking the muzzle off the target. The man went down and he swept left, still moving forward. Never stop in the kill zone. The SEALs' guttural shouts clashed with the keens of the Ashaarans. He caught another figure, triggered again, missed. Assad's boys were pulling back into a shadowy warren beneath the house they'd so confidently dropped down into. Fucking intel never got it right.

"Tunnel back there someplace," he grunted.

"Tunnel?"

"Gotta be why they're pulling back. Some back-alley way out."

"Shooter, left," Kaulukukui grunted. Teddy swung to glimpse a retreating back, occluded by a low wall. He tried for a head shot, missed again. He switched to burst and hosed the dark. Sparks exploded, red and fading, but he couldn't swear he'd hit anything. He crouched, sucking dusty air as he reloaded.

The clatter of something heavier than a Kalashnikov. An RPD or an RPK, something that could let off burst after burst without overheating. What was a light machine gun doing down here?

"Door! Left!" his partner shouted. Without thought he swung and fired again, through it, till the bolt gave a hollow-sounding *pock* as it locked open on the empty magazine. His right hand had the fresh mag ready. He dropped and swapped, considered for a fraction of a second—grenade? Only one left.

They had to go through that door, but he didn't want to. Trading glances with Sumo, across it, he saw the Hawaiian felt the same. That was the advantage of training together, fighting together, so long. They didn't need to speak. Just the flick of an eye, the lift of an eyebrow. The angle at which a muscled arm tilted a smoking barrel.

He squinted and winked. Kaulukukui nodded. Together, they went through.

He was in the doorway when the machine gun chattered again, close, half hidden in a recess his retinas registered for a millisecond in the crucifixed flare of its muzzle flashes. He was down and rolling, head over heels, then up again and slamming off the wall on the far side. Pushing his weapon light left to right now, registering scattered pistol fire in a space much larger than expected. The ground floor must push out into one of the attached buildings. It smelled dank, cellarish. A face, *fire*, a chest, *fire*, the glint of a rifle turning his way, *fire fire*. Faster than conscious thought, like a Wimbledon player moving in for the kill. Kaulukukui's huge bulk beside him in the balletic dance they'd perfected over so many missions.

Another doorway, and their last grenades. Kaulukukui swept left to right, Teddy right to left. Then he stopped, chest heaving, air sawing in and out through a throat dry as hot iron. Looking around. Not understanding.

The room was empty. But bullets were still slamming down around them. "What the fuck?" he howled. A burst cracked into the ground, spewing up dirt and stones.

He spun, looking up.

They were above, on a balcony or catwalk. All he could see was shifting shapes, then muzzle flashes in the dim. Down here, no cover. Nowhere to go. No way out except back through the doorway, where the machine gunner waited, between them and the other team.

They'd suckered the SEALs in, and pinned them in the kill zone. At least four shooters, pushing muzzles over the catwalk and firing down without exposing themselves. Not aiming, but sooner or later one of those bullets would hit. He snap-shot back, but with nothing to aim at. Beside him Kaulukukui was hugging the left wall, returning fire too, but the shooters had a clear shot down at him. Bullets ripped across rock walls, spewing chips. Hot brass spun through the air. Dirt flew, and something hard spattered his goggles.

"Obie! Y'in there?" Bitch Dog, yelling past the machine gunner.

"They got us stone, babe," Oberg shouted back. "Set us up righteous. Some fucking assistance here."

"Can't get to you, man. Guy's got us cold."

He groped for a grenade, the only way he could think of to take the shooters out, then remembered: not even a flash-bang.

A shooter stuck his Kalash over the railing and emptied it wildly, spraying in their general direction like a garden hose. A bullet clipped his boot, another his harness. He couldn't believe they hadn't been hit yet, but it was only a matter of seconds. "Shit," he muttered, backing toward a corner as he kept the sight on the balcony, waiting for the next weasel to pop up. "You bastards. Pop the fuck up, fuckers." But they didn't expose themselves, just kept sticking rifles up and spraying the room. Sooner or later—

Head lowered, he was slamming in another mag when

something flew down from the darkness. It struck the ground and took a lopsided bounce. A small green spheroid. His peripheral vision identified it as a grenade at the same moment it struck the wall beside him and glanced off.

It rolled between them, spinning, and rocked to a halt midway between them. The drill was to duck or roll, but there was nowhere to duck or roll to. Kick it away. But there was nowhere to kick it. This whole end of the room was empty. A turkey shoot, with two SEALs as the prize gobblers.

His eyes met Kaulukukui's across the four feet of space between them.

The big Hawaiian said, "War's a motherfucker, ain't it?"

Before Teddy could react he stepped over it and crouched, putting himself between Teddy and the grenade.

"No! Sumo!"

The shattering crack of high explosive interrupted him. Kaulukukui shuddered. He half turned, a smile still curving his lips.

Then he toppled, exposing the raw bleeding mass into which the fragments had chewed his back.

Teddy couldn't grasp it for a long second. "SEAL down," he croaked, reflex again, because he was still staring. Then he sucked a breath, kneeling beside his friend, pumping burst after burst blindly up at the gallery. *"SEAL down!"*

A sudden tremendous bang shook the walls, filled the air with flying debris, and he dropped next to his swim buddy. The gallery separated from the wall and pitched downward, throwing screaming men to the hard-packed floor.

The smell told him it was C4. Giving up on getting past the machine gunner, the other team had set its remaining explosive against the wall closest to him and blasted it down.

He got to his feet, drew his pistol and shot both insurgents, double taps to the chest and a head shot, then charged up the ramp that the now-collapsed gallery made to the upper floor. Arkin and Kowacki bulled through the doorway below. He twisted as he ran, screaming down into their upward-aimed muzzles. Then twisted forward and fired to take down a man aiming from the opposite gallery. Behind him came boot thunder as the other SEALs buffaloed after him up the makeshift ramp, which shuddered and swayed beneath them.

Another door, which he simply crashed through, pistol extended at eye level, and took each target as it presented itself.

Suddenly it was over. No tunnel. Only a final bunker where those left living had taken cover. Metal thudded and jingled on a scarred wooden floor. Those not already dead were on their knees, hands raised. Panting, Oberg put his sights on one forehead, then another. He could kill them all. Article 556 them, like the major said. But then there'd be no one for intel to interrogate.

Fuck intel. They'd killed Sumo.

No. *Professionals.* They were *professionals.*

"Where's Assad? Assad?" he shouted so hard phlegm flew and they closed their eyes. *"Wayn fareek? Fareek? Wayn Abdullahi Assad?"*

With a shaking hand, a kneeling man pointed. Kowacki, still covering them, bent to put a hand on a uniformed body. Felt the neck. Then, making sure he was on the far side, in case anything explosive lay underneath, levered it over.

The face was that of the man in the photo.

General Assad was off the board.

The killing fever ebbed. Teddy sucked thick gas freighted with smoke and the stench of blood and voided bowels and earth. That putrid stink seemed to underlie everything in this fucking stinking country filled with stinking, treacherous skinnies. He raised the pistol again, then cleared his throat and spat. "Sumo took a grenade. Stepped in front of it. So it wouldn't get us both."

"Go take care of him, Obie. We'll zip 'em."

He ran back to the killing room. Swung his way down the collapsed gallery, the beams creaking and groaning, to where the Hawaiian had dragged himself against the wall. He unslung Kaulukukui's weapon and put it on the dirt. Then knelt.

His swim buddy was still twitching, but his eyes were rolled back and the twitches felt wrong, as if something were trying to get out from beneath those big soft muscles. Teddy searched frantically. He stripped off his harness and e-bag and belt. Kaulukukui shuddered, breath fast and shallow. Teddy got Sumo's body armor off and felt the wet under it. Unbuttoned his blouse and pulled it out.

Wet and sticky, right where the armor ended. This was bad. Kidneys, liver, maybe spine. He'd turned his left side to the grenade.

Behind him came shouts and blows as Bitch Dog and Whacker pushed their captives down onto the dirt. "How's he look?" Arkin said. "Gonna make it, right?"

"I don't know."

"That was Assad, all right. What about these guys? We really need 'em for intel?"

They'd suckered them in. Trapped them. And killed Kaulukukui. "I don't need 'em," he said thickly. "You want to fuck 'em up, okay by me."

He was shaking even as some obscure corner of his mind fabricated a justification. They couldn't get Sumo up to the roof and guard prisoners too. And they had to get him up there, now.

When the firing stopped he keyed the handheld. "Mountain Air, Rogue Hammer. SEAL down. SEAL down. Medevac, roof of Building A. Over."

"This is Mountain Air. Get him to the roof. Bushido Six One inbound for casevac."

They hoisted Sumo to their shoulders, three on one. His buddy's head lolled onto Obie's chest. His open mouth snagged on his spare knife, rigged to his harness. Teddy gently unhooked it. His shooting gloves were slippery with blood, Kaulukukui's or the Ashaaran's, it was all over the room where the high-velocity bullets had blown it.

Through the door. Left turn, everyone suddenly energized again after the agonizing intensity of the fight.

The man they gripped heaved, seemed to ripple. His arm flung out. His eyes blasted open. He muttered something in a fluid language too fast to understand.

Then he died. Teddy knew; he'd seen it enough. Smelled

it, too. Still they pressed on, up the stairwell, hustling, until they emerged into dust-whipped air and strobing lights, the flutter-thump of blades and the reek of exhaust. Tears slicked his face. "You fucker," he kept saying. "You rat bastard. You fat-ass Hawaiian asshole, you fucking prick."

"We got him, Teddy. Nobody left behind. We got him."

"Take it frosty, Obie. Corpsman'll fix him up."

He bowed his head, trying to breathe around something in the way. A howl like an animal would make being crushed welled from his gut and almost made it out before it died behind clenched teeth.

A guy swung out of the helicopter. "We got him. Slide him in. Anybody else? Prisoners?"

"Nobody else. Don't take him—Yeah. Take him, the stupid motherfucker." He stepped back and lifted his gloves, realizing only then they were empty, somehow he'd done the unimaginable, left his primary weapon on the dirt floor, by the bodies. "Fucking asshole," he said, punching the flaccid shoulder as the crewman rolled the body into the helo. "Fucking asshole. Fucking asshole." Hands gripped him, pulling him back. The strobes made him blind. He stared up into them as the shrieking filled his ears.

Dan still had an operational Pioneer at five thousand feet. The DSs patched it through to the central screen as Ahearn boosted himself into the commander's chair. The picture jumped like an amateur horror film, but showed the ridgelines pinching into a defile a mile ahead of the convoy.

The very place he'd picked as the most likely ambush site.

Juggling windows at his terminal, Dan estimated the point Humvee of Viper was less than a mile from the pinch-in. He put the headphones on in the middle of a transmission from the drone pilot in the control van and his next-level supervisor. ". . . to fourteen."

"Sure they're not sheep?"

"Gettin' so I can tell sheep from goats, and these ain't hoofies. Unless sheep carry things."

The image trembled and zoomed, monochrome in chlorine and charcoal, but now he saw them: pale blobs, undulating across the desert. Shapeless and fuzzy-edged, Michelin Man rotund in the poorly focusable infrared. One bent for a moment, put down something long that glowed less brightly. Its arms worked around its head. Then it bent again and, like a white cell engulfing a bacterium under a microscope, sucked up the long rod into the central blob. The frame pulled back. He counted ten, twelve, fourteen, maybe more, undulating in clots toward the overlook. Some blobs smaller than others, moving differently, though he'd have been hard put to say how.

He took deep breaths, fighting a bad feeling. Not wanting to be here, in the seat he was occupying.

The corporal was still talking to the UAV. "Still seeing movement . . . catch the four guys on the left. Back and forth, then they go down prone."

"Aiming?"

"Don't know. Doin' something weird."

Dan was rechecking the coordinates reading out at the edge of the Pioneer download against a paper UTM chart of central Ashaara. The numbers matched, but his unease deepened. He knew where it came from. Years before, he'd had to defy an incompetent commodore to save a column of marines inside Syria.

Was Commodore Isaac Sundstrom's indecision, the wavering Dan had rejected with a young man's contempt as incompetent dithering, now infecting him?

The murmuring grew louder. Dan toggled to audio, hopped channels. Thirty-eight miles to the north, in Fenteni, the quick reaction force was hitting resistance at Assad's western headquarters. The J-3's voice: *"This is Desert Darkness, Desert Darkness. Is Arrowhead Two One on station?"*

"Two one, copy, on station."

Dickinson asked for an ordnance-remaining report and got back seven hundred rounds of twenty-millimeter and all eight Hellfires aboard the Cobra. As the J-3 acknowledged,

Dan switched channels to the AC-130H Spectre, orbiting far overhead.

Ahearn got up and came to the watch officer's terminal. Dan felt the two fingers on his shoulder, like being seized by vise grips. "Can we divert the gunship yet?"

Dan wasn't sure whether he meant the Cobra or the C-130. Both were called "gunships" in different contexts, by different services. He said carefully, "We've got a problem on the ground in Fenteni, sir. But the Cobras have IR capability too. And so far it's localized to one building."

"You're saying, put Jockey over the convoy? Commander?"

"Jockey" was the Spectre's call sign. "Yessir. My recommendation. But I have to check with the aircraft. Their fuel state's close to bingo, I know that."

Ahearn muttered, "Fuck." Then added, "Do it. If you can."

Dan spent the next minutes relaying that order to the Air Force special tactics sergeant controlling the AC-130H. The okay came back, but it sounded reluctant. "We only got twenty more minutes on station," the sergeant told him. "It's a long flight back to Mombasa."

"Right, the general understands. Can they vector?"

"Vectoring now. Time on top, time three seven."

When he got back to his seat Ahearn and the J-3 were back to the UAV imagery. "Can we get lower?" Ahearn called, elbows on knees, intent on the screen.

Dan made out the convoy. The lead vehicle's hood was a glowing glob, with a tenuous, ever-shifting ghost from the exhaust. Rocks coruscated, pinpoints of solar energy retained from the bake-oven day.

And above them, gathered in a ragged line, the milling, faceless biped amoebas that could be identified no more closely than as human. Dan conned back and forth between the image, the overlay, the paper map. The overlook wasn't that high. Ten, fifteen meters.

But made to measure for an ambush. Once into the pinch, the convoy was committed. Pick off the lead Humvee with a rocket-propelled grenade, and they could shoot up the thin-skinned trucks at their leisure. If the civilians fled on foot, they'd be lost in the desert, miles from water or help. Many of the aid personnel were in their fifties or sixties, volunteers who'd finished one or two careers and gone out to the wastes of the Third World to give back.

But who were these onlookers? If he could just catch one clear image. If it were only daylight. But of course, they wouldn't attack in daylight. In the constantly jerking scramble of motion he caught one queer frozen image. A blurred figure, head tilted back, hesitated between craggy rocks. Was that an RPG it carried? Or sticks picked up for a fire?

Would women be out this late picking up firewood? Not from what he'd seen of Ashaari society. They kept close to home after dark.

Complicating everything was the village. It lay north of the road, on another slow slope upward. No gunship fired straight down. Grazing fire was most efficient, impacting at a shallow angle to the terrain. Because of the convoy, they'd have to fire south to north.

Any overshoot or ricochet would put high explosive in the village.

His fingers raced over the keyboard, querying both the lance corporal flying the UAV, miles to the west, and the duty force J-2, the intel weenies, four terminals away. Answers glowed on the screen. *Unsure, possibly hostile*. The J-2: *Probably hostile*. Dan hesitated, fingers poised, brain searching for certainty.

There was no certainty.

The fog of war lay thick over the battlefield.

On the screen, a bloom of incandescence. The lead vehicle careened off the road. Small figures detached from it and staggered back toward the body of the convoy. Dan frowned. What was going on? He'd seen no flash of heat from the gaggle on the hilltop. A rocket motor put out thousands of degrees and an immense backblast. He switched channels, put the convoy on one ear, the AC-130H on the other, processing visual, double audio, and at the same time keeping half an eye on Ahearn. Voices streamed through his head, text scrolled, images blurred. He hovered above the battlefield like a god of war, the finger of death pointing where he willed.

Nothing was in his hands. Everything was in his hands.

He felt immense doom, immense responsibility. His heartbeat expanded as his mouth went dry. He fought for the rationality that had come before in battle. But this didn't feel like battle. He didn't know what it felt like.

Something like cold steel chilled his back. This was the war of the future. Where machines and computers watched, judged, executed from afar. What Admiral Contardi and Dr. Fauss were striving to perfect. It felt not just inhuman, but antihuman. Not antiseptic, but profoundly evil.

From the stream of frenzied voices he plucked IED. An improvised explosive device. Something about a pile of debris that had concealed something less innocent.

"Those insurgents?" The raw-onion odor of Ahearn's sweat, his breath in Dan's ear.

"That's the consensus. But they haven't made a hostile move yet."

"Blowing up a Humvee's not a hostile move?"

"In charge of movement called that as an IED."

"So that was what they were watching for." Ahearn looked at the wall clock.

Dan said, "But maybe not."

"What?" The general switched his attention back.

"They might not know about the IED. And there's the village."

"Range?"

"Six hundred meters. Easy for a ricochet from a 105."

Ahearn studied the screen; then him; then the screen again. "In ten minutes we won't have the Spectre. If they turn hostile then, we lose everybody in the column. Take them for action, twenty-millimeter only, as high an angle as possible."

His right ear: "JOC, Spectre control. Locked in awaiting fire order. Eight minutes."

Dan licked his lips. The massive aircraft's guns were tracking as it swung in its miles-wide orbit. The targets had been laser ranged. Only three words were necessary to destroy the shimmering creatures on the screen.

Most likely, hostiles. But maybe not.

The hell of it was, there was no way to tell. No way to be sure.

He knew by now, midway through his existence, that evil was the inevitable result of ignorance multiplied by power. Even as human beings attempted to do good, the outcome was all too often bloody.

He cleared his throat again and forced out, "Spectre Control, JOC: Jockey 05, cleared in hot."

"Video from Jockey," a disembodied voice announced. In front of the room the screen flickered and changed, to another image, like that from the UAV, but steadier. It seemed to be from a low light sensor rather than from IR, for the figures were more detailed. Dan even caught the shaded blur of an upturned face. But he still couldn't tell age or sex, only that it was lifted, sensing perhaps in its last moment of existence that it was observed.

The picture shuddered for a second. Two seconds later intensely bright specks bloomed to the right of the blobs, turning instantly to dust clouds. Some of the specks flew off the top of the screen. North, toward the village.

The specks moved to the left, over the blobs, and suddenly pieces detached. They seemed to fly apart, like overripe tomatoes thrown against a wall. Then dust obliterated the view. The speckles of light moved past them, ceased.

The wind picked up the dust and smoke and carried it off at a walking pace. The blobs lay still, amoebas exterminated by some potent biocide. Here and there one still squirmed.

"Reacquiring targets, going hot," the voice said. The screen juddered again, and light and then dust reblossomed. Dan forced himself to keep watching. This time when it drifted off none of the forms moved. Those on the outskirts were already fading.

"Fire mission 0105 complete. Jockey 05 is Winchester

and RTB," said the voice, flat, as if another piece of metal had been stamped out. Dan sat with shoulders hunched, staring at the screen. When he looked around, every man and woman at a terminal was too.

There was no cheering, the way it was in the movies. The whole JOC was completely silent. Until the next radio call came in.

28

ASHAARA CITY

Spayer woke to the rumble of artillery. Or at least it sounded like it, low and distant.

It was the LAVs and amtracs starting up for the day's attack. He rolled out of the shelter of a shattered rubble wall, where he'd cocooned in his poncho just after midnight. He sucked thirstily on his camelback, pushed the last of the crystallized instant coffee into his mouth, and rammed a dip in on top. Fire lifted a chin from his overwatch above on the rubble; the rest of the team stirred in the gravelike holes they'd dug. He crawled to the side of the wall and darted a glance out in the predawn light.

Ashaara City was burning, the smoke visible for miles across the desert. He wondered what the nomads thought of that. Probably made them smile.

The Marines had gone into war-fighting mode, breaking through the thin shell of insurgent resistance around the Zone, then aggressively pushing west toward and then through Darew. For days they'd fought their way through demolished, horrific miles of smashed homes, breached compounds, frightened, dirty, ragged people, dead animals. The usual smells of raw shit and smoke were flavored now with old blood and rotting flesh. This village had been fought through before by one or another militia, and the new owners had put up huts amid the wreckage of the homes of those they'd displaced.

Interesting, that they didn't move into the buildings themselves; just pitched huts between. The huts were bent poles or looted conduit covered with WFO rice sacks, the omnipresent UN blue tarps, goat hides, or whatever would keep sun out. Under them huddled families, children, eyes white in the dim hooches, who shrank back as heavily loaded, filthy, on-edge marines slogged past, eyeing each heap of shattered bricks or drift of trash for IEDs, sweating and coughing in the smoke and dust like lung cases.

Caxi hitched up his load-bearing equipment, cleared his throat of the night's nastiness, and spat. He looked around for the kid, then remembered: Little Team was gone. Fire'd seen him talking to some skinnies on a corner. He'd never come back. Spayer missed his antics, that smile, the happy way he'd inspect their cartridges and load their magazines.

He tried to look on the bright side. Maybe Nabil had found his family. Hey, he could hope.

"Squad leaders, front," his handheld crackled, the sergeant's hoarse voice. Spayer pulled himself together, starting with a convenience pack of baby wipes. Close as anyone had gotten to a shower since the start of Tet Two, as the troops were calling the instant insurgency.

A little later he took a knee with the other squad leaders, holding a cup of MRE coffee, its rim crawling with flies, as the company commander gave them the big picture. He was sandboxing it on the ground, the sergeant and the corpsman watching off to the side.

The Blue Zone stretched from a left flank anchored on the Victory Bridge, along the Fenteni ring road. The right flank ran to the sea, to keep RPGs or mortars from interdicting the sea approach to the marine terminal. The battalion held the road out to the airport, too, and a mile-wide circle around.

The first few days of the insurgency had been a hasty scramble to get all the NGOs accounted for and back inside the Zone.

During that hectic two weeks, Raven had deployed west, then leapfrogged back along the Durmani escorting convoys, guarding bridges, establishing OPs along the high ground and checkpoints along the road. At one their corporal had taken a bullet through the leg that UPS'd him back to the World. Now Spayer was acting squad leader, and though he'd never done the ISLC course it would still go on his Page Eleven. He had three fire teams now, but still thought of Raven Eight as his.

He and Ready and Team and Fire had survived the southern quarter, cordon-and-knock operations that had degenerated into house-to-house fighting, rooting out the Waleeli fanatics who fought like they wanted to die. They'd had to kill and kill. This was what marines did, but he felt it sinking inside him like heavy ice. He'd taken a hit in his Kevlar combat-stacked at a doorway, when an insurgent leaned around a corner and let loose. They'd done night ops too, though the Ashaaran dogs made that difficult. Hard to sneak up on an insurgent when a bunch of mutts were yapping their heads off. But after two days all ROEs had come off except Laws of War and after that they'd managed to push through. With wounded, but to everyone's satisfaction, not one marine KIA. So far.

The company commander was still at it. "Higher's confident we've broken the insurgents' back. The next step's to reopen the main highway and link with the airfield. Like yesterday, the ass will lead off. Kickoff at zero-six."

"Ass" was the armor. "Stay clear of those RPG magnets," another squad leader muttered beside him. Spayer drank off his coffee and actually lowered himself to sit. A moment of luxury in the midst of hell. A guy went around with more coffee and a box of only partially melted Twix. The captain was earning points.

He went over the phase lines and axes of advance as they took notes. "Keep your heads on those brass swivels, hooyah? When we roust 'em, take 'em away with shock and firepower. Any questions?"

The expressions around him reflected what Spayer felt: be nice if it came that easy. So far, it hadn't. Their enemies weren't marksmen, but they were brave and they had unlimited RPGs and grenades. Another squad had found a burlap-wrapped Dragunov, the first sniper-type rifle they'd seen in country.

The chain-saw whine of a Pioneer overhead. So familiar now, no one looked up. Spayer put up a hand.

"Lance corporal?"

"Sir, we keep hearing about the northerners and the Council forces, but the guys we're fighting are all Brotherhood. Where are these northerners? We gonna see them behind us one of these days?"

"Intel thought the Governing Council was behind the insurgency. That's why we had a special ops team take out Assad." The captain looked across smoldering acres. "Doesn't matter who they are. We're even hearing about foreigners, coming across the border. We fight anybody who fights us. And did I say, keep your guys hydrated. Hooyah?"

He got his "Hooyah" back and a few scattered "Kill"s and "get some"s, but not as rousing as it could've been. The meeting broke and Spayer eased to his feet, feeling eighty years old. Sleeping on bricks wasn't doing shit for the back he'd strained falling down a cellarway. Fortunately the S-4 was bringing forward plenty of everything they needed: Ibuprofen. Batteries. Ammo. Antibiotic salve for their eyes. Meds for the drizzly shits almost everybody had. Plenty of water too, Egyptian, in liter bottles.

He took the plans for the day back to his team leaders, made sure everybody had ammo and MREs and batteries, then got them into position. First and third fire teams to the left, second to the right. He reminded them to interlock fields of fire and hold position when they got close to the LAVs. The sun leered over the jagged roofs of shattered buildings, greeted by a chorus of barking and the revving of the armor. He checked his rifle and made sure everyone had extra water. He leaned against a broken wall before he shouldered his ruck.

Suddenly he realized: *he'd been here before*. He remembered these shattered bricks, the orange fog, the smells of shit and smoke. The breach in the building opposite, as if some giant had bored through it with a sharp iron rod. But he didn't remember being himself, or wearing this strange uniform. Didn't remember carrying a weapon like this, black, short-barreled. Though at the same moment he still knew it intimately, he remembered other weapons, smooth-hafted, longer, heavier . . . man, he almost had it. . . .

It slipped away. He sighed, bear-scratching his spine against the masonry. The hell was that all about? Getting loopy. Like everybody else. What the fuck were they doing here, anyway? Half the skinnies hated them, the other half had their hands always out. Nobody back home gave a shit.

But that wasn't why marines did what they did. The mission. The guys. The Corps. If you didn't understand, no point explaining. Looking around at the unshaven chins, leaking noses, infected eyes, askew helmets, dusty, worn-shiny magazines, the faces—some pale and some dark but all the same color now under the cocoa-powder dust—*he* knew why.

"Zero-six, El-Corp," Fire yelled.

"Yeah, dog." He jerked awake, checked his watch. Flicked out the signal: advance in fire team wedges, squad wedge. It was open enough here, at least for a couple hundred yards. At the same moment the racket began, the whipcracks and gunrattle as the armor cleared ambush points ahead.

Flung across what had once been a street, covering each other with short hops forward more like weary trots than rushes, the squad advanced.

The air hummed in the JOC. Dan rubbed his face. It felt gray. Down in front Dickinson had put up a plastic-covered map for Operation Chicago, the linkup of elements from the Zone and the airfield. They had the same map on the terminals, of course, but when a general wanted a vertical display, he got one.

The attackers were Brotherhood. Assad had certainly supported the initial attacks, and the northern clans had taken advantage of them to carry out looting, raids, and reprisals. But hours after his death, the Governing Council had offered to cooperate. A meeting was set up for today. He'd heard Peyster berating the J-2 for the bad call, but Dan thought the embassy was equally at fault. Shouldn't State at least be able to tell them, if a group began attacking foreigners, who it was likely to be?

He cushioned his head on the keyboard. Had to get out of here. No night or day in the JOC. Infinite connectivity, but no link to the world outside, where for several days there it had seemed like they were losing this unexpected war.

The enemy had followed the departing aid people down the roads to the city. The JTF had abandoned observation posts and support airfields, needing the troops for the retrieval effort, and fed them into a defensive perimeter as they trickled back. The insurgents had tested it over two days with vehicleborne stabs out of the desert preceded by barrages of RPGs. Each time they were cut to pieces by the Marines' organic weapons, 155s, 60- and 81-mm mortars, and the MEU's air element.

Nor was that all. Ahearn and Dalton had screamed loud enough that Centcom had handed the mission to the Air Force. The 506th Air Expeditionary Group had self-deployed from Texas to Ashaara International, and flown its first A-10 strike four hours after arriving. That wasn't the only USAF contribution. The Spectre had returned, roving the Line for the entire night, breaking up groups and any transport it caught on the move.

The MEU had its own fire support coordination team, but he'd been able to fold in; he'd filled a similar billet years before. Ahearn had tasked him to set up on-call Tomahawk missions, in case they got a bead on whoever was directing the enemy's operations.

After several days and hundreds of casualties, the enemy had learned his lesson. The U.S. Marines could not be dislodged by force, no matter how many suicidal young men they expended.

Now Chicago was kicking off, to break out of the pocket they'd been compressed into and link up. They were turning everything west of the city to rubble, and the place hadn't been far from it before.

The presidential candidates had debated the previous

night, carried live on Armed Forces Television. One said he'd withdraw U.S. forces as soon as the ground situation stabilized. The other promised to pull out as soon as he took office; nation building wasn't an American responsibility, especially with no Ashaara left to build.

Dickinson stood from his terminal. He spotted Dan. "How's that Tomahawk strike going, Commander?"

"*Chancellorsville*'s on call. All we need's a target worth a half-million-dollar missile."

Dickinson took his wraparounds off and examined the plot. Without them his eyes looked small and weak. "How about General Al-Maahdi?"

"Seems like we put one general down, another pops up," Dan told him. "Anyone ever think it's not the guy, it's just the way it is out here?"

"They're making a case at the head shed he's the one ordered the whole shebang up in flames."

"In that case, I could probably treat him to a TLAM strike. Where is he?"

"Would it were that simple."

"Thought not. What's this meeting I'm hearing about?"

"Want to sit in? Take my ticket."

"I better stay on the support side. This is with the Council guys?"

"Peyster thinks they could help."

"After we blew away their warlord?"

"Maybe they never liked him much. Or it was a wakeup call. Anyway, they're gonna drop in for tea. Ahearn's tent." The J-3 kneaded his chin. "I better shave."

"Stay with it. The terrorist look's popular."

Dickinson gave him a tight smile and turned away. Maybe it wasn't that funny, after all.

A saffron flash, a gigantic jet of dirty smoke, a staggering thud ripped the sky a few hundred yards away from where they followed the deputy ambassador off the helicopter. It was so loud Aisha stopped in her tracks and couldn't help cowering slightly.

When the bellow shook the ground again she recognized it as artillery. There was no road communication between the city and the airfield, unless you were in a tank. The helo trip had been low and fast, barely giving glimpses of troops moving forward in the suburbs, volumes of smoke, lines of new refugees winding north: the only way out of the fighting now that it had blocked the westward roads.

She was in her trademark flowered abaya, headscarf, and running shoes, carrying a huge shaggy purse made of worn carpeting. Erculiano had abandoned silk shirts, gold chains, and designer slacks for combat boots, a white Oxford shirt worn under a flak vest, and his SIG tucked into the waistband of his Levi's.

"Damn, that's a big cannon," he said. "Wonder what it is?"

"M198 one-fifty-five-millimeter medium towed howitzer," said the marine waving their party through a barricade. "That's RAP rounds they're firing."

"Ah, thanks, man. Just wondering."

She'd been here before, but each time the camp seemed more permanent. Wire and bunkers perimetered the airfield. Concrete antitruck barriers protected the terminal. She caught stares from troops as they threaded labyrinthine alleyways between dozens of Conexes.

Inside she blinked, barely recognizing the once-shabby interior where a frightened man had welcomed them to Ashaara. If the idea was to impress the Council, this was the place, with the earth shaking as the artillery fired, jet transports turning up on the tarmac, and heavily armed helicopters lifting, twisting in the air like dancers, then hurtling overhead.

Terry Peyster was already in the JOC. A colonel in sunglasses briefed them on the day's movements on a plot board. So far, good news. No U.S. casualties, and where the tanks pushed, the insurgents fell back, decimated by artillery and air strikes. When they got to Ahearn's tent, though, there seemed to be a mixup. They wanted only the lead agent. Erculiano said no problem, he'd check out the PX.

They sat for an hour, drinking bottled tea, until the flap

was raised and a group entered. She stood to greet them, then focused on the tallest.

He was in starched French-style fatigues and field cap. This time he didn't stink of sweat and whiskey. But his face was still a white man's molded onto a black man's skull, and he still towered over everyone, with hands that looked like baseball gloves. He was smiling, rubbery bluish lips stretched in what must have been meant as reassurance, but that came across as terrifying. She couldn't imagine being married to him. Seeing that face straining above her.

There were worse things than being single. She should remember that.

But hadn't he been a sergeant, that time at the gate? When Peyster had handed him a briefcase full of money. So he wouldn't kill.

"This is General Olowe," Peyster said. "General Ahearn, commander of the Joint Task Force."

They shook hands, the marine a slim child next to Olowe. The other Ashaarans smiled nervously when Peyster turned to them. They waved their hands, palms out. They didn't want to be introduced. But Olowe stood tall, shoulders back, almost at attention, as Ahearn introduced Dickinson, Erculiano, and Aisha. The Ashaaran enclosed each hand softly, nodding. But when it came her turn his gaze didn't even pause, just slid past. Allah, yes, the unreconstructed African man. They made American jerks look like models of chivalry. He pulled over a sturdy-looking chair with that huge hand, stretched out his boots and crossed them at the ankles.

She stared. Not only was he wearing brown top boots, there were *spurs* at his heels.

"Tea, General?"

"Thank you—General." Olowe smiled more broadly, pale cheeks flushed pink. It was distinctly possible she'd never met an uglier human being. Yet his very hideousness transcended the usual classifications. The first time, at the gate, she'd thought him a thug. Now she wondered if he wasn't even more dangerous.

If so, you wouldn't have judged it from the deputy's smooth

patter, the general's relaxed bonhomie. The only thing missing was cigars. Wait, the deputy was handing them out. She smiled at minus twenty degrees. Peyster fired her a warning glance.

The deputy launched into a statement. The U.S. was implementing UN decisions. Those who helped would be remembered as patriots, humanitarians. Olowe smoked, legs crossed. A man translated in a rapid, stumbling voice, looking too scared to sit down.

When the deputy finished, the "general" replied at length, gesturing with the cigar, waiting between sentences as his words were forged into English. The Governing Council had offered to place its forces at the disposal of the Americans, to protect aid shipments and ensure efficient distribution. Yet they'd been pushed aside while the Coalition built up exiles, Communists, labor leaders, others who'd lost the trust of the people. Not only that, they'd targeted the respected Abdullahi Assad. Errors could be forgiven. However, fanatics had stepped into the vacuum. They were the true enemies of the Ashaari, directed by foreign interests, dedicated to setting up a radical regime like that of Iran or Afghanistan.

"We're attriting them now. They won't stand," Ahearn put in, and Olowe trained that horrifying countenance in his direction. "But they've halted the aid effort. There's grain piling up at the port, ships waiting to offload."

"The general says, these are rebels you are talking about. Rebels against the legitimate government, the Governing Council."

She lifted her head, understanding now what this discussion was about. Ahearn wanted armed manpower. The deputy ambassador needed a local client. The RSO wanted . . . something, she wasn't sure what. And Olowe wanted recognition of what was all too obviously now his personal regime. The starving people in the hinterlands were secondary to the struggle for power. She started to speak, but Peyster put one hand over hers. "Not now," he muttered.

The deputy was saying, "We'll need protection for the food shipments."

"We have many technicals and also armored cars," Olowe said, through the interpreter. "Place distribution in our hands. Give us fuel and ammunition. Then you can withdraw your troops to your base. No more American deaths. That's what Washington wants, isn't it?"

She tensed again—what about the other clans?—but Peyster was already making that point. "Food aid must go to *all*. Not only Diniyue, Jazir, and Xaasha. If we don't see it happening, our partnership will end."

"That must be very clear," the deputy agreed. "If there's to be cooperation."

Olowe listened tolerantly, then spoke. "The general guarantees it will go to all the clans," the translator said.

"Southerners as well?"

"Terry," she murmured, but he waved her off, leaning to hear what the translator was saying.

"The general says he is a soldier. A simple man. You will find, a man of his word. But you must also be men of your word." The translator stopped, frowning. Was beginning to speak again when Olowe leaned forward. He tapped the deputy's knee.

"Kill Al-Khasmi," he said. In English.

The deputy smiled uncertainly, glancing around. Olowe tapped again, harder. *"Capisce?"*

"The general is saying—"

"We understand the general. But we don't assassinate leaders."

"He says: You assassinated General Assad."

"Assad's protective detail resisted his arrest. He died accidentally in the melee."

"Kill Al-Khasmi. Kill the false Maahdi." Olowe flicked a cylinder of ash to the floor, then sucked moodily on the cigar again.

The deputy rose. He said a few more words about how glad he was to have this exchange of views. He hoped it would lead to a free and prosperous Ashaara. A liaison would report to discuss concrete measures. Olowe stared grumpily and at last lumbered to his feet. He squeezed out a smile and shook hands again. Ahearn held the flap and he ducked out, the other Ashaarans trailing.

Except for the translator, not one had said a single word.

As soon as he left she had Peyster's arm, hissing in his ear, ignoring Ahearn's curious glance. "Why are we talking to *him*, Terry? Don't you remember what he wanted when he came to the compound?"

"What?"

"You don't *remember*? Your local employees. Some were southerners. He wanted to kill them!"

"That's your reading, eh?"

She rounded on Ahearn. "General? Does he strike you as trustworthy?"

Peyster took her elbow and steered her out, then down an alleyway to the camouflaging burr of a generator. "We're out of democrats, Aisha. Maybe they never were actually a viable alternative."

"*He's* our alternative?"

"Maybe what this country needs right now's a soldier. Anyway, we don't have a choice. If we don't get at least some of the clans on our side, we're just an occupying army."

"Taking sides won't make us popular with the sides we don't take. And we already know he's corrupt."

"Olowe's corrupt?"

She spluttered. "*You* bought him off with a bagful of cash."

Peyster said mildly, "He sees reason. That gives him long-term potential as a supporter of U.S. interests. He's not involved in weapons dealing or drugs, far as we know. Yeah, he has clan loyalties, but I've never seen an Ashaari who didn't. Have you?"

"Dr. Dobleh didn't."

The RSO bared his teeth. "Dobleh's dead, Special Agent. We bet on him, and lost. Sometimes even a dictator's better than nothing. We've still got to get something that looks like a government running. Preferably, leaving somebody in charge who's not totally anti-American. But that's right, we're not here to promote U.S. interests, are we? Maybe you'd rather the whole country fell to this Messenger of Allah, or whatever he calls himself?"

She steadied her voice. "That's not a fair thing to say, Terry. Don't equate all Muslims with people like Al-Maahdi. And don't put me in the same category as him."

"Then don't equate all soldiers with whoever you're comparing our new friend to. Don't worry, Agent Ar-Rahim." Peyster patted her arm, mild-mannered again. "Believe me. Everything's going to be fine."

In the tent, flaps drawn, alone except for his J-3, Cornelius Ahearn rubbed his missing fingers and stared at the secure phone. Finally the light glowed and it purred. He picked it up and waited for the sync. "General Ahearn."

"Hello, Corny. Steve Leache here. Watching your progress on Geeks. When do you expect linkup?"

Centcom himself, calling from Tampa. "By dusk, sir."

"Casualties?"

"Light."

"We're not seeing much media. Maybe that's good—I've got enough pressure to pull you out already. Your marines kicking ass?"

"Pushing hard, but the enemy's not standing. They're withdrawing."

The distant voice dropped. "No chance of a mop-up, then."

"No sir. They're in for the long haul. Classic guerrilla tactics."

"Can we localize leadership elements? A decapitation strike? You got Assad, right?"

"He was a player, but apparently not *the* player. Intel's trying."

"I'll see if we can do better here. Anything else I need to know?"

"Had a Warthog pilot drop his M9 in the port-a-john here at the airfield."

"Ha, ha! That'll teach him to use his lanyard. How's the nation building? Thought you had that all set up. Before this Al-Maahdi pissed all over it. Who is this guy, anyway?"

"One of our agents met with him, before he went nuclear on us. A homegrown charismatic. May be tied to al Qaeda, maybe not. Bottom line's the same." Ahearn waited out a pause, then went on. "I just met with a possibly cooperating faction leader. I don't like him. But the Agency does."

"I can't feed you any more assets, Corny. Tie a bow on this pig and kiss it good-bye. I need everybody ready to move when the whistle blows in Iraq. Tamp down the insurgency. Hand over to local leaders. The next game's not going to be against bandits with AKs."

"Aye, aye, sir."

"Love that salty lingo, Corny. Have a good battle." Leache signed off.

Ahearn set the handset back. He scratched the stubs of his missing fingers again, looking at the tabletop. Sighed, checked his boots, then his blouse. Wiped the ever-present dust out of the corners of his eyes with his thumb, straightened his back, and strode out.

29

IN THE SOUTHERN MOUNTAINS

Gráinne woke as she had every night since they'd captured her: with a moment of disorientation, of hope it'd all been a bad dream.

It never was.

They'd moved her from place to place, from hand to hand. Not really abusing her, as she'd first feared, but not taking great care of her, either.

She pushed back the torn blanket and stretched, looking around the campsite as dawn cracked the world open like a raw egg.

After the men at the roadblock pulled her out of the

Rover she'd never seen it again. They'd kept her overnight at a campfire, surrounded by baaing sheep, the occasional distant bark of shepherd dogs. The next morning, after a long argument she couldn't follow—and which earned her a swift backhand to the mouth the one time she'd tried to speak up—they'd marched several miles from the road and turned her over to another group traveling by camel. They'd given her to the women, who after much critical discussion and pulling of her hair stripped off her boots and clothes down to her underwear, threw a stinking black wool robe over her, tied a black scarf over her hair, retied her hands, and hoisted her onto one of the camels.

Two days of torment followed. The beast's rolling gait made her sicker than she'd ever been on any boat. Her thighs bled from rubbed-raw sores big as her palms. The only disinfectant she had was her own urine, since they left her on the animal even when they stopped to rest. From time to time helicopters hurtled overhead as she watched helplessly, unable even to wave. And what would a wave mean, from a black-clad sack?

She remembered a story, or was it a movie, about a professor captured by a desert tribe. They'd cut out his tongue, dressed him in hammered-out tin cans, and forced him to dance and caper, the tribe's fool, until he lost his mind.

Weaving in the heat for hour after hour, fading with thirst, she toppled off and came to facedown in the sand. They hoisted her again and lashed her on. With hands bound tightly behind her, legs tied to the wooden saddle, she became the professor, mutilated, helpless, carried deep into a savage land. Was that what they planned? Or something even worse, passed from tribe to tribe to rape and torture as some horrible prize?

They were headed southwest, by the sun. Toward Sudan? There was still slavery there, Arabs kidnaping black Christians and Animists, backed by the Islamic government. Even humanitarian workers had been "disappeared." What would she be worth?

One thing was certain: wherever she ended up, she'd

never be allowed to leave alive. She cursed her foolishness. Efrain had warned her not to leave the camp without an armed escort.

The heat increased, the ravines danced, the rocks sang. A tinny jingle grew in her ears day by day, till it became louder than her breathing, louder than the pain from blood- and lymph-weeping thighs, raw-chafed wrists. A blue Bonneville convertible pulled up alongside her, with three blond starlets calling up, sipping champagne from flutes. Next came a horned, copper-plated being, from some ancient bestiary; then a cone-spired blue-and-terra-cotta temple, twisting upward like a ziggurat, in the wastes. She blinked through furious tears at swarms of flies that bit and bit at the edges of her eyes. With hands tied, she was powerless to stop them.

Finally she rode unconscious, slumping, held on only by the rope. And knew nothing until she was dragged down and forced to drink muddy water from skins, then pushed into a stinking stable as dusk fell on another day in Hell.

One by one, others joined her, a trickle that grew into a stream. Women, mostly, but not all. Aid workers, nuns from the far west, nurses. A French aid worker smeared a bit of antibiotic salve where it would do Gráinne the most good. The detritus of war, some crazy with disorientation and fear, sobbing under their black tents. Others—the nuns, principally—seemed composed, as if this was exactly what they'd expected someday, just part of the job. They prayed together and over the days many aid workers joined them.

The procession grew into a migration, with camels, donkeys, even a cart the guards used to haul water and captives who'd grown too weak. By then Gráinne was off the camel and walking. The guards treated them more like slaves each passing day. Each evening their captors found an overhanging scarp, a cave, an abandoned hut or village sheep pen they could all huddle in. They seemed to fear the open sky.

She tried to speak to the Ashaari women, establish a bond. But the women and children inflicted cruel, painful tricks on the captives, throwing their food in the fire, giving them lice-ridden blankets. One old woman slapped them and pinched their ears, sneaked up behind and burned their necks with brands from the fire. Gráinne suspected she was insane, but that didn't make it hurt less, or dilute the hate in the sodding cow's bleary old eyes. The men—there was always a guard not far away—just called encouragement, or laughed.

She dragged a stinking black wool sleeve across festering eyes, uncertain of what she saw. But it was true. Just now, no one was around. None of the women. None of the guards. Not even the kids.

A hiss. She whipped her head round so fast she almost keeled over. The French nurse, Frédérique Trézéguet. They'd slept together to stay warm, and memorized the addresses of each other's parents. She looked almost like an Arab woman, small and bent in dark clothes.

They'd realized it at the same moment. For the first time in days, no one was holding a gun on them. From down the ravine came voices: ecstatic shouting.

"*Que'est-que ce'st que ça?* What's going on?"

"*Pas d'idée.* No idea," Gráinne muttered, glancing around the night camp. No other captives were awake. Exhausted, they huddled under thin blankets. "But they're not watching."

Their eyes met, and in the nurse's she saw hope and fear. She was beautiful, or must've been, in a delicate dark style. "D'you know where we are? Can we escape?"

"I don't know. Maybe."

They'd crossed a road the day before. At a guess, fifteen kilometers back. Too far, in their condition, under the blazing sun, without water.

The answer of course was not to hike it in the sun. They'd have to hide, till the caravan pressed on. Then make their way to the road in the dark, and persuade, threaten, or bribe whomever they ran into to let the army know about them.

Not a great chance. But better than whatever lay at the end of this trail.

All this flashed past more quickly than anything had for days. But Trézéguet must have thought she was hesitating. She stood with fists clenched. *"Viens avec moi?"*

"Fuck, yes." She scrambled out of the blanket, ran a step or two, then stopped. Not only did her thighs feel like they were on fire, but she needed that blanket.

They climbed the side of the ravine, torn feet slipping on rocks and scree. She poked her head up cautiously.

Her heart sank. Beyond lay undulating desert, dotted in the quiet sunrise with rounded purple humpings of sand like surfacing whales. To the south, mountains; to the west, mountains, but more distant. She oriented by the sun. Pointed, and they began running, or, rather, shambling.

After they passed the first patch of loose sand, she looked back to see their tracks. She cursed and headed for gravel, but the damage was done.

The men caught them before they'd hobbled a mile. Perhaps they'd left the captives unguarded on purpose, to see which would run. They swung off the camels and pushed them down in the sand. They beat them with large sticks, then began tearing at their clothes. She screamed, but the stick made her quiet. She almost wasn't conscious of the rape.

As the men took turns, Frédérique bit one. They beat her again, so hard that when they pulled her up and let her go she tumbled down like a broken mannequin. Her eyes were rolled up into what was left of her skull. Her black hair was clotted with blood. They dragged her back to the ravine and made the other captives bury her.

The next day they tied Gráinne on the camel again.

This continued for days. Finally, far from the last road, the camels nodded to a halt and drifted one by one, as if knowing they were home, down into a black scar in the white hardpan; a jumbled ravine dotted with ruins. Something about its shape pulled at her memory, but not enough to unravel the skein. She was pulled down one last time, her ropes unknotted. The cloth was jerked from her head, and her captors recoiled as her red hair tumbled out.

She took a deep breath of light, of air. Then had to squat, whimpering as the scabbing on her raw thighs cracked open. At the bruises from the beatings and what was probably a cracked rib, a stabbing that made her gasp each time she leaned. Her eyes itched so badly she wanted to claw them out of her head. Fluid ran from them, thick and stinking.

They lay in a cavern with light glimmering in under an overhang. Less a ravine than a chain of linked sinkholes. She lay examining the sunbeams that flickered as people walked by the entrance, throwing queer writhing shadows on the back wall. Listening to the coo of doves.

There'd been water here once. Most likely still was, in water holes, maybe too in deeper caves, level on level of sinkholes, chambers, worming passages like the intestines of the earth. The piles of karst, broken and eroded limestone, at the back of the cave told her that. The rock around her was dolomite. Over many ages the rain had slowly eaten it away. The striations on the walls told of alternating wet and dry periods, dating back probably twenty, thirty thousand years. She saw no stalactites, but there would be, deep in some secret chamber sunk in the fathomless dark.

They gave them corn mush and alkaline-tasting water. Her stomach hurt, but she made herself eat and drink it all.

The next day she woke with mind empty. She thought fleetingly of the mad professor and of Efrain. Of her mother, her husband, Frédérique. Her eyes were gummed shut. After she worked through the anguish of opening them—it felt like tearing open a scabbed-over wound—she looked around for the professor. It took a while to remember: he wasn't there. The caravan had led him off jangling and cavorting, his tin armor sparkling. Really, some of his antics had been so funny. She'd miss his company.

Away with the fairies again, O'Shea?

Breakfast was mush and a cupful of dirty water.

The captives sat or lay all morning. She crept to the mouth of the cavern, blinking in the painful light; then retreated.

From time to time the guards came and took someone away. No one came back. Once they heard far-off shots.

She sat uncaring. She wished only they'd hurry up and get to whatever scheme they had for her. Maybe they'd let her drink a little more water before they shot her. She giggled, making the other captives glance her way. Water was all she wanted now. While there were billions of liters deep beneath her, beneath them all.

She remembered and tried to straighten. To retrieve her mind from wandering. She had to tell someone about the water. Above all, whatever happened to her, she had to live to do that.

They came for her a little after midday. Led her stumbling, a hand tented over her eyes, up a rocky trail. They stopped by a blue plastic jerrijug, the kind the nomads had left lined up as they waited for the Seabees to finish drilling. They made motions; wash your face, your hands. She obeyed, slurping a furtive palmful under the guise of rinsing her mouth. The guard pulled the black cloth over her head and led her down again, into a depression dotted with tents. An ancient collapsed sinkhole. Goats stood about, ridiculously small, watching her hobble past with insolent eyes. The guard shouted and pushed her head down.

They halted. The guard said something dismissive, and pushed her forward.

She raised her eyes to an extraordinary gaze. Black, burning eyes above a tangled beard with something strange in it. No; the jaw itself was swollen, shockingly so. Realizing she was staring, she dropped her eyes.

Silence. A mechanical click. Then a hand waved at a camp stool. Someone said, in accented but well-educated English, "You may sit."

The stool was rickety, but when she hobbled over and let herself down it felt lovely. She sighed, then raised her eyes again.

The man looked as if he'd once been tall, but huddled now in the shadow of a tent flap he didn't seem so. The most shocking thing was that grotesque facial distortion, disfiguring, worse than a goiter. In back a small desk with the legs sawed off stood on a threadbare green-and-scarlet carpet in a Walled Garden pattern. At it sat a neatly groomed chubby man in Arab robes. And to her right, another, focusing a video camera.

"Your name." The cultured voice came from the robed man. The one with the misshapen face didn't speak, only gazed at her.

"Dr. Gráinne O'Shea."

"A doctor?"

"Of hydrology. Yes."

"Would you be willing to examine this man's jaw?"

"Hydrology is a geological specialty. I'm not a physician. There was a nurse with us, but she—was raped and killed."

"I am sorry. In war, such things happen. We lose many friends as well, to your soldiers."

"They're not my soldiers. Ireland's a neutral."

"What were you doing in the Empty Quarter?"

"Research."

Now she realized what they were staring at. "What is that symbol, on your neck?" the small man said politely.

"The claddagh."

"A Christian symbol?"

"No."

"Jewish?"

"It's a Gaelic friendship sign."

" 'Gaelic'?"

"Irish."

"What does this symbol mean?"

"It means friendship. Love. Loyalty. My husband gave it to me."

"You have a husband. Where is he?"

"In Ireland."

"Yet you work here?"

"Correct." She explained about the International Hydrological Programme. He waved her to silence before she was done. "Yes, the UN. We know. What is your relation to your husband? That he's in Ireland, and you're here?"

"We're estranged."

He sighed. "Are you a Christian, a Muslim, or a Jew?"

"I'm not a Christian or a Jew, no. Nor a Muslim."

"Then what religion are you?"

She tried to keep her tone level, soft, the way the guards liked the captives to speak. "I'm a scientist. I don't believe in religion, I'm afraid. I have aunts back home who do."

They exchanged glances. Finally the fat man said, a bit sadly, "You will not say you are a Christian?"

"That wouldn't be true. As a scientist I value the truth, you see."

"That is what we also value. You must become Muslim, then."

She almost smiled, but tried to make it look sympathetic rather than superior. "I've no reason to do that."

The man in robes shifted; the one squatting in shadow remained motionless. Could this be the one they called Al-Maahdi? He was supposed to be very dangerous. The steadiness of his stare was disconcerting. Could he be mad?

"I believe you have a very good reason, Doctor. You see, if you are a Christian, or a Jew, that would not be a problem. Unless you attempt to proselytize, of course. Proselytizers must be put to death. However, we are not required to make People of the Book convert. So long as you submit, you may stay Jew or Christian. But a pagan must convert."

She shifted on the stool; her infected thighs felt like the skin was being peeled off. Her eyes itched madly. "Right. Or else what?" she managed to say, not really following. No question, she'd showed a better game once.

"Otherwise you must die," the little man said, still apologetic, a customs official explaining a silly rule. "It is not difficult. All you need do is say: 'There is no god but Allah, and Muhammad is his prophet.' That's all that is required. See those others, over there? They have converted, have joined Islam."

She saw them: the ones who'd been called away before her. At least, some of them. They sat a few yards away, bowls before them, though they weren't eating. She started to laugh, then found she couldn't. Could these gobdaws be serious?

They seemed so, absolutely, as did the red light of the video camera. She swallowed, mouth suddenly devoid of the water she'd stolen. "Please, may I have a drink?"

"Water's precious. You were given some when the sun rose. You should not need more."

"There's something wrong with my eyes. I need medical attention."

"We'll discuss that after you convert."

"My aunts are Catholic. I was raised Catholic."

"No, Doctor. You already renounced Christianity. But if you think we're asking you to renounce Jesus—Issa—we too hold him to be one of the great prophets."

The man on the carpet interjected a few words, leaning his face on his fingers. Looking at him, she thought through her terror: It must hurt. Must hurt terribly. But he didn't seem in pain. Or perhaps just didn't mind.

"You must decide now," the little man said regretfully, as if to imply, I'm really sorry to put you to all this trouble. She wanted to say, *Wait a minute, let me think*, but the guard was already hauling her up. He walked her twenty paces to the lip of another, deeper sinkhole. The videographer followed, silently, as if he were only a great eye.

She was thinking now, though, reasoning desperately with each hobbled, pain-filled stride. She'd decided years before religion was pants. At best a prescientific way of explaining the world by imaginative but ignorant desert tribes. At worst, a cynical scam, selling tickets to a nonexistent afterlife to yobs too credulous to see through the mumbo jumbo. Virgin births, invisible angels . . . bollocks.

On the other hand, if the alternative was death, and she didn't believe anyway, why not recite a few ridiculous words?

She stopped at the edge. Down there, at the bottom, lay bodies. Fresh ones. She recognized the nun who'd led the prayer group.

"The proselytizers," the fat man said. "Those who brought lies to our land. Even now, we would have forgiven them, had they come to the truth. Will you?"

She wanted to say, Science is the search for truth. Not religion.

But you couldn't martyr yourself for science. The very idea was a contradiction.

She opened her mouth, to find something else stopping her. Church as a child? Her aunts' humorless explications of how a merciful God sent all non-Catholics to Hell? Whatever it was, she couldn't form the words. She felt more violated, more deeply defiled, than after the rape.

This was ridiculous! It didn't matter what she said to some fundamentalist fanatic! She had to survive. Without her, no one might ever know about the life that waited beneath the desert.

She bowed her head. "There's no god but Allah," she tried under her breath. It didn't taste very good.

"Louder, please. Face the camera."

"What then? What'll you do with us? Those you haven't killed."

"We'll release you. Why not? We're getting in touch with your friends in the city. Now, confess the truth."

"There is no god. But Allah. And Muhammad is his prophet."

Had they caught it, that hesitation? Even as she spoke she'd been unsure; it had come out of a tangle of urges and fears that tried to pick and choose the next word past cracked lips. But they didn't seem to notice, or didn't care. Once the magic words were spoken.

They smiled, and led her from the edge. Took her to the others, and served corn mush, flat bread, a little gristly goat meat, and as much water as she cared to drink. She and the other new converts sat not meeting one another's eyes. She made herself swallow. But the food had no taste, and her hands trembled so, water slopped from her plastic cup onto the lifeless goat-churned sand.

30

ASHAARA CITY

Have you seen my assistant? Nuura?"

The Ashaaran at the reception desk bowed. "No, ma'am. She did not come in this morning."

Aisha frowned. Her small, modest translator was dependable as the sun. But today she was nowhere to be seen.

She stopped at a window. The day was bright, but past the compound wall smoke darkened the sky. The embassy staff carried themselves with new jauntiness, calling cheerful greetings. Everyone looked relieved, though the host country employees seemed guarded.

For now, the rebels had been pushed back. Chaos was at a safe distance. Others were suffering, not they.

But where was Nuura? She glanced at her watch, then dismissed the question till later. She found the right door, next to the deputy's office, and gimlet-eyed the GrayWolf guard, impassive behind his wraparounds, as she flashed her pass. He seemed familiar—the one who'd hassled her at the conference?—but said nothing as he stepped aside.

Peyster was already sitting with Jolene Ridbout and the ambassador. The deputy too, the AID director, and several other counselors. She grimaced inside; the ambassador, by protocol and custom, arrived at meetings on time and expected everyone else already seated. She'd planned to be early but had gotten sidetracked searching for Nuura.

Dalton looked more rested than at their last encounter. He half rose, smiling icily; she nodded and hastily took the last seat. The attaché was in the battle dress she'd worn since hostilities had begun, sleeves rolled up, holstered pistol riding on a nylon belt. Peyster wore a white cotton kurta, like a Pakistani guayabera, with slate slacks and woven leather shoes. She owned some herself, from Morocco. "Going native, Terry?" she whispered.

"Love the scarf."

"Why're we here, Terry?"

"The news is good."

"I read the cable."

"You did?"

"You info'd NCIS and DIA."

The deputy put a finger to his lips. She quit whispering and focused on Ridbout. The attaché was giving the daily report. "The Marines have retaken the Victory Bridge. The rebels are in retreat. They counted on overwhelming us. When that didn't work, they had no staying power. They're fading back into the desert. We have road communication from the Zone to Camp Rowley and bulldozers are clearing the ring road. The marine terminal's bringing in their first ship this afternoon. With luck, we'll be able to discontinue rationing and resume food, fuel aid, and electrical power to the city very soon. That completes my report, Mr. Ambassador."

"That leaves the rest of the country," Dalton said. "WFO's predicting thousands of deaths."

"We can't be held responsible, sir. Not in the face of a major attack. Force protection had to come before the humanitarian mission."

"I suppose so, Jolene. What's General Ahearn doing now? Are they . . . in pursuit?"

"Not exactly, sir. He plans to push up the highway toward Fenteni, reestablishing order along the way in coordination with the Governing Council."

"Olowe?" Aisha put in. Heads swiveled like high-speed sunflowers.

"General Olowe, correct," Peyster said. "I know you don't care for him personally—"

"A mass murderer who takes bribes? One of my favorite people."

"Aisha," the ambassador whined.

"Actually he's our last chip," Peyster observed. "So let's take what we're dealt and make hay, shall we? As I was saying, the GC troops are establishing order. Rooting out rebel sympathizers—"

"Meaning, massacring the southern clans—"

"Aisha—"

"Those militias cooperated with the insurgents, Agent," Ridbout pointed out. "We can't expect our marines to distinguish a friendly Ashaari with a rifle from an enemy Ashaari with the same rifle. It may be necessary to rearm the GC, by the way. To bind them more closely to our interests."

Aisha coughed, choking on the phlegm from her congested lungs and the sickness at her heart. She'd argued with Peyster after the meeting with Olowe at Ahearn's headquarters. Tried to point out how contrary to common sense it was to ally themselves with the very clans that'd supported the corrupt and repressive former regime. The RSO had said equably that Olowe had been a bit player then. He'd be dependent on his new patrons.

More and more, she was wondering who Peyster actually was. Did he really work for State? The Bureau of Diplomatic Security? Or something darker? The NCIS ranked low on the federal peeing pole compared to this other agency.

"Okay, next topic," Peyster said. "The unaccounted-for aid personnel. The good news: they're alive, most of them. The bad: we have a communication from the Waleeli. Through Al-Jazeera, interestingly enough."

She occasionally watched the all-Arabic satellite news channel, based in Qatar. The rapid colloquial language was difficult, but usually she could follow. Seen as independent, it had become a channel for Islamicist groups throughout the Middle East. The RSO said the station had passed the message to the special representative in New York. Someone in his office had sleight-of-handed it to Dr. Dobleh's former e-mail account, with info copies to Leache and Dalton.

Dalton said, "There's no ADA left, then?"

"None to speak of, sir. The Cosmo bombing took down the whole leadership, except for three wounded."

"Where are they?"

"They left the country, Mr. Ambassador."

"Oh . . . hell."

"Yes, sir. Now: the aid personnel. The quote, Waleeli National Resurgence Council, unquote, says they're holding five women and three men. They're being treated well and will be turned over unharmed on delivery of a five-million-dollar ransom."

"Not more ransoms," muttered Dalton. "Isn't this a UN matter?"

"Well, sir, I called Mr. Kazuma's office and they feel it's in our area of responsibility, since the implementation on the resolution entrusts us with physical security of international relief personnel. He quoted paragraph 9(c) at me. I could argue with their legal staff but I'd probably lose."

"Meaning what? *We* have to pay?"

"We could do a stakeout if we did," Aisha put in.

Peyster raised his eyebrows at her but kept speaking to Dalton. "Not that we specifically have to, sir, no. My own recommendation would be not to. I read New York as saying basically that since we were responsible for protecting them in the first place, getting them back's up to us as well."

"How do they propose we do that?"

"They were unwilling to provide guidance. Said we were closest to the problem."

Dalton rubbed his scalp furiously. For a man whose siege had just been lifted, he looked distraught. "I have a call with the SecState at ten. I'll mention it, see if they have any guidance."

"Yessir, but right now I don't think we can avoid at least passing the ball to someone else. I suggest General Ahearn."

Dalton perked up. "Will you call him, Jolene? For me? He could stage a commando raid. That'd be best, I think."

Ridbout said reluctantly, "If you authorize me to speak in your name, sir. For a raid, well, hostage rescues are hard to do right. We'd have to know exactly where they're being held. But I'll ask. . . . What should I say about the funds?"

The ambassador said stiffly, "During his tenure as secretary, Henry Kissinger established as policy that we never pay ransom to foreign kidnappers or terrorists. Nor would our embassies facilitate such payments. I recall he fired our ambassador to Tanzania for allowing his staff to assist in the payment of private funds to rescue U.S. citizens. Even though that rescue was successful.

"I believe this policy still stands. And I certainly don't have such funds at my disposal. Regardless of my personal concern for these unfortunate captives. So if someone does pay, it's going to have to come from their home churches, or the WGO. In no way is that a State responsibility."

Dalton stood, and the rest did too. When he left they looked at one another. "Will he really ask?" Aisha said.

Ridbout shook her head. "Probably not. But you have to hand it to him. Back when they were at the gates? Most ambassadors would've decamped. Dalton stayed." She grinned at Aisha. "Didn't actually man the ramparts, though, like you, Agent Ar-Rahim. Which reminds me, who do I call about putting you in for some kind of NCIS award?"

"I don't need an award. They were just poor people who saw a chance to get something they'd never be able to own otherwise."

Both the others were silent and she read their minds: What kind of bleeding heart have we got here? Peyster said, "Before we break, I wanted to run something by you. What you said about a stakeout. What'd you mean?"

"Standard procedure in a hostage-ransom situation. The FBI Hostage Rescue Team has it down to a science."

"More."

"What happened to 'please'? Still the magic word, Terry."

"Sorry, Aisha. How would you set up a stakeout on somebody like Al-Maahdi? Please."

"Well, use the turnover meeting—where he gets the ransom and we get the hostages—to move in and take him into custody."

"If we knew where he was."

She said patiently, "Terry, that's the point. We have to know that in order to get his money to him. All I'm saying is, maybe we should try. Or have you not thought about doing an Assad on him?"

"Assad resisted arrest."

"Well, maybe Al-Maahdi, or Al-Khasmi, or whatever he's calling himself these days, won't."

"Would he show up at the exchange site? He's a slippery character."

"At the least we'll get one of his deputies. Maybe we can persuade *him* to tell us where his boss lives."

"Well, thank you both," Peyster said, getting up. They were all headed for the door when he said, "Oh, one more thing . . . for you, Jolene. Thanks, Aisha. We'll keep you in the loop."

He eased the door closed behind her. She stood in the hallway. Had he just gotten rid of her?

"Agent?" The familiar-looking GrayWolf, with the Ashaari whom she'd asked about Nuura. He held out a folded paper. "He says this just came in the gate for you."

When she unfolded it she recognized the handwriting. It was Nuura's, yet not. Hers was exquisite, like the little translator herself: each tiny letter executed in painstaking block print. This was hastily scrawled with a soft pencil whose tip had broken off halfway through, then pressed so hard the last few words ripped the paper.

Miss Rahim. Emergency. Emergency. You come help us please. This man knows where.

"Do you know where she is?" she asked. The Ashaari shook his head, backing away.

Until she held out the money.

When the door shut Peyster waited a moment, standing by the window. Then said in a low voice, "What if she's right, and he comes out of his hole?"

"Localize and neutralize a leadership node," Ridbout said, scratching the tabletop and looking at her nails. "He's a legitimate target, far as I can see. What would you do with him, after? There's no judiciary to turn him over to. Do you want him?"

"Definitely not. I have no problem targeting him. But you guys have the assets. Could you do it? Speaking theoretically."

"Theoretically," said the colonel, "we could. If he showed up. That's the nub, isn't it?"

"That's the nub. How would you do it? Bomb?"

"Not with hostages in the impact area," the colonel said. "The most effective means would depend on the location of the exchange. Who shows up, how many . . . Anything else for me?"

"Nothing else," said the security officer. "Keep me posted."

"Sure," said the colonel. They looked away from each other, then got up and left.

Dan's face was pressed into the keyboard again when someone shook him. "Let's talk," Dickinson muttered.

"Here, sir?"

"Out in the terminal."

They strolled through the canvas screening, boots echoing. Another aircraft came in, turbines blurring out all other sound. The ops officer said, "You mentioned a possible way of localizing this Al-Khasmi."

"A software program we've been working on at TAG."

"We just got a tasking to find him. Basically, at all costs. And the J-2's shit out of ideas. They got intel out the ying yang, everybody from the A-guys to NCIS looking, but he's not there. What have you got that's gonna rock my world?"

Dan gave him the short version. CIRCE was sophisticated but still beta-version software TAG had developed from a commercial circle-of-contacts product. The original intent had been to integrate multiple near-chaotic inputs in a littoral environment to locate quiet submarines. From there, Henrickson had developed it into a multiagent model that integrated not just comms and intel but social and spatial relations. A stochastic modeling agent reasoning framework predicted not just the location, but the likelihood of a unitary actor—a submarine captain, a pilot, an enemy general—taking certain actions as against others.

It wasn't magic, merely the same thing deeply expert human beings had always done, often unconsciously—with "intuition." But CIRCE's data-mining capability, with its ability to elicit second- and third-degree relationships, could tease out leads that might otherwise slip under the radar.

When Dan was done the J-3 said, "Can it give us a specific location? Where he is, or will be, at a given time?"

"Well, *sometimes*. If the data's there. Sometimes humans just can't put together enough hints. Occasionally CIRCE can. It actually works pretty well with an object with three-dimensional locations, fixed movement rates—like a submarine."

"Can it focus down on one specific individual?"

"What've we got to lose?"

"The guy who's giving us all this trouble. Al-Khasmi, Al-Maahdi—whatever he calls himself. The one behind the Brotherhood. Could it find him?"

Dan stuck his fingers in his back pockets. "His home base, you mean? Or where he's at, at a given moment?"

"I'll settle for either. Right now, he's a fucking phantom."

"There's a fair chance of localizing his stomping grounds."

"How soon can you set up? Need computers, equipment?"

"I need to get my team leader here. Anything else, he can bring. We don't need computers other than our notebooks—CIRCE runs on our Sun there at TAG; we can uplink on your satellite broadband." He gripped Dickinson's arm. "But what happens if we find him? If we get a datum?"

"A what?"

"Sorry—naval terminology. If we come up with a locus of probability. Then what?"

"We smoke him," Dickinson said. "What the fuck else? He's the king vulture. Blow him the fuck away, and body-bag as many of his second echelon as possible."

Dan took a silent turn, making sure he had no problem with this. It was probably the Waleeli who'd blown up the hotel, nearly killed him and Blair. Was he getting hardened? He hoped not. But just hearing it from Dickinson wasn't enough. "This tasking, it's from who? Specifically."

"From Higher."

"What exactly did the CG say?"

Dickinson didn't answer. Dan looked at him. "Okay, I'll rephrase that. What *will* Ahearn say? Because I've gotten burned on this kind of word-of-mouth mission before."

"You just got an order. From me."

"Which I asked for clarification on, Colonel. All right?" The J-3 grimaced but Dan went on. "We're happy to respond to the requirement, but I've got to present this to my commanding officer as a legitimate support request from a deployed, in-combat task force. It doesn't have to say exactly what's going on, and I'll be happy to draft the request, but COMJTF's got to be on board. It can't just be something you and I hatched one night."

"I can tell you what he'll give you. If we can localize the guy, he's a legit target. Directing a rebellion, targeting UN forces? Definitely. We're not in the assassination business."

Dan felt strange, detached, as if watching actors in a film having this discussion. "I don't like even hearing that word."

"It's not *me* saying it. It'd be the JAGers."

The military lawyers. "Who'd say . . . what?"

"That it's more how it's done than that it's done."

"Not sure I grok you, Colonel."

Dickinson stopped in the middle of the empty terminal and jabbed Dan's chest, with a rigid forefinger. His eyes were rimmed with blood as if he'd been chewing qat, though it was probably just sleep deprivation. "It's *gray area*, Commander. Okay? A politician, he's off limits. Military, he's fair fucking game. Which is Al-Maahdi? You tell me. Are the Waleeli a political party? To us they're fucking guerrillas, insurgents. To Olowe they're rebels, but he's not the government, not yet, and *this isn't a war.* We're here under a UN mandate. If it looks like we're taking out faction leaders, even violent ones, there'll be sheer fucking *hell* to pay. But if we call him as military, hit him with a Hellfire from a Predator, it's legitimate. If we pay somebody to put poison in his tea, *that's* assassination."

"How about a sniper team? Don't tell me. Gray area."

"Big time. That's why I think what we'll get from the general will be, 'I never got this briefing.' Not because he's a bad guy. Ahearn's as straight a shooter as I've come across. It's an inescapable element of an ineluctable situation."

Dan pushed his finger away. "I guess that's as plain as it's going to get. So?"

"All right." Dickinson looked grim, even for a man with a shaved head. He took a deep breath and rubbed his eyes. "So. Let's take it in to the general."

Aisha had driven them herself, strictly against regulations, without an escort, and without protective vests either, in an embassy van she'd found parked behind the fueling station. The desk clerk who'd given her Nuura's note sat petrified in the passenger seat, the stink of his fear filling the car. He kept counting the money she'd handed him. Then would point to a missed turn, and she'd have to back up and maneuver the van around in some narrow alley.

The streets were spooky, deserted in the artificial twilight the smoke made. The wind smelled of burning rubber and trash. But at last they were there.

This street wasn't deserted. People bustled about, carrying things out of the houses. Like a gigantic neighborhoodwide garage sale, though there were no card tables with housewives and cash boxes. What she did see was tracks, huge ones. The unmistakable knobby wide treads of military tires.

The door he pointed at hung wide open. The house was hand-patted brick, yardless, indistinguishable from the ones around it. She'd known Nuura was poor, but this mud hovel made the shed behind the embassy look lavish.

When she reached the door her guide bolted. She shouted, but he never looked back. She hesitated, peering through, only noticing then the hinges were broken. It had been battered open.

Under cover of her abaya, she pulled her purse around and extracted the SIG.

Inside clothes lay scattered across the dirt floor. Someone had shat on them. Flies rose in a droning cloud as she skirted the pile. Deep scrapes showed where heavy things had been dragged out. That might account for the lack of furniture, though there couldn't have been much to start with. She gripped the pistol in both hands. "Nuura?" she called. She couldn't remember the husband's name. "I'm here. Nuura?"

The second room was totally dark and smelled foul. She felt the wall for a switch. Her fingertips found only gritty dried mud. Duh, Agent Ar-Rahim. She barked her shin on a piece of rickety furniture. She really should carry a flashlight. But her purse was already so heavy. . . . She called again and again; no one answered. She was turning away when something squeaked, back in the dark.

She took another step back toward the entrance. Then stopped.

She felt her way into the dark again, stooped, feeling with a free hand. Glass grated under her shoes.

A rear door stood partially open. She pushed the pistol through, then worked her upper body after. A galvanized washtub boomed as it toppled.

A little rear laundry room. A hole in the wall admitted dusty light. Broken reed baskets lay tumbled. The smell of rust and dank water. Dangling lines overhead. More clothes, threadbare, stained, piled in the corner. Rags.

The squeaking came again. From the corner. She lowered the muzzle of her pistol very slowly, and hooked the top rag with the front sight. An old dress, torn and stained. She lifted it.

It looked quite inhuman. Its head was misshapen, pointed, eyes squeezed closed. Tiny gray fists waved feebly. It couldn't be more than a few hours old. Catching her breath, Aisha flipped the dirty cloth aside.

It was a *she*. Nuura's baby girl.

31

QRFVILLE, CAMP ROWLEY

Teddy Oberg swung over the wall and dropped, hard.

Then bent, catching his breath where the others couldn't see him. Sweat rained off his face onto his boots. A filleting knife twisted deep in his liver. He took five seconds, then straightened and headed for the next wall. Up and over, huffing and blowing.

"Wet and sandy," Whacker grunted, slamming down next to him so hard dust whiffed out of his gear, then wriggling under the wire. "Dig deep, boy. Dig deep."

"Whyn't you go . . . find a goat and dig deep in his fucking ass, Whacker."

"Because they all fucking smell like you, Yo-Berg. You feelin' all right? Sure draggin' ass today."

A hundred twenty in the shade and the team was out in full gear doing an obstacle course the marines had improvised out of a couple of ruined houses and a shitload of busted concrete slabs from something that'd gotten blown up or bulldozed down. Berms, tires, wire, barriers made out of old telephone poles, chest-high walls, the works. Hell in the Desert, the way only the U.S. Marine Corps could brew it.

It was him and Vic Cooper and Aleks Kowacki and a new guy, Donoghe, pronounced Donahee, fresh out of quals and paratrooper and sniper school. *The kid's first mission.* Yep, a real SEAL pup, twenty years old, all "like awesome" and "that's sick," who cocked his head when he listened to you, like a smart dog. They'd taken one look at his earnest blue eyes, bulging biceps, and protruding incisors, and named him Chipmunk Cheeks.

And here he was, right beside him. "You okay, Obie? Obie, dude, doin' okay?"

"Get the fuck off my face. *Dude.*" He scrambled up and lurched for the dangling rope, went up hand over hand for the second floor, cleared the top and worked his way down the stairwell, switching off with Kowacki.

Sweating was good. Kept him from thinking. From remembering what Kaulukukui had done during the raid on Assad's compound weeks before. He couldn't shake his buddy's last smile. The big round face creased into a dusty, grit-smeared grin.

Before the grenade cracked.

Could he have saved him? If he'd thought ahead, not charged them into a trap? No, it was Sumo who'd charged. Who'd saved his ass back on the Iranian sub and a couple other times before that.

Before he'd saved it for the last time, and paid with his own. He blotted his face with his sleeve. Christ. "Some fucking fluid here, Cheeks," he croaked, and caught the bottle the kid tossed his way. Hot from the sun, but that was supposed to kill the germs. The concern in the kid's face put a snarl on his own. "Shut the fuck up, Donoghe," he said. The fucker was always talking. If he was breathing, he was talking.

They were out by the north end of the airstrip, near the helipads, where the quick reaction force had set up. Tents, modulars, even a shower. A range, too—they put in an hour there every day. Word was they were getting ready for a hostage rescue. But everything was on hold while the head shed figured out where. Obviously, they couldn't drill the rescue till they knew the layout, but he and the gunny had hammered out a training schedule heavy on pistolcraft and teamwork through typical Ashaaran compounds and nomad camps.

Teddy was lukewarm about marines. They were gung ho but they weren't dedicated hunters, silent lethal killers. They were noisy and gear-heavy and didn't move fast enough. Training was fine, but you could plan everything in anal detail, and maybe half the mission would go that way. You had to stay light on your feet, react instantly and right.

It got worse when hostages were involved. The SAS and the Deltas, the IDF and the Russian Alpha Units, trained for it 24/7, with live ammo, and even they didn't bring everybody home alive. When a bad guy saw he was fucked, his buddies being taken out, it was too easy to flick the selector to auto and hose down a roomful of helpless people. That's where speed counted, being able to put two in the chest and one in the head without taking time to aim.

Did he want marines on his six? If they stayed back there unless he yelled for help, sure.

Did he want Cheeks on his six? He was pretty sure that he did not want.

They'd had a sit-down with the major in charge of the QRF, Freidebacher. And Lenson, whom Teddy knew from two TAG missions. He'd walked out knowing less than he had going in. Only that Operation King Vulture might start with a helo feint. The insurgents feared helos. They'd learned that during what the marines were calling the Battle of Ashaara City. A helo insert was out; the Waleeli had a makeshift warning net that made it almost impossible to stay covert, but the Hammer Force might chopper in after the direct-action team pinned Al-Maahdi's party down.

Teddy had probed for some idea of where they were talking about—mountain, desert, north or south—but Lenson kept that close hold.

They staggered out of the ruined house and headed for shade. His gut rumbled and stabbed. They'd sent Arkin back with worms. Diagnosis: "Eosinophilia, possible helminth infections." Teddy had to shit all the time, and often, if he cared to look, it was streaked with bright blood. Now he was trying to keep up with twenty-year-old jarfuckers.

Grunting, he let himself down to his haunches, propping his back against a wall hot as a pancake griddle. A flimsy plastic bag tumbled by on the hot wind, writhing as if in agony. Teddy watched it gloomily. By definition, you fought in hellholes, but Ashaara took it to a whole new level. The flies, the human shit all over, the wasted stinking animals, the fucking dune coons—he was no racist, but he was getting there. And now, hooyah, fucking worms.

The SEALs sat in the shade and watched. Till a Marine

sergeant came over. A big one, with rock jaw and caveman brows. "Your spec ops pogies sittin' this dance out, Oberg?"

Teddy stared at him for a second, then heaved up. "SEAL Team Eight, comin' through."

A mile away, in the Special Compartmented Intelligence Facility, a wired and guarded cluster of choos and modules, generators and antenna farms that formed the secret brain of the JTF, Dan put a hand on Monty Henrickson's spindly shoulder, then took a seat where the little analyst patted.

For the past week he'd alternated between the JOC and the SCIF, working with Dickinson and the light colonel in charge of the QRF to write the op order for King Vulture. Now they had it signed off. All that remained was to frag, or modify, it when they had the final location.

Now they might. "Pioneer?" he said, leaning to see.

The scene was backlit, taken just after dawn. A lander shot of Mars, except not in color. A fissure, a pursed mouth, a crooked vagina across the screen from upper left to lower right. Boulders lay as if tossed by a giant bocce player. Dan peered as Henrickson zoomed in. "Those bomb craters?"

"Not sure. Too small to be volcanic. Some kind of sink-hole?"

"Where is this?"

For answer he toggled to a map of Ashaara, then zoomed, hurtling down in a dizzying drop shot till Dan had to look away. "That's the Tanagra," Henrickson said, and Dan looked again. The crosshairs were between the southern mountains and the river, fifty miles west of the Tanagra Delta at R'as Zalurah. Not even the small red dots of hamlets on the map, and the dotted trails that meant dirt roads were missing too.

"No population?"

"The OGAs mention bandit hideouts in that area, back when they were fighting the Italian colonial government. A tributary of the Tanagra used to come out of there. Just a wadi now, no water at all. But"—the analyst called up another screen, a graphic with arcs leaping from a shimmering circle of streaming data—"we have intersections from local merchants, cell phone calls, camel trails. There's a salt mine not far away. At first we thought the trails ran to it. Most do, but not all." He shifted back to the Pioneer video and rotated it, moved an arrow across the screen with his mouse. "Between these rectangular rocks, winding down into this gap. You can only make it out only at sunrise. Otherwise the light flattens it, reduces the contrast till it disappears."

Dan peered as Henrickson went on. "We couldn't think of a reason for a trail there. Especially with no water and no salt. But guess what's on that trail?"

"What?"

"Camel droppings. It's in active use. So we started watching." Henrickson nodded to two Air Force enlisted who sat listening. "Tysheka and Ronshende've put in many, many hours beyond their normal workdays on this. And we've had to fight for the overhead assets all that time. Finally Tysheka just happened to be watching when this happened."

The same tortured rent in the desert floor. But now, at the east end, a tiny star. Henrickson clicked, zoomed, and in the grainy mosaic of overenlarged pixels, a picture grew.

"AK's are notorious for this. The 'glint,' it's called. "

Dan nodded. Blurred, at maximum magnification, but the figure was clear. A man, legs extended, looking off to his left while the rifle on his lap, picking up the sun overhead, reflected it into the lens. "A sentry."

"Right, and whatever he's guarding's under these overhangs here, here, and possibly here. You see their shadows at midafternoon. Here's someone's leg sticking out. And here, a cookpot. Everything else is under cover, hidden from overhead surveillance. We e-mailed photos to a geologist. It's called a karst topography. Could be be deep wells, caverns, cenotes. Caves big enough to hold a battalion."

Dan clasped his knee, wondering why he was underwhelmed. Maybe he just didn't want to believe it. It'd be a nightmare to send troops into: a lunatic labyrinth of chaotic stone. Bombing, strafing, would be useless. You could pour troops in, but whoever knew the topography could chew them up and spit them out. "Anything point specifically to Al-

Maahdi? These could be like you said, just bandits. Or villagers, holed up till this insurgency gets settled."

"CIRCE says it's him. Probability above seventy percent. Based on the social-contact algorithm." Monty looked up anxiously; keys rattled. "Here's the chart. The lines are isoprobabilities; see how they stack up as we get closer to the site. There are other centroids, here in this refugee camp, Camp Number One, another down in the southern mountains. But they seem older. Maybe where he holed up previously. These indications are much more recent."

"What's Dickinson think?"

"He asked what you thought. That's when I called your choo."

Dan rubbed his head, reluctant, but at last got out his cell. One more guy to run it past before they went to the general. Major Freidebacher answered on the first ring.

Not too much later, the QRF leader was looking at the same screen, with the same expression Dan figured he'd had. The enlisted had left; Henrickson busied himself with his notebook.

"No place I want to assault," Freidebacher said flatly. He was surprisingly small, but with massive arms, a neck like a bull's, sad dark eyes. "Troop on troop . . . be a meat grinder. The best way to winkle them out would be gas."

"Tear gas?"

"Of course, tear gas, Commander. Blocking force here . . . reserve force here." A forefinger sketched lines of advance, fields of fire, on the screen. "It's heavier than air. Sinks into caves and ravines, and they won't have masks. But it'd take massive concentrations. If there are spaces without good air circulation, some will die." The marine sniffed. "But the ROE on gas . . . it's tight. Clearance all the way up. Thinking about it, we don't stand a chance. Getting approval, I mean."

"Well, how else do we do it?" Dan chewed the inside of his mouth, trying to grasp an elusive concept; something about infiltrating the caves from behind or below, moving the hostages out without alerting the mass of the Waleeli.

"What about SEALs? They do hostage rescue, right? Can we get them in there in the dark?"

"SEALs? Those guys aren't Superman. Far from it. Hotshots. Arrogant cowboys. Need a good dose of military discipline, in my humble grunt opinion."

Dan wasn't sure this was accurate, he'd seen them in action, but it wasn't the time to argue tactical philosophies. "Then how? We'll have to go to Ahearn with this, Pete. Tell him we know where the hostages might be. More than that, where Al-Maahdi's probably holed up. He's going to want a plan."

"I'll tell you one thing: I don't want my guys in there." Freidebacher made a fist, blowing into it. "I mean, if he says go, we go, but we'll carry a lot of body bags out. And they're not all gonna be insurgents."

"So what do we tell him?"

The major rictused a smile. "That, we'd better think about. Long and hard."

32

THE PALAIS DE SÉCURITÉ

The van buffeted in the wind as they slowed, pulled ahead of their escort, and turned in. Aisha felt strange being back after all this time. This had been her first stop in Ashaara, and even in the midnight darkness the spear-pointed fence, the abandoned moat, the outlines of mansard roofs and corner towers, brought creepy memories of meeting Assad in the basement lair of the SDI.

The red-and-white-striped barrier was history, as were uniformed guards. Instead sandbagged machine-gun bunkers flanked the entrance. In the pulsing glare of generator-driven floods through windblown dust, hard-faced black men in coveralls waved the GMC to a stop. Their driver stared back, locked in some testosterone-fueled facedown. "Olowe's personal security," Peyster murmured. "Remember: We're here to listen. We don't promise anything. We don't make offers."

She didn't answer. A guard peered in, then jerked the rear door open and clambered in, shoving her to the middle of the backseat. A sharp object jabbed her ribs: the front sight of his rifle. She gripped her purse, feeling the outline of the SIG. Without a word, he waved them forward.

Their minder pointed them to a back court, an entrance new to her. The hallways were spookier, if possible, than on her first visit. No desks anymore, no chain-smoking clerks with haunted eyes. Whatever had stalked them had come and gone. All that remained was drifted paper, toppled file cabinets, side rooms whose very doors had been stolen off the hinges. Broken glass, smashed plaster, holes where copper had been mined out. The overhead fans were gone too. The intensely close air smelled of dust and mold, slow rot and terror.

People had a habit of suddenly disappearing, in this country. She'd never found Nuura, either, though she'd asked every Ashaaran she knew. Most just shook their heads, not even daring to speak.

The baby . . . she couldn't leave Nuura's newborn girl there to die. She'd taken her in through the compound gate with her huge carpet-purse riding in the passenger seat, the clasp undone. Fortunately the infant hadn't made a sound. Tonight she was with one of the cleaning women, in a makeshift crib in the employees' shed.

The guard led them up a stairwell, AK at port arms.

Olowe received them in a partially restored office in a corner tower. Tall windows with bowed antique glass that distorted the lights outside looked down on the forecourt, the fountain, all semiobscured in the wavering veil the wind drew, then pulled back. A desk lamp was tilted up to reflect off the freshly painted ceiling. In the corner a crone with a widow's hump sang to herself at a desk, tapping slowly at an antique cast-iron Olivetti with a platen a yard long. Aisha did a double take. The transcriptionist who'd spoken Italian to Erculiano. As indestructible and enduring, apparently, as the brick walls.

The general appeared less imposing tonight, almost ingratiating as he came forward with hands outstretched. But he was still too huge to feel comfortable with indoors. He wore not a uniform but a dark blue civilian suit, buttons straining over his massive chest. His black tie was inexpertly knotted. He enveloped Peyster in a bear hug from which the RSO emerged with sandy hair tousled and shirt spotted with the general's sweat. To her surprise, he reached for her hand too. Aisha tried both to meet his eyes and to not stare at his face. Was this the man whose troops were evicting whole neighborhoods? Could that pale patch of unpigmented skin have grown?

Olowe spoke sharply to the guard, who about-faced smartly, British-style, and took up a position in the hallway. Aisha met the old woman's sly glance over the typewriter; they exchanged minute nods.

A slim shadow hesitated at the door. The young man looked uncomfortable in the short-sleeved white shirt and dark slacks that seemed to be business formal in East Africa. Olowe spoke and the old woman tottered to a side table. She served tea and biscotti. The young man shifted on his chair, not meeting their eyes. He gazed at the moving shadows outside the window, then at his tea. Steam rose, curling in the dim hot air.

"Ali Wasami Hasheer," Peyster murmured. "One of Al-Khasmi's closest associates."

"Actually, we've met. In the desert." She smiled at the young man, who dropped his gaze to her feet. Oh, yes, she remembered him. The last time she'd seen him, he'd been pointing a rifle at her GrayWolf bodyguard's head. He looked away, then back, as if reluctantly drawn to her shoes. She set her purse on the floor, the unclasped top facing him.

Olowe began speaking. This time, to Aisha's surprise, in crude English. He'd obviously been studying. When he hesitated she or Peyster would suggest a word and he'd repeat it, slowly, as if tasting it, then resume. He introduced the young man as Ali. "He is with one some call Al-Maahdi. One of his young *fedahin*."

"We know of Mr. Hasheer, and his high position with the Waleeli Brotherhood," Peyster said. "We're looking forward to exchanging views. If that's the purpose of this meeting."

Of course it wasn't. All four knew that. Peyster had explained on the way. "One of Al-Maahdi's boys wants to come in from the cold. Our job's to milk him for all he's worth, then see if we can turn him like Whiteface thinks we can. If we can recruit him, he may be the key to your hostage-swap takedown. Olowe wants to be the go-between, but doesn't want it known. That's why we're going at night. Just us, him, the guy, and his personal SS."

"Can you trust him?" she'd asked.

The RSO had just smiled. "Can I trust you? Can you trust me?"

"I hope you can trust me."

"Of course I do." He'd patted her hand, and a chill had skittered up her back like an icy-footed roach.

Olowe had explained as the insurgent listened impassively. Now Hasheer began speaking, in Arabic. She took over the conversation, understanding it better than Olowe's Ashaaran. The piebald general sat back, lighting a cigar and listening intently, though she wondered how much he was picking up.

"Our official"—she nodded to Peyster—"welcomes you and wishes to know you better. We are both the general's guests tonight, as we are your guests in your land."

"What's he saying?" the RSO asked.

"Just getting through the preliminaries, Terry. It won't pay to rush this, believe me. I've got to build empathy first."

The Ashaaran mumbled compliments in return, and gradually they got down to business. "The general tells us you've grown from being a supporter of Al-Maahdi, or Al-Khasmi as he is called, to believing it's better for the Ashaari to cooperate with the UN until the famine ends. Correct?"

The young man leaned from side to side in his chair and explained in great earnestness that he'd fought at Ghedi's side—

" 'Ghedi' is Al-Khasmi?"

"Yes. I fought by him in many battles. But he was wounded at Uri'yah, when he defeated the troops of your—your democrats. Since then, he's changed. For a time I believed truly that the Waleeli brought life to the people and did the will of God."

She nodded, urging him on. To hear from a jihadist what made him tick—she didn't have to feign interest. "That's what I find difficult, discerning God's will for me. It's hard."

"Yes. Very hard."

He met her eyes for the first time. Compassion and empathy: that was what made an informant useful. She'd be his big sister—no, his fellow searcher for Truth. "What is it for the Brotherhood? As Ghedi understands it?"

"That the Americans are here to take over our country. We must resist their godlessness and evil. That is the great jihad the holy Sheekh Nassir, peace be with him, declared before you killed him. We Waleeli would unite all Ashaarans and eject the foreigners, then govern in accordance with the Book. To teach righteousness, and enforce the holy law."

"You took great risks for this goal. The Waleeli are brave fighters."

An eye flick to Olowe, then back to her shoes. "I did. There's been so much suffering. How could a government of God not be better?"

"What changed his mind?" Peyster asked. So he was following at least a word here and there.

She said to Hasheer, "The high official thanks you for coming with your heart open. He respects your devotion to your suffering people. Will you tell a bit more about your leader? He's of great interest. One who fights us, yes, but who is in his way a great man. A patriot, too." She said a *du'a* to ask forgiveness for that lie.

Peyster asked again what was going on. She told him to

be patient. Olowe shifted behind his desk, tapping cigar ash onto the floor.

Hasheer said his master was from the south, orchard country. His family had been broken up during the time of the Morgue and he'd grown up fighting. He could barely read, but was a man of honor. He was brave and noble. His men loved him. But the wound had changed him. He'd begun killing without reckoning the cost, even ordering his own brother beheaded. The man he admired had gone mad.

She nodded, as if disillusionment with a once-worshipped leader and no other motive lay behind his presence. She asked about his master's other lieutenants, and he described them. Peyster stirred and sat forward as Hasheer went on to describe a Saudi who served one he called the Prince of Believers.

"This Yousef. He's not from Ashaara?"

"No. He's Saudi. Very well dressed, courteous. His family is rich, I think. His plan is to use the Waleeli to install a Shura council dominated by the Arabs. After which, they'll have no more use for Al-Khasmi, so I think they will kill him. If by then his mouth, his wound, does not cause him to die." The slight young man spread his hands as if to say, *It is not my will.*

"Interesting. So you don't want Ashaara dominated by Arabs, any more than by Americans."

"The Arabs have brought us great suffering in the past."

"Do others feel as you do?"

"Perhaps, but no one dares speak of it."

Her fingers itched for a pen, but they'd have to depend on the digital recorder noiselessly eavesdropping in her purse. If the scratch and hiss of dust on the windows didn't blur his words, obliterate his speech. Then she'd take away only what memory could carry. "I can understand that," she said encouragingly. "Tell me, who is this 'Prince of Believers'?"

"I have heard, an Arab named Usama bin Laden. For that reason, I asked to see General Olowe. The honored general answered courteously that he'd like me to meet his friends, the Americans." He eyed her. "I did not think they would be like you. You speak very good Arabic. Where are you from? Kenya?"

"New York City."

His mouth actually came open. She used that moment of astonishment. "Yes, many things they say about America are not true. We wish only prosperity for Ashaara, for a peaceful world means peace for us too. Then our soldiers can leave. Though I hope we'll remain friends.

"Now let us speak of the hostages your master holds. Have you seen them? How many? Are they treated well?"

The next half hour yielded a good deal of useful information. Ali Hasheer stated firmly that he'd personally seen the hostages. Some had died, of various diseases, but fourteen were alive. Where, he refused to say, since that would reveal his master's location. Nor would he give figures on troop strengths or organization for the insurgent forces. She didn't push too hard. Her main concerns were the hostages, and Al-Maahdi himself.

Plus one question for Olowe, before they left.

The general had been sitting back, puffing out smoke. Now he cleared his throat and got up. "Mr. Peyster," he said, interrupting Aisha in midsentence.

"Yes, General."

"Here are my thoughts. You know why Al-Maahdi wants ransom?"

"To buy weapons, is our guess."

"Correct, to buy helicop'er missiles."

"Um, to buy—I'm sorry—?"

Olowe mimed pointing a shoulder-fired weapon, pulling a trigger. Aisha grimaced. "Antiaircraft missiles?"

"From China."

Peyster said, "Is this true?" Hasheer hesitated, then nodded. The RSO sat back, looking grave.

The general said heavily that in view of their new alliance with the Americans, the Governing Council could not allow such weapons in the country. Hasheer was prepared to cooperate in arranging Al-Maahdi's capture. If the Americans would agree to furnish the ransom, the insurgent lieutenant would arrange the turnover of the hostages. In return, he, General Olowe, pledged to reward Ali Hasheer with a high position in the new government.

"And the money?" Aisha asked him. He smiled, waved his hands as if to say: immaterial.

Peyster seemed to agree. All he asked was, "Can he guarantee Al-Maahdi'll be there? At the turnover?"

She translated. Hasheer said he could, if the Americans made it clear they'd turn the ransom over only to him in person.

"You'd be in charge?"

"His other lieutenant doesn't come to the city. I can travel back and forth."

Meaning, she thought, Hasheer had a safe conduct from Olowe past the roadblocks between the rebel-held hinterland and the GC-controlled areas along the main roads. Which also hinted their relationship wasn't as recent as presented.

Did that matter? Probably not. A lot of her work, dealing with informers for example, wasn't that appetizing. You held your nose and got on with it. She nudged her purse an inch closer to him with her toe.

Olowe perched on the corner of his desk. He rumbled, "Hasheer makes where you meet. Al-Maahdi comes. Then you take."

"He's not to be harmed," said Hasheer in Arabic. "The general has promised this. Only captured."

Aisha gestured to the old woman, pointed to their cups. The old woman wagged her head at her own slackness, muttered apologies in Italian. As she tottered from one to the next on ancient high heels Aisha explained to Peyster, who listened with fingers locked. Till at last he rose, said, "Excuse us" to Olowe, and strolled out. The guard watched, but didn't move to follow.

They paced the length of the darkened corridor before Peyster murmured, "Now, you've met the guy? This Ghedi, the one we've been calling Al-Khasmi?"

"I interviewed him in the southern mountains when we were trying to get him to join the coalition. The reaction, well, it wasn't positive. Our informant's right. He spoke of the ulama, of sharia law."

"Does he trust you? Al-Maahdi?"

He wanted to marry me, she thought of saying, but didn't. "I doubt he *trusts* me, but he knows me. With Ashaarans, that's a big step forward."

"What do you think? This Hasheer. He the real deal?"

"I see no reason to doubt he can do what he says. Or has a reasonable chance, properly managed."

"The JTF thinks he's holding the hostages north of the Tanagra. It'd be too costly to take him out where he is. But if Hasheer can lure him out into the open, we can intel-drive a direct action mission. Get the hostages back, zip-tie him, and park him somewhere he can't rally the Waleeli. Best case, Hasheer succeeds to the leadership, and we've got our own man in charge." Peyster smoothed his hair and lowered his voice even more. "That'd be desirable for any number of reasons—including some leverage on Olowe."

She looked at him, no longer wondering what agency he actually worked for. "And charge him with—what?"

They came to where strips of light lay against the ceiling, shining up from the floods in the courtyard, and stopped. Peyster blinked, as if she shouldn't need to be told. "Conspiracy to murder. For the Cosmo bombing. Or don't you think he was behind it?"

"We've assumed so. That was the word on the street."

"Did you ask Hasheer?"

"No. But I can."

The RSO shrugged. "Let it go, why rattle the teacups? In case he planned it himself. There's enough on our plate."

"So what do I tell them?"

"Tell him we're in. Set up the meet, but he's got to let us know *where* as far in advance as he can. Just make sure Al-Khasmi's there, in person. This Yousef the Arab—we'll take him too if we can, but I think I know who he is. We'll have our friends in Saudi talk to him next time he goes home. Okay, he knows you, we'll stipulate you want to personally hand him the cash, to ensure it's really going to him. Make it personal, you and him."

"Right." She turned and they started back. "We take him, and then?"

"We hold him till Olowe gets a court set up. They try him, we don't. I don't think the general will mind shooting him in a courtyard someplace." Peyster shrugged. "Slam dunk, far's I can see. Let's get Olowe's chop on the deal, and get out of here."

Outside, in the back courtyard, she stopped to gather herself. Trying to stifle the sense she'd crossed some obscure but fateful line. She'd finally asked the question she'd held in reserve all through the interview. Where the southerners Olowe's troops were evacuating from the city were being taken. But the big man had just smiled blandly, looking off at nothing, answering not a word as Peyster pulled her away, apologizing.

The wind gusted, rattling sheet metal close by. The lights dimmed as the generators wound down. The stars shone out from equatorial black. They were brighter here than she'd ever seen them. They were all but invisible in New York, with its never-sleeping beacons of the electric future.

They seemed to move as she watched, whirling in interstellar cold. Staring up, she felt that chill again despite the lingering heat. As if everything rushed onward faster and faster, a blind gallop toward some horrific denouement no human effort could delay by a microsecond. Was this how God had written the book of their lives?

She didn't think this terrorist in the desert was anything more. An ignorant insurgent, fighting what he didn't understand. The age of prophets was past. But wouldn't it be ironic, if what they said about Al-Maahdi was true. Then she'd be the Muslim who'd set up a Judas to betray the Messenger of God.

"You okay?" Peyster, holding the van door. "Look like you saw a ghost."

She grimaced without speaking, and got in.

33

FROM THIRTY-FIVE THOUSAND FEET

The gunners hugged themselves beside their weapons, sucking oxygen from tanks strapped to their waists. Freezing their asses off, but keeping clear of the SEALs, who took up most of the rear of the aircraft.

Builds character, Oberg thought. At thirty-five thousand feet, in the unpressurized, unheated, almost unlit fuselage of the Spectre, the cold was intense. The 110-knot slipstream howling back from the open gunners' stations didn't help. He wore fleece and underarmor pants and tops. A face cover too. Bulky, but he was glad of it now and would be even gladder outside. He'd been sucking oxygen for forty minutes, but still the lack of air made his heart hammer as he finished dressing out. Not to mention the stabbing in his guts, the worms, or dysentery, whatever he'd picked up. And the impossibility of getting his gear off, or for that matter back on, if he had to shit again.

Which he was going to have to soon. Freidebacher had eyed him when they fell in for the chalk, asked if he was all right. He'd given the major a hearty grin and a cheery aye, aye. No way he was missing a combat jump, even if his bowels were tearing free and getting ready to drop out.

The four SEALs were finishing their preps between the gunners' stations, the forty-millimeter forward and the howitzer farther aft. Obie's arms felt like lead. His lips and face were frozen beef. His back felt close to breaking, and his gut . . . Don't think about that, Teddy. Not till you're on the ground.

No, it didn't get much better than this.

He eyed his watch, getting concerned. They'd been on oxygen longer than usual, since it'd taken longer than scheduled to get to altitude. SEALs prebreathed for high-altitude jumps, to purge nitrogen. If they didn't, the rapid compression as they fell could starve the brain of oxygen. No static lines on HAHO jumps; blacking out meant you cratered. So they breathed pure O_2, connected to an oxygen console. In a few seconds they'd transition to the bottles they breathed from during the long drop. Trouble was, they couldn't take even a single breath of ambient air as they switched, or the nitrogen content of their blood would jump right up again.

None of this was guesswork. It'd been learned the hard way, in death after death.

He illuminated the little square screen on the GPS wrist unit. Course: 274 degrees. They were forty miles south of the Tanagra, paralleling it. In four minutes they'd be over the drop point.

This would be a high-altitude insertion. No need to worry about radar, but they did need to prevent anyone on the ground hearing the unmistakable cracks of five chutes snapping open a couple hundred feet overhead. They'd free-fall for ten thousand feet, then deploy the chutes and go in silent from there.

"Stand by," the copilot said in their ears. The last blue lights went out. They stood crouched and burdened, like cave bears with blackened faces, in complete darkness. He gripped the safety line and watched a dark slot appear a little above eye level.

As the ramp dropped and the cargo door rose the stars glittered, unearthly bright at the edge of space. Teddy took a deep breath, held it, flipped the switch, and disconnected his hose. Sucked warily, and got a click and the hiss of dry gas. He checked the gauge, sucked a deeper breath. Good.

He gave the jumpmaster a thumbs-up and waddled toward the maw where the dropped ramp of the C-130 led off in a single long step into the roaring blackness of a thirty-five-thousand-foot fall. Behind him Donoghe and Cooper and Kowacki dragged their 105 pounds each across the aluminum deck: oxygen masks, packs, drop lines, separate pack with double parafoils, weapons, bipods, ammunition, medical packs, radios, knives. The Spectre's loadmaster pushed a square bulky pallet of Oh Shit gear on casters after them:

machine gun, rations, water, batteries, more medical consumables, everything else they'd need for a mission that might last a week. No Walmarts where they were going. Just empty desert, and skinnies eager to kill them.

Dickinson and Freidebacher and Lenson, all the gold braid had planned Operation King Vulture. The silent, covert insertion. The helo feint miles to the north. A second diversion, *Squall* and *Shamal* getting under way and heading south along the coast. The intel, about where the turnover would take place. A lot of smart folks had put their heads together. But it was up to Teddy Oberg to bring back the trophy head for over the fireplace.

That was fine. That was the SEAL way: self-discipline, not discipline from above. Why they didn't always play so nice. And how they got things done some people said were impossible.

His bowels squirmed. Sweat prickled his forehead. He had to get his pants down, or things were gonna get messy. But the timing . . . it *really* couldn't be worse.

"On my count," the copilot's voice crackled. Usually there was a green "go" light, but teams didn't usually jump from Spectre gunships, either. But there were only four of them this time, and the Spectre could circle to cover them on the way down, should they land somewhere unlucky. Such as, in the middle of an insurgent encampment.

He concentrated, squeezed. . . . Twisting his upper body he searched the faces behind him. Cooper, no problems there. Kowacki, a steady regard back. But Donoghe's eyes were jittering like greasy marbles behind the jump mask. Teddy gripped the web of his shoulder. Bent his helmet to put them together, like spacemen in a Mars movie. "We cool, dude?"

"Way cool, bro."

"Up for this? We can do it without you."

"Fuck, no way, man. Let's bounce."

The copilot's voice echoed. Teddy faced front again and bent slightly. Eyes open. Chin down. . . . "Five," the voice said. "Four. Three. Two. One. Go! Go! Go!"

He couldn't hold it any longer. His sphincter let go.

Screaming inside the helmet, he charged for the square of darkness. Proper exit. Check body position. As the last metal dropped away beneath his feet, as his guts emptied in a liquid stream, he tumbled, locking his knees back, spreading his arms. Batman, falling out of the Gotham sky.

Facing the black and enormous Earth as it sucked him down.

The universe spun, then stabilized as he picked out a bright planet and slipped left and steadied on it. The roaring air buffeted his ears. The agony in his belly ebbed. He didn't fall, he floated. His heart pumped harder, slamming in his ears, but under the mask he was smiling so hard it hurt. The desert shimmered for uncounted miles, burnished to mercury by the starlight, the horizon faintly visible as a blacker threshold where the stars began. Nothing better than a jump. Except a jump followed by a firefight.

There'd be no nights like this in LA. Just chasing dreams other people owned. This was living. If he caught a bullet, or a grenade, like Sumo, it'd been worth it. To hang here, an eye suspended in infinite night.

He just hoped nobody collided with him. He hated being first out, low man, but he was team leader. The stick would be following him, all the way down.

The biggest danger after lack of oxygen was one SEAL tracking through another as they descended, either before or after deploying chutes. That'd happened to two team guys not long before, on a training mission. One had fallen right through another's chute as it was opening. The first man had two thousand feet to think about how hard he was going to hit.

Teddy had told them over and over again in the prebrief: spread out, don't track on each other, open up like the fingers of a hand. "And I'm the fucking thumb, down here. None of this skydiving shit. I don't care if we land a fucking mile apart, as long as we're all walking when we get up off the ground."

The grin beneath the mask held, though. He swallowed, vibrating as if charged with a thousand volts. The old SEAL saying: "Hey, if it don't suck, why would they need us to do it." But this didn't suck, it was great, dropping at 120 miles an hour, terminal velocity, fixed on Jupiter, through a black and silver night into the great swelling pit of Africa. He tilted his body and rotated 360 degrees, catching jagged darknesses that must be the southern mountains. Above him, less presences than hints, specters, other absences, falling swiftly as murderer angels banished from an already forgotten Heaven.

Yeah, he was a fucking poet, fucking Dante or whoever. Get with the mission, Teddy. He checked the glowing screen on his wrist. They needed to come left. He reoriented to put the planet above his floating, buffeted right glove, and fell slanting so he made a hundred feet forward for every thousand feet they dropped. The altimeter flickered. They'd redesigned them with numbers, not needles. In hypoxia you couldn't read a dial, but numbers still penetrated. But those were blurring too. He had oxygen, what was wrong? He slammed his wrist against his faceplate and squinted. Better.

Thirty thousand. Every seven seconds, another thousand less. His sodden trou and underarmor were icy cold. Ignoring it, he made one more rotation. The air was thicker. Warmer. It slashed and cut, its voice a growl now where it had been shrill.

When he looked up the horizon was rising around them like a hydraulically powered black cylinder. Now he gazed up at the stars from the bottom of a well. The tornado buffeted him but he rode it, arms outstretched as he plummeted. Twenty-six thousand.

Five hundred.

Twenty-five. He slammed his hand across his chest and grabbed the toggle, sensing the others above, behind, willing them and the cargo not to be in the wrong place when he popped. Got his fist tight, and yanked.

The opening shock on the parafoils was much softer than with the T-10s he'd first trained on. He glanced up; the black squared-off arch arced reassuringly.

A flash of motion against the stars. Cooper, if he was in the right place. Teddy examined the foil again, steering experimentally right, then left, making sure he had the stable sink regime that meant all the cells were inflated. It responded, so he concentrated on the GPS, lining himself up on the "roadway." With a lift-to-drag ratio of three to one, from this altitude they had a covert run in to the LZ of almost fifteen miles. He wasn't going to stretch it that far—the meteorology wasn't favorable for the next couple of days—but they'd be able to fly in to less than five miles from the meet point.

The next few minutes glided as smoothly past as the foils whispered through the air, trailing edges faintly luffing. He had a good sink rate. They were on course. Opening at twenty-five thousand, at this rate they'd have almost twenty-five minutes in the air.

After a while he looked around. This time he caught two shadows, one to the left and another almost directly above and a little behind him, enough so he could glimpse it around his own canopy. He checked glide path and the sink rate again, obsessing a little, but you didn't want to land short. Or go long, either.

He took another little vacation in his head. Not exactly nodding off. Still monitoring the situation. But enjoying the view. Mile after mile of shining desert. Mountains, slowly rising to meet them below his dangling boots.

Some time later he checked again, then focused on the ground, matching his approach course with what the surface wind had been briefed at. But the wind was never what they told you it would be, and he slipped right, slipped a little more, trying to sense it through the risers without being able to feel or see it. The ground rushed up, closer every moment, but it was just a confused jumble of shadow and starlight, much rougher than he'd expected given the long study of the overhead imagery.

Then it was on him. Prepare to land . . . boots together, knees together and slightly bent, elbows tight to flanks, chin down. In the last seconds he scanned the ground to either side of what he'd picked out as his landing point, for movement or any hint of light.

The rock came up at the last minute, hidden by some trick of starlight and shadow that made it suddenly jump into existence only two or three seconds before he slammed full length into it. He spilled air, trying to pull up. It reduced his forward speed but he couldn't avoid the darkness that expanded to fill his mask.

He hit hard, stamping his whole body backed by the load he carried into the rock face at thirty feet a second. Stunned, he still registered his faceplate cracking, something snapping in his upper chest, things breaking all over his body. He tried to grab the rock but his fingers slipped off. He stuck there for a moment, molded to stone, before the chute refilled and yanked him off, smashing him into another stone face, then dragging him along the ground before he fought through the stun and got his fingers hooked in the release assembly. Then he was prone, panting. Plastic shards fell from his face mask. The pain arrived, from shins and kneecaps, ribs and face.

When he could breathe again and took stock he got back various bruises and scrapes, a hell of a lump on his shin, but apparently nothing serious broken. Unbelievable, hard as he'd hit. Apparently helmet, faceplate, and gear had taken most of the impact.

He got to his knees and starting fighting the harness off. A rustle and scrape told him someone else had come down, but he was too busy to look. Working silently as possible, he shucked goggles and mask and bottle. In sixty seconds he had his pants down and was scrubbing them out with handfuls of sand. He pulled his skivvies off, scooped a hole and buried them.

With belt buckled again he breathed easier. Sand grated his crotch, but he could live with that. He pulled his rifle from its padded case and swept a 360. Why did his left arm feel weak? A luffing of nylon grew in the sky; ended in a scuffing thud. A third SEAL safe on the ground.

"Obie. Obie!"

"Over here, Whacker. Who's that over there?"

A shifting shape, face black as the darkness. "Coop. See your buddy? Where's Donoghe?"

"Cheeks. Cheeks," Teddy called, keeping it low. No answer. "Fuck, anybody see him?"

"He was above me when we exited."

They'd come down on a sloping hillside bare of rocks, except for the one he'd managed to locate with his nose. They oriented with his GPS and their compasses, formed a search line, and began sweeping back along the line of descent. After a hundred yards Cooper spotted the luminescent tape on the cargo pod. This was excellent, but Teddy was getting worried. Granted nothing went as planned, but you didn't start by losing a team member, even a dickhead newbie. In fact, you were supposed to take special care of first-timers. "Cheeks," he yelled softly. "Donoghe! Where the fuck are you?"

They froze as hollow metal hit rock some hundreds of feet away. It sounded like an aluminum tent pole, a distinct *bong* that floated on the wind like a bell. "The fuck was that," Kowacki muttered.

"Might be him."

"Might not be, either."

"D'you bury your shit?"

"When've I had time? We just fucking got here."

"I want this landing site sterile. *Sterile*. Don't say it."

"I wasn't gonna say anything."

"You stay with the pod, Whacker. Coop, go downwind, I'll come upwind."

"Man, somebody shit his drawers. You smell that?"

"Goats," Teddy said. He cleared his throat softly, hooked to the right, and came around downhill on where he thought the sound had come from.

A kneeling shadow spaded industriously in the sand. Obie came up behind it and hissed, "That you, makin' all the fuckin' noise? Sounds like you're putting up a fucking carnival tent."

"Why you all in a knot? There's nobody out here." Donoghe

smoothed the soil over where he'd buried his chute and got to his feet. "Everybody make it?"

Teddy told him yes, the cargo pod too. They circled back cautiously, dragged the pod to the base of Teddy's rock, and buried it. Then all the other chutes. This took about half an hour, with two guys digging, the other two on security. Teddy felt something grating in his chest while he dug. His left arm felt weak. Fuck, had he broken his collarbone?

When they had the site sanitized he took another GPS fix, to be super sure. They passed a bottle of water around, drinking all they could hold before they left the cache. He checked his watch. Time to get going. He set a rally point and thought about how to move. He decided against a bounding overwatch, what they'd normally use to cross relatively flat terrain, because of the danger of getting separated. They'd move in a compact wedge, together, trusting to speed and darkness for concealment.

He rose to a combat crouch, weapon at low port, and signaled them out. The others oriented and moved after him, the only sound the crunch of boots in sand, the occasional click of a rock. From now on, no one would speak. They'd use hand signals or whispers.

The mission was to see without being seen, kill without being killed. They had to use every minute before dawn to reach their position, do a hasty search, then a more detailed one. And if it seemed suitable, dig in.

Trouble was, Al-Maahdi or his men had picked a meet site that presented almost no possibility of an overlook. Even on the map, it looked bare; satellite imagery—they hadn't dared send anything as noisy as a Pioneer in—had backed that up.

Plodding along, he reviewed the terrain, wondering how he was expected to get off a shot. They had a hide site picked out, but only inspection would tell if it was tenable.

Some minutes on, his stomach spasmed again. He held up a fist and squatted. So did Kowacki. The wind was rising. That was all they needed, a dust storm. On the other hand, he could pick up the pace. That'd leave them more time to prep the hide.

He rubbed his face with his free glove, jaw clenched. His belly felt like soft pieces were tearing out. Whatever the medic had slipped him, it wasn't doing the job. He thought again about the little blue pills in his kit every SEAL carried on mission. Then decided to hold off. If he had what he suspected, he didn't want to put his gut worms on speed.

Over a slight rise, down a slope; then the ground rose again. They saw only more desert. This was good, but the lack of cover worried him. If the sun came up before the hide was ready, they'd stand out like burning bushes.

An hour and a half later they came off the last rise and down into the gentle saddle just north of their goal. He tripped and fell as the ground gave way; a canal, or ditch, concealed by drifted sand. The desert was a lighter green now in the NVGs, which meant they didn't have long before light, so he picked up the pace, thighs grating with sand. Regular protrusions poked up as they walked along. At first he thought, *Shit, mines*, but finally recognized ancient stumps. He kept taking fixes and at last picked it up ahead: low walls like broken teeth.

They'd discovered the ruined village on the overhead imagery. Then Henrickson had located it on an Italian map dated 1924. It lay north of the saddle, where there'd once been a road. No trace of one now. Just sloping desert rising to the foothills, and to the east to a flat-topped *djebel*, a lone hill. The meet site was a kilometer south, at what'd been a well or watering hole.

He signaled Kowacki and Cooper to hold as a fire element and pointed at Donoghe. *Follow me*. They jogged forward twenty meters apart, and dropped when they reached the first wall. Lower than it'd looked in the NVGs, barely two feet of dumped stone. He waited ten minutes, then slowly raised his head and began observing, in overlapping fifty-meter strips. He cupped his ears and listened. Ten meters away Donoghe was looking and listening too.

When they agreed it was clear he signaled Donoghe *Stay put* and low-crawled forward, cradling his rifle, belly dragging over sand and pebbles. As he passed the corner of a wrecked foundation something slithered out, hissing angrily. He froze and counted to sixty, staring at the sand close to his eyes. Distorted and blurred by the night vision, furrowed by the wind, it reminded him of the scallopings of the sea bottom near a surf line. When nothing else happened he altered his course a little, giving whatever it was a wide berth, and crawled on.

Into the center of what once must have been a thriving little hamlet. Sand lay in smooth patches between foundations. An iron pipe stuck up at an angle. Rocks grated and shifted under his weight. He slithered to the highest point and surveyed again, a slow 180. Nothing. He signaled Donoghe forward, watching as his buddy passed the hand signal back, bringing the other two into the ruins.

Fifty meters on he came to the outliers of the village and lay prone for a long time looking over what lay beyond. The dust obscured vision past seventy or eighty yards, but out to there was flat desert furrowed by the gullies he'd fallen into during the approach. Once this land had been irrigated. Now it was moonscape. Fine sand whipped his face. He hoped this wind died down before he had to shoot. He fumbled out his GPS, fumbled up his goggles, concealing the glowing screen against his chest. They were a klick and a half northwest of the meeting point. He didn't like locating the hide in these ruins, the first place an enemy patrol would look. But in the absence of any other cover, it was the best he could do.

A pebble rattled. Donoghe. He twisted and signaled him up.

The newbie's harsh breathing rustled in his ear. Teddy pointed down and covered his eyes. Muttered, "Hide site."

"Right here?"

"In the corner. Start digging. But keep it fucking quiet, hear?"

The folding shovels had plastic-coated blades, to keep the ring of metal on stone from carrying. Still, he winced as Donoghe sliced into the pile. "Belay that, fuck that, Cheeks. Just use your hands, till you're down past the rocks."

A scrape, a rattle. Kowacki slid on his belly like a snake over the foundation and down into the lee. Teddy left Cooper in overwatch as the rest set to work. This had to be good. By the time the other side sent its patrols out, they had to be invisible. And the stars were fading.

Still, they were in position, and even early. Today, tonight, then another morning. A low murmur from fifteen yards away told him Cooper had the satcom up and was transmitting their "on station" report. He farted painfully. He found the tube of his camel and allowed himself two slow sips. Then took out his camo compact and used the baby wipes tucked inside to sponge off the greasy blackface.

He began again, glancing from the shallow cups of paint to the sand and rock around him. A light tan base coat. A darker stripe to disrupt and conceal features the eye would otherwise pick up. Lightening areas that usually formed shadows; darkening nose, forehead, chin, what tended to shine. He scooped up sand and patted it there and there. He cupped the mirror and checked the result.

He crawled to Donoghe and grabbed the shovel. They needed to go deep, and be totally concealed.

The sky began to pale an ominous dusty tan.

The man all the world now calls Al-Maahdi stands in his cave cradling the massive stone embedded in his jaw. He can't open his mouth anymore. Only sip goat's milk and a little water. He mutters thickly, "No. I don't want to take them."

Round him in the cave squat the four on whom he's depended during the uprising. The jihad that went so well at first, then so badly. But for every fighter killed two more stepped forward. A wonder, a sign his path is blessed. He rubs his lower face and walks toward light and then back into darkness, where he sits at the desk. It's all, aside from his rifle and the drab clothes and scuffed boots he wears, the headcloth he wraps as the nomads do, that he owns. Though he's taken to wearing a green one, rather than the Waleeli black.

He closes his eyes, and God whispers in the pain and

darkness. He says he is His messenger, His chosen one. But is the Voice real? Is it truly Him?

Juulheed stirs. His counselor and friend, turned in strife-filled months from wayward madman to tempered fighter. He wears a headwrap as a sling; he was wounded by American counter battery fire on a night raid, when they fired rockets against the airfield. Ghedi smiles. "Yes, speak, go on. Do you find fault with me too?"

"No, my friend. I do as you order. Take the hostages or not, it's all the same to me. I only think, we should not meet the Americans where we say we will."

"Then *how* will we meet them?" Hasheer says angrily, rolling over to face the older deputy. Juulheed eyes him like a mastiff facing an obstreperous kitten. "Are you afraid? It will be perfectly safe. They've given their word. Backed by Olowe."

Fiammetta grunts, "You seem close to Olowe. Who picked it out, this place?"

"He did," Hasheer says, nodding toward Ghedi and arguing in the stubborn way Ghedi loves in him. "You can set up machine guns on the hills, in case they attack with helicopters. You can get there in a technical. We can march, but the prisoners—some can't even walk."

Ghedi paces, locking his hands behind him to keep them from his mouth. He loves his young men, all of them. "What about the Lightning?"

The aircraft that flies in the dark, destroying everything that moves. During the battle for the city it came every night. The only defense was to move always behind walls and inside buildings, and never to gather in groups under the open sky. Hasheer takes a deep breath to reply.

"You're right, Honored One," says a new voice, and they all look deeper in the cave. "You give up your power over the Westerners when you give up your hostages."

The Arab perches on a wobbly folding stool of planed wood he brought with him. Yousef's less chubby now after weeks in the field, face darker, beard ragged and much longer than when he first came among them. He no longer wears braided leather but the boots of a dead enemy. His white teeth have yellowed, and he's proven himself a fierce, resourceful fighter with rifle and grenade.

But Ghedi knows this man whispers against him, saying he's not the Maahdi, that such talk is idolatry. He persuaded them to attack those who gave aid, knowing the result would be starvation and full-scale war. He too has followers among the Waleeli. Soon there will have to be a choice, and only one faction can win.

This doesn't bother him. If he dies, his jaw won't wake him with such agony that only pride keeps him from howling like a dog smashed by a truck. He murmurs, "What would your master the Prince have me do?"

Yousef shrugs. "Kill Americans; that's our jihad. If enough hands throw enough stones, we can topple the largest pillar. Then we will restore the Great Caliphate, as the Hadiths promise. This I believe."

"I too," says Ghedi, but he makes his tone ironic, and searches the faces in the gloom.

What should he do? The question gnaws at him like a desert rat. He's pulled his men back from the city. To face the Americans means losing them in prohibitive numbers. On the other hand, he still holds the countryside, south, west, and in a great half moon around the Governing Council territory. On the third hand, his people are starving. God has not sent rain. The drought's iron, unshakable, a doom from Heaven. Yousef promised food, but little has arrived, only a trickle of trucks from Sudan. Barely enough to feed his fighters, let alone their families.

He rubs his face, keeping his fingers from his jaw. Things were better before. Everyone fed, with the Waleeli secretly controlling distribution. The Americans had tried to disarm and trick him. Sent the Muslim woman to tempt him. But he'd attacked instead. It's Yousef's doing, that subtle perfumed voice in his ear.

But Yousef is his comrade in jihad . . . and jihad's the will of God.

Yet it's destroying the very people he's fought to save.

It's so confusing sometimes he finds it hard to breathe. He must pray more fiercely.

What he does know is that his friends and comrades will stand with him. If he's wrong they'll die beside him. He reaches to fondle hair, knead shoulders, grasp their hands. Hasheer stands back, gaze troubled. Ghedi grabs him and pulls him close, smelling an elusive scent on his clothes. Cigar tobacco? But he never smoked.

"The whiteface, Olowe, wants you to make peace," his friend murmurs into his ear, clinging in the embrace, so the others might think they are kissing.

"How does that benefit him?"

"If you return the hostages, the Americans will forgive. Why not? It's no sin to stop fighting. In a year or two, when the rains come, they'll leave. You've shattered the clans, destroyed the democrats. When the foreigners go, it'll be you against the Council."

Ghedi isn't sure the rains will ever come again. Has God cursed them? Is it not God who speaks to him, but some desert demon? But no demon would ask him to fight in God's name. And why does the boy say "you" instead of "we"?

But he voices none of this. Then those thoughts too flee, eclipsed as an idea occurs. A way out. Could it work? He resolves to think it out, alone with God, and maybe his sister. He's never admitted this to his men, but he talks things over with her.

"Yes?" Hasheer prompts, still embracing him. That tobacco smell again.

"We'll see," he grunts. He rumples his hair, then pushes him away. The young man grins, gazing at him.

Deep in the cave, Zeynaab's buttered fingers spin a flat thin square of dough on the smoking griddle. The heat scorches her face; the spitting oil sputters, stinging as she drizzles it on the bread the men will eat when they're done talking. She glances now and then at them in the flickering dim, and never says anything at all.

* * *

Daylight came slowly, ebbing from the ground into the dusty sky. Everything was hazy, like a morning mist in California, but it was dust. Metallic-tasting, fouling Teddy's throat and itching in his nose. He rotated his head in tiny increments, only when the wind gusted. He sucked a grudging sip from the tube. He judged the wind as fifteen, twenty miles an hour, from the southeast. Each gust whipped up minute grains from the shattered stonework in which he lay buried. Only half his face showed. Their camouflage capes and uniforms blended with weathered stone, powdery sand. He knew exactly where Kowacki and Cooper were, but even so could barely make them out under the piled stones. They lay motionless, curled around their weapons, so no straight line showed to distant binoculars. They'd lie like that through the entire day.

His own weapon lay under his right arm on pebbles and shattered rock. The rocks shone in a muted rainbow. Pale crimson. Violet. Quartz white. Among them as light came, he noticed a shard of porcelain, blue and white. A gust blew sand from it, revealing the eroded ghost of a leaping rabbit, hind legs gone forever.

He drew the rifle to his face, a millimeter at a time, ignoring the grating pain from what he was pretty sure now was a cracked collarbone. Lay motionless for a long while, scrutinizing the ninety degrees of sand, rock, and downward-sloping ground in front of him, stretching out to what he'd tentatively decided would be his firing position: a depression he could reach via one of the sand-choked canals.

He turned his attention to the rifle. It was no longer black, as when "Doctor Dick" Skilley had checked him out on it, but spray-painted in wavering splotches of earth and lavender; handguard, buttstock, barrel, suppressor, magazine. Even the heavy belled scope and its flip-up covers were painted. He hooked his thumbnail over them and flicked up, then migrated it to his eye. Rotated a switch, and peered.

He saw at once that the reticle was skewed, the image blurry. When he focused it didn't improve. The laser-ranging diode blinked on when he pressed the button, but pointed at a rock a stone's throw from the hide site, it read 450 meters, then 3600. The image stabilization didn't work either. He shook it. The tinkle told him all he needed to know.

Just. Fucking. *Great.* He took a slow breath, closing his eyes. Let it out between his teeth.

The scope was junk. He'd totaled it, slamming into that rock when he landed.

Okay, he had to fix this. But how? Kowacki had a sniper rifle too, but it wouldn't stabilize the extra-long, extra-heavy rounds Skilley'd given him. They had standard ammo, but it wasn't accurate enough at extreme range for the shot he'd planned.

He'd have to get closer. A lot closer, across terrain hard as shit to blend into.

He started to sweat, seeing the mission circle the toilet bowl. He wiped his face, then stopped; didn't want to smear his camo. Maybe he could swap scopes, put Kowacki's glass on his rifle? But the zero would be off. Without several sighting shots that wouldn't work either.

He lay motionless, ignoring the sand fleas biting, rocks knifing into his chest, bruised knees, the chafing burn in his crotch.

After all, he had all day to think about it.

34

Dead right there, Teddy thought.

Oh, yeah. Easy.

As dawn came again, their second in the ruins, he lay half covered with rocks, curled into the corner of the foundation. He was concealed by a camo cape that matched the sand around him. It *was* the sand around him, sticking to a special adhesive layer. He was indistinguishable from the jumble of pebbles and occasional tuft of dead grass. He was the Invisible Man.

He sure as fuck didn't feel like it, though. He felt like a

chancre on a bridegroom's dick. As that asshole submariner he'd done the Korean mission with would have said.

They'd lain up in the abandoned village all the day before, with the total motionlessness only long training made possible. Only once, when the wind rose and gusted haze up from the desert floor so thick they couldn't see thirty yards, had he half risen, stretched agonizingly cramped muscles, and sipped from his gradually deflating camelback.

During the night just past he'd done a leader's recon. He'd left his rifle, taking only knife and night vision goggles and the little binoculars from his cargo pocket. He'd moved by inches, scouting every yard ahead through the NVGs, in case this was all a setup and some canny skinny had planted something nasty. Freidebacher had told them the intel was solid, from a no-shit internal source, but he'd been burned often enough to take nothing Intel said at face value. It took three hours to crawl eight hundred yards. By the end of that time he could feel the sharp end of his fractured collarbone chewing through the muscles of his chest.

He'd spent an hour at the firing point, glassing every outcrop and bush right up to the well, a low tumble of rocks with what looked like Abraham's hut collapsed some distance away. No sign of water, no bushes or trees, though again there were stumps, the long-dead orchards they'd walked through the night before. But that was good. A clear field of fire. He averaged what the radian lines and his GPS were telling him and came up with 850 yards.

A very long shot with Cooper's M24—a bolt-action Remington, a modified varmint rifle—but doable if he held for the chest rather than the head. That made for less than a certain kill, but a solid hit with a 180-grain open-point boat-tail would ruin anybody's day without a skilled trauma team on hand. And he didn't see any out here.

Usually you avoided torso shots on a high-value target. But no better plan suggested itself. He'd lain for another half hour, listening to the wind. Then crawled back, reaching the hide just before dawn. He'd gestured, and they'd stirred and crept in. He went over the final things, actions on contact, their E&E plan.

He'd drunk a little water, munched a protein bar, then dozed under his cape. His stomach rumbled but hunger seemed to dull the pains. Keeping the worms quiet? Whatever worked.

Not long after dawn pebbles grated close by. He opened his eyes and found himself staring at a sandal.

Teddy was impressed. The guy had come up out of the haze without a sound. Tall, black as licorice, with a peanut-shaped head in a black, sloppy turban-wrap. He wore a long shirtlike robe, cotton pants, tire-tread sandals. A cloth magazine bag was draped over one shoulder, a canteen over the other.

Holding a shorty Kalash, he stood atop a pile of rubble, looking around. The deliberation with which he scanned told Teddy he was a hunter. Behind him two more shapes writhed in the haze, trotting left and right while their boss watched directly ahead. One was headed for Kowacki's hide.

Teddy hadn't checked his paint yet, had been planning to when there was more light. He hoped the shine of his skin didn't give him away. A millimeter at a time, he moved his hand up to shield it. He squeezed his eyelids tight, pulled the rifle in a little, and slipped the safety off.

Rocks crunched as the flankers pelted past. The tall one moved at last, in a slow zigzag down what had once been the main street of this abandoned hamlet. He went on through the ruins and Teddy relaxed.

Then he came back. Striding across the sand, shirttail flapping in the wind, he crossed their front with long easy strides. He looked downhill, away from Teddy's hide, toward the meet site by the well.

Then he stopped, and faced them. Faced the ruins, cocked his head, and shaded his eyes.

Teddy stopped breathing. The guy was looking at him. Right into his eyes, from fifty yards away. He didn't look back. It sounded mystical, but every sniper knew some targets could sense another's gaze. He lowered his eyes, focusing on the porcelain fragment. The rabbit's ears quivered in the heat rising off the ground.

Seconds were born, lived, drew long retirements, then died at last of old age.

The tall man stepped forward, frowning. Oberg's grip tightened on the rifle.

A dust devil passed between them, nodding this way and that as it whirled across the ground. The man stepped back, making a hand gesture. It swayed toward him, and he shrank away. Then it changed its mind, and spun off across the flat land in its unsettling simulacrum of purposeful life.

The Ashaari called to his buddies. They answered with yips and wails, some sort of code. Like yodeling. He gazed about for another moment, then burst into a run. Sandals flipping up puffs of dust, he sped off in an awkward, lanky lope, as if Abe Lincoln had taken up jogging.

Teddy allowed himself a very slow intake of breath, but didn't move, not even his pupils. He held still for a full hour, until full day had come and the sun burned across the open desert, throwing long shadows at them from the motionless rocks.

The technical rattles and shakes. It bounces across the ragged land, far from any road. Three other vehicles speed along with it, raising skeins of dust that mingle with the haze.

Ghedi fingers the smooth shape in his pocket, examining the sky. Two other fighters watch it too, clinging to the mount of the machine gun as the pickup sways. At last, satisfied there's little risk, he takes out the cell phone, slips the cover off, and inserts the battery.

As soon as he flips it closed, he holds it out the glassless window. Another truck swerves in, a gaunt boy stretching out one hand, the other wrestling the wheel. The two vehicles lurch and collide, jolting everyone. As they separate he tosses the cell into the other vehicle. It instantly turns sharply, accelerating toward the horizon.

"It's clear," he tells Hasheer, beside him. Then looks

behind him, to meet his sister's troubled gaze. He's told her this is men's work, but she insisted there are women among the hostages. She needs to come too. No point arguing, he's learned that.

He grips the side of the door and stands, braced against the hot breath of the wind. His whole face and throat throb. It's getting hard to swallow, or see. Or even breathe. Again uncertainty gnaws. He glances back at the truck grinding after him, rocking side to side on worn-out springs. Ten women, four men. He can turn them over. Give the money to Yousef for the new weapons, missiles to strike back at the fire from the sky.

But what then? Until they arrive it'll be dangerous to move, by day or night. The nomads have known about the subterranean oasis for centuries. From Ottoman times, Italian times, British, it's been a bolt-hole. But that was before eyes that see even in the darkest night. Sooner or later, the Americans will discover it. He has to be gone before then.

But where? The Arab expects him to fight it out here. So, no sanctuary in Afghanistan or Sudan. Djibouti's controlled by the French. Ethiopia's unlikely to offer refuge. He clings as the jolting ignites agony in his head and neck. His swollen face feels as if it's been poured solid with molten lava. All his back teeth have fallen out. He feels light-headed. Hasn't eaten solid food for weeks. Only a little goat's milk, a little of the soft yogurt his sister coaxes him to swallow.

Can his idea save them? He's fought for an Ashaara free of the unending warfare of the clans and the interference of the foreigners. One nation, united under God.

He stares into the burning sun. Are You there? Do You truly write what we do in our lives? You have to be real. If Al-Maahdi goes down to failure, perhaps this Prince will triumph. Centuries may pass, but the people will be victorious.

All will be as God wills. He tries to draw comfort from this. But today it feels more like a sentence, a grim condemnation handed down by a pitiless judge.

A low hill grows ahead. The day's turning hot. Mirages dance over the desert floor between one hill and another, miles off. Memory stirs. Can this be his old village? But where are the orchards, the homes, the eddying canals that laced fertile fields? A chill furrows his spine. What is this wasteland?

"Where are we going, younger brother?"

His deputy points and Ghedi shades his eyes. Yes, perhaps he does remember . . . distantly. . . .

A figure emerges from the wavering, striding with elephantine legs through the mirage. The driver swerves to meet it. They close fast, then brake and skid, pebbles banging into the underpan. The elongated figure suddenly shrinks to become merely grotesquely tall.

Juulheed jogs the last few yards to them, breathing harder than usual, but that's all. His Kalash is slung across his back. He leans into the truck and they wrap their arms around each other.

"Beloved brother. They're not here yet?"

"I came early. I don't like where you arranged to meet."

"We can see in all directions," Hasheer says.

"True." Juulheed points. "But I don't like those ruins. Or that outcrop, on the hill to the west. Either could harbor a sniper."

"They didn't know we'd meet here. And that's too far to shoot. But, my friend"—Ghedi slaps his shoulder, raising dust—"I am so fortunate, to have two I trust as I can my own blood. Tell me what to do."

"That hill." The deputy nods. "The rounded one. We can see the road from there. Anyone approaching has to come uphill at us."

"That would put the saddle between us and retreat," Hasheer points out. Ghedi considers. Looking from one to the other: the lean, ascetic disciple he'd once thought crazy; the young, affectionate one he once suspected as a northerner. He picks up binoculars and examines hill, crag, village.

"We'll do as Juulheed suggests," he decides, kneeing the driver. "Top of that hill." The engine snarls, and the truck grates into motion once more.

* * *

Half a mile away, flat in the ditch with the sand blowing over him and Cooper, behind him, as spotter-observer, Teddy rolled the scope away from his eye and cursed.

It'd been the TI. "Target of interest" was the antiseptic way the operations order referred to the man they were here to shoot. Just as "standard operating procedure" translated into killing prisoners captured on a raid. The asshole they wanted, with the swollen jaw. In dark glasses and a green headwrap instead of a black one, but him. Too far for a shot, and the mirage was a jumbled boil, but for one millisecond he'd seen clearly enough through the 10–40 Leupold to be certain.

Then the truck had rolled out to the left, not toward them, and the other vehicles followed. But not toward the well. Instead, trailing dust, they were climbing the rise. He tracked them through the scope. It was Cooper's rifle, not his. His super scope on his super fucking useless rifle was still busted; it hadn't healed itself. He didn't expect it would. "Range now?"

"Fifteen hundred yards. Seventeen. Two thousand. Two thousand five hundred."

The truck was still climbing. He deshouldered the rifle in disgust. "Fa-a-u-ck. Where are these bitchass motherfuckers headed?"

"Somebody tipped 'em off," Cooper muttered below him. Whacker was back at the hide, transmitting the SPOTREP with Cheeks.

"You didn't laze 'em, did you?"

"Fuck no. Those were reticle ranges."

Did the turn away mean the enemy was aware of the team's presence? Or just a last-minute change of plan? He didn't think they'd given themselves away. The patrol at dawn, he'd have sworn it hadn't made them. If so, the tall guy in charge had been remarkably cool about it. Teddy had watched him closely, and seen no sign of surprise. They'd low-crawled to the final firing position with infinite care, keeping their faces in the sand, using the ditches for the approach.

He inspected Cooper critically. The spotting scope was netted and hooded, garnished with dried grass. They had black plastic grates over every piece of optical gear, so no flash could give them away. They had contingency plans, escape and evasion plans. But when the target decided to go somewhere else, you couldn't plan for that. You just had to roll with it.

"They're turning again . . . no . . . dust plume's stopped. They're parking up there."

Teddy squinted through the blowing dust. The hill rose maybe thirty meters above the saddle. A pimple, in terms of relief, but in terms of dominating the approach, it was formidable. They'd have to cross over a mile of upward slope, with only a few rocks and bunches of dead grass for cover. The natural folds of the land might be enough to conceal a prone sniper perfectly camouflaged, but he hadn't been over that terrain. Like a climber ascending a sheer face, he'd have to find his footholds in the tiniest cracks and faults, as he came to them.

And if he couldn't . . . but looking at the hilltop, and the saddle below, one thing was clear as the morning sun. Any possible shot would be at a much longer range than he'd expected. So long, in fact, considering the wind conditions, he wouldn't be able to make it with the bolt-action. The bullet would get there, but it just wouldn't be accurate at that range. As it shed velocity the gusts would grab it, and wrestle it farther off target with each hundred yards it traveled.

He needed a bullet that would buck the wind.

Skilley's wonder bullet. And since Cooper's rifle couldn't stabilize that heavier bullet—the twist rate was too slow—he could shoot it only from Skilley's wonder gun.

But he still had no scope. Cooper's Leupold was in working order, but you couldn't jerk a scope off one rifle and slap it on another and expect to hit anything.

He frowned, shaking his head so slightly no observer would have seen it from twenty yards away.

He rolled the scope to his eye again and raised his head, very slowly. The sun was behind him; there'd be no warning flash off the lenses. How to do this? His solution wavered, like a distant target in the heat-boil. No matter what, he had to get closer. A lot closer.

But very carefully. Sandals or no, that patrol leader had looked like a dangerous opponent. One who used his eyes and his brain, who didn't just spray and pray like most of the insurgents.

He looked down at Cooper. The spotter/observer raised his eyebrows, cocking his head toward the hill. Teddy shook his very slightly. He glanced back toward the hide site; signaled *keep low.*

Cooper began backing around. Teddy slid to the bottom of the ditch. Then followed, on his belly, sweating in the close heat, dragging himself back yard by yard.

Gráinne huddled in the rattling bed of the lorry. Her stinking pajamalike trousers were torn in back, so she had to keep her face to any male or risk a beating. The light hurt her eyes. The wind burned through the crusts. She could see only a little, peering painfully, and only close up. It felt like things were uncoiling inside her eyeballs.

But they were going to be released. Traded. Redeemed. Or so someone had told the hostages that morning. Too late for one older woman, an Oxfam volunteer, who'd been sinking for days. They'd buried her yesterday, two hours after she died, just before nightfall. An Ashaari custom, apparently. Her husband sat on the other side of the truck, clutching all she'd left when she died: her purse, a little address book, her passport. He looked very old and totally bereft.

Her hand rose to clasp the claddagh before she remembered it was gone. After her conversion, one of the women had snatched it off her neck. A pagan symbol didn't belong on a Muslim woman.

After her mumbled conversion at the ravine they'd taken her back to the caves, but not the one she'd been in. The women had brought bowl and rag, and begun to bathe her eyes. She'd thought that was good, until she'd caught a whiff. Then the pain came, so incredible she'd fought and kicked as they held her arms and legs. It was salt, and camel urine, and who knew what else. When they returned she'd fought and screamed again until they let her alone. Not about the prayers, though. They'd brought her outside and put her in a line with the other new Muslims, forced them to bow, tried to teach them the routine. She'd been too sick and exhausted to even pretend. Just knelt with her head down until they jerked her up and pushed her back into the shadows.

She loved the darkness now. It didn't hurt. It was friendly and cool. Some spring or lever had snapped inside her. At that ravine, seeing the bodies . . . she wished she believed in something that strongly. Enough to die for.

Science *is* truth, she told herself. This other's rot. And anyway, she had to live. She still held the great secret that would transform the country. Once she passed that on, she could die if she wanted to. Most of all, she just wanted to lie down.

She was in hospital, in a bed, all light and white. There were tubes in her arms and down her nose and up her growler, but she didn't mind. The light came through the window so lovely. Specks of dust, floating with immense beauty. So clean, and she could see. She felt pleasantly languid, like lying on the beach after a long swim in the surf at Youghal, her favorite place on the South Coast. What they called the Irish Riviera.

Then the lorry jolted and the smells of shit and dust rose through gaps in the floor. It braked and the hostages slid and clutched at each other, or just lay, resisting neither the jolting nor the skids. She wanted to brace herself, but didn't have the energy.

Suddenly she wasn't there, or in the hospital bed. She was in Cobh. The bed-and-breakfast they'd stayed in when she and her husband first fell in love, high on a little lane that led up to the cathedral. Waking drowsy in the Victorian four-poster with Limerick crocheted lace coverlets. Knowing just from the smell they were setting out a full table of Irish fry downstairs. Eggs, grilled tomatoes, black pudding. Hot steaming oatmeal with cream. Fresh-baked scones. Great lashings of bacon, and bangers glistening with grease. She got up eagerly, pulled on jumper and slacks, and went down in stocking feet. Slid a sparkling Belleek plate from a stack and reached for a serving spoon.

. . . And came back to men shouting and pulling at her. They were dragging the hostages out, one by one. Some they had to carry. The goateed old man blinked at them, holding his dead wife's purse. They dragged him up and thrust him toward the back, lowering him roughly to the ground.

They came for her. Whatever favor she'd gained from converting was lost on these ladhbs. They handled her even more roughly than they had the old man, and one wasn't above sticking his hand between her arse cheeks for a feel. Good luck to him. She lost her footing on the sandy metal and nearly pitched headfirst, but got a grip on the tosser's sleeve to break her fall. She forced one eye open, gasping, but saw only light and sand.

A hand on her arm; a Kensington toff's accent but gentle. "This way, miss. I'll guide you."

"Thank you."

"The Yanks are here. I see their jeeps coming up the hill."

"Thank Christ," she muttered, then bent over and retched. Not much came up as she stood trembling, the old man's hand warm on her back. He patted her, then cupped a palm under her elbow.

Together, they tottered toward the top of the hill.

A mile away downslope, Teddy and Cooper wriggled in infinitesimal increments along a dry ditch drifted with sand. The ditch crossed the gradient at a diagonal. He figured it must once have brought water down from somewhere beyond the hill. They were crossing their target area's front, moving slowly right to left and gradually closing. It would be a long crawl.

The SEALs had stripped off all their gear except for rifles, knives, pistols, and optics. They also had water, but not enough for a long stay. Everything else was back at the hide. Dried grass stuck out from their boonie covers. Their faces matched the sand. They carried the rifles slung beneath their bodies, muzzles aft, so they wouldn't come up clogged.

Kowacki and Donoghe were crawling too, making for

overwatch positions out to the flanks. If anyone stumbled over the sniper team, or came after them following the shot, they'd provide cover. He didn't think these guys had much countersniper capability, but the other team would still be watching for movement, for glare, dust, the telltale sparkle of glass.

Right now he was worried about a lot of things, but the worst, maybe, was the up angle he'd have to shoot at. Not in terms of the hold correction—that was simple to calculate—but the fact that, looking up from below, he might not be able to see the turnover. And if he couldn't see, he couldn't shoot. The well would have been so much better.

But the well was history. He came to a shallower part of the ditch and raised his head in minute increments, cocked sideways. The gully petered out ahead. There really was zip for cover. The wind blew, gentled, blew. He looked long on the terrain and finally his head sank as slowly as he'd raised it.

The SR-25 had backup sights that flipped down out of the way when the scope was installed. (He'd buried the busted scope back at the hide.) It would be a difficult shot, but iron sights were more accurate than most shooters thought, if you knew how to use them. No magnification, but with them he could use the new rifle, with its faster twist and heavier, long-range bullet.

He still had to get forward at least another two hundred yards. He pointed to the ground and made a patting motion to Cooper: *Stay put—five minutes—then follow me*. Then pushed off with his toes, hugging the rifle, his busted collarbone jabbing, moving with excruciating slowness up over the lip of the shallow depression that until now had shielded him.

In the open, he moved with a deliberation that made his previous progress seem like a sprint. He didn't jostle a single pebble. Nor a blade of the dead grass-clumps he gradually wormed between. He kept his cheek to the sand, head turned sideways to further lower his silhouette as he oozed along a half inch at a time, matching each movement to the wind. Making its rhythm his own. It wouldn't be the same at the top of that hill. It'd be different still where he'd fire from. It was switching, blowing first one way, then another, gusting till streamers blew off the sand humps that dotted the undulating slope up which he inched.

A lizard froze, eyeing him. Its leathery lids flickered. He didn't move. Neither did it. A standoff. He flicked his little finger and it blinked again and vanished. The hilltop above, the battered trucks, seemed close, but weren't. Not in terms of a bullet's flight. It would be a half-mile shot.

A tug on his boot sole. "There's the hostages," his observer muttered, lips pressed to the ground.

He squinted. Distant forms were exiting the far truck, but when they dropped below the lip of the crest he lost sight of them. The lead vehicle was parked on the side of the hill closest, but so far there was no movement from it.

He tilted his watch. The ransom party would arrive at noon. He had to be in position then.

He swerved in his snailing to put a head-sized rock fifty yards upslope between him and the silently waiting white truck. Wondering, meanwhile, how long it would take to swap a suitcase of cash for fourteen heads. Not long, probably, but he couldn't take the shot until it was done. Otherwise, even if he connected, the insurgents could mow down the hostages.

He'd have to hold fire until they were out of the way, yet act before Al-Maahdi climbed back into his vehicle. The window of opportunity could be very narrow. But "mission failure" wasn't a welcome phrase in the spec ops world.

The heat grew intense, focused by the saddle below. The sun cauterized his pupils. His gut cramped and voided. He felt as if he were leaving a trail of slime behind him, like a slug. The sharp ends of broken bone ground and sliced each time he extended his arm. Every muscle in his upper body screamed. If anyone up there had glasses on them, if they shook a branch at the wrong time or sent a rock rolling, they were prime targets. It'd be a long shot for the skinnies too, but at the rate four or five AKs sprayed bullets, they wouldn't make it back to the ditch without getting hit.

He oozed from gully to gully like a torpid snake. No one

could see him. No one could stop him. He was the Invisible Man. He was Death, inching closer to the one whose time left on earth was ticking away.

Teddy Oberg couldn't stop grinning.

Hours later, lying full length on a slope littered with shattered quartzite, he understood. This was as close as he was going to get. Pushing it even a yard farther would be like crawling across a tennis court and expecting to surprise the server. He estimated they were at least eight hundred yards from the crest. From time to time, when the wind was right, he heard voices.

He glanced around, moving only his eyes, and waited for a gust. When it kicked up the dust he scraped a little rampart of rocks and sand and dead sticks together in front of him.

That done, he began working the rifle around. When the barrel got within reach he slipped off the muzzle cap. He grasped the tab of the tan gaffer tape over the ejection port and peeled it off. He slipped a lemon candy out of his pocket, shucked off its silent waxy paper, and slid it into his parched mouth. Then reached down again, and came up with a disposable lighter and a flimsy white plastic MRE spoon.

Holding the lighter down by his thigh, he lit the spoon. The tiny orange flame flickered in the wind. He passed it under the inverted front sight, playing the smoke over it. Then pushed the spoon into the sand.

He pulled the rifle the rest of the way up. Peered. Carbon from the smoky flame had blacked the front sight, eliminating reflections. It was tapered aft to forward, so there wouldn't be any shadows. He just hoped the jump and all the marching and crawling since hadn't knocked the backup sights off kilter too.

Very slowly, he slid the rifle up and along his body until the suppressor poked out through the sticks and straw and pebbles.

"Not very far now," said the driver, listening through headphones to an intraconvoy intercom. He tapped instant coffee out of a packet and crunched it between his teeth. "That's it, between those two hills up there."

Aisha peered through the windshield, dazzled by light and heat. Their convoy had left the embassy just after midnight: two Marine armored cars and four Humvees, one the ambulance version, spearheaded by two Cobras that scouted ahead. The money was in a valise in the backseat. It wasn't State money, and it wasn't Navy. When she'd asked, Peyster had just said he had funds. And when she probed, said he could hide them "within the bureaucracy" as used to purchase information leading to the capture of a senior terrorist.

When she'd asked what bureaucracy, he'd smiled and changed the subject.

They'd crossed the dry bed of the Tanagra, shortcutting the coast road, miles back. Now they were climbing. The foothills rose around them, at first just gentle slope, but growing ahead into the southern mountains. Not tall enough to be snowcapped in these latitudes, but tall enough to impress. The Humvees were cramped, packed with the coveralled medical personnel Ridbout had insisted had to come. Only they didn't act like medical personnel. They talked like marines, and the cases by their boots were shaped more like weapons than medical equipment. She sniffled and blew her nose.

The LAV ahead slowed. Its lights flashed as it turned right. The other herringboned to the left, leaving the Humvees to pass through and onward as the camel track they'd been following grew steeper. She checked the map. It was new, put out by the Defense Mapping Agency, in beautiful full color. The well was clearly marked. She peered closer at faint blue dotted lines identified as abandoned irrigation canals. Abandoned villages too. Apparently this area had once been heavily populated. Was it the desert's steady advance, the repeated droughts, or the Morgue's ruthless "national communism" that had erased what must once have been a fertile, well-watered region?

"There they are," said the driver. Young, with stubbled skin the color of creamy coffee. His name tag read Spayer. "Hold on. Could get rough."

It did. The Humvee jolted and banged over rocky outcrops. After a painful body slam off the door into one of the medical personnel—who carried something hard in his side pocket—she clung to him to avoid getting bruised like an eggplant in a grocery bag. Her own service sidearm was in her purse. Peyster had looked at her funny in the floodlights inside the embassy gate. "A *purse*? And you're wearing—that? Into the desert?"

"They're designed for the desert, Terry. Not coming?"

"Not me, this is your show. You look like . . . I don't know."

"How about this? Better?" She pulled the chador up over her face. Not really an abaya, a georgette caftan in teal her sister had gotten her at Barneys, but kind to someone who, to be blunt, was packing more weight than she liked. She wasn't looking forward to the annual fitness test. "I can wear Level Three protection and nobody'll suspect."

"Right, but—"

"And the best thing is, there's this cute little Arab with them. Believe me, he'll come in his pants when he sees me. They know how to appreciate a good-looking woman."

The marines snapped their shaven heads around. Peyster seemed lost for words. Finally he'd just waved. "Good luck, everybody. Bring 'em back alive."

Once she wouldn't have said such words. She thought about asking for forgiveness. But she didn't.

Something was happening, all right. The longer she stayed in the Mideast, the less pious she felt.

Wasn't that what her mother had been afraid would happen? When she'd told her she wanted to be a cop? "You'll get hardened. Fall away from the faith."

It wasn't that she didn't believe. But the more evil she saw done in God's name, the more horrors justified with twisted religion, the less she felt like invoking Him herself.

Like the sticker she'd seen on a bumper: *I love God. It's His fans I can't stand.*

The Humvee lurched and tilted, climbing. Diesel noise filled the compartment, and of course there was no air-conditioning, unlike the embassy vans, or the massive SUVs the GrayWolf personnel drove. Jolene had asked if she wanted them along, and she'd put her foot down. She had more confidence in the marines. There were disturbing rumors out of the Washington office. A whistle-blower had implicated the security conglomerate in arms dealing and influence peddling. So far just rumor, but she felt more comfortable with real military protecting her.

She shifted, trying to get some air in under the protective vest. She was sweating like a pig. They had to keep the windows closed or dust infiltrated everything, so they were all cooking, sweat glazing their faces. The bad thing was Kevlar degraded to a lower level of protection when wet.

"There they are," said Spayer. She peered through the dirty glass. Four vehicles, parked in a rough circle. Flags flying. Two larger trucks, a white pickup, a strange-looking contraption that might once have been a Land Rover. "Thought the deal was no weapons, Special Agent."

She peered. Both pickup and Rover mounted machine guns. Beside her Erculiano was examining them through binoculars. "Abort?"

"No way. We're committed. Which truck's he in?"

"I'd guess the white one," Spayer said. "He won't be with the hostages, which is probably the one that looks like a stake truck."

She wasn't sure what a "steak truck" was but figured it was the one that looked as if it were built to haul livestock. "Stop a hundred yards out. I'll walk the rest of the way. You're coming with me? Spayer?"

"Absolutely, ma'am."

"Special Agent."

"Hooyah, Special Agent."

The Humvee crested the rise and came out on a hilltop twice as large as a football field. It was littered with rocks and dwarf bushes that looked corkscrewed into the ground. As they approached, men in light-colored clothes dropped flat. Spayer muttered under his breath but kept rolling. "They aiming at us, Ready?"

"Looks like it, Team."

"Fuck. Fuck."

"Just keep driving," Aisha told him, clutching her purse. They must know that if anything happened to them there'd be aircraft, helicopters on call. They'd be hunted down and exterminated.

But maybe fanatics, desperate for martyrdom, wouldn't really care.

She put her hand in her purse, then took it out. The trucks loomed in the windows. The men stood as the Humvee braked. They weren't armed. What she'd thought were rifles were sticks, like Ashaaran goatherds carried.

She got out, knees shaking, and tried to hold her skirts down as the wind whipped them. That would make a great impression, to Marilyn Monroe them. She hobbled toward the trucks, wishing she hadn't told the marine to park so far away. The landscape shimmered, as if they were all submerged in some hot thin fluid heated by gas jets beneath their feet. Far above, specks soared between her and a swollen, white-hot sun that occupied half the sky. So bright and hot it seemed to spear down into her brain. Hawks, buzzards? She blinked up, but the birds kept the sun behind them, circling so slowly and so high they hardly seemed to move at all.

As she neared, a figure detached itself. Green-turbaned, and even thinner than she remembered.

When she saw his face she gasped.

His eye sockets were those of a skull. Most horrible, though, was the enormous swelling that disfigured his whole lower face. He was probing his mouth with two fingers as he came forward. He worried something out, examined it, then tossed it away.

Had that been a *molar*? Three lieutenants ambled forward with him. She knew them now by name. The tallest, the most dangerous, in her book: Juulheed. Hasheer, the Judas, in Western-style jeans and short-sleeved ocher-and-sunflower-striped polo shirt. The Arab, Yousef, fussy in spotless white turban, white robe, and *thobe*. The latter spread his arms as he approached, as if to embrace her, though of course he didn't. She called greetings as they came within speaking distance, keeping her tone demure. She was acutely conscious of Erculiano behind to her left, the marine to her right. Another woman, black-burkaed head to toe, trailed the approaching party. She kept her gaze on the ground save for one glance up. When their eyes locked Aisha caught her breath at the hatred in them, a flaw at the heart of a black diamond.

Al-Maahdi swayed as he walked. They stopped a few feet apart on the hot ground, and she saw he was terribly ill. He trembled, leaning on one of the camel prods.

Then he spoke. She concentrated but couldn't make out a word of the slurred mumble. He opened his hands and held them forward, as if thrusting something out. Then half turned, and waved behind him.

"The money," she told Erculiano, without looking away from the insurgent chief. The plan was to get the hostages clear, then helicopter-land the anvil force behind the Waleeli and their retreat. She looked steadily into Hasheer's eyes. He dropped his gaze.

Erculiano brought the suitcase up. He popped the latch and held it open like a counterfeit-Rolex vendor on Fifth Avenue. The men opposite stared in.

Their chief put his hands in front of him, palms down, fingers spread. He drew them apart, then twisted his open hand. She frowned. The twisting hand was a signal of refusal. He spoke again, but once more, she couldn't make it out.

"I'm sorry, I don't understand," she said in Arabic, more or less to Yousef, but the Arab wasn't smiling anymore. He was frowning at Al-Maahdi.

The sick man took a stride forward, rocked on his heels, then steadied. He put his hand on the lid and closed the case. Made that rejecting motion again, and stepped back. When the Arab spoke he rounded on him, speaking angrily through clenched teeth. Bloody fluid trickled down his beard. He spoke on, to her now. She stood bemused, not understanding. Was he refusing payment? But wasn't that what had drawn him out of his den in the first place?

She looked away, at the sweep of dead horizon all around.

The purple loftings of the mountains, far to the west. The ruins the map had shown, below, to her left. Down there somewhere, the well they'd been supposed to meet at. She shaded her eyes and looked toward it. The men followed her gaze.

"Got the TI." Cooper, behind him on the scope.

"Wind?" Teddy grunted.

"Effective, ten to fifteen right to left."

"Pass that up here."

Very slowly, the spotting scope crept up. Making sure the black plastic grid and sunshield were in place, Teddy aimed it at the hilltop.

He studied the man leaning against the truck. Graving not so much his face—he wouldn't be able to see features through the aperture sight—as his clothes, his height compared to those around him. The turban. The others' were black, but his was green. Once Teddy knew him he defocused, pulling the plane of sharpness back three-quarters of the way to his eye, then halfway, then a quarter.

The mirage eddied and flowed, first this way, then that, a disquieting shimmer of heated atmosphere pushed by the breeze. At three hundred meters it simply seethed in place. But there wasn't just one wind. It was different at a hundred yards than what it was at five or six or eight hundred. The farther the bullet got from the muzzle, the more velocity it shed, the more the wind at that point would affect it.

"I get about a mil and a half right."

Teddy didn't answer, still squinting into the eyepiece as his fingers rested on the focusing knob. The spotter made recommendations, but the shooter was in charge. The spotter kept a roving eye, in case a perimeter guard wandered up the slope, or a circling buzzard read two motionless forms wrong and landed for lunch. It had happened.

After a while the TI got in the truck again and sat back, one leg sticking out. Teddy put the front sight on him and practiced snapping in. He dry-fired ten times, visualizing the way the sight looked when the snap came. Making sure he had the top plane of the front post perfectly centered in the peep. Every few seconds he put a click or two on the windage, this way or that. Picking up the rhythm as the flags straightened or drooped, angled this way or that.

Some time later, Cooper pointed at a dust cloud bleaching the sky. They watched as the vehicles diverted from their course for the well, turning for the trucks atop the hill, the flags flapping in the hot breeze. Saw bobbing heads, but nothing more, as the ransom party dismounted.

He waited, wishing fervently for a better angle. All he could see was the tops of heads, no, just distorted, shimmering blobs that now and then, in the moiling overheated atmosphere, detached from their bodies and floated upward, bobbling like helium balloons. If they stayed there, no way he could take a shot. He'd just draw doom down on them for nothing.

He had to act. SEALs didn't wait around scratching their asses. They made things happen. He pulled his consciousness out of the sights and looked left and right. Cooper must have thought he was doubting his backup, because he muttered, "I got your six."

"I know. But I can't see. We gotta get closer."

Cooper's look said: *You're shitting me*. Teddy wasn't that sure himself, but he knew one thing: he didn't have the shot. And that was what this whole fucking mission was all about.

Reslinging the rifle along his side, he started crawling. Out from behind the last bush, from behind his little concealing rampart.

Out onto open ground.

Hasheer seemed very excited. "He says he doesn't want the money," he said, in Arabic. But Aisha was watching the Saudi. This guy didn't like what he was hearing. He kept trying in his polite way to butt in. But the leader raised a hand and he stopped. Al-Maahdi mumbled a few more words through his bleeding mouth.

"He wants a cease-fire."

"Holy smoke," muttered Erculiano.

Aisha caught her breath. The guy was linked to the Cosmopolite bombing. To the deaths of Buntine and the marines, the rocket attacks on the airfield. In one way or another, the man before her had caused the deaths of thousands, pitted himself against the United Nations and every concept of civilized behavior. He was beyond the pale.

And yet . . . his militias were still in the field. They still occupied great swaths of the hinterland. If he was willing to cooperate, allow the aid workers to go back, they could save many lives.

"Yeah, a cease-fire. Just what they'd want," Spayer murmured.

"What do you mean, Sergeant?"

"So they can regroup. Recruit. Rearm. Come back and hit us again." He glanced at the sun, then down at the valley. "We better get those hostages, ma'am."

Which was absolutely correct. That was the number one priority. "We need the hostages in our custody before we discuss anything else," she told Hasheer. "I have no power to negotiate a cease-fire. But I can relay the word to General Ahearn. If that's what your leader wants. Let's do that now, transfer the hostages, and we'll leave the money issue on the table for a few minutes."

Al-Maahdi waved to the Waleeli by the livestock truck. They began shouting, herding the gaggle of men and women forward with sticks. The hostages milled, then limped forward eagerly.

Gráinne heard a queer moan and was startled to realize it came from her own throat. "They want us over there," the old man told her. His clawlike hand fixed in her shoulder as if a falcon perched there. The other hostages were chattering like an after-theater crowd, the same bright accents, the same sudden animation after a passive trance.

"I'll steer you. Like walking a bicycle. Can you move a little faster?"

"I can't." Her thighs were weeping fluid. It was running down her legs. Like when she'd felt her period trickling down her leg in algebra class. Had to press her binder over her skirt. Thank God, the school uniform had been dark blue skirts and a white blouse.

"Don't worry, I'll be right here. Let them jog ahead if they like."

Prying an eye apart with finger and thumb, she made out the drab angularity of military vehicles framed by a gauntlet of Waleeli in tattered jeans and looted camos and black head-wraps. She nearly wept, then nearly laughed. She stumbled and the old man caught her. "Not far. Keep walking, old girl."

For a moment she thought he was her father, there beside her, and murmured, "Okay, Da." Then, "No, no, I was confused, I thought—"

"That's all right, love. Call me whatever you like. Another hundred steps. The first people are already there. They're giving them something to drink. One foot in front of the other."

She felt sick to her stomach, faint. Maybe she wouldn't make it. Then she thought, I must. Not for herself, but the secret she carried. It would transform the desert. Transform the lives of everyone in the country. Give them food, plenty, the certainty of a tomorrow instead of eternal famine and war.

For that, she could force bare bleeding feet across burning-hot sand. She heard murmuring ahead. It slowly drew closer. She was passing whoever was speaking. There were three voices. One was a woman's. The sounds drew abreast of her, then fell behind. She heard motors idling.

"I see a camera," the old man said. "Chin up, then, let's look good."

She took a deep breath. Lifted her head, and tried to paste on something like a smile.

"Eight hundred and twenty yards," murmured Cooper, behind him. Teddy breathed in slowly, held it, forcing oxygen into his bloodstream. Then breathed out, letting the tension go. Sucked it in, let it go.

He made sure the safety was on. Then pulled the charging

handle back and slipped the long slim cartridge, nose-heavy with its black moly-coated projectile, into the chamber.

Very quietly, he eased the bolt forward and heeled it closed.

He fitted his finger around the trigger. Sensing the wind, how it enveloped and embraced the land. It flickered the flags on the distant hilltop.

"Hold two and a half minutes right. Five clicks right, by the tables."

They were lying full length with no cover, out in the open, trusting to their sand capes and the camo paint to evade any searching eye. Even so he was at the far limit of his marksmanship, his weapon, and his ammunition. He hoped Skilley's bullet would hold the half minute of angle the old sniper had promised. That it wouldn't tumble, way out there, or let the wind seduce it off course. He'd get one chance. Then the shitstorm would descend.

"Got the TI?"

"Got him." The green headwrap definitely helped.

Only seconds now. The hostages, a herd moving left to right, were almost at the Humvee with the red cross on the side. He'd built his position. His natural point of aim. The blackened post of the front sight rose and fell as he breathed to center precisely on the TI's headwrap. Like a green bull's-eye, but smaller than any he'd ever fired on at the SpecWar range at Dam Neck. A beautiful range, overlooking the ocean, the waving sea oats on the dunes giving you wind dope right on the target line. Like the black-and-green flags were now, rippling up there on the hilltop. He watched them. Hesitated. Then reached up and put one more click on the windage dial.

His spotter began the chant behind him, low and rhythmic. "Fire. Fire. Fire."

Teddy breathed in again, very slowly, taking up the slack in the first stage of the trigger as he looked off to the right, at the pebbles and dirt, to relax his eye.

He looked back. The post came down as he exhaled. The TI shifted his feet, as if to turn and walk away.

The trigger broke. A surprise, just like it was supposed to be.

Bang.

As the sights came back down from the recoil, he saw the flags had foreshortened. He cursed, hurriedly shoving the second round into the chamber.

Spinning at three thousand revolutions per second, the bullet leaves at over 3000 feet per second. At a hundred meters out its velocity is 2,800 feet per second; at three hundred, 2,500; at six hundred meters, a fraction under 2,000.

All this can be known, calculated in advance; corrected for barometric pressure, altitude, humidity, temperature, the rotation of the earth. But as it arches outward the wind sways its unwinding trajectory through space and time and moving air first this way, then that. Pushes it half an inch to the left at a hundred yards, two inches at two hundred, twenty-two inches back to the right between two hundred and six hundred.

From moment to moment the wind shifts and folds on itself in a thousand whirls and pleatings, like sheer cloth dropped fluttering through the air. There's no way to predict density, speed, direction ten seconds from now. Each molecule batters the flying metal with its own will, each impact infinitesimal, but numbered in the trillions.

There's no way to predict the wind. Or even to measure it, until the present's passed into history.

By the time the tapered slug reaches the hilltop it's dropped 158 inches below a line drawn level from the muzzle. The wind has drifted it 50 inches off its original course. As it reaches its target, one and a quarter seconds after it was fired, it's still moving three hundred feet per second faster than the speed of sound.

Ghedi watches the sky, the moving specks up there, as his finger works at a loose bicuspid. Crows were messengers of *waaq*, of an evil death. That was the old way, the old belief. Like the *wadaaddo* some said inhabited Juulheed. The way of the clans. Not the new way.

He's offered the foreigners peace. Now God will determine whether they accept. If not, there'll be more war. Whatever He decides, he will accept. The wind cracks and snaps in the flag above him.

He's looking up at it when someone shouts. It's Juulheed. Ghedi shades his eyes. What's he yelling? He's pointing, calling out about hearing something. Another voice joins in. His sister. What's she saying? But if there are helicopters . . . he starts to turn, to see what's wrong.

The bullet comes out of the sun and explodes through his head.

The superheavy metal barely slows as it traverses the eight inches that hold his dreams and terrors, and wipe them away. All memories evaporate in the instant liquefaction of fat and brain tissue. His skull flies apart. His body still stands, shaking with sudden palsy, but he no longer exists.

The bullet drills on, barely slowed by bone and flesh. But that resistance alters its course. It spins off to one side and downward in a spray of blood and fluid that creates for a fraction of a second a halo of pink spray, all around the shattered head it has just emerged from.

"Shot one, TI, good hit. Head," Cooper said from the scope. No longer murmuring. Just a normal everyday business voice. "But he's still standing. Refire, same dope."

Teddy was surprised. He'd expected that wind shift to push him off target. And he'd been aiming center mass, not head. He put in one click down and tripped the bolt release.

An obliterating white flashed behind her sealed lids. Something heavy and hard struck her so hard in the back her body went numb. Gráinne heard a hollow, abrupt sound, like a slab of oak being chopped in two.

The bullet enters her lungs and tumbles, slowed by the transition from air to solid. It exits, blowing blood and tissue out onto the sand.

* * *

Her knees buckled and she sank, the old man clinging bewildered to her arm, trying to hold her up. No time even to wonder what had hit her. But she grasped with that instinctive wisdom of the body that it was something very bad. Just when she'd thought they were safe.

Then she was down, the sand hot against her face. The old man was cradling her head in his lap. He was crying, asking why someone had shot her.

So I was shot, she thought drowsily. Starting to go.

Then she remembered. She forced her eyes open to see his grizzled chin above her face, between her and the sky, which was very bright. She opened her mouth and tried to force her throat to speak, but there was no air. When she tried to breathe nothing happened.

She tried to form words with her lips. Had to say it. He could tell New York. No one knew but her. It didn't come out, though.

She tried again. Just a sentence? No. Then, one word. Just one.

Her lips were still parted when the black birds flew in from all the edges of the world, faster than any bullet, rushing in on her more rapidly than she could ever have believed anything could move.

Aisha turned at a muffled clap, like the sound you hear when one car backs into another, not hard enough to crunch metal, but an impact.

"What the fuck," Erculiano said.

Her mouth opened but nothing entered her mind except what her eyes drank in. Rooted to the ground, she stared as the pink mist bloomed and faded, as the still-living but headless body stood jerking. A second clap sounded and it folded and fell. A few yards away one of the hostages, a woman, trailing the others in the company of a bent little man, sagged to her knees, holding her chest. The old man howled.

The bolt release snapped forward, feeding the second round. Teddy settled back into position, left elbow in the same cup of sand, biceps dead in the tight sling. Inhale. Exhale. Align sights. Slow pressure.

Slam and recoil and dust. Could they miss seeing that dust? He didn't think so.

"Shot two, center hit, TI down. Call the cleanup crew. Shift to secondary target."

Teddy shifted but they were running now, ducking or hitting the ground. Were those distant screams? He tracked another bad guy, a white turban this time. Fired, but was pretty sure he missed.

But he'd gotten the principal. The asshole who'd blown up the Cosmo, started a war, killed a hell of a lot of marines. No reason to waste tears on him.

"That's it," he grunted, looking around for any trace they might've left. Brass sparkled in the sand. As the first return fire cracked out from the hilltop he scooped up empty shells. One, two, three. They burned his palm. He slid along the ground, crawfishing back into cover.

"Let's haul ass."

Above them, above the men who stood firing downhill, the others who hustled shivering hostages into vehicles, above a wailing woman in black who crouched by a motionless body, the crows circled. They called harshly to each other, as if denying what they'd just witnessed.

THE AFTERIMAGE

JOHN F. KENNEDY INTERNATIONAL AIRPORT, NEW YORK CITY

The admissions area was hot, crowded, a Babel in a hundred tongues. Aisha cradled the warm bundle in her left arm, maneuvering her carry-on with her right and wishing her purse weren't so heavy. She felt both not herself and as if she were only now commencing real life. In only three weeks her existence had realigned itself as radically as if the force of gravity had suddenly shifted ninety degrees.

She jiggled her new burden, looking down.

Dark eyes met hers with a welding that made her heart stop. A button nose needed wiping again. A dimpled cheek. Warmth gushed again, a fountain of sheer selfless pleasure. Better than sex. Better than anything she'd ever felt. A tiny hand rose, waved about, then fastened to the satin border of the pink blanket. The sweet scents of formula and powder enfolded her. Each time she picked her up it seemed more natural.

Peyster had leaned back in his chair when Aisha said she needed a special favor. Quirked his eyebrows, pursed mouth reluctant. Until she'd pointed out how much she knew—or rather, how she'd helped score a major success against the insurgency. Al-Maahdi was dead, shot in a fracas among his bodyguards during the hostage exchange. A huge thorn in the side of U.S. policy in the region plucked out, and all the hostages safely returned. Except for the Irish geologist, of course. A tragedy. Hit by a stray bullet, dying before a medic could stabilize her.

"All right," he'd said. "Let's hear it. What do you want? Job with the Agency? Letter of commendation? You're right, we couldn't have done it without you. He'd never have trusted us enough to turn up."

That hadn't felt so good, the intimation she'd betrayed a trust. But she'd stuffed that and simply said, evenly as she could, "There's someone I want to take back with me, Terry."

An old Jewish woman smiled at her, cooed at the baby, who regarded her with startled eyes. The woman gestured Aisha ahead of her in line. With her red official passport and federal ID, Aisha could have bypassed this line altogether. But she wanted this on the record. She wanted a paper trail.

Finally she was face-to-face with a heavyset, skeptical-looking woman with a Customs and Immigration badge on her blouse. Aisha laid her blue passport on the counter and shoved it under the glass. It was brand-new, uncreased, just issued by embassy staff in Ashaara City. The photo showed her and Tashaara. Trying to look bored, she slid the CROBA through too. The woman glanced at it, then up at her.

All bureaucratic, not very exciting. Not nearly as dramatic as smuggling Nuura's baby home in a duffel, her fallback plan. But like a magician, Peyster had angled his lopsided smile and all difficulties had fallen away. "You *have* gained some poundage lately," he'd said. "And those awful tents you wear—let's just say this won't be too hard for anybody around here to believe."

The Consular Report of Birth Abroad, which the woman behind the glass was now examining, documented the out-of-wedlock birth of one female child, Tashaara Ar-Rahim, to one Aisha Ar-Rahim, U.S. federal employee and citizen on duty abroad. The legal equivalent of a birth certificate, it entitled the child to U.S. citizenship based on her mother's nationality.

Tashaara began fussing, as if sensing how much was at stake. Aisha hugged and kissed her, inhaling the sweet clean smell from the crown of her little head. Would the woman object? Sense something unusual, wrong? Her uninterested gaze as she held up the passport, comparing it to their faces, said she didn't much care. She was a light-skinned sister, a bit heavy herself, cheeks dotted with large freckles. Maybe even a Muslim, to judge by her close-cropped hair. Aisha smiled at her. "Salaam," she said, on the off chance.

"You shouldn't be in this line," the immigration officer said. "Next time, just go through the U.S. Citizen line. With your daughter."

"I'm sorry. I wasn't sure."

"That's all right. By the way, I love your scarf. Is that from Africa?"

"Yes, from Ashaara. Thank you."

Aisha almost offered it to her, then remembered: officials here didn't require gifts. Two thumps of a rubber stamp and her new daughter was legally in America. She crammed the paperwork awkwardly into her purse, turning away so the woman wouldn't pick up on her welling eyes. She'd never found out, might never know, what'd happened to Tashaara's mother. Vanished, like so many others. But Nuura's little girl had a future now.

And a family. Aisha's sisters and mother stood waiting outside the barrier. She walked toward them heavily, feeling new weight on her hips, in her arms. Feeling her new gravity, a different, slower sway to her walk. There'd be questions. Reproaches, no doubt. But the excitement in her mother's eyes told her none of it would be vented on the baby.

Yeah, Maryam would go crazy pampering her new granddaughter. What would be hard—much harder, now, than she'd anticipated—would be leaving the baby with her mom in Harlem while she went back to Washington. Still, she could ask for leave. Maternity leave? That might be pushing it. Keep it under the official radar. At least for a couple of years, till everyone was used to the picture on her desk, a smiling little girl in pigtails, and how her daughter was living with her mother in New York.

"We couldn't save them all," she whispered to the tiny face that stared up with frightening intensity. "But I saved you, my sweetest and dearest. You'll never be hungry, or afraid. And now you're home."

"Aisha! Aisha! Over here!"

"Is that her? Is that the baby?"

She lifted her head, and smiled through the tears.

ESKAN VILLAGE, SAUDI ARABIA

Teddy came so hard his head felt like it was about to explode. It lasted and lasted, which didn't surprise him. It'd been forever since he'd gotten any.

"Did you come already? Did you?"

The captain's voice was concerned. He grunted and rolled off, hoping she didn't reach for another cigarette. Since he'd called and said he was back, to get somebody to cover for her at the site and come to his room, she'd been dewy-eyed and acquiescent. Not even any complaints about how often he had to rush for the can.

Like right now. "Back in a minute," he muttered, and rolled out and padded across the floor.

The diagnosis had been worms, all right, but the cure was almost as bad as the disease. Resting on the throne, looking around the unadorned bathroom, he let himself sag until he was resting against the wall.

He came to with barely knitted collarbone aching and the wall slamming beside his ear in a rhythmic syncopation. He must've zonked out right there on the shitter.

He and Kowacki had adjoining rooms. The other SEAL had picked up an Army nurse at the PX. A little butt-heavy, but perfectly serviceable for field use. Sounded like Whacker was catching up on his missing pussy time too.

Good for him—they'd earned it. Since they'd pulled out of Ashaara the team had been in Park, assigned to Centcom but without anything to do. It did seem like things were quieting down in the Mideast, though.

He got up reluctantly, washed his hands, hawked phlegm into the sink, a slick tan wad of coughed-up sand.

When he went into the darkened bedroom she was snoring. Turned on her side, legs drawn up, dark bush sticking out like a little tail. He looked down, feeling nothing. She was getting clingy. They did that. First outraged, then all lovey, and finally, into full barnacle mode. You enjoyed it while you could, and let go when it got to be too much.

A clang outside. He dropped into a combat crouch, heart suddenly slamming, head up. Listening.

The pistol was in the drawer with his skivvies. Cradling the weight in his right hand, safety off, he waited.

Was that breathing, outside his door?

He covered it, picking up the night sight, until he half reluctantly concluded it wasn't breathing. Just his own pulse slamming away in his ears. He straightened and padded to the window. Standing out of the line of fire, he twitched the drapes back. The street was empty. He couldn't see whatever had made the noise. The lights buzzed with a coral glow on naked asphalt, the cookie-cutter roofs. Beyond them the sky hung dark.

Out of nowhere, he was back in that house. Trapped in the kill zone, flashes of gunfire above. Then the grenade had come arcing down—

His hands shook. He took deep slow breaths, staring at his reflection in the dark glass. Pale eyes gazed back, filled with things he didn't want to remember. The air force officer had brought some Johnnie Walker. It was in the kitchen nook.

The grenade arced down from the flashing darkness. Hit the ground, and bounced—

No. He didn't want to get like the old warhorses back at

Dam Neck, running on ethanol like a Brazilian bus. Smelling of Jack Daniel's at 1500, backing their pickups into the younger guys' cars in the lot, crashing in the empty barracks at the National Guard base up the road instead of going home.

Maybe he should reconsider getting out, making that movie. But even as he thought it he knew he wouldn't. Acting, directing, were just illusion. Dreams. Make-believe. He'd grown up in that fantasy world, and as soon as he was old enough, run as far as he could. What good were fantasies, when you could live the adventure? Be a fucking SEAL, ripped, cool under fire, better than 007, the man every woman wanted to get creamy with, the man every man you met wanted to be?

But in the movies, only the bad guys died.

He gripped the curtain rod and pressed his forehead against the glass. Even at night, it was hot. He didn't like air-conditioning.

A small green spheroid. His peripheral vision identified it as a grenade.

And Kaulukukui gave him that look.

"War's a motherfucker, ain't it?"

Yeah, Sumo. Yeah. It's a motherfucker, all right.

But we were supposed to be the meanest motherfuckers in the valley.

"You bastard," he muttered. "You fat bastard."

What had Sumo died for? To put another Idi Amin, another Mugabe, in power? Teddy didn't like what he was hearing about this new boy, the black one with the white face. He and his men had sweated, bled, risked their lives to take down Assad, then Al-Maahdi. But what was different? What had changed?

That wasn't what Sumo Kaulukukui had died for. Not freedom, or democracy, or any of the gratuitous bullshit the Navy chaplain had drizzled over his grave. Teddy had stood there in his dress uniform, facing the family as the squad fired the traditional three blanks into the air. They'd flown him back for the funeral. All the way to Hawaii, if you could believe it, with a twenty-four-hour turnaround. The SEALs took care of their own.

Sumo had died for him.

"What'd you say?"

When he turned she was awake, drowsy, dark hair masking her face like a burka, peering up through it. "What're you doing?" she said, smoothing it back.

"Nothing."

Her eyes widened. "Is that your gun?"

"Thought I heard something."

"What?"

"Nothing. Dog in a garbage can, probably."

When he slid it back into the drawer and turned she'd rolled over on her back and pulled up the T-shirt she wore to bed. A green one, one of his. "Come to mama," she murmured, lifting her knees, reaching down to spread herself with her fingers. "She's got something you like. Right here. I can see you're interested."

Teddy blinked and looked away. The resemblance to the torn, swollen flesh of an infected wound was too disturbing. He stared out into the darkness again.

The grenade arcs down—

He shoved it away, reeling back to the bed. His gut cramped, but he didn't let that stop him. Fuck you, ghosts, fuck you, memories. She didn't ask for preparation, and he didn't feel like waiting. Ramming away, slamming the headboard against the wall in raucous countercrescendo to the rising storm from the other room, he battered his way past her panting, then her screams, toward a bursting lightless self-obliteration as complete as it would be momentary.

USS *SHAMAL*

Dan leaned over the lifeline, coughing in the brownish white smog as the diesels warmed. It was so thick he could see for only a few feet around him; the lifelines leading fore and aft, the uneasy, sand-scummed chop below; a gutted fish, floating as if more exhausted than dead. So opaque it darkened the day, the smoke streamed up from the waterline exhausts, filling the basin as Geller, in the pilothouse, argued with the Ashaaran pilot.

They were headed out. Down the length of the Red Sea into the Gulf of Aden, around the barren coasts of Yemen and Oman, then into the Strait of Hormuz. A week of maintenance in Bahrain, then she'd head for a new assignment: antipirate patrol off Somalia. The chaos of that failed, unfortunate state was metastasizing across East Africa.

But not to Ashaara. At any rate, not yet.

"Take in lines two through four," Geller yelled. Dan backed against the superstructure as the line handlers hustled past. The smoke thinned. Cranes and trucks emerged from the murk, and the towering cliff of a cargo ship unloading in the next berth. A whistle blast. "Under way. Shift colors."

No one was on the apron to see him off. Henrickson and McCall were gone, flown back to TAG. Ahearn had said good-bye with a three-fingered handshake at Camp Rowley, which would be handed over to the Pakistanis, Bangladeshis, and Indians, the hired hands of most UN peace missions. Still, on some obscure impulse, Dan lifted a hand in farewell as the gap widened, the engines thunked into gear, and the staring fish circled in a lazy eddy as the jetty began moving aft.

A day or two in Bahrain, then he'd fly home to brief Admiral Contardi on the results of his study. And also, testify before an investigating subcommittee looking into how the insurgent attack had taken the JTF by surprise. The Pentagon was still negotiating what questions he'd answer.

The surviving leadership of the Waleeli had signed a cease-fire. The Governing Council, now accepted as the de facto government, had asked the United Nations for a peacekeeping force to oversee militia disarmament and aid distribution. But there were disquieting rumors about General Olowe. Hints that the former sergeant major was only biding his time. Building up security apparatus and army for the final showdown with the clans still hostile to his rule. People who'd angered the new strongman, or become too close to the Americans, were quietly disappearing.

They'd tried hard in Ashaara. Had they succeeded? Or failed? They'd hoped to restore democracy, but turned the country over to another budding dictator. Tamped down violence, but only by imposing a terror of their own.

He listened to the roar as giant machines sucked grain from the cargo ship's holds. They'd averted mass starvation, at least. Maybe that was the important thing.

The new, extended jetty slipped past, and he thought: No, that's too pessimistic. We're leaving some good things. Buntine's legacy, what the gruff constructor had died building: a functioning, expanded terminal, capable of handling cargo for all upper Africa. For the airport, a lengthened runway, dozens of new buildings, radars and generators. Scores of new wells, generators, water and septic systems, clinics, and schools throughout the country.

Whether they'd still be standing stone on stone ten years from now depended more on Olowe and his successors, and Ashaarans at the local level, than on America or the UN.

The outside world could help, but only Ashaarans could build Ashaara. As had been true of every country on earth.

He strolled forward, stepping over the ground tackle, and looked out as the city slipped past. The baking rocks of the jetty. Behind them, the citadel and pullulating slums of the Old Town.

What would he report to Contardi, whose bidding had precipitated him into this maelstrom of drought and famine, war and anarchy? What did the admiral's vision of transformation mean?

He couldn't say technology didn't have a place. He'd been impressed by the neural network's success in teasing Al-Maahdi's subterranean den out of a welter of background noise. CIRCE was a powerful tool, nearly as all-seeing as the witch for whom it had been named.

But its knowledge wasn't perfect. And could never be.

The engines' mutter lessened.

The little pilot clambered down, a bundle clasped in one

hand. Food, most likely, though wine and cash were acceptable tips too. "Left twenty degrees rudder," Geller said in the pilothouse.

Dan turned and walked aft. He pulled himself up a ladder, past the bridge, to the open cockpit atop it. Up here the warm air was clean, the exhaust streaming aft as they accelerated. Signal flags fluttered. The Stars and Stripes snapped on their halyard. He looked down on Geller's shaved skull as the skipper shaded his gaze shoreward. Dan swung the Big Eyes that way too. Taking a long last look at the city; the embassy, windows flashing in the sun; the white beaches and rolling dunes as Africa fell astern. Sunlight flashed from the blue sea.

Maybe that would be his final report to Contardi. The admiral's premise had been that a decision maker could achieve perfect knowledge. Predict the trajectory of every bullet. Identify every target that moved in the darkness. Penetrate the intentions of every tyrant.

But no matter now fine the digital net, chance would slip through. The wind changed. The human heart defied logic.

Which left human beings with . . . what? The conclusion that, since no result could be guaranteed, no effort should be undertaken?

No. Turning away would be a greater evil. When starvation and war threatened, those who could had to act. Or abandon any pretense of humanity.

To act at all was to accept that the outcome would be mixed. Proceed with caution and faith, doing the best they could, without selfishness and without fear—that was all mortal men could do.

Shading his eyes, he saw they were passing the sea buoy. Shoals to starboard, between them and the coast. Shoals to port, between the channel and Jazirat Shâkir. Shoals all around, and to guide them, only the marks human judgment had anchored here and there amid the boundless sea.

He hoped it would be enough for a safe voyage.

Read on for an excerpt from David Poyer's next book

GHOSTING

Available in hardcover from St. Martin's Press

Jack got the cover off the mainsail and raised it, but jammed the battens into the spreaders. He lowered it and raised it again, but the halyard caught. He lowered it a third time, cursing the winch, and raised it again. This time it went all the way up and filled. He sheeted in until the trailing edge stopped luffing, the way he'd learned as a kid. The autopilot hummed, yawing as it adjusted to the new thrust, then understood and settled back to their course. The sail surged them along, wake creaming out behind them. He had a little trouble setting the radar, but finally picked up a blip several miles to the west on almost the same course and speed. He called them on the VHF, channel sixteen. Nigel Gutkind's voice came up at once. "This is *Hamadryad*. That you, Jack? Over."

"Sure is. How do we get together?"

"This is the emergency channel. Let's clear it and go to sixty-eight."

"Uh, right. Switching to channel sixty-eight."

He punched in numbers. When the display changed, Gutkind was saying through a low crackle, "*Slow Dance, Hamadryad*. I've got a sail four miles to the east. Can you see me?"

"No, but I have you on radar."

"Putting my helm over. Coming left. Is that the one you're looking at?"

"Right."

"Stay put. I'm coming to you. Over."

"Roger," said Jack, uncertain about the etiquette on the radio. "Over and out."

"I see a mast," Ric called back. "Off to the right."

"To starboard, Ric. At sea, it's starboard, not right."

His son didn't answer. Jack kept looking where he pointed and after a while he saw a white patch of sail. He was suddenly glad he'd hoisted his own. He bent to the panel and pulled the kill switch on the engine.

When it died silence rushed in, leaving only the cries of the gulls that trailed them. The steady ripple of the wake. A dry creak from below as the boat worked, everything new aboard her, parts not yet comfortable with their neighbors. He searched the horizon, shading his eyes from the glare of the rising sun off the waves. Save for that distant sail, they were alone. The last fumes of the diesel faded and the air was clean.

The distant sail became a boat, became *Hamadryad*'s green hull and white cabin and buff, age-stained sails. A cramped, heavily built Pearson with an antique engine Arlen said made everything aboard stink of gasoline. Nigel had owned her for many years. Then Jack made them out, two figures waving from the cockpit, and he waved back.

They ran alongside thirty yards apart. The swift water slid between them like a black river. Up close scuff marks and patches of mismatched paint marred the other boat's hull. Rust bled from a stanchion base. Nigel and Dinah Gutkind waved and smiled. Jack didn't see their granddaughter. Torrie must be below. She was the only one of the Gutkinds' numerous offspring who was interested in sailing, a compact blond girl with enormous energy.

"No jib?" Gutkind yelled, long gray hair ruffling in the wind.

"Waiting for you to catch up."

Nigel nodded. "Smooth transit out?"

"Pretty easy. Ric had it most of the night."

"Good for him," Dinah yelled in her high voice. "How you doing, Ric?"

His son waved but didn't answer. He'd assumed that dissociated look Jack didn't like. When the boy seemed to withdraw, looking at something the people around him couldn't see.

He pushed that worry away. Never think about your troubles. Think about your successes. "Want to take the lead?" he yelled.

"I'll stay in visual range. Check in on the VHF every couple hours. Channel twenty; we'll leave sixteen clear." Gutkind bent to something inside the boat, then straightened. "Looks like it might get a little heavy tomorrow."

Jack frowned. "What's that?"

"The weather, Doc. Looks like we could get some wind."

"The better to sail with. Right?"

The Gutkinds nodded. Nigel hauled in on the mainsheet and the old Pearson slowly forged ahead. Jack watched them go. Instead of a chartplotter, they used moldy paper charts from years back, which Gutkind kept under a seat cushion. Instead of a wheel, an oak tiller Nigel had laminated himself. No radar. No autopilot, either. He'd read you could trim a boat to sail herself if the wind was right, but he couldn't imagine having someone on the wheel twenty-four hours a day. Just hunching over the tiller would give you a permanent kink in the spine.

"So long," Ric said, with volume turned up, startling him. He made a waving gesture after them, a writhing of both arms Jack found disturbing. Choreoathetosis, from the antipsychotics?

"Did you take your meds this morning, Ric?"

"Not yet."

"D'you take 'em last night?"

"Think so."

He shoved down angry words. "Well, take 'em now. And another half dose in case you forgot last night. Then get some sleep."

After the boy went below, Jack checked the chartplotter again. He shaded his gaze at *Hamadryad,* a mile ahead now, and checked the instruments for wind direction and speed. He unfurled the genoa, pushing the button a little at a time. He wasn't sure how much to put out, so he stopped when it was three-quarters unfurled.

Slow Dream heeled, and the voice of her wake changed from a ripple to a soft roar, leaving the sea dotted with flecks of rocking foam behind her. What had Nigel said? He'd have to check the weather channel. He balanced on the heeling deck, watching the waves. Black as obsidian, smooth-humped as the backs of whales. He checked the knot meter. Eight? *Hamadryad* seemed more distant than last time he'd looked. Gutkind was clipping along. Maybe they could go a little faster. He let the mainsheet out just a bit. Bent to let out just a bit more jib by hand.

He blinked.

A line led aft from the bow, under the lifeline on the port side. "What the hell?" he muttered. He let go the furling line, then grabbed it again as it began to run out. Tied it off, made the sheet fast, and climbed out of the cockpit. He edged forward, handing himself from boom vang to stay, so a sudden heave wouldn't cost him his footing.

It was the port jib sheet, a line that wasn't in use unless the wind was coming from the other side of the boat. The black-and-red braid led over the gunwale down into the water. Jack gritted his teeth. Steve had warned him not to let lines trail over the side. They could go into the propeller, wrap themselves around the shaft or the strut. A bent strut would explain the boat's wanting to turn to port. Planting his feet carefully, hooking an arm around a stay, he bent and tugged.

It was rigid; there was a strain on it. Quite a considerable one, since it didn't yield at all. A rushing burble alongside waxed and waned as *Slow Dance* alternately surged and slacked to the swells. He shifted his grip on the stay and lay out over the gunwale, looking over the side.

And froze, staring down.

For a moment his eyes didn't make sense of it. Beneath the shadow of the davited inflatable, a drab object was tangled in the trailing sheet. It rotated as the line towed it through the water. It drifted into the hull, bumped, rolled. A pale thing attached to it by a short stalk came into view, then vanished.

Recognition penetrated whatever incomprehension or disbelief had stood between his sight and his understanding, and he saw a body being towed along by one leg, the other doubled back by the resistance of the water, limp arms streaming on either side of the head. It was on the opposite side from where *Hamadryad* had approached, or the Gutkinds would have seen it. As he watched, the turbulence slowly rotated it, till it stared up again. Not at him, but at the hull, only inches away.

It was the old man, Hagen. And there was no doubt he was dead.

Jack eased himself up—the deck was slick with spray or dew—and climbed back up over the center cockpit coaming. He refurled the genoa until only a slip showed. He racked off on the main sheet to slack the big sail off the wind. The sloop straightened. She ceased charging through the water, and her pitching eased. He waited until the autopilot had caught up and was steering straight again. Looked ahead, at *Hamadryad,* and around the horizon. The tanker he'd seen that morning was long gone. No other ships were in sight. The only witnesses were the laughing gulls who darted and canted above *Slow Dance*'s wake.

Back at the gunwale, full length on his stomach, he hauled in on the sheet. The body was astonishingly heavy. He couldn't lift it far out of the water. He slacked the line and it dropped back, submerged, then rose again as the line tightened once more.

He pulled it forward again, then gathered in smooth nylon as it extruded dripping out of the sea and took a couple of turns of the slack around the port winch. He climbed into the cockpit, took the handle out of its locker, fitted it to the winch, and cranked the body up out of the water, legs first.

When it was at the gunwale he knelt again and rolled the corpse onto the deck. It lay face up, pondering the sky, the left globe shrunken, too deep in its socket.

Jack fingered a torn dungaree shirt, then angled the head from one side to the other. Contusions on the scalp. Along with the fractured socket, deep blue bruises on the face. Or, no, not bruises; he could wipe them off the cold suety flesh with his thumb. It was bottom paint, off the hull that face had been smashing into for some hours.

He checked the pockets and found nothing, no change, no keys, no wallet. Most likely the old man hadn't carried anything of consequence. He returned his attention to the head. The cranium was dished in over the left eye. A blow to the skull? Or from repeated bashings against the hull? You'd need a pathologist to answer that one. He hadn't done an autopsy since med school. They were for butchers, not surgeons.

It had to be an accident. But how did the old man get aboard? More to the point, how did he get *overboard*? He hauled the leg up again and looked closely at the line, where it circled the frayed dead-white flesh of the puffy, sockless right ankle. Either an accidental tangle, or a bowline—he *did* know bowlines—botched by somebody who didn't know how to tie a proper one.

The old man had come back, after the party. Sneaked aboard when he and Arlen were asleep, intending to stow away in hopes of a job. Maybe the salesman, Steve, had even sent him back to ask again; the guy had seemed to think Jack needed help. But then what? He stared down, trying to see as the gulls flitted and shrieked, their shadows drawing closer.

Then . . . he'd slipped. Or tripped on the sheet, which would explain why it was around his ankle. Hit his head, and fallen overboard. He'd been drunk enough. As anybody at the party could testify.

But what if that was a deliberate knot around his ankle? What if that dish in his skull was from a blow?

It would have had to be somebody aboard *Slow Dance*.

The shadow of a gull flicked across the dead face. Jack felt cold, as if at the first breath of a squall.

Ric had been up all night.

Ric hadn't slept at all.

And every study he'd ever read said the fastest way to a psychotic break was sleep deprivation.

Jack was reaching for his Leatherman to cut the line when another, larger shadow fell across the deck. He let go the sheet and jerked back, but not quickly enough.

"What have you got there?" Arlen said, yawning, behind him.